To Whisper Her Name has everything a fine histo........ characters we truly care about, struggles that really matter, splashe........ d details that bring the past to vibrant life. Ridley .... es and disappointments tucked in their traveling ba........ o-ries and make room for the Lord's cleansing tou........

—Liz Curtis Higgs, *New York Times* bestselling a........

Tamera has taken 205 years of Belle Meade history and brought it to life in *To Whisper Her Name*. The mansion becomes vibrant again with family, the grounds alive with guests and staff, and the thoroughbreds are once again saddled and ready to take the reader on a rollicking ride!

—Alton Kelley, executive director of Belle Meade Plantation

To Whisper Her Name has everything I love in a Tamera Alexander book: great sense of place, multilayered characters, and a romantic plot that kept me up way too late. This post-Civil war novel is a terrific story by one of the top authors out there.

—Colleen Coble, author of *Tidewater Inn* and the Mercy Falls series

From the beginning of the prologue to the end, the story captured my excitement to keep reading and discover what was next in the lives of Olivia and Ridley. I did not want to put the book down at times when I had to! Relaxed, fun reading! *To Whisper Her Name* reminded me once again of how life must have been back when my maternal ancestors walked the Belle Meade Plantation grounds and of their dedication to the plantation thoroughbred farm and its owners.

—Luvenia Harrison Butler, MSP, board member of Belle Meade Plantation

To Whisper Her Name is another compelling novel from the pen of Tamera Alexander, revealing that though times have changed, human emotions and relationships never will. A cast of characters you'll fall in love with, and a beautiful story of redemption and hope.

—Deborah Raney, author of *The Face of the Earth* and the Hanover Falls novels

To Whisper Her Name will grab you and not let go. It's a beautiful, powerful story with unforgettable characters who face the unthinkable with honor while a captivating romance blooms where seeds should never have been scattered.

—Cindy Woodsmall, *New York Times* bestselling author of the Sisters of the Quilt series

To Whisper Her Name draws you in on a journey to redemption and love between two people who have suffered deeply from others' judgment. This is a story of love, but mostly of God's grace and His ever-present hand in restoring the lives of those who seek him. A romance so deeply satisfying, both to my heart and to my soul.

—Christy Jordan, author of *Southern Plate*

Rich in history, romance, and human drama, *To Whisper Her Name* is a book to be savored, like a sumptuou........ kills as a master story-teller have never been m........

—Robin Lee Hatcher, be........

Books by Tamera Alexander

A Belle Meade Plantation Novel
To Whisper Her Name

A Belmont Mansion Novel
A Lasting Impression

Fountain Creek Chronicles
Rekindled
Revealed
Remembered
Fountain Creek Chronicles (3 in 1)

Timber Ridge Reflections
From a Distance
Beyond This Moment
Within My Heart

Women of Faith Fiction
The Inheritance

A BELLE MEADE PLANTATION NOVEL

TAMERA ALEXANDER

To Whisper Her Name

ZONDERVAN®

ZONDERVAN

To Whisper Her Name
Copyright © 2012 by Tamera Alexander

This title is also available as a Zondervan ebook.
Visit www.zondervan.com/ebooks.

This title is also available in a Zondervan audio edition.
Visit www.zondervan.fm.

Requests for information should be addressed to:

Zondervan, *Grand Rapids, Michigan 49530*

Library of Congress Cataloging-in-Publication Data
     Alexander, Tamera.
          To whisper her name : a Belle Meade Plantation novel / by Tamera Alexander.
          p. cm.
     ISBN 978-0-310-29106-0 (softcover)
       1. Widows—Fiction. 2. Veterans—Fiction. 3. Tennessee—History—19th
     century—Fiction. 4. Belle Meade Plantation (Tenn.—History. I. Title.
     PS3601.L3563T66 2012
     813'.6—dc23   2012034386

All Scripture quotations, unless otherwise indicated, are taken from the King James Version of the Bible.

Scripture quotations marked NLT are taken from the *Holy Bible, New Living Translation,* copyright © 1996, 2004. Used by permission of Tyndale House Publishers, Inc., Wheaton, Illinois. All rights reserved.

Any Internet addresses (websites, blogs, etc.) and telephone numbers in this book are offered as a resource. They are not intended in any way to be or imply an endorsement by Zondervan, nor does Zondervan vouch for the content of these sites and numbers for the life of this book.

Cover design: Michelle Lenger
Cover photography: Mike Heath / Magnus Creative
Interior design: Sarah Johnson

Printed in the United States of America

For the ladies of Coeur d'Alene . . .
I hope heaven has Julys.

There is no longer Jew or Gentile, slave or free, male and female. For you are all one in Christ Jesus.

Galatians 3:28 NLT

Preface

Most of the novel you're about to read is purely fictional, though there are threads of actual history and people woven throughout. For instance, there is a Belle Meade Plantation in Nashville that still welcomes visitors today. The Harding family, characters in *To Whisper Her Name,* lived at Belle Meade and many of the events included in this story were drawn from their personal history and were then fleshed out in my imagination.

In addition to the Harding family, many of the former slaves who served at Belle Meade inspired characters in this story. In nearly every instance, I used the real names of the former slaves and the positions they held at Belle Meade. However, the characters' personalities and actions are of my own creation and should be construed as such.

After two years of research and writing *To Whisper Her Name,* I invite you to join me on yet another journey into the postbellum world of Nashville, Tennessee. Thank you for entrusting your time to me. It's a weighty investment that I treasure and will never take for granted.

Most warmly,

Tamera

Prologue

August 17, 1863
In the hills surrounding the Union-occupied city of
Nashville ...

*F*irst Lieutenant Ridley Adam Cooper peered through the stand
of bristled pines, his presence cloaked by dusk, his Winchester
cocked and ready. Beads of sweat trailed his forehead and the curve
of his eye, but he didn't bother wiping them away. His focus was
trained on the Negro hunched over the fire and what he was certain—
if his last hour of observation proved true—the slave had hidden just
over the ridge.

Best he could tell, the man hadn't spied him, else he wouldn't be
going about making supper like he was. Beans and pork with biscuits
and coffee, if Ridley's sense of smell proved right. *Real* coffee. Not that
foul-tasting brew the Rebs scalded over an open flame until it was
sludge, then drank by the gallons.

Rebs. His brothers, in a way, every last one of them. Two of them
the blood kind. And yet, the enemy. He hoped Petey and Alfred were
all right, wherever they were.

A northerly breeze marked evening's descent, but the air's movement did little to ease the sweltering heat and humidity. Someone
raised in the thickness of South Carolina summers should be accustomed to this by now, but the wool of the Federal uniform wore heavy,
more so these days than when he'd first enlisted.

Yet he knew he'd done the right thing in choosing the side he had.
No matter what others said or did. Or accused him of.

Ridley felt a pang. Not from hunger so much, though he could eat if food was set before him. This pang went much deeper and hurt worse than anything he could remember. *God, if you're listening, if you're still watching us from where you are … I hate this war.* Hated what this "brief conflict"—as President Lincoln had called it at the outset—was doing to him and everyone else over two bloody years later.

And especially what it called for him to do tonight. "At any cost," his commander had said, his instruction leaving no question.

Jaw rigid, Ridley reached into his pocket and pulled out the seashell, the one he'd picked up on his last walk along the beach near home before he'd left to join the 167th Pennsylvania Regiment to fight for the Federal Army. The scallop shell was a tiny thing, hardly bigger than a coin, and the inside fit smoothly against his thumb. With his forefinger, he traced the familiar ridges along the back and glanced skyward where a vast sea of purple slowly ebbed to black.

It was so peaceful, the night canopy, the stars popping out one by one like a million fireflies flitting right in place. Looking up, a man wouldn't even know a war was being waged.

When his commanding officer had called for a volunteer for the scouting mission, the man hadn't waited for hands to go up but had looked directly at Ridley, his expression daring argument. Ridley had given none. He'd simply listened to the orders and set out at first light, nearly three days ago now. Ridley knew the commander held nothing personal against him. The man had been supportive in every way.

It was Ridley's own temper and his "friendly" disagreement with a fellow officer—a loud-mouthed lieutenant from Philadelphia who hated "every one of them good for nothin', ignorant Southerners"— that had landed him where he was tonight. The fool had all but accused him of spying for the Confederacy. Their commander had quashed the rumor, but the seed of doubt had been sown. And this was the commander's way of allowing Ridley to earn back his fellow officers' trust again, which was imperative.

Ridley wiped his brow with the sleeve of his coat, careful not to make a noise. He'd tethered his horse a good ways back and had come in on foot.

He didn't know the hills surrounding Nashville any better than the rest of his unit, but he did know this kind of terrain, how to hunt and move about in the woods. And how to stay hidden. The woods were so dense in places, the pines grown so thick together, a man could get lost out here if he didn't know how to tell his way.

They'd gotten wind of Rebels patrolling the outlying areas—rogue sentries who considered themselves the law of the land—and his bet was they were searching for what he'd just found. So far, he hadn't seen hide nor hair of them. But he could imagine well enough what they'd do to a Union soldier found on his lonesome—especially an officer and "one of their own kind" to boot—so he was eager to get this thing done.

Gripping his Winchester, Ridley stepped from the tree cover, still some thirty feet from the Negro. He closed the distance—*twenty-five feet, twenty*—the cushion of pine needles muffling his approach. *Fifteen, ten* ... But the man just kept puttering away, stirring the coffee, then the beans, then—

Ridley paused mid-step. Either the Negro was deaf ... or was already wise to his presence. Wagering the latter, Ridley brought his rifle up and scanned his surroundings, looking for anyone hidden in the trees or for a gun barrel conveniently trained at the center of his chest. It was too late to retreat, but withdrawal of any kind had never been in his nature, as that cocksure, pretentious little—he caught himself—*lieutenant* from Philadelphia had found out well enough.

He tried for a casual yet not too pleasant tone. "Evening, friend ..."

The man's head came up. Then, slowly, he straightened to his full height, which was still a good foot shorter than Ridley. He was thicker about the middle, older than Ridley too. In his thirties maybe, or closer to forty, it was hard to tell. The Negro was broad shouldered, and judging by the thickness of his hands and forearms, Ridley guessed that years of hard labor had layered a strap of muscle beneath that slight paunch. He hoped it wouldn't give the slave a false sense of courage.

"Evenin'," the man answered, glancing at the stripes on Ridley's shoulder. "Lieutenant, sir."

Not a trace of surprise registered in his voice, which went a ways in confirming Ridley's silent wager. The man's knowledge of military rank was also telling.

The Negro's focus shifted decidedly to the Winchester, then back again, and Ridley couldn't decide if it was resignation he read in the man's eyes or disappointment. Or maybe both.

Ridley surveyed the camp. Neat, orderly. Everything packed. Everything but the food. Like the man was getting ready to move out. Only—Ridley looked closer—not one cup but two resting on a rock by the fire. He focused on the slave and read awareness in the man's eyes. "How long have you known I was watching?"

The Negro bit his lower lip, causing the fullness of his graying beard to bunch on his chin. " 'Bout the time the coffee came back to boilin', sir."

"You heard me?" Ridley asked, knowing that was impossible. He hadn't made a sound. He was sure of it.

The man shook his head, looking at him with eyes so deep and dark a brown they appeared almost liquid. "More like ... I *felt* you, sir."

A prickle skittered up Ridley's spine. Part of him wanted to question the man, see if he had what some called "second sight," like Ridley's great-grandmother'd had, but the wiser part of him knew better than to inquire. He had a job to do, one he couldn't afford to fail at. Not with his loyalty to the Union being called into question by some. "I take it you know what I'm here for."

There it was again, that look. Definitely one of resignation this time.

"I reckon I do, sir. It's what all them others been lookin' for too." The slave shook his head. "How'd you find me?"

Only then did Ridley allow a hint of a smile. "I don't know that I can say exactly. We got rumor of horses being hidden in these hills. I *volunteered*, you might say, and then just started out. I followed where my senses told me to go. Where I would've gone if I was hiding horses."

The man's eyebrows arched, then he nodded, gradually, as if working to figure something out. He motioned to the fire. "Dinner's all ready, Lieutenant. Think you could see fit to eat a mite?"

Ridley looked at the pot of beans and meat bubbling over the flame, then at the tin of biscuits set off to the side, his stomach already answering. The man was offering to feed him? All whilst knowing what he was here to do? Ridley eyed him again, not trusting him by any stretch. Yet he had a long journey back to camp, and the dried jerky in his rations didn't begin to compare. "I'd be much obliged. Thank you."

They ate in silence, the night sounds edging up a notch as the darkness grew more pronounced. The food tasted good and Ridley was hungrier than he'd thought. He'd covered at least seventy-five, maybe a hundred miles since leaving camp in Nashville.

Just four days earlier, Union headquarters had received rumor of a slave out in these hills, reportedly hiding prized blood horses for his owner. Word had it the horses were bred for racing and were worth a fortune. Ridley would've sworn they'd confiscated every horse there was in Nashville when they first took the city. But he'd bet his life that the man across from him right now was the slave they'd heard about.

He lifted his cup. "You make mighty good coffee. Best I've had in a while. And this is some fine venison too."

"Thank you, sir. My master, he got the finest deer park in all o' Dixie. Least he did 'fore them no-good, thievin' — " The Negro paused, frowning, then seemed to put some effort into smoothing his brow, though with little success. "I's sorry, sir. I 'preciate all your side's tryin' to do in this war, but there just ain't no cause for what was done at Belle Meade last year. 'Specially with Missus Harding bein' delicate o' health, and Master Harding packed off to prison like he was. Them Union troops — " He gripped his upper thigh, his eyes going hot. "They shot me! Right in the leg. I's just tryin' to do what I's been told, and they shot me straight on. Laughed about it too. And here we's thinkin' they come to help."

Reminded again of another reason he hated this war and why the South no longer felt like home and never would again, Ridley held the man's gaze, trying to think of something to say. Something that would make up for what had been done to him. But he couldn't.

Ridley laid aside his tin and, on impulse, reached out a hand. "First Lieutenant Ridley Adam Cooper . . . sir."

He knew a little about the slave's owner — General William Giles Harding — from what his commanding officer had told him. To date, General Harding still hadn't signed the Oath of Allegiance to the Union, despite the general's incarceration up north last year at Fort Mackinac — a place reportedly more like a resort than a prison — and the lack of compliance wasn't sitting well with those in authority. Not with Harding being so wealthy a man and holding such influence among his peers. It set the wrong precedent. Union superiors hoped the outcome of this scouting mission would provide General Harding with the proper motivation he needed to comply with the Union — or suffer further consequences.

The Negro regarded Ridley — the crackle of the fire eating up the silence — then finally accepted, his own grip iron-firm. "Robert Green, sir. Head hostler, Belle Meade Plantation."

"You been at Belle Meade long, Mr. Green?"

"Since I's about two years old, sir. My folks and me, we was a present to the first Missus Harding on her and my master's weddin' day. Been at Belle Meade ever since."

Ridley nodded, then stared into the fire as the man's comment settled within him. *We was a present* ... It didn't settle well. According to a proclamation from the president eight months earlier, most of the slaves had been freed. But words on paper didn't always match the reality of a situation. Especially when newly freed slaves attempting to exercise their freedom ended up shot in the back or hanging by a rope.

"You must'a met with some of them Rebs, Lieutenant."

Ridley looked up to see Robert Green gesturing toward him.

"Seein' them bruises, sir, looks like somebody got a piece of you 'fore you took 'em down."

Ridley fingered his cheek and chin, his jaw still tender and now roughly bearded with several days' growth. "Actually this was from a fellow officer. He and I had a ... difference of opinion, you might say."

Green chuckled. His laughter had a comforting sound about it. "From the size of you, Lieutenant, I be guessin' that man looks way worse off than you do."

Ridley shook his head. "He got a few good punches in before he went down."

"That may be, sir. But with one good lick from you, I'm bettin' he done stayed down. For a week!"

Ridley allowed the trace of a grin, then felt the need for sleep creeping up on him and sat straighter to keep his wits about him.

"Lawd ..." Robert Green sighed and stretched. "I used to love me a good fight. I used to could hold my own too. Don't you think I couldn't just 'cause I's built low to the ground."

"No, sir ..." Ridley shook his head, humored at the way Green described himself. "I wouldn't begin to think that."

Robert Green locked eyes with him then, and the man's smile faded. Green blinked, as if just now seeing Ridley in his uniform again and remembering why he was here.

The brief ease of conversation between them left as quickly as it had come.

Feeling precious time slip past, Ridley rose, bringing his Winchester with him. "I thank you for dinner, Mr. Green. And now ... I need to ask you to show me the horses."

Robert Green rose as well, reaching for a knobby cane to steady himself. He grabbed a nearby lantern and lit it, then picked a path through the darkness. Ridley followed, still wary and more than a little watchful.

Slivers of moonlight fingered their way through the trees, lending the night a silvery glow. When they reached the top of the ridge, Ridley peered over and counted three — no, four — horses. His gaze narrowed in the pale moonlight. Their size and stature. Their build . . . Though he wasn't an expert on horse flesh, he knew enough to realize everything his commander had said was true. *Magnificent* was the foremost word that came to mind.

If these horses were worth a dollar, they were worth a thousand. Each. Easy. And they flocked to Robert Green like newborn pups to their mama. All of them. The man whispered low and stroked their necks, scratched them behind their ears. The gentleness of the animals in contrast to their brute strength was something to behold.

"You open to me askin' you somethin', Lieutenant Cooper?" Robert Green turned back, and as if on cue, the horses lifted their heads. All seemed to look directly at Ridley.

Ridley got a spooked sort of feeling. A little like . . . if Robert Green were to give the word, those thoroughbreds would charge that hill and stomp the life right out of him. All because Robert Green wished it so.

Hearing in his mind the question Mr. Green had asked, Ridley pulled his thoughts taut again. "Yes, sir. Go ahead."

"Where you from, Lieutenant? I know by your speakin' you ain't from nowhere north."

"No, sir. I'm not. I'm from South Carolina."

Robert Green whistled low. "I's guessin' what you done ain't gone over too well with your kin."

Ridley pushed aside the painful images of his father and younger brothers. "No, sir. It hasn't." He turned his thoughts to figuring how he was going to get these thoroughbreds back to camp. He was a fair rider, but he'd never been especially good with horses. Not a fact he'd been eager to share with his commanding officer. He'd handled this many horses before, but not spirited blood horses, and he certainly lacked the knack for it this man possessed.

"But still . . . you's fightin' for what you think is right, Lieutenant. Speaks high of a man to do that, sir. 'Specially when it costs him dear." Robert Green paused. "Anythin' I can do to change your mind on this, Lieutenant Cooper? These here are the general's favorites. And he trusted 'em to me special, sir. To keep 'em safe."

Ridley leveled a stare. "I appreciate that, Mr. Green. But no. There's nothing to be done. I've got my orders."

The older man bowed his head, nodding. "Mind if I water 'em up 'fore you take 'em?"

"No. Long as you don't mind if I come along."

Robert Green took hold of the leads of two of the thoroughbreds and led them to the stream. The other two horses trailed behind. Ridley followed, rifle in hand.

The largest of the thoroughbreds, a black stallion, nudged up beside Green similar to how Ridley remembered Winston—his hunting dog as a boy—doing. He hadn't thought of that ol' dog in years, buried on the hill behind the house back home.

But it was how Robert Green leaned into the stallion that caused Ridley to study the scene. He'd never witnessed anything like it. Animal like that reacting toward a man this way. And he felt a disquiet inside himself, one he tried to dismiss. But couldn't. He had a direct order. He had no choice but to do this. He couldn't return without these thoroughbreds. And wouldn't.

He followed Green back to where the horses had been.

Green turned to him. "You know anything 'bout horses, Lieutenant?"

"'Course I do." Ridley heard the defensiveness in his own voice, for some unknown reason eager to prove himself to this man. He gathered the reins of two of the thoroughbreds, noting they were none too eager to follow him over the ridge. But finally, with firm insistence, they did.

"Blood horses like these," Green said, coming down the hill behind him. "You gotta take special care with 'em, Lieutenant. They got high spirits, and they can—"

"I *know* about horses, Mr. Green."

Green didn't say anything, but his silence did.

"Lieutenant Cooper?"

His patience thinning, Ridley paused and looked back.

"If you got a mind to let me, sir, I go with you, a ways anyhow." The man looked at the horses with fondness akin to what Ridley had felt for old Winston. "I go as far as the road runnin' north of here, then I turn back. That rebel patrol … they catch me out in these woods—" He shook his head. "I be better off bein' trampled by Olympus there." He thumbed toward the black stallion. "Either way, I be dead."

"If the Rebs catch either of us, Mr. Green, we'll likely both be dead."

Surprisingly, Green chuckled. "That's God's honest truth, sir. I's thinkin' they might just take to killin' you 'fore they kill me."

Ridley considered that possibility and found no comfort in it. But having Green along to help with these horses did have advantages. Finally, he nodded, and Green packed up the camp.

They were on their way inside of fifteen minutes.

Ridley was grateful—and also not—for the full moon. It gave them light, but did the same to anyone else in the woods. He led the way, reins to a dark bay stallion and a handsome chestnut in his grip. He glanced back at Robert Green every so often. "We'll head north about a quarter mile to where I left my horse, then we'll take the path over the next ridge. There's a deer trail running through there that I followed a day or so back. Unless you know of a better way?"

"No, sir. That's the best way. And fastest."

The thoroughbreds were surefooted and grew easier to lead as they went, which Ridley knew better than to attribute to his own skill. "When I came into camp, Mr. Green, you looked about packed up, ready to move out. Where were you headed?"

"I got me some good hidin' spots in these hills. I move around some. Mainly at night. Ain't seen nobody for a while."

Almost back to where Ridley had tethered his gelding, he heard the horse whinny, then felt a touch of relief when he found the mount as he'd left him. The gelding was a mite high-strung. Temperamental at times too, even obstinate, and Ridley wasn't overly fond of the animal.

The thoroughbreds tossed their heads, as though hesitant to welcome the newcomer to their ranks, but Green quieted them with soothing whispers and a touch.

"May I, sir?"

Ridley glanced up to see Robert Green gesture to the gelding. Gathering what he was asking, Ridley granted permission with a nod.

Robert Green walked to within three feet of the gelding then stopped and stared. Just stared. The gelding stared back, its withers rippling. Then with an outstretched hand, Green closed the distance between them, moving slowly, patient as sunrise in winter, never breaking the stare. The horse suddenly blew out a breath and stomped. Green halted and lowered his arm.

Ridley watched, not knowing what the man was doing but about to tell him in no uncertain terms that they didn't have time for this foolish—

"You's a good boy," Green said, his voice low and soft. "Little scared sometimes, I'm guessin'. But we all is. We all got somethin' we afraid of . . . You ever talk to him?"

Ridley blinked. It took him a second to realize Green was speaking to *him* now and not the horse. "Beg pardon?"

"You ever talk to this horse, sir? Tell him what a fine boy he is? How grateful you are for what he done for you?"

Ridley stared at Robert Green, wondering now if the man was a mite touched in the head. And knowing he was wasting his time with the gelding.

"Horses are like women, Lieutenant. You gotta talk to 'em, let 'em see what's inside you 'fore they can start to trust. You kin to that understandin'?"

Ridley started to admit he wasn't, then decided his personal experience was none of this man's business. "Mr. Green, I'm sure you mean well, sir, but we don't have time for—"

The gelding took a decided step toward Green. And another. Then lowered his head as if giving Green permission to touch him.

Ridley exhaled. "Well, would you look at—"

High-pitched laughter cut through the darkness and Ridley instinctively brought his rifle up. He put a finger to his lips. Robert Green nodded. The stallions tossed their heads as though sensing the tension around them, and the gelding edged closer to Green.

Ridley motioned to Green to gather the reins of the thoroughbreds, but the slave already had them in hand, as well as the gelding's.

More cackling laughter and occasional whoops annoyed the night's silence, the telling sound of liquored-up Confederate soldiers. Ridley crept through the trees to get a better look, betting they weren't as drunk as they sounded. It occurred to him again that, with one hearty shout, Robert Green could use this chance to turn him in. The slave might try to work a bargain—the Rebs would get the thoroughbreds, the gelding, and one Federal lieutenant, and Robert Green might go free.

But Ridley knew the chances of Green going free were close to nil. He only hoped Robert Green knew that.

Watching through the trees, he could see the patrol passing by on horseback not twenty feet from where he stood. The rhythmic plod of their own mounts provided coverage, but if the thoroughbreds—or the gelding—spooked . . .

One of the Reb's horses snorted and pulled up short, no doubt smelling—or at least sensing—the thoroughbreds. Ridley tensed.

The soldier swore and dug his heels mercilessly into the mount's flanks, spewing a curse-laden tirade about "the worthless piece of horseflesh" beneath him.

Ridley didn't dare look away but wondered how on earth Robert Green was managing to keep their horses so quiet. Then a thought occurred. He jerked his head back to make sure Green hadn't—

The slave and the horses were just where he'd left them.

Not realizing he'd been holding his breath, Ridley slowly let it out and then filled his lungs again, willing his pulse to slow. He waited. The patrol passed. As did a full minute. Then another. But he knew better than to let relief come quite yet.

These Rebs ... they were sly, some of them. This could be a trick.

Ridley allowed a full five minutes to pass—silently counting and glancing back on occasion to check on Green.

"I think they's gone, sir," Green finally said, his voice a feather on the wind.

"I think they are too," Ridley whispered back. "But we can't go the way I was planning." Not when that way meant trailing the patrol party.

"What you gonna do, Lieutenant ... with the general's horses?"

"I'm taking them back to camp, near the capitol building."

"Aw, no, sir. Please, sir. These is too fine'a horses to be cavalry mounts, Lieutenant."

Ridley sighed, admiring the man's stab at persuasion. "They're not meant for cavalry mounts. They're to be presented to officers as gifts." At least that's what he'd been told, but he wondered again, as he had at the outset. His commander had said they wanted to make an example of General Harding. How far his superiors would go to do that, he didn't know.

But looking at the thoroughbreds now—at what fine animals they were—he questioned those lengths.

One thing beyond question was the trust this slave had earned with these animals. Looking at the black stallion—Olympus, Green had called him—Ridley would've sworn the animal was thinking something intelligible. What, he didn't know. But the disquiet he'd felt earlier that night returned a hundredfold.

He couldn't define it. He only knew he couldn't set it aside. Not without a cost. And for reasons he couldn't explain—and knew were a far cry short of sane—he walked over and reached out to touch the stallion.

The animal flinched and took a backward step, the whites of its eyes visibly stark against black pupils. Then Green's voice came, hushed and gentle, whispering whatever it was he said to calm them.

Green looked over. "You ain't earned his trust yet, Lieutenant Cooper. That's all. Trust takes time and lots of doin'. You got to prove yourself worthy of it, sir."

Feeling rebuked by this man, yet appropriately so, Ridley said nothing at first. "You didn't try to bargain with the patrol, Mr. Green. Or turn me in."

"Oh, I thought about it." Green's smile was briefly lived. "But I knowed me too many white men who's thirsty for blood. I reckon I best take my chances with one who don't seem so eager to spill it ... sir."

There it was again. That sense of unease. Ridley looked at the thoroughbreds and felt a deliberation inside him, warring against his judgment, against what he knew he should do as a Federal officer. "Has it always been this way for you, Mr. Green? With horses?"

Green didn't answer immediately, his focus on the thoroughbreds. " 'Fore I could walk, I knew how to ride a horse. That's what my papa said anyway. I was right about three years along when my mama woke in the night. Couldn't find me nowhere. She and Papa went lookin'." Green's smile was full of memory. "Say they found me sleepin' in the barn. Hunkered down with a stallion, right between his hooves."

Ridley studied him. If anyone else had told him that story, he'd have discounted it without a second thought. But he couldn't. Not with it coming from this man.

"God made a wondrous thing when he made these creatures, Lieutenant Cooper. In some ways, they's smarter than we is. They know things. They remember things too."

Ridley stared, his decision made. He just didn't know how to go about explaining it to this man. Or what he would tell his commander.

The sky to the east showed a pearly gray slowly giving way to dawn. "It'll be light soon, Mr. Green. If you aim to keep these horses in your possession, I suggest you find another good hidin' spot." He phrased it much as Green had earlier. "And find it right quick."

Green stilled. And stared. "Are you sayin' that—" The question in his features melted into cautious gratitude. "Why you doin' this, sir?"

Ridley laughed and took the reins of the gelding. "I have no idea. I only know I can't be responsible for destroying so—" How had Green put it? "So wondrous a creature as these animals are." Ridley briefly looked away, the tightness in his throat betraying his weariness, both in body and soul. "Not when there's so little wondrous left in this world."

Weary and eager to be gone, Ridley mounted the gelding, aware of Green closing the distance between them.

"I thank you, Lieutenant Cooper. And I promise you, sir, as sure as God is listenin' to me right this minute, I be prayin' he pays you back for your kindness. And that he keeps you safe, sir." Green extended his hand.

But Ridley only stared at it. "Thank you, Mr. Green … But I don't believe God hears our prayers anymore. Or if he does, he sure doesn't seem to be heeding them."

Sensing Green's argument, Ridley urged the gelding in the opposite direction of the patrol and didn't look back.

Two hours later, he stopped by a stream to water the horse, still thinking of Robert Green. Part of him wished he'd seen the man safely back into the hills. But then … the slave had seemed to be doing all right on his own, he guessed.

As he refilled his canteen, the tug of a tattered dream returned. One that had taken root deep inside him awhile back and that he'd acted on earlier that spring. But foolishly so, now it would seem. The past months of brutal bloodshed had shown him that. Yet, here he was, still coddling it like a stillborn child. Odd, how death could sometimes feed a dream.

If he got through this God-forsaken war alive, he vowed again to get as far away from these blood-drenched hollows and hills as he could. He'd head west, far beyond the banks of the Mississippi, past the borders of Missouri, to a place he'd seen a painting of once. A place called the Rockies where the mountains were so high, they disappeared into the clouds. He'd never seen the shade of blue the artist had used to paint the sky, but a man standing next to him that day, who'd been to the Colorado Territory—or so he'd said—told him that God himself had chosen that color special, just to go with those mountains.

The memory of the painting acted like a blade to his hope and slit its throat clean through. Ridley was certain that if he looked down, which he didn't, he'd see his dream pooling in a puddle of blood around his worn leather boots.

A snap of a twig drew his gaze up and his rifle with it. He listened, still as an iced pond in winter. One silent minute stretched into two, and he finally decided the longing inside him was making him edgy. Shrugging off feelings best left alone, he rode on for the better part of the morning, circling wide to avoid meeting up with the patrol.

The sun rose high in the sky, hot and relentless.

He reached back into his saddlebag and fished out a piece of jerky. It felt good to chew on something besides what was gnawing at him on the inside. First, how was he going to explain to his commander about returning without the thoroughbreds? And second—he felt a traitorous twinge of a smile, the next thought was so ludicrous—he was actually jealous of Robert Green. A Negro. A *slave*. But he couldn't deny it.

In a different time and place, worlds away from this one, he would've appreciated a chance to learn from that man. To study his ways. Because Robert Green knew more about—

An explosion rent the air, and the gelding beneath him stumbled.

A second blast ... and pain ripped through Ridley's right shoulder and across his chest. The gelding buckled forward and the ground came rushing up with a force that knocked what little air remained from Ridley's lungs. He fought for breath as another rifle blast sounded. The gelding convulsed beside him and let out a mournful cry Ridley knew he'd carry to his dying day.

Ridley struggled to stand, but a blow to his back rendered him prostrate. Dirt coated his tongue and he heard laughter floating somewhere above him, along with taunts in thick Southern drawls.

"Look'a here! We got us a lieutenant, Cap'n!" More laughter.

Ridley gasped, the simple effort excruciating. He managed to lift his head and saw the gelding looking straight at him, a flow of blood pulsing from a hole in its side. And with a certainty that knifed his gut, he sensed the animal's confusion, its struggle to understand. Its silent, numbing question of why.

Heat shot through Ridley's veins, filling him with a fire and strength that surprised him. Somehow, he gained his footing and—fists clenched tight—plowed into the corporal closest to him, managing to take him down. As well as the officer next to him.

Movement flashed on his left, but Ridley couldn't react quickly enough. The butt of the rifle connected with a *crack* and pain exploded across his skull. His eyes felt like they were coming out of his head. He was falling again, except this time, the momentum pulled him under. Hard and deep. He struggled to form one last conscious thought, Robert Green's promise returning to mind. He wished he could believe it, but he knew Green's prayers for him would be wasted. God was deaf to them. Deaf to it all.

God had given up on them a long time ago.

Chapter ONE

May 10, 1866
Nashville, Tennessee

*O*livia Aberdeen bowed her head as she hurried to the waiting carriage. Stares from people on the street bored into her like rusty nails, but she averted her gaze, certain if her eyes met theirs, the passersby would glimpse traces of guilt and would rush to heap further blame on her for what had happened.

Clutching an envelope in one hand, she accepted the servant's assistance into the carriage. Despite what her late husband had done to the people of Nashville—and to *her*—she couldn't bring herself to spit in the face of propriety. So while her heart was far from grieving the untimely passing of Charles Winthrop Aberdeen, she was properly adorned in the widow's garb befitting a woman of her station in life.

Or what used to be her life.

Settled on the carriage seat, Olivia drew in a deep breath, the first in what felt like five years. She knew it was wrong, what she was feeling. Because a widow of only a week shouldn't wish to dance a jig. But God help her, that's precisely what part of her wanted to do. Not on the grave of her recently deceased husband, of course—that would be considered rude. Just off to the side would suffice.

A swift stab of remorse accompanied the disparaging thought, and she bowed her head again, feeling the hot prick of tears. Merely imagining someone might guess her true feelings scathed her conscience. The duplicity of her circumstances wore on her already-frayed emotions, as did the knowledge that those watching her were also judging her.

But one thing she knew they would agree with her about—including the men who had successfully plotted to kill her husband—Charles Aberdeen had been among the basest of men, lacking in morals and ethics and loyalty to the Confederacy.

She'd never wished Charles dead. But she *had* wished to be severed from their marriage almost from the moment they'd become man and wife in God's eyes. The marriage had been arranged by her father in one of the final decisions of his life—an *irrevocable partnership*, as he'd explained—and Olivia had determined from the outset that what God had joined together, even without her consent, she had no right to put asunder.

Yet it would seem God himself had finally undertaken that task and had performed it with exacting precision and finality. So much so that, despite lingering doubt, she'd begun to wonder in recent days if he really did hear everything, even the silent desperate whisperings of a disillusioned soul.

The possibility brought a measure of comfort, but a greater feeling of unease when considering how little she really knew about his nature. She'd tried to be the very best wife she could be to her late husband, and *this* is how God repaid her.

"I got one trunk already loaded for you, Missus Aberdeen. But where are all the others, ma'am?"

Olivia sat straighter on the carriage seat, struggling to remember the servant's name. He'd only been sent to collect her. "I'm only taking the one trunk ... Jedediah. I have everything I need in there." And nothing her brother-in-law had forbidden her to take. He'd been named the sole beneficiary of her husband's estate—every last cent of which Charles had gained by cheating, lying, and swindling nearly everyone they knew. Even their friends, as it turned out. Those friends who—thanks to Charles's elder brother, the last of the Aberdeen family—now believed she'd known all along about the far-reaching extent of her husband's shady dealings.

Which she hadn't.

But one thing could be said for Charles Aberdeen ... he'd not been a respecter of persons when it came to taking advantage of someone. In that regard, he was no better than one of those Union sympathizers or fortune-seeking Northerners. And she wanted nothing that his greed and hypocrisy had garnered. Not even the wedding band—a family heirloom—Charles's brother had demanded she relinquish.

Jedediah peered up at her, his dark brow knitting tight, and she wondered if he understood what was happening to her, if he'd read the newspapers, if he could read at all. She wasn't about to try to explain it to him.

"Everything is fine," she assured, glancing down at the letter in her grip. Or soon would be. Surely Aunt Elizabeth would know what to do to help her navigate these unknown waters.

The carriage leaned to one side as Jedediah climbed to the driver's perch, and Olivia took one last glance at the handsome red-brick two-story house that had never been a home. Something went rigid inside her, and although it was ludicrous, she could've sworn she heard the scrape of mortar being spread on brick. Another layer being added to the wall she'd erected within herself. A wall that distanced her from every shed and unshed tear. Every unmet need. Every harsh word, look, and blow her strikingly handsome husband had bestowed upon her. And as much as she hated how the protective wall had changed her, hardened her, the wall also kept her safe, guarded her from being hurt again and from the sting of betrayal. She'd vowed to never place herself in a position where that could happen again.

And in the somber reflection of the moment, she silently pledged it for a second time.

She looked away, but recklessly so, for her gaze collided with that of a woman standing not ten feet away. The woman, older in years, draped in black, her pale skin sallow, her eyes sunken deep, stared at Olivia, unblinking. The woman's lips moved and Olivia braced herself for whatever she might say. Or scream. But it wasn't words that came from the woman's mouth.

The carriage started forward with a jolt, and Olivia tore her gaze away. But not before she saw the woman wipe the spittle from her chin.

Rigid as stone on the outside, Olivia trained her gaze straight forward as the carriage bumped and jarred over the rain-rutted road, purposefully not looking to the left or the right. A recent newspaper article had reported in detail about the entailment of Charles's estate onto his brother, so no doubt people were aware of her circumstances. Likewise, judging from their reactions, many of them were savoring her comeuppance.

Down Elm Street first, then Pine and Poplar, until, finally, the number of gawking pedestrians mercifully thinned.

Charles.

A traitorous tear edged the corner of her eye, but she put a swift end to it, unwilling to shed one more drop of grief over that man. She didn't miss him, so what was this ... emptiness she felt inside?

Realization gradually dawned, and with difficulty, she acknowledged what she was feeling. Though she hadn't loved Charles, a part of her did miss what they might have had together if he'd been a different kind of man.

The carriage passed a school, one she'd walked by often and always with a yearning. Though not for what most women might have wanted. Oh, early in their marriage, she had asked God repeatedly for children, truly wanting a child and believing it would help her and Charles's relationship. But God had not granted that request and wisely so, looking back. Charles had blamed the lack of conceiving on her, as he had with everything. And though she still hoped for children someday, *if* she was able, what she wished for now—what she'd wished for growing up—was a chance to nurture in another way.

But even that, Charles had taken from her. Along with everything else. She watched the school disappear from view.

Street traffic was light, so stops and starts were few. But recent summer downpours followed by days of oven-like heat had left the roads deeply scarred and ill-fit for travel. The carriage lurched to one side as a rear wheel slipped into a rut, and Olivia grabbed hold of the door, her stomach knotting. The walls of the carriage seemed to close in, and the horses' struggle to gain footing didn't help her already taut nerves.

If it wasn't so far a distance, she'd get out and walk. As it was, she tried to focus on something else, turning her gaze outward.

The war-torn city was gradually coming back to life again, though the number of boarded-up buildings stood as testament to how far a stretch remained on that journey.

A line of pedestrians trailed out the door of a bakery and that of a telegraph office, while a woman draped in black, like so many others, cradled a squalling infant in one arm and pulled two more children along behind. Men clad in tattered clothes—some still wearing their Confederate coats, now turned a dingy, defeated gray—stood clustered together on street corners, their shoulders thin and stooped beneath invisible burdens.

Olivia swallowed, tasting a bitterness, hating what the war had done. And to think her husband—and her, by association—had profited from the less fortunate, by helping others to "invest" what little money they had left. No surprise people looked at her with such disdain.

The last image she had of Charles rose in her mind, and she squeezed her eyes tight, wishing she could erase it from memory. The way they'd killed him ... His body so brutalized and—

Swallowing hard, she pressed back against the cushioned seat and focused on the buildings passing in a foggy blur. She steered her thoughts toward her destination, all while fingering the letter in her lap. *Aunt Elizabeth.*

Her mother could not have had a finer friend in this life, nor could her mother have chosen a finer woman to help fill the gaping hole her own passing left. Elizabeth Harding, "aunt" by friendship, was the closest thing to family Olivia had left. She clutched the envelope as if it were her ticket to a new life. *Thank God for you, Elizabeth.*

Where would she be right now if not for this kind and generous invitation?

One might think that going from the wife of Charles Winthrop Aberdeen to being the Harding family's head housekeeper was a far fall. But managing the day-to-day household activities sounded like a haven to her. She would cook and clean too, if it came to that, and do whatever else was required to repay the Hardings for their kindness in taking her in.

Well, almost anything else ... The only part of the arrangement that didn't sit well was having to live in close proximity to General Harding's spirited thoroughbreds.

She ran a hand over the sleeve of her left arm, still able to feel a slight bump, even through her suit jacket, where the bone had mended thirteen years earlier. She'd been only ten at the time, but the events from that afternoon remained vivid. The pain of the break was memorable enough, as was the unsightly scar. But the excruciating *snap* when the doctor reset the bone had haunted her for years. She hadn't ridden a horse since. Not until Charles had insisted a year ago.

"Get on the horse, Olivia!" Teeth clenched, he'd gripped her arm tightly.

"Charles, *please* ... I don't want to do this. You don't understand what—"

"You're embarrassing me. And yourself! Now get on the—"

Her cheeks burned as she recalled his harsh words. A queasiness clenched her mid-section. She'd told him the stallion was too much horse for her. He hadn't listened. Or cared. The horse had thrown her for no apparent reason, then turned and almost trampled her in the process. It had taken weeks for the bruises on her hip and thigh to heal.

She hadn't been on a horse since.

She managed riding in a carriage well enough but didn't like it. And a wagon too, though the nearness the open conveyance afforded to the four-legged beasts was much less preferred. She wished no ill will on the breed as a whole, she simply wished them to be kept far away from her. Which shouldn't be an issue, even at a stud farm like Belle Meade. Not with her serving as head housekeeper to the Hardings.

The terrain outside the carriage window gradually included fewer and fewer buildings until only rolling countryside filled the frame. The air inside the carriage grew overly warm, and Olivia leaned closer to the door, letting the breeze blow across her face. She longed for fall and cooler temperatures, the crisp air and crunch of leaves underfoot. Something about summer giving way to autumn always made her think of new beginnings. Odd really, when nature was going dormant for a season. But she loved the fall and desperately needed a new beginning in her life.

Despite everything that had transpired with Charles and his death, Nashville was the only home she'd ever known. And as certain as fall passed into winter and spring gave way to summer, she knew she would live and die here.

The South was a part of her, and — for better or worse — she would always be a part of it.

The carriage slowed, and Jedediah negotiated a path onto a washboard road leading to the Harding plantation. Within seconds, Olivia was certain her teeth would be jarred completely out of her head. Wealthy as General Harding was, he couldn't dictate the weather or control its aftereffects. Aunt Elizabeth had written to her more than once about the general's determination to pave this road with macadam, and right now Olivia would've wholeheartedly seconded the plan.

After a mile, then another, the ruts seemed to lessen.

She'd been out here only once in the past five years since she and Charles had married, and once with Charles and General Harding in the same room had been more than enough. She remembered

General Harding's exact words: "A man so keenly tied to the Union's interests in both action and opinion smacks of betrayal to the Confederacy and to his fellow countrymen. I'll extend no welcome to him in my home, nor will I claim association with him in any public forum."

Aunt Elizabeth—though she too disdained Unionists—had been more understanding and had written faithfully, even suggesting they meet in town. But Charles had swiftly squelched that idea. Olivia touched the side of her temple, remembering their ... "discussion."

The letters between her and Elizabeth had been a lifeline, and she cherished them. But she'd been less than honest with her about the intimate details of her marriage. After all, it wasn't proper for a woman to speak of such things. Once, in a letter to Elizabeth, she'd penned the truth of her relationship with Charles. But the very thought of him laying claim to that letter had sent her to the hearth posthaste, and she'd watched the fire devour the engraved stationery, the flames licking up the truth still locked tightly inside her.

She leaned forward on the seat, her anticipation growing at the thought of seeing Elizabeth again. "We'll be waiting for you with open arms, Livvy," Elizabeth had written. "You are like a daughter to me. As much as my own Selene or Mary is." Olivia took a deep breath and held it, smiling on the inside for the first time in she didn't know how long and awaiting that first glimpse of the Belle Meade mansion and its beautiful—

Something caught her eye. Some*one*. A man. Walking up the road a ways. And something about him drew her in.

He carried a ragged-looking pack, like that of a soldier, slung across his back. His gait was measured and unhurried, a fluid confidence accentuating each step. And he was tall, at least as tall as Charles had been.

His hair, dark, with a touch of unruly curl, reached past his collar in a manner more suited to that of a vagrant than a gentleman. Yet his clothes didn't look threadbare like those of the other men she'd seen in town. Still, his trousers were caked in dried mud six inches deep, like he'd been walking for weeks—if not months—on end.

She wondered if he knew where he was going and that this road led to the Hardings' plantation, then on down south through much of nothing, all the way to Natchez, Mississippi. And that, only after traversing the fifty-three hundred acres of wooded meadows and hills that comprised the Belle Meade Plantation.

As the carriage drew closer, Olivia leaned back into the shadows of her protective confines, not wanting the man to see her watching as they passed. But at that very moment he turned and looked back, and their eyes locked.

The distinguishing features of his face were hidden behind a thick beard, one that hadn't seen a trim in weeks, if ever. And although she couldn't pinpoint exactly why, she sensed a determination in him, in the resilient set of his shoulders perhaps or the steady gait of his stride—maybe in the way he carried himself. But he had a wildness about him too, like something caged, recently set free. And that untamed quality made her glad she was in the carriage and he was not.

As the carriage drew closer, she told herself to look away. Too late.

A flash of acknowledgement registered in his eyes. He waved to Jedediah—a short, succinct gesture—then looked back at her. One side of his bearded cheek edged up as though he found her attention amusing, and his teeth showed white in a slow-coming smile. He brought his hand to his forehead—just as the carriage passed him—and snapped a smart salute, then he—

Olivia felt her mouth slip open. He'd *winked* at her? Her face heated. She focused forward, gripping the cushioned velvet beneath her as the carriage bumped and jostled down the road.

For a moment, she wondered if she'd imagined it, yet knew she hadn't. The audacity. The nerve of that—

As Jedediah guided the carriage around a narrow bend, she half turned on the seat, wanting to peer back out the window. But she resisted the urge, somehow knowing he would still be watching. And smiling! She sighed. The war had taken so much from them, not the least of which, it seemed, was chivalry.

But General Harding, who held honor in the highest regard, would send that scoundrel packing soon enough. Belle Meade had more workers than they could use. Elizabeth had said as much in a recent letter, and the general was particular about who he hired.

Another mile passed before it occurred to her . . .

She looked out the window and exhaled. Her view to the right was now blocked by a hillside creviced with Tennessee limestone. Watching him had caused her to miss the first glimpse of Belle Meade. Now she'd have to wait another mile or so before seeing the—

Without warning, a thundering crack exploded somewhere behind her and the carriage swerved hard to the right. Thrown from her seat, Olivia grappled for a hold as the conveyance seemed to drop out from beneath her. Wood groaning, shuddering in protest, the carriage jerked, and she fell hard against the door—and felt it give way.

She scrambled to grab onto something, *anything*, as the ground rushed up to meet her. But it was the feral scream coming from somewhere in front of the carriage that sent a chill straight through her bones.

Chapter TWO

*A*fter what felt like a lifetime, the carriage slammed to a halt, and the deafening crunch of wood siphoned the air from Olivia's lungs. Eyes clenched tight, she waited, still as stone, to make sure it was over.

No matter how she tried, she couldn't get that scream out of her mind. It had come from one of the horses, she felt certain.

She wanted to move but was afraid whatever part of her body she commanded to obey wouldn't. An erratic *thump-thump-thump* came from somewhere nearby, and it took her several breaths to realize it was her own heartbeat.

"Missus Aberdeen ... Can you hear me, ma'am?"

Recognizing Jedediah's voice — far away though it sounded — Olivia blinked her eyes, but her *yes* came out a strangled whisper as she found herself staring at the carriage ceiling. The conveyance was tilted back, hulked to one side as if squatting on its wounded right haunch. The window to her left framed a swath of blue sky, but the view to her right, more ground level, was obstructed by a slab of limestone cratering in the side of the carriage — just where she'd been sitting.

Feeling the walls close in around her, she was reaching for the door when her world suddenly lurched again. The carriage shifted and one of the horses let out a high-pitched whinny. Olivia braced for another onslaught but the rock wall refused to relinquish hold.

"Whoa there, girls. Steady now, steady ... I just need to cut you loose ..." Jedediah's voice carried over the horse's complaints.

Olivia prayed he would hurry, wanting nothing more than to be untethered from the wild beasts.

Her skirts—and emotions—in disarray, she pushed herself up and gave the left door handle a quick yank. It held fast. Determined and fighting a closed-in feeling, she put more weight behind the effort, not easily done with gravity working against her. Pain shot through her shoulder, cutting the attempt short.

A familiar panic, one she loathed, began to thrum deep within. She debated on gathering her hoop skirt and trying to climb out the window, but that would hardly be proper. And she doubted she'd fit anyway, not with her bustle. Pulling in a calming breath, she took quick mental inventory.

Other than the ache in her shoulder where she'd hit the door, she didn't think she was injured. Not seriously anyway. Certainly nothing was broken.

A hasty tread of footsteps, and Jedediah appeared in the window. "Missus Aberdeen!" With the carriage tilted as it was, he could barely see over the edge. "Is you hurt, ma'am? Cuz if you is ... oh, Lawd—" He mopped the sheen of sweat from his brow with a wadded bandanna. "Missus Harding ain't never gonna forgive me."

Olivia summoned calm she didn't feel. "I'm not hurt, Jedediah. A little sore, perhaps, and bruised. What happened?"

"It's that confounded wheel, ma'am." He gestured. "It done cracked and gave way. 'Bout scared the mares to death, and me too. One of 'em done run off." He motioned. "The other's hurt pretty bad. Got a busted up foreleg. Tried to take a chunk outta my arm when I cut her reins loose. She can be downright mean when she puts her mind to it. Won't let me come near her. I'm guessin' we might have to put her down." He shook his head. "General gonna be none too happy 'bout that. But here ..." He stuffed the bandanna back in his pocket. "Let's get you outta there, ma'am. I hate to say it, but we be havin' to walk the rest of the way. But it ain't too terrible far. And I heard Missus Harding say they'd be waitin' to greet you."

Jedediah gripped the door latch, but it didn't open. He tried again. Nothing. Olivia could've sworn the cramped space inside the carriage shrank by half.

"Can't you get it open?" she asked, smoothing the angst from her voice.

He worked the latch repeatedly. "This door's good and stuck, ma'am. It just ain't wantin' to give."

Feeling more corralled by the second, Olivia pushed her shoulder hard against the door, more for want of control than thinking anything might come from the effort.

"It ain't budgin', ma'am. But I'm bettin' that if I had me some tools, I could spring it."

"And do you have these tools with you, Jedediah?"

"Not the ones I need, ma'am. They's back at Belle Meade."

"Well ..." She let out a breath, not relishing the prospect of being stuck inside here for an hour or more. But then ... perhaps—she eyed the width of the window again, wondering—she might not have to wait after all. "Jedediah." She smiled. "I suggest you go ahead and be on your way, then you can retrieve the necessary tools and return for me."

His forehead crinkled. "I can't be leavin' you on your lonesome, ma'am. Why ... the general, he'd—"

"I'll be fine, I assure you." She put on her most polite yet insistent smile. "And—" She glanced down the road toward Belle Meade. "The sooner you go, the sooner I'll be freed."

Not looking at all convinced, Jedediah shook his head. "It just ain't right, me leavin' you here, Missus Aberdeen. I don't fancy the—"

"I'm a grown woman, Jedediah, and am perfectly capable of taking care of myself in your brief absence." She held back a smile this time and could tell by the deep furrows bridging his nose that she was getting her point across. "And what's more, I hate the thought of Mrs. Harding standing there on the porch, waiting and watching. You said yourself she'd be looking for me."

"Yes'um, I did say that." He rubbed his jaw then sighed. "Got a crate of apples up top, if you want one 'fore I go. If you's hungry."

"Thank you, Jedediah. But I'm *not* hungry. I just want out of here."

"Yes, ma'am." He nodded. "I be runnin' the whole way, Missus Aberdeen. So you just sit tight." He set off down the road at a hasty clip.

Olivia waited for a couple of moments, making certain he was gone, then took several deep breaths, sizing up the window. And then herself. She'd never taken part in tree-climbing, a tomboyish pastime that her mother, God rest her soul, had frowned upon. And with good reason, Olivia knew. But right now, she wished she'd at least attempted to scale the lowest limbs of a friendly dogwood. The experience would have proven helpful.

She peered through the window to the ground below. It was farther than she'd anticipated, but the thought of being prisoner inside this carriage bolstered her courage. She could do this. She'd never done anything like it before, of course. But she could do it.

She gained her footing and hitched up her hoop skirt, gathering the yards of black fabric and lace around her waist. Holding on to the side of the window, she eased her leg through, but quickly discovered that the bottom of the window was higher than she'd thought. The lace on her pantalets caught on the window's edge. She tugged the fabric, but it held fast.

She pulled harder, determined, and felt the material rip just as she felt herself falling backward. Frantic, she grabbed the side of the door to steady herself. Then laughed, thinking how foolish she must look.

With renewed courage, she stretched her leg as far as she could down alongside the carriage until she felt the rim of the step beneath her boot tip. She tapped it with her toes, testing its strength. Then took another breath and put her full weight on it. She scrunched her upper body and had just managed to get her head through the window when—

She heard whistling. And looked up.

It was *him*. The man they'd passed on the road earlier. He'd rounded the corner but was looking down and, judging by his lack of reaction, hadn't seen her—yet.

Faster than she would have imagined possible, Olivia dragged herself back into the carriage, snagging her hair, her pantalets, her petticoat, and nearly everything else in the process. She backed away from the window, but her heel caught in her hem and she fell, nothing but air behind her. She went down hard, landing on the cushioned seat and whacking the back of her head on the wooden paneling.

Lying on her back, her head throbbing, nearly drowning in a sea of whale bone, crinoline, and lace, she gritted her teeth and recalled a word Charles had used all too frequently when frustrated. Knowing he would have used it helped her not to.

Footsteps refocused her attention just as a somewhat-familiar face appeared in the window. But instead of the slow-coming smile he'd worn earlier, concern lined his expression. "You're still in here!" He was winded from running and his gaze moved over her in an appraising fashion. "Are you all right?"

Aware of her state, Olivia tugged the folds of fabric down over her underskirts and pantalets, grateful he had the decency to look away, albeit not long enough. "I'm fine," she said, smoothing the front of her dress. "For the most part anyway."

"I looked up and saw the carriage, and—what happened?"

"It was the wheel." She gestured behind her. "We hit one too many ruts, I'm guessing."

"And your driver? Where is he?"

"He went for help."

"And left you here? Alone?"

His query gave her pause, as did his forthrightness. Both made her aware of just how alone she was. Correction. How alone *they* were. And she began to question the wisdom of having sent Jedediah ahead. Yet she knew better than to show uncertainty. Or fear. Revealing weakness to a man gave him power. Power she would never give a man again.

She straightened and made herself look him in the eyes, grateful for the barrier between them. "It was at my insistence he took his leave, sir. The door is jammed and he went to get help. But I'm certain he'll be returning posthaste!" She glanced beyond him as if expecting to see Jedediah any second, knowing full well there was no way the servant would be back this soon. But *he* didn't know that.

Piercing eyes of hazel—or were they blue? She couldn't quite tell—met hers, and she found herself wanting to avoid the gaze of this man who seemed far less like a vagrant upon closer inspection—and yet somehow, even more *untamed*.

He tried the door handle—*once, twice*—to no avail. And somewhat to her relief. "It's stuck all right."

"As I said."

There it was again, that slow-coming roguish smile. "I'm glad you're all right, ma'am. The horses ... what happened to them?"

"Jedediah cut them loose. He said they ran off."

He eyed the carriage. "I've seen my share of these fancy rigs turn over on roads not nearly as torn up as this one. And you're lucky too, seeing which wheel snapped, that you didn't go sailing right out that door."

She trailed his gaze, saw the carnage of crushed wood and bent metal again, and frowned. She clearly remembered that door coming open and the sensation of falling. So ... how then had she *not* fallen out?

"I need to offer you an apology, ma'am."

That brought her attention back around.

His gaze swept her dress, then lifted. "A few minutes ago ... back on the road, I—I winked at you, ma'am." His grip tightened on his pack. "I didn't realize you were in mourning. The inside of the carriage was dark and all I saw was how you were staring at me and—"

"I was not *staring* at you, sir." The words were out before she could catch them, and Olivia did her best to appear appropriately affronted. "I was merely looking at you as the carriage passed." But she had to glance away as she said it, knowing it wasn't the full truth. Or even a partial one.

"Of course, ma'am. I didn't mean to insinuate anything on your part. I'm sorry." His mouth didn't turn but she'd have sworn he was smiling on the inside. "But even if you *had* been staring, which you weren't, I realize," he added quickly, "I shouldn't have winked. It was—"

"Improper," she supplied, daring herself not to blink.

"Yes, ma'am. And therefore—" He tilted his head, a ghost of a smile showing. "My offered apology."

Sensing his sincerity only made her feel more guilty about the lie, which in turn made her more eager for him to leave. "And your apology is kindly accepted. But now ..." She looked beyond him, hoping he'd take the genteel hint. "Understanding that help is already on the way, you needn't feel any obligation to stay with me. I'm quite capable on my own."

"I have no doubt about that, ma'am." He stepped back and studied the window. "But if you're game, I'd be happy to help you climb through there."

Not about to admit she'd already tried—and still intended—to do that very thing, Olivia drew herself up. "Climbing through a window is hardly behavior suitable for a lady."

He laughed and rubbed his bearded jaw. "Perhaps not ... *m'lady.*" He said it with a touch of haughtiness, bowing at the waist like some English lord. "But you'd be out of there and on your way again. Which *is* your objective, is it not, Mrs.... ?"

Olivia leveled a disapproving stare, something she'd done once with Charles but never again, having paid for that mistake dearly. But this man wasn't Charles, and she didn't appreciate his taking the liberty of asking for her name instead of waiting until they'd been properly introduced. She had the feeling he'd done it intentionally too, knowing it would rile her.

She wasn't taking the bait. "I thank you, sir, for stopping to ascertain my well-being. But I believe it would be best to wait until help arrives. And—if you will allow me—I also believe your assistance would be best lent in going for help as well."

Laugh lines crinkled the corners of his eyes. "You want me to leave."

"I didn't say that."

"No, ma'am, you didn't. Not outright. But you said it well enough just the same."

Olivia didn't know how to respond. He was so direct. So free with his opinions—and his apologies, but she swept the latter point aside. There were proper rules of etiquette to be followed between a man and woman, especially when they were strangers, and this man seemed bent on plowing through them all. "What I'm attempting to say to you, sir—"

"I know what you're saying, ma'am. So I'm only going to ask you this once more. Do you want me to help you climb out of there or not?"

She drew herself up. "I do not."

"No one's going to see."

"I don't care who sees, it's the—"

"Suit yourself then." He took a step back. "After all, this seems like a safe enough road, and you *are* locked inside a carriage. By my calculation, we can't be more than a couple of miles from Belle Meade, so it shouldn't be long before your driver returns."

Olivia eyed him. "So … you *know* where you're going then?"

He looked at her as though she were daft. "Generally I try to make that the case, yes, ma'am. Don't you?"

She suppressed a sigh. "What I meant was … you're aware that this road leads to the Belle Meade Plantation?"

"I am."

"Well." Feeling as though she had the upper hand and enjoying it, Olivia smoothed her skirt. "If it saves you any trouble, I can tell you that General Harding isn't hiring right now. He has all the help he needs."

"Is that right? So you're privy to General Harding's business, are you? You must be close to the family."

Olivia read bemusement, rather than disappointment, in his expression and found it irritating. Same as she found him. Yet she hesitated, not wanting to overstate her relationship with the Harding family, especially considering the conditions of her coming to live with them. "I'm acquainted with the general, sir. But I enjoy a much closer friendship with his wife. It's through her knowledge of her husband's dealings that I'm privy to this fact."

He nodded, obviously weighing the information. "I thank you for your counsel, ma'am. But with all due respect, I've come a long way to get here. I think I'll take my chances."

Olivia bristled at her advice being so summarily dismissed. And by someone like him. "I was simply trying to spare you further wasted effort. It seems such a shame"—she peered over the window's edge and down at his mud-covered trousers—"considering how far you've apparently traveled."

He smiled even as the bluish hazel of his eyes darkened. "Your *kindness* is duly noted. And while I may not get what I've come for, ma'am, I won't consider my effort in getting here wasted." He looked up the road toward Belle Meade, then back again. "If I'd never tried to get here ... now *that* would have been the real waste."

Reaching up, he tipped an imaginary hat and strode on without a backward glance. She followed him with her gaze as he rounded the bend and disappeared from sight. But his words resonated inside her.

I may not get what I've come for ...

She hadn't wanted him to stay with her. She preferred him gone. So why this unexpected interest in knowing what had brought the man to Belle Meade? She couldn't account for it, but one thing she knew. She wasn't waiting for Jedediah to return. She wanted out of this carriage.

Spotting Aunt Elizabeth's letter below her on the seat, she retrieved it, stuffed it in her skirt pocket, then hiked up her skirts. Gripping the door, she maneuvered her leg through the window, more smoothly this time than before. She smiled. This wasn't going to be as hard as she'd thought. But the trick was ... how did she get the rest of her through without falling?

The mounds of fabric only served to slow her progress, bunching around her waist and making it hard to get a good hold. Taking a deep breath and letting it out, she tucked her chin against her chest and tried to make herself as small as she could. Then she forced her head through the narrow space and was almost through when her shoulder caught.

She tugged and pulled, but it was no use. The opening was too small. She groaned, the muscles in the back of her neck burning. She was loathe to admit it, but her plan of escape was ill-concocted.

Tucking her chin again, she ducked her head to push it back through—but her hair caught. She huffed a breath, wishing she'd never started this. She managed to free her hair only to discover she was hung on something else from behind. She reached around, feeling for where she was snagged when she caught movement from the corner of her eye.

One of the horses.

It broke through the pine trees lining the opposite side of the road and limped toward her. Blood ran down its leg from a gash, ugly and deep, and another line trickled down the side of its neck. The horse paused near the middle of the road, lowered its head, and exhaled a blast of air that sent dust and dirt flying. Olivia went weak inside. Scarcely able to breathe, she made herself go perfectly still. If she didn't move, maybe the animal wouldn't see her.

As if reading her thoughts, the horse raised its head and looked directly at her, then snorted and pawed the ground. All Olivia could think about was that stallion nearly trampling her. And though the thought was absurd, she knew, she sensed accusation in the mare's actions and recalled what Jedediah had said about the horse... *Tried to take a chunk outta my arm when I cut her reins loose. She can be downright mean when she puts her mind to it.*

It started toward her again, limping, and Olivia fought to free herself. With every step the horse took, Olivia's efforts grew more frantic. "It's just a horse, Olivia. Just a horse," she repeated, words her father had said to her years ago, the day following the accident, her tiny arm throbbing and bandaged. "It won't hurt you if you treat it right," he'd said.

But her father had been wrong. She had treated that horse right, and it had thrown her. She'd treated Charles as best she could too. And he'd hurt her. Over and over and over again. And no amount of bandages or salve was going to heal the wounds he'd left behind.

Not wanting to, Olivia forced herself to look back, and the painful knot at the base of her throat twisted tighter. The horse was close now—too close—and was sniffing the air, chomping at the bit. No doubt wanting to chomp into her, just like Jedediah had said.

Tears burning, the scar on her arm aching, Olivia tossed pride and propriety to the wind and screamed for all she was worth.

Chapter
THREE

*R*idley shook his head again, smiling. It'd been a long time since he'd met a woman so hard bent on being proper. The years of war and loss had taken their toll on everyone, himself included. And getting by on little to nothing had thinned the starch of even the most properly bred of Southern society.

Or so he'd thought.

After all, who gave a horse's tail about how the woman got out of that carriage? He certainly didn't. But her expression when he'd suggested she crawl through the window had said it all. And when he'd intentionally asked for her name, able to guess at the kind of reaction that would draw ...

He laughed, recalling how those eyes of hers had flashed. That pert look on her pretty face was enough to make a man—

He paused, hearing something. He turned back in the direction he'd come and waited, head cocked, listening again.

But ... nothing. So he continued on.

If he ever had the pleasure of crossing paths with the young widow again, he promised himself he would—

There it was again. A scream. No mistaking it this time. *Or* the direction from which it came. He reeled and broke into a run. An image flashed into his mind of someone forcing his way into the young woman's carriage, and Ridley fully blamed himself for leaving her unattended. No matter that she'd made it clear she wanted him to leave.

He rounded the corner he'd passed just moments earlier and wasn't prepared for what he saw. And heard.

The prim and proper young widow was hanging half out the window of the carriage, her skirts hitched high and her petticoats—and other frilly unmentionables—on view for all the world to see. But it was hearing what she was saying and who she was saying it to that made him slow his steps.

"Shoo! Go away! *Shoo!*" she half-screamed, half-cried at a pretty little bay mare he remembered seeing earlier.

The mare inched closer, and when Ridley spotted a few apples beneath the carriage, he soon guessed the animal's motivation. Still, the mare watched the woman with a curiosity Ridley understood and, frankly, shared. The woman continued to give the mare a good goin' over, as his grandfather used to say. But the only question in Ridley's mind was why.

He made a quiet approach. "Ma'am, is everything—"

No sooner had he spoken than the mare bolted. Ridley tried to grab the horse's harness as she passed, but she veered away, favoring her right leg as she went. And he soon glimpsed why. Her leg was busted up. But still, she ran. Knowing he'd never catch her now, Ridley turned back.

The young widow looked up at him, blinked, then quickly ducked her head. Her breath came in staggered sobs. Not knowing what to make of the situation, Ridley stayed his ground, uncertain if she'd welcome his presence after dismissing him so soundly. Not to mention the embarrassment of being caught in such a predicament. From the look of things, he guessed she'd tried climbing out the window after all. Now she'd gotten herself good and stuck.

But one thing was certain, that was one shapely calf attached to one very shapely thigh.

He still couldn't see her face—her intention, no doubt—but he couldn't hide his smile. Not that she was looking. "Ma'am . . . may I be of assistance to you?"

A few thready breaths, a sniff, then finally she nodded, her head still down. "Yes . . ." Her voice came out small, muffled, the folds of her dress all bunched up around her. "Would you—" She took a quick breath and he saw her grip tighten where she held on to the window. "Would you please help me get out of here? I'm stuck . . . as you can clearly see."

Ridley stepped closer. The halting lilt of her voice told him her fear was—or had been—real, but the edge to it let him know she hadn't completely swallowed her pride. Choked on it was probably more accurate.

He dumped his pack and assessed the situation. "It'd be my pleasure, ma'am. Where're you hung up?"

"My hair and then ... somewhere along here." She gestured toward her back end, her gaze still averted.

"All right then, let me take a look." He put a foot on the carriage step and pulled himself up. He untangled a strand of dark brown hair from the rivets along the window then ran his hand around the top side, pushing aside the obstinate hoop skirt and pressing down yards of fabric as he went. His exploration extended the length of her back, though he took care not to touch her any more than he had to. He had to admit, however ... this task wasn't too terribly unpleasant.

He quickly ascertained the problem. "It's your bustle, ma'am. But I'm afraid I'm going to tear it if I try to—"

"Do it, *please*. Just get me out of here."

"All right." It was dark inside the carriage which made it more difficult to see. He quickly realized what he had to do and grinned, but tried not to let it show in his voice. "Ma'am, I'm going to need to ... *feel around* a little to find where you're hung up."

She nodded, but he felt her tense.

He reached inside the window, much closer to her now, and caught a whiff of lilac and something else sweet and womanly. He located the bustle—not hard to do on a woman—and gingerly felt through the folds of dense fabric, a somewhat trickier task to manage without being able to see well. But harder for her than him, he realized.

"You headed to Belle Meade too?" he said, feeling a need, for her sake, to make conversation.

"Yes ... I'm the Hardings' new head housekeeper."

"Oh ... well, that's good." Though it wasn't what he had expected her to say. From the look of her—her fine clothes and the highfalutin way she conducted herself and from what she'd said earlier—he'd have figured her for a rich friend of the family, not an employee.

But then, the war had changed things for everyone.

If anyone had ever told him he'd be in such a predicament— feeling his way around a woman's bustle—he would've guessed he might have enjoyed it a little more. As it was, he sensed the young woman's discomfort and hurried to finish the task. But it took longer than he thought. It was a right fancy bustle. He cleared his throat, needing a diversion.

"May I ask you a question, ma'am?"

Seconds passed.

"Yes."

"Why were you screaming like that just now? At the mare, I mean."

She exhaled. "I don't care for horses."

Thinking back on the scene he'd come upon moments earlier, the pieces slowly fell together for him. *I don't care for horses.* So much said in so few words, and the truth being understated, if the fear he'd witnessed from her was any clue.

He found where the material was snagged and pulled. The fabric ripped in his hand. "Now ..." He stepped back down. "If you'll crawl back inside there then come out head first, we'll have you out of there in no time."

She finally looked at him then, her eyes red-rimmed, clouded with embarrassment. Wordless, she maneuvered her body back inside, then her leg. Ridley helped push the voluminous folds of her skirts back behind her, glad now that she hadn't seen him smiling.

Wasting no time, she stuck her arms and head through the window. Ridley guided her hands to his shoulders, then gripped her about her waist and pulled. She didn't weigh much, not when considering the shapeliness of the curves beneath his hands — and the curves at eye level, which he couldn't help but notice and tried not to stare at.

Her skirt got hung up again, but he didn't wait for her instruction. He just pulled. Her feet cleared the window and gravity did its work. Her body fell against his and there was a moment — when he was holding her eye-level with him, his hands about her waist, hers on his shoulders — when he became aware of just how long it'd been since he'd touched a woman. Much less held one. Her eyes were so deep a blue they looked almost violet in the afternoon sun. Her dark lashes lay soft and pretty against her skin, and her hair — a glossy dark brown, like the finest aged whiskey swirling in the glass — was piled atop her head, but for a few strands that had come unhitched in the struggle. Ridley swallowed hard. Widow or not, she was one beautiful wom —

"*Please* ... put me down."

The simple command snapped him back to attention. He felt heat rushing through his body, most of it ending up in his face. He cleared his throat and promptly set her on the ground, where she took two hasty steps backward and wobbled. He reached out to steady her, seeing her boot caught in a rut, but she yanked her arm away—and went squarely down on her bottom.

This time he didn't even try to curb his grin. Not even with the dark look she threw him. He tried to help her up, but she batted his hand away.

"I can do it myself."

He laughed, seeing a storm gather behind those violet eyes. "Yes, ma'am. I can see that."

She dusted off her skirt, then started poking her hair back into place. She was taller than he'd first judged. Still a good few inches shorter than him, but the height looked good on her. Her expression was guarded. Not that he blamed her. And color heightened her cheeks. Whether from crying or embarrassment, he didn't know. Probably both.

"I'm sorry I had to tear your dress, ma'am."

"I don't care about that. I—" She took a breath, her hand hovering at her midsection. She looked up at him. "I'm indebted to you, sir." Her voice was just above a whisper. "I thank you for helping me get out of there."

Well able to imagine what nick her pride had taken with that admission, Ridley nodded once. "You're welcome, ma'am. It was my pleasure." He caught the quick rise of her brow but didn't respond, not having intended anything by that last comment. But he could clearly see that she thought he had. This woman ...

Remembering the promise he'd made to himself earlier about her, he decided to keep it. "No one's here to introduce us properly, ma'am, but it seems to me that—under the circumstances—we should know each other's names. Don't you agree?"

She stared up at him.

Not hearing a protest, he proceeded. "I'm Ridley Cooper, ma'am. Mr. Ridley Adam Cooper, if we want to be formal about it." He waited, half hoping she would offer him her hand, so he could greet her properly—with a kiss—like a gentleman. But she didn't.

She opened her mouth. Closed it. Then took a quick breath. "Nice to meet you, Mr. Cooper. I'm Mrs. Charl—" She stopped as if catching herself. Her features tensed. "I'm ... Mrs. *Olivia* Aberdeen."

Ridley did his best not to react to her correction and to what it revealed. She was a widow, after all, like scores of other women in this town and a hundred others like it, still missing their men and trying their best to carry on without them. He could tell by the way she firmed her mouth and looked away that she was carrying a load of grief. Understandably so.

"It's a pleasure to meet you, Mrs. Aberdeen. And for what it's worth, ma'am, I don't think one bit less of you for coming through that window. In fact, I'm impressed."

He was pretty sure she tried to smile, but the gesture couldn't seem to take hold. She lowered her gaze again. A rustle in the trees drew their attention, and he saw the mare peering through the branches.

Olivia Aberdeen stiffened.

"It's all right." He held up a hand. "She's just hurt, that's all. And a little scared." He walked over and grabbed his pack, dismissing the idea of trying to catch the thoroughbred. "Is there anything you need before we start walking?"

Ridley caught her staring at the trunk still strapped up top. "You want your trunk?"

"No, it's all right. Jedediah will get it when he comes back."

But the way she said it—same as his mother used to when she wanted something but didn't want to be a bother—told him otherwise. He retrieved the trunk and got a closer look at the damage to the other side of the carriage. Imagination kicked in, and he sighed. It was a wonder the woman hadn't been seriously injured. Or worse.

He shouldered his pack, then the trunk, which wasn't as heavy as he'd thought, and they fell into step together.

Neither spoke, and he left it that way, figuring she preferred it.

After almost a mile, he shifted the trunk and looked over at her. Traces of sweat beaded her brow. "Why don't you take off that jacket, ma'am? It'd be a lot cooler for you."

"I'm fine." She tugged on her left sleeve. "I'm not warm at all."

Ridley nodded, deciding to leave it alone. "Where are you from, Mrs. Aberdeen? If you don't mind me asking."

"I'm from here." She walked on, face forward. "From Nashville. I've lived here all my life."

He waited, giving her time to pursue the conversation if she wanted to. Though he didn't mind the silence either. After all he'd been through, he didn't think he'd ever tire of quiet again.

"What about you, Mr. Cooper?" she finally reciprocated, more out of politeness than interest, he suspected. She didn't look at him. "Where's your home?"

"South Carolina. On the coast."

"The coast?" She turned, slowing. "So . . . you've seen the ocean?"

He laughed, liking the way her eyes lit up. "Yes, ma'am. Many times. I've swam in it too."

"What's it like?"

"Wet. And salty."

She laughed—a light, musical sound—and he sneaked another look at her. "Maybe you'll see it for yourself someday."

"Oh no. I don't think so." She shook her head. "Tennessee is my home. I don't expect I'll ever leave. And I don't wish to . . . I love it here."

Something about the way she said it made him wonder if she really felt that way, or if she was trying to convince herself it was true.

On impulse, he reached into his pocket and withdrew the seashell. "I've carried this with me for a while now. I picked it up along a stretch of beach not far from my home."

She slowed, looking at it like it was a rare jewel. "May I hold it?"

Liking the way she asked, he nodded. "Sure."

She paused and turned the shell this way and that in her palm. "It's so pretty." She held it up it to the light then waved her forefinger behind it. "You can see through it." She rubbed her thumb along the smooth inside.

How many times had he done the very same thing?

"And it was just lying there? On the beach?"

"Along with about a thousand others."

She exhaled as though unable to imagine such a thing.

Her gaze never leaving it, she handed it back to him. He returned it to his pocket, wishing he had another shell he could give her. They walked on, and after another half mile, he started wondering where the driver of the carriage was. Surely the man had had time to get back to Belle Meade by now.

The temperature was climbing but at least it wasn't raining. Traveling by foot and sleeping beneath the stars was as familiar to him now as home used to be. So was having his clothes soaked clean through. But he preferred the dry.

Thinking about being wet through and through made him recall a night he and his brothers had spent out in the woods. He'd only been eleven at the time, which meant Petey and Alfred couldn't have been more than nine and seven. A bittersweet pang knifed him just thinking of their faces again, of how they'd given their mother fits at that age, and of how Petey and Alfred had died. In battle.

Ridley narrowed his eyes, feeling the burn of hurt rising up behind them. The war had taken so much. And his father, sickly and worn from worry, had laid most of the blame at his feet before dying himself a handful of months later.

The trunk started digging into his collarbone and Ridley shifted its weight, wincing at the needle-sharp pain in his shoulder and at the memory that always came with it. Almost three years had passed, yet what had happened that night on the mountain still lived inside him. As did the grueling events of the months following. He only hoped he hadn't kept his sliver of a near-starved dream alive for naught. But he guessed he'd find out soon enough.

"What is it that brings you to Belle Meade, Mr. Cooper?"

Ridley looked beside him, not surprised by the question so much as the curiosity edging her tone.

"Earlier," she continued, "you said that you may not get what you've come for." She peered up. "I'm simply wondering what that is."

Sensing more than casual interest on her part, Ridley felt his own guard nudge upward. After all, she was, by her own admission, close to General Harding's wife and therefore likely felt a sense of protectiveness toward the family. He understood that. He also understood what was at stake for him should anyone at Belle Meade learn the truth about him. Namely, about his allegiance during the war.

Just this week, he'd glimpsed some news about a man — a "Northern sympathizer," the Nashville paper had labeled him in capital letters — who had been shot in broad daylight. Murdered. His halfnaked body dragged through the streets behind a horse, then hung from a lamppost, the words *traitor* and *scalawag* — words Ridley knew only too well — scrawled in blood on a scrap of wood above him. And that man had been one of Nashville's own.

"It won't sound like much to you, Mrs. Aberdeen, but ... I heard about General Harding's place, about his thoroughbreds, and decided to have a look, that's all. I'm just passing through, ma'am. I won't be staying long." He focused forward, but it was a full eight strides before she did. He counted.

To her credit, Olivia Aberdeen kept pace with him, and other than pulling on her black lace collar once or twice, she didn't complain — something he would have expected from her, based on their earlier encounter. Those fancy-heeled boots she was wearing made the going more difficult, and she stumbled a time or two. But he didn't dare try to help.

The squeak of wheels drew his attention, and a buggy rounded the corner ahead, moving at a good clip. "My guess is, Mrs. Aberdeen, that's your driver."

The Negro slowed the conveyance — an extravagant little thing, big enough to hold maybe two people and not much else — and reined in alongside them, his gaze firmly on Ridley. "You all right, Missus Aberdeen?"

"Yes, Jedediah. I'm fine."

Hearing suspicion in the man's voice, Ridley offered his hand. "Ridley Cooper, sir. You passed me on the road a ways back."

Jedediah nodded, the tension in his features easing a little. "Yes, sir. I 'member you now." His focus shifted to Mrs. Aberdeen. "How'd you get yourself outta there, ma'am? Y'all get that door open after all?"

Seeing Mrs. Aberdeen struggle with her response, Ridley jumped in. "That door was good and stuck, all right. But we managed somehow." He motioned behind them. "We saw one of the mares. Looks like her leg is tore up pretty badly."

Jedediah wiped his face with his sleeve. "Don't I know it, sir. Pains me somethin' awful. She bein' such a fine horse. I need to see to her and the other one too. But first" — Jedediah shifted — "I best get you to Belle Meade, Missus Aberdeen. I told Missus Harding about what happened and that you was all right, but she's eager to see for herself, ma'am."

The mare hitched to the buggy snorted and pranced. Jedediah held the reins taut but Ridley didn't miss the look of panic that flashed across Olivia Aberdeen's face.

"Thank you, Jedediah," she said, forming a smile that didn't reach her eyes. "But I think you should go on and see to that mare. I'm fine to walk the rest of the way. I enjoy walking."

"You sure, ma'am? Won't take me long to skedaddle you right on back to the —"

"I'm sure, Jedediah." Her smile deepened, but Ridley would've sworn he saw her shudder. "It's not that far and I'll enjoy the fresh air. I insist," she added with finality when Jedediah made no move to leave.

Looking like a man who'd been told what to do by a woman,

Jedediah continued on his way, and Ridley did the same, letting Mrs. Aberdeen set the pace.

She seemed determined to stay at least a half stride ahead of him, and he let her, considering it gave him a chance to study her unhindered. She was pretty, that had already been established. But she had a cuteness about her too. A spunk. A way of carrying herself that made him wonder what she'd been like as a little girl. He guessed she'd been a real spitfire. Then again, he found that image difficult to marry with what he knew about her conventional bent. But whichever way he looked at her—and he did, with appreciation—he liked what he saw.

They rounded a bend in the road, and a long, shrub-lined drive came into view. At the very end sat a mansion reigning queen-like over a meadow that sprawled out in all directions, the land rising and falling around it like incoming tide. Six square columns stood tall and proud, framing the front of the two-story estate, and at the peak of its roof sat a cornice that looked remarkably like a crown from this distance.

The Queen of Southern Plantations ... More than one person had used those words to describe Belle Meade. And now he knew why.

Mrs. Aberdeen slowed beside him, so Ridley did the same.

He lowered the trunk to the ground, welcoming the respite but seeing her frown. "Something wrong, ma'am?"

Her attention stayed fixed ahead. "No," she whispered. "It's just been a long time since I've been here. And it's—" She bit the inside of her cheek, an unconscious gesture, Ridley knew. "It's so much lovelier than I remembered. So fine a house and grounds." She looked down and grimaced, then started brushing the worst of the road dust from her dress.

"You look real nice, Mrs. Aberdeen. You needn't worry in that regard, ma'am."

She looked at him, and he half expected to see a hint of *tsking* in her eyes. But instead, he detected gratitude.

She quickly looked away. "We'd better be going. Jedediah said Mrs. Harding was waiting for me."

Halfway up the road, she peered over at him. "Don't be surprised, Mr. Cooper, if General Harding asks if you were in the war. Aunt Elizabeth says he talks about those years often."

Ridley nodded but said nothing, surprised she was offering him this insight. But the war wasn't a topic he welcomed.

"You did fight, didn't you?"

He took his time answering. "Yes, ma'am. I did."

She nodded, as if considering that a good thing. "I haven't seen the general in over four years, but his wife tells me he made a vow not to shave his beard until the Confederacy claimed victory." She glanced toward the house, where a group of people gathered. "I guess we'll see soon enough whether he's softened any in that regard."

Ridley followed, glad to be spared further questions about the war and feeling slightly out of place when looking around him. He'd never seen so handsome an estate. The main house, the corrals, the stacked rock walls stretching for miles ...

And the land. It went on forever.

Trees bordered a vast meadow, thick and hearty with pine and oak, an occasional dogwood crowding in, stretching its gangly arms low and wide. Numerous outbuildings dotted the grounds, including a blacksmith shop and not one, but two stables, each at least ten times the size of the house he grew up in. And—if he was seeing correctly—a race track in the distance.

He spotted a group of Negro men standing around a horse trailer beside an adjacent corral. From the back, one of the men looked familiar, and Ridley's half-starved dream drew a faltering breath. Then the man turned. Ridley saw his face and exhaled in disappointment. It wasn't him.

A crowd of people comprised of both Negroes and whites, gathered near the end of the long drive by the corral, and as Mrs. Aberdeen drew closer, they broke into applause. An older woman stepped forward and waved a handkerchief in their direction. And like a young schoolgirl, Olivia Aberdeen chuckled beneath her breath.

Ridley couldn't help but lean down. "Well, Mrs. Aberdeen, this is quite a welcome. I'd say they're mighty happy to see you again, ma'am."

Color rose in her cheeks and a smile blossomed on her face. "I'm certain Mrs. Harding put them up to it, Mr. Cooper. I doubt most of them even remember me. But ... I must admit—" She gave a little shrug. "It feels nice to know—"

"Three cheers for Jack Malone!" a man called out. "Hip, hip—"

"Hooray!" the crowd cheered.

"Hip, hip—"

"Hooray!"

"Hip, hip—"

"Hooray!"

Whoops and hollers went up in swells. Olivia Aberdeen stopped, as did Ridley, just now seeing a chesnut stallion being led down a ramp from the horse trailer. A reprise of celebration rose again and Ridley's gut twisted tight, realizing who—or rather, what—the enthusiastic welcome was for.

Even before he stole a glance beside him, he could feel Olivia Aberdeen drawing inside herself. Gone was the radiant smile and rosy bloom of color. Her face went pale, her dark dress making it more so by comparison. He tried to think of something to say to fill the awkward silence, to take away the hurt in her expression, but he'd never been good with words that way.

Just then an older man, distinguished and with an air of wealth, stepped from the crowd, and Ridley felt a stab of recognition. A pencil drawing of the man had circulated during the war, and Ridley saw now that whoever had drawn it had captured a remarkable likeness.

It was Confederate General William Giles Harding in the flesh, with a beard that nearly reached his vest.

Chapter FOUR

*O*livia struggled to mask her disappointment, feigning interest in the horse being unloaded from the trailer. She knew better than to think Ridley Cooper was fooled by her performance — not with him knowing how she felt about the animals. Still, she sustained her stiff smile, unwilling to let him or anyone else see how bone weary she was of feeling so small, so foolish and insignificant. All the things she'd felt with Charles.

"Livvy!"

Hearing her name, Olivia turned, welcoming the distraction and the chance to remove herself from Ridley Cooper's all-too-close attention. Aunt Elizabeth hurried toward her, and it was all Olivia could do not to run the rest of the way.

Arms outstretched, her aunt wrapped her in a hug, and Olivia held on to Elizabeth Harding like a buoy in a storm. Over four years had passed since she'd seen the woman. Olivia knew she was probably imagining it, but Elizabeth felt thinner. Frailer. Considering what she'd been through, what she'd suffered in light of General Harding's imprisonment at the hands of the Federal Army, it was to be expected. Olivia didn't realize she was crying until she pulled back. Tears pooled in Elizabeth's eyes too.

Elizabeth reached up and brushed back the hair at Olivia's temple. "It's so good to see you, Livvy. And it's been so long. Too long. It feels like another lifetime, my dear."

Olivia gave her another hug. "It's so good to see you too, Aunt Elizabeth," she whispered. "Thank you for allowing me to come and live here. I don't know where I'd be right now without your kindness. And the general's too, of course."

"Oh, my dear ..." Elizabeth drew back and framed Olivia's face in her hands. "You are family now, and we're all grateful to have you with us." Her brow furrowed. "You've been through so much, Livvy. Just this past week alone. I can't begin to imagine. I'm so sorry—" She gave Olivia's hands a gentle squeeze. "About Charles, about the newspapers ... And then the accident on the way here today. Jedediah told me about it. I'm so glad you're all right. You've been given far more than your fair share, Livvy."

Determined not to cry again, Olivia tamped down the emotion rising inside. "I hope my coming won't cast you and your family in a bad light, Aunt Elizabeth."

"Nonsense." Elizabeth waved aside the comment. "We're no strangers to gossip. One doesn't live with a strong-minded man for twenty-six years without becoming accustomed to such things. Besides"—she leaned closer—"I've explained the circumstances of your marriage to the general again. He understands."

Olivia smiled her thanks, the meaning of what Elizabeth had said not lost on her. Elizabeth had explained it all to the general *again*, meaning General Harding had inquired about her. Which Olivia took to mean he likely hadn't been in favor of her coming to live here—before Elizabeth persuaded him. Olivia didn't find the news comforting.

"Ah!" Elizabeth glanced to the side. "Here are my girls. They're eager to welcome you."

Olivia lifted her gaze. But instead of seeing the Harding daughters she remembered, she saw two decidedly more mature young women making their way toward her.

"Olivia, you remember Selene and Mary." Elizabeth's countenance shone with motherly pride. "And girls, you remember Mrs. Aberdeen, the daughter of my dearest friend, Rebecca."

A very womanly looking Selene—her dark hair arranged elegantly atop her head and her figure having blossomed in all the right places—offered a genteel curtsey. "Welcome to Belle Meade, Mrs. Aberdeen. How very nice it is to see you again. And"—her voice lowered—"may I offer my sincere condolences, ma'am, on your recent loss."

Olivia dipped her head. "Thank you, Selene. And please, call me Olivia." She looked next at Mary, who at sixteen—four years younger than her sister—was attractive as well, though perhaps a tad plainer and lacking the poise and grace of Selene.

Olivia smiled, remembering the clinging awkwardness of youth only too well. But Mary merely curtsied and looked away.

"Mary." Elizabeth's voice was soft but instructive. "I'm certain you have a word of welcome for Mrs. Aberdeen as well."

With the slightest hesitation, Mary looked back. "Of course ... Welcome, Mrs. Aberdeen." Her smile was as abbreviated as her curtsey had been. "My heartfelt condolences on your loss, ma'am."

Elizabeth gave the girl a look, but Olivia acted as though she hadn't seen. "Thank you, Mary. I'm grateful to you and your family for allowing me to come and live with you. And to serve as your head housekeeper. I'll do my best to—"

"But you're not the head housekeeper," Mary blurted. "Cousin Lizzie is." Mary looked at her mother. "Papa said this morning that he promised the—"

"Mary!" Elizabeth's voice tightened. "We can discuss the details of everyone's duties later. Now ..." She nodded toward Selene. "Why don't you two go see how your father's getting along with his newest addition. And please remind him that dinner is at six thirty this evening." She gave a feather-light laugh. "We all know how he loses track of time with these things."

As Selene and Mary carried out their mother's request, Olivia felt a rising sense of dread. General Harding had given the position of head housekeeper to someone else. A *real* family member. Where would she go if the Hardings had changed their minds? If the invitation from Belle Meade had been withdrawn?

"Livvy, dear." Elizabeth linked arms with her. "There is something I need to explain to you, but—"

"Excuse me, Missus Harding?" A servant—a Negro woman Olivia recognized as the head cook, as delicate-looking a woman as she was energetic—leaned close to whisper into Elizabeth's ear.

Olivia looked away to give them privacy, but also to pull herself together. She'd started to shake, deep down inside, like the day her mother died, then her father. Like she had when Charles left their bedroom, so abruptly, on their wedding night, after ...

Feeling a chill, despite the heat, she pressed her hands against the knot in the pit of her stomach, trying her best not to remember while also trying to prepare herself for whatever Elizabeth would say next, when something—or someone—caught her attention.

Ridley Cooper. On the front porch of the Hardings' home.

He deposited her trunk by the door, then worked his right shoulder for a minute as he looked out over the yard. She had to admit, the man had a presence about him. And could be considered somewhat attractive, she had to concede, if a woman liked that kind of look in a man—feral and brooding, undomesticated—which she didn't.

But it occurred to her, watching him stand there, alone on the porch, tall and confident—overly so on the latter—how easy it was to imagine him in uniform. In the familiar gray wool of the Confederacy. He hadn't wanted to talk about the war, that had been clear. And she hadn't either. She'd simply wanted him to know the general would.

She still didn't think General Harding would hire him, but considering how he'd helped her out of the carriage, then covered for her with Jedediah, she felt like she owed him something.

He stilled, and she realized he was looking at her. He nodded once, motioned to the trunk, and she saw one side of that unruly beard of his edge up the tiniest bit, as if he were smiling. Much like he'd smiled at her when he'd helped her out of the carriage. When he'd held her entirely too long. Longer than a gentleman would have.

She tried to imagine what he might look like clean-shaven and kempt and had to admit—

A tug on her arm brought her back around.

"Livvy, forgive me, dear. My attention is required in the house. But please ..." Elizabeth cradled Olivia's cheek. "Listen to me. There was a slight misunderstanding, that's all. Unbeknownst to me, the general entered into an agreement for his cousin's daughter to become the head housekeeper. And it's an agreement that, I fear, cannot be set aside. However—"

"It's all right," Olivia heard herself saying, bowing her head. "I understand."

"Livvy, darling, look at me."

Clenching her jaw so her chin wouldn't quiver, Olivia did as asked.

"This in no way alters our arrangement with you. You are welcome to live here with us for as long as you like, no matter how long that may be."

"But ..." Olivia swallowed hard, mindful of others around them and unwilling for them to hear. "How can I live here, Aunt Elizabeth, and not contribute to the family? To the household, in some way?" She shook her head. "It's not done. It wouldn't be proper. And ... I can't help but question whether the general really wants me here."

"He does want you here, Livvy." Elizabeth's expression changed, and Olivia knew whatever Elizabeth was about to say next was the unvarnished truth. "He was hesitant at first, I admit, with everything happening so quickly. But he's warmed to the idea. Especially in the last day or two. And don't you worry one bit about contributing, Livvy. You'll do that simply by being with us." Elizabeth gripped her hands. "So we'll have no more talk of this, all right? Now ... help yourself to the refreshments on the table over there. Susanna made her beaten biscuits with ham. They're delicious. Then come on inside and we'll show you to your room."

Not at all convinced, but grateful to have a place to call home, at least for now, Olivia nodded. "Thank you, Aunt Elizabeth."

Ridley followed Olivia Aberdeen's progress through the crowd, grateful for the vantage point the porch provided, as well as the partial concealment of a lilac bush. He still felt bad for her about the confusion over her welcome. But she'd received a cordial enough greeting from the first lady of Belle Meade, which surely made up for some of the disappointment.

From what he'd witnessed, he'd have to say the two women were indeed close, as Mrs. Aberdeen had claimed. He'd also have to say there was more to Olivia Aberdeen than he'd originally thought upon first meeting. Not that he had any business thinking about the woman in the first place.

Focusing on his task, he descended the porch stairs, both eager—and also not—to see if his reason for coming all this way was still here. He could've asked Mrs. Aberdeen, to see if she knew Robert Green, but Ridley didn't want to draw any unnecessary attention to himself. Not with her being so close to the Harding family.

He cut a path around the crowd, instinctively keeping an eye on two people—Mrs. Aberdeen and General William Giles Harding. The general stood with a host of other suited men, nodding and accepting pats on the back while he admired his new thoroughbred. Harding appeared older than in the drawing that had circulated during the war, and—if his beard were any indication—even more stubborn.

Ridley scanned the crowd, hopeful when he saw a group of Negro men gathered at another corral. He closed the distance, staying to the fringes and trying to think what he'd say to Robert Green when—*if*—

he saw him again. He discreetly searched faces as he went, but none of them was Robert Green. His hope waned. He spotted a skinny boy carrying a load of wood. The lad was short and barefoot, his pant legs hovering above his thin ankles. But it was the cap the young boy wore tugged down close to his ears that was most distinguishing.

Ridley approached. "Excuse me, young sir."

The boy stopped, looked at Ridley from beneath the curved bill of his old worn cap, then turned around and glanced behind him before speaking. "Is you aimin' that talk my way, sir?"

Ridley had to smile. "I am. I have a question for you."

The boy came closer. "Then I do my hardest to know the answer, sir."

"You know a man here by the name of Mr. Robert Green?"

The boy cocked his head. "Can't say I know *no*body by that color name, sir."

"How long have you been here, son?"

"Nigh onto a year. I come from Georgia, sir. With my mama. She be a dairy maid, workin' with them cows. I work in the stables." The boy's chest puffed out. "I exercise them racehorses ... When I ain't totin' wood or doin' nothin' else."

Feeling hope siphon away, Ridley thanked the boy and turned back to the estate. If the lad worked with horses and hadn't heard of Robert Green, it pretty much depleted any hope of finding the man. Still, he'd come all this way.

He saw two stables—one south of the mansion and one north— and was leaving no stone unturned. Since Belle Meade was a stud farm, he assumed one stable housed stallions. And the other, mares. He headed for the one closest to him.

When he stepped through the open doors, his gaze was drawn upward to the massive beams that supported the weight of the high-pitched roof. This place looked more like a cathedral than a barn. He glimpsed a tack room off to his right and shook his head at the number of stables and abundance of horse tack. Saddles, bits, bridles, and blankets lined the walls and shelves, all neatly arranged and far finer than anything he'd ever owned.

Numerous barrels containing feed, and others containing water, were set every few feet down the length of the building. He blew out a breath. These thoroughbreds lived better than most people he knew, himself included.

"You got the general's permission to be in here?"

Ridley turned to see a man standing in the doorway of one of the stalls, a pitchfork in his grip and a squint of unwelcome in his eyes. Ridley quickly sized him up. The war had taught him many things, mostly how to read people, and rarely was he wrong. But the thing he noticed most about this fellow was how he resembled one of the corporals from that fateful night on the mountain, the first—and last—time he'd seen Robert Green. He wasn't the same man, Ridley knew. And yet, staring at him, it felt like he was.

Ridley felt an instant dislike for him, yet forced a pleasantness, reminding himself why he was here. "I'm wondering if you could help me. I'm looking for—"

"I asked you … Do you got the general's permission to be in here?"

Ridley held his gaze. "No. I don't. But all I'm looking for is—"

"I know what you're lookin' for, stranger." The man strode toward him. "Same as what that fella we caught sneakin' round here last week was lookin' for. You tryin' to scout out what General Harding's doin' with his stock so y'all can take it back to Renfroe's farm and give that ol' man a leg up before the next race." He came within a yard and stopped, pitchfork raised. "I got my pay docked for that, so y'all ain't doin' that on my watch, partner. Not again. You best turn around and use that door before I poke your belly full of holes."

Ridley held his ground and the man's stare, knowing he shouldn't. Men like this were animals. Edgy. Territorial. Easy to draw off. You stared at them long enough, they felt a challenge, and he could tell by the way the man fingered the pitchfork's handle, turning it, working to get a better grip, that he was an easy mark. With steam to blow off. Ridley knew the feeling well. He also knew provoking this man wouldn't serve his cause.

He made a half-hearted attempt at a conciliatory tone. "Listen, I don't want any trouble." He laughed. "And I don't even know who Renfroe is, much less—"

The man lunged, pitchfork aimed chest high, and Ridley spun, wincing when one of the tines grazed his upper arm. So much for filling his belly full of holes. The fellow was about his height, heavier with muscle, but a little slower. With a sweeping motion, Ridley under-cut his legs, and the man went down hard on his back, dropping the pitchfork. But he didn't stay down.

Ridley kicked the pitchfork aside, dropped his pack, and braced himself as the man came at him. Momentum drove them backward, and Ridley slammed into a wall. The back of his head smacked with a thud he knew he'd feel later, and a horse let out a high-pitched whinny somewhere behind him.

He shoved the man back with force. "Listen to me! I'm here looking for Robert Green, that's all. And I—"

The fellow came at him again, swinging hard. His fist connected with Ridley's jaw, and Ridley would've sworn the guy's hand was made of granite. He shook off the buzz from the blow and swung with his left—intentionally missed—then jammed a right hook square into the man's chin. The man's head whipped back. He staggered, dazed and bloody, but still didn't go down.

Ridley flexed his hand, shaking off the sting, starting to enjoy this a little, though he knew he shouldn't.

The man wiped his face, blood oozing from a gash on his chin. "I'm gonna show you what we do to cheats and thieves around here."

"I'm not a cheat. And I'm not here to steal anything either. I told you ... I'm here to see Robert Green. If you'll just—"

The man came at him again.

"Grady Matthews!"

The man skidded to a halt, his focus beyond Ridley now, enraged. Ridley, his breath coming hard, turned to glimpse who was back there, while still keeping an eye on this Grady Matthews, just in case.

Chapter
FIVE

*R*idley blinked and wiped sweat from his forehead, surprised when his hand came away bloody, but even more surprised by the emotion tightening his throat. A slightly older looking—and unarguably livid—Robert Green strode toward them, clad in a white apron, a slight limp hindering his gait.

"What in tarnation is goin' on in here? Grady, you best start talkin' or I'm goin' to the general. And this time, he'll send you packin'!"

"U-uncle Bob," the man sputtered, pointing to Ridley, who took notice of the name he used. "It's another one from Renfroe's camp, come to spy us out!"

Robert Green turned dark eyes on Ridley. "Is that true, sir?"

"No, sir," Ridley said. "It's not."

"Then what's your business here?"

Ridley didn't detect even a hint of remembrance in the man's expression. He knew he'd changed some. Lost weight, mainly, which he was working to gain back. That, along with the muscle—not easy to do with meat so scarce and expensive. "I'm actually here to speak with you, Mr. Green, about ..." He hesitated, glancing at Grady. "About a private matter, sir."

Green studied him a minute. "Grady, go wash up. Then see Rachel about sewin' up that chin again."

Grudgingly, Grady took his leave, throwing Ridley a scathing glare that said this wasn't finished yet. Ridley returned it.

"You said a private matter, sir," Green continued once they were alone, his tone suspect, his expression still void of recognition.

Even so, Ridley felt a lightness he couldn't quite account for. Seeing this man was like seeing an old friend again. And friends were something he'd been running mighty low on lately. "It's been a long time, Mr. Green." He cleared his throat, his voice not sounding like his own. "But I still remember your coffee, sir. And the venison you shared with me that night ... on the mountain," he added softly. "Best I'd had in a while. And ever since too."

Green's eyes narrowed, causing the traces of wiry gray in his bushy brows to stand out even more. "Sweet Jesus," he finally whispered. "It can't be." He searched Ridley's face, warmth moving in behind his eyes. "Lieutenant Cooper? Is that you behind all that hair and them whiskers?"

Smiling, Green extended his hand and Ridley gripped it tight. For several heartbeats, Ridley just stared at their clasped hands, thinking how long it had been since he'd seen this man and how much had happened. And what he'd come to ask him.

Green's hold tightened. "Every day I prayed for you, sir, 'til the war was done, and then after too, askin' God to pay back the kindness you showed me. But ..." He laughed, his gray-touched beard pulling taut on his chin. "I can't believe you's standin' here. Right here in front of me now." He exhaled. "God kept you safe. Yes, sir, he did. Just like I asked him to."

Ridley released his hand, the warmth he'd felt cooling a mite. "I appreciate your prayers, Mr. Green. But ..." He exhaled a quick breath, looking to make sure they were alone. "I'd hardly call the time I spent at Andersonville 'God keeping me safe.'"

Green regarded him, his features going solemn, and Ridley gathered he'd heard of the place.

"How long was you there, sir?"

"Fourteen months. They held me at Richmond first, then moved me down to Georgia when the prison opened come spring."

"How'd they get you?"

"Ambushed me the morning I left you. On my way down the mountain."

The lines wreathing Green's eyes and mouth deepened. "Andersonville," he whispered, looking away. "The general don't speak much to me 'bout the war. But sometimes, when men he served with are here, like today, there's talk among 'em. So I heard things 'bout that place." He looked back at Ridley, his gaze unflinching. "I'm sorry you was there, sir, and that they got you like they did. Sorry as I can be."

Ridley appreciated the honesty in Green's response, yet it made him uncomfortable, eager to change the subject. "What happened to you? After that night?"

"I kept the general's favorite thoroughbreds hidden 'til the end of the war. I still had to move 'em 'round from time to time, but them horses—the ones you let me keep—they's the reason Belle Meade's doin' so good right now, sir. Cuz the general had somethin' to start with after the war, thanks to you."

Ridley shook his head. "Belle Meade's success right now is due to you, Mr. Green. Not only because of what you did for the general, but because of your gift with horses. I saw it that night in the way you handled the thoroughbreds. I have to admit, though ..." Ridley smiled. "It sorta spooked me at first, seeing how they just came to you like that. I've never seen anything like it before."

Green bowed his head. "Thank you, sir. That's mighty kind of you, but ... it ain't me. I's just doin' what God put me here to do, that's all."

The statement struck a chord inside Ridley, and he remembered what Green had told him about his mother finding him in the barn sleeping with the horses when he was just a boy. Ridley also knew, without a doubt, this was where he was supposed to be—for now, at least. Learning from Robert Green.

He only hoped Mr. Green would agree.

A horse whinnied in the stall beside them and poked its head through the opening. Ridley thought he recognized the black stallion. "Olympus?" he asked.

"Good memory, Lieutenant." Green walked over and gave the animal's neck a good scratching. He looked back at Ridley. "I's sure glad to see you again, but what brought you all this way? Didn't you say you was from South Carolina?"

Ridley told him about returning home, about learning his younger brothers had been killed and about his father. "He was a skeleton of the man I'd left four years earlier, his body all eaten up with tuberculosis. And he—" The words caught in Ridley's throat. "He was still just as bitter toward me, even in the end."

"For the choice you made," Green said quietly.

Ridley nodded, able to see, even now, how his father had looked up at him from his deathbed. That same old ache began to throb again. "I think he blamed me for my brothers' deaths too. Putting myself in his place, I might have felt the same."

Seconds passed in silence, bits of indistinct laughter and conversation drifting in through the open entry.

"What about your mama?"

"She died a few years back, giving birth to a little girl. They both went together. Preacher said it kind of seemed fitting to him, but ... I didn't much believe that. Still don't." Ridley shifted his weight, again eager to get onto another topic. "A little over two months ago, my father died. I buried him, sold the house and what little was left of the farm, and set out."

"Where you headed?"

"West, eventually. Colorado Territory. But I need something first— from you, Mr. Green. If you're willing."

Green's brow furrowed.

Ridley took a breath, focusing all his hope. "I've come here to ask you if you'll show me how to handle horses. How to work with them like you do. How to make them do what you want."

Green's laughter was immediate and full. "Lawd, sir ... I'd sooner get my wife to do what I want than I could these blood horses. If I had a wife. Which I don't." His smile waned, but the spark in his eyes didn't. "I don't *make* these horses do anything, sir. I just listen to 'em, let 'em tell me what they need to. Then I help 'em do what God created them to do. Run, strong and hard. Fast as the wind."

Ridley stepped closer to the stall door. "Can you teach me how to do that? How to"—he felt a little silly actually saying the words—"*listen* to them like you do?"

Green sighed. "I ain't never had anybody ask me that before. Shoot ..." He shook his head. "I ain't even sure it's somethin' I can teach. And what's more"—his expression grew serious—"I'm not sure you's ready to learn ... sir."

"But I *am* ready. I've come all this way. And ..." Ridley hadn't spoken of this to anyone, and talking about it now brought back memories he wished would stay buried. "When I was at Andersonville ... thinking about this, about learning from you, Mr. Green ... it's all that kept me going some days. That, and the dream of getting out of there and leaving the South for good."

For the longest time, Green didn't speak, didn't even look at Ridley. He just kept rubbing the horse's forehead. Finally, he lifted his gaze. "I'm guessin' you know how the general feels about things. With the war, I mean. And the Federal Army."

Ridley thought of General Harding's beard and of what Olivia Aberdeen had told him about it. He also considered the risk Robert Green would be taking if he said yes. It wasn't that he hadn't considered it before. He had. He'd just never done it while in the company of the man himself, and the close proximity brought the risks into a harsher light.

Ridley picked at a knothole in the side of the stall. "I don't figure General Harding would take kindly to the idea of me being here."

"Lieutenant Cooper, that don't even come close to the truth. If I was to say yes to you and the general was to learn who you are—or *were* ..." Green exhaled. "We'd both be long gone from here. Maybe end up dead somewhere too. Not by the general's hand. He ain't that kind of man. But some of the others 'round here ... They hold a grudge for a mighty long time." He sighed, rubbing his beard. "I been here at Belle Meade all my life. Everybody I know is here. I got nowhere else to go, sir. And I don't want to. This here's my home." His hand stilled on the horse. "And ... if the general see fit to lettin' me stay, I wouldn't mind dyin' here neither."

For a second time, Ridley found himself envious of this man and what he had. But he was also mindful of all Green had to lose. Hearing the man's answer and seeing it in the watery sheen of his eyes, Ridley straightened. "I understand, Mr. Green. And I don't fault you one bit for your decision." *Disappointment* didn't begin to describe the roil of emotion inside him, but Ridley did his best not to let it show. "I thank you for your time, sir. And"—he held out his hand—"for what you gave me that night on the mountain."

Green gripped his hand, tighter than before. "And just what was that, Lieutenant?"

Ridley felt his eyes start to burn. "Hope," he whispered, his throat closing tightly around the word. He walked to where he'd dropped his pack earlier and retrieved it, looked back one last time, nodded a thank-you, and headed for the door.

Once outside, he took a deep breath. Well, that was that ... He sighed. The crowd of people had thinned. General Harding was still standing near the thoroughbred, flanked by supporters. But nowhere did Ridley see Olivia Aberdeen. The trunk that he'd set by the door was gone, and he felt an unexplained regret, thinking of her. He wondered if she'd find what she wanted and hoped she would.

The sun had moved on across the sky and the air had cooled

some, but not by much. An aroma drifted toward him, something smelling like ham and fresh-baked bread, and his mouth watered. His stomach was empty, but that was nothing compared to the loneliness within. He started walking, thinking about Petey and Alfred and his father, about his mother and little Emily—the sister he never knew—and how much he missed them. How much he missed having a place to call—

"It ain't gonna be easy to learn, Lieutenant Cooper."

Ridley slowed his steps as the voice behind him registered, as did the words. He turned them over in his mind, then turned back to see Robert Green standing in the doorway of the stable, looking straight at him.

"It's gonna take time too," Green said.

The man wasn't smiling, Ridley noted, but that didn't keep *him* from suddenly wanting to. "Time is something I have, sir." Within reason, he thought, knowing he could learn quickly if he put his mind to it.

"And you have to really want it." Green was unyielding. "This ... *gift*, as you call it."

"I do." Ridley walked back toward him. "I give you my word, I do."

"You gots to do what I say too. You gonna have a problem with that?"

Ridley smiled. "No, sir. No problem."

"You good with a whip?"

"Actually, I'm very good with a whip. Even as a boy, I could—"

"Well, you ain't gonna be usin' that thing here." Green fixed his gaze on him. "We *never* take a whip to a horse. Or a stick. So I hope you got patience. And lots of it."

Ridley paused, not because he didn't have a ready response, but because it wouldn't be the truth. Furthermore, he had a hunch Green already knew patience wasn't his strong suit. "I'm willing to learn that too, sir."

"You can't just be willin'. You have to set your mind—and heart—to it. It's gotta come from here." Green touched his chest. "And that ain't easy."

Ridley nodded. "I understand." Though not certain that he did, he wasn't about to admit it. He needed and wanted to learn what only Robert Green could teach.

Green met him where he stood. "General Harding ain't a perfect man, Lieutenant. Ain't no such thing as that. But he's a good man. Been right fair to me, and I feel like I owe him." Green looked toward the main house where General Harding now stood on the porch with some other men. "But the way I see it ..." He sighed. "I feel like I owe you somethin' too, seein' what you did for me and for the general. So ... I teach you everythin' I know, best I can. But somethin' we need to be clear on, Lieutenant. General Harding is the one who does the hirin' and firin' 'round here. I'm willin' to teach you, but I won't do it behind the general's back. I'm guessin' your pockets could use a little linin' while you here."

Understanding the unspoken question, Ridley nodded. "I've got a good amount saved up, but not enough. I could use a paying job, for sure."

Green thought on this for a minute. "Then you need to meet the general and ask him for work, formal-like. General Harding's mighty particular 'bout who he hires. I sent a man away earlier today. Loner type, angry. Wouldn't o' done well here." Green gestured toward the house where Harding stood. "You tell the general you done spoke to me and that I give you a nod. But if he says no ..." Green shrugged. "Then I reckon I can't do this after all. 'Cause the only way to learn from me is to work with the horses, and it's his stock I be usin' to teach you. So it's only fair the general gets the final say."

Although he didn't like this new angle Green had thrown in, Ridley didn't see that he had any choice. He held out a hand, and Green shook it. "Fair enough. I'll look forward to meeting him."

"And meet him you will, soon enough. He's usually in the saddle ridin' the plantation from dawn 'til dusk. But there's somethin' you got to promise me 'fore we agree to all this, Lieutenant. And it's not somethin' I'm willin' to budge on."

His interest piqued, Ridley waited, watching. "And what's that?"

"No matter what, you can't ever tell anybody what side you fought for, sir ... And General Harding can't ever know that you and me met on that mountain."

Chapter
SIX

Olivia, dear, please have a second serving." Elizabeth gestured to the servant holding a bowl of mashed potatoes beside Olivia. "You're hardly eating enough for a bird."

The young Negro girl tried to scoop another dollop of potatoes onto her plate, but Olivia held up a hand. "They were delicious, thank you. But I've had plenty." Glad Elizabeth didn't force the issue—like she had with the buffalo roast—Olivia sipped her water and tried not to stare at Cousin Lizzie, the new head housekeeper, who had arrived shortly before she had that morning. But with the young woman seated directly across the table from her, it made the determination a challenge.

Olivia glanced down at her own gray ensemble, which she'd changed into before dinner. Wrinkled though it was, this dress was in better shape than the other she'd worn here. A servant had already claimed the black dress for cleaning and mending, assuring her it would be back in her wardrobe by morning.

Conversation whirled about the table, as did the variety of topics discussed, and the spirited exchanges all but abandoned the customary etiquette of formal dinners Olivia had attended here before. It occurred to her then that she'd never actually attended a family dinner at Belle Meade. The stinging realization as to why didn't help her feel any more welcome.

She was an outsider.

Surely everyone else around the table was thinking the same thing. Even Aunt Elizabeth—who appeared weary from the day's events—treated her more like an honored guest than someone who would be living here permanently. Selene was politely cordial and attentive—painfully so. And Mary ...

Olivia sneaked a look at the youngest Harding daughter. Mary Harding rarely met her gaze at all, yet was thick as thieves with Lizzie, despite the difference in their ages. Even now, the two had their heads together, smiling and whispering about something.

Lizzie was older than Olivia had expected. In her mid-thirties, Elizabeth had confided earlier. Lizzie's parents were deceased and she'd never married. The hope of matrimony for a woman of such years was paper-thin these days, or so Elizabeth had shared, what with so few men among them. From every indication, however, the young woman seemed nice enough.

The greatest infraction Olivia could lay at Cousin Lizzie's feet was that she'd requested a third serving of cinnamon apples. But the apples were delicious. Prepared to perfection, like everything else. So there was little fault to be found with the woman.

Everything about the meal was exactly as Olivia imagined a real family dinner should be. So unlike the dinners of her childhood, which had been quiet, proper, and in order. No one talking over anyone else. Sentences never touching. No dramatics. No outburst of laughter like here.

Having been an only child born to an older couple, she'd never experienced a family dinner like this and likely never would—not with the reputation Charles had left behind. A reputation yoked as snuggly about her neck as the rope that had been tied around his.

The thought of Charles, the reminder of how he'd died, made her squirm. She didn't desire to marry again, so why even a passing wish to experience such a setting as this for herself? Yet, looking around the table, seeing the smiles, the warmth, the familiarity and ease with which this family interacted, she knew why.

Because she'd once held such hopes for what marriage and family might be.

As a girl, she'd daydreamed about it. As a young woman, she'd been groomed and prepared for it. And as a bride, she'd swiftly realized it was nothing like she'd imagined.

There would come a day, she knew, when she would have to remarry. If only to avoid burdening the handful of people around this table who still welcomed—or at least tolerated—her company. But she prayed that day was a long way off. At least a year, if not two, abiding by the customary grieving period for a widow.

And the next man she married—if given a choice, a choice

she'd fight for this time—would be nothing like Charles. He would be feeble, paunchy, and dull. Scarcely able to raise his voice to her, much less his hand. If she was fortunate enough, she'd feel for him a kindly sort of affection. Not the depth of love and longing she'd once dreamed of. Those were the childish dreams of a little girl who hadn't known any better and a young woman not yet acquainted with life and its realities.

And disappointments.

Olivia studied the napkin in her lap, smoothing out the wrinkles and fingering the elaborate *H* embroidered on one of the corners. Other attributes she'd wish for in a husband—if given the right to choose—were loyalty and honesty. And beyond question, he'd be a Southerner, dedicated to rebuilding all that was lost when the Confederacy fell.

Laughter echoed around the table, bringing Olivia back to the moment, and she thought she heard her name. She lifted her head to see Elizabeth watching her, as was everyone else.

"I was just asking you, dear ... Have you heard the general tell this story before? It's quite amusing and goes along rather well with our dessert this evening, which our Susanna makes to perfection."

Olivia blinked. "Ah ..." Having absolutely no idea what Aunt Elizabeth was talking about, she forced a smile, seeing the young server from before setting bowls of syllabub in front of each of them. "I don't believe I have, Aunt Elizabeth. But I'd certainly love to!"

Olivia guessed, by the general's satisfied expression and the way he settled back into his chair, that she'd answered correctly. Eager to taste a spoonful of the whipped-cream dessert—so light and airy, one of her favorites—she waited for Elizabeth to take the first bite, as etiquette dictated.

"My late father, John Harding, God rest him," the general began, "was quite a man who lived quite an adventuresome life, as my family well knows. Not only did he carve out the beginnings of what is now Belle Meade, but he was instrumental in shaping the framework for the city of Nashville. He and my mother used to entertain local and national dignitaries, and on several occasions—"

"Oh, hurry, Papa," Mary cajoled, "and get to the good part."

"And be sure to do Grandpa Harding's voice too," Selene added.

He held up a hand. "Patience, daughters, patience." Then he sneaked them a wink.

Olivia saw the other ladies smile, so she did too. Until she saw General Harding looking at her.

"I'm assuming you've heard of David Crockett, Olivia? The famous bear hunter and Tennessee congressman?"

She nodded. Every child in Tennessee was taught about Davy Crockett.

"Well, shortly before Crockett left Tennessee for Texas" — General Harding leaned forward — "my father and mother entertained him. Right here, at Belle Meade." His smile grew wistful. "Mr. Crockett was one entertaining storyteller, ladies. After dinner we'd sit around for hours and listen to him weave his stories. One night ..." He grinned. "My mother, Susan, served this very dessert."

As if on cue, everyone looked at their bowls then back at him.

"When Crockett asked my father what it was, my father said ..." General Harding lowered his chin a fraction. " 'The ladies call it syllabub, I believe, Mr. Crockett,' " he said in a deeper register, his drawl thicker than usual. " 'Do you like it?' "

Selene, Mary, and Lizzie giggled. Elizabeth's eyes sparkled, and Olivia found herself grinning too.

"Crockett," the general continued in a normal voice, "whose reputation as a witty man was known far and wide, replied, 'Well, I don't know. I took a snap or two at it but I reckon I missed it!' "

Laughter erupted around the table and Olivia joined in, a sense of relief inching back toward her. The general included her in his gaze.

Elizabeth took the first bite of syllabub and the rest of the table followed suit. "Olivia, I wish you could have met Mr. Harding, the general's father. He had such a gentle presence about him, so mild in manner and speech."

"And what was his motto, girls?" the general asked.

Selene looked at Mary, who paused her spoon mid-air. " 'If you had tried a little harder,' " they said in unison, and even Lizzie joined in, apparently familiar with family history too, " 'don't you think you could have got a little further?' "

Once again, everyone laughed. And once again, Olivia felt like she was on the outside looking in.

"Selene ..." The general sipped his coffee. "Was that your young friend Roberta here today?"

"Yes, Father, it was."

"And did you finally coax her into riding?"

Selene shook her head. "She would scarcely set one foot inside the mares' stable, much less get close enough to touch one. Or ride. She kept insisting they wanted to do her harm."

Everyone around the table laughed. Everyone except Olivia.

"The next time she's here"—the general looked pointedly at his eldest daughter, his voice holding firm resolve—"you must let me know. I'll take it upon myself to get her seated and riding immediately. Every young woman should know how to ride and handle a horse. We must face our fears instead of running from them. And you may tell.her I said as much."

Silence reigned as though everyone were taking the general's edict to heart. Olivia kept her gaze glued to her bowl, praying with a fervor no one would ask her about riding.

"And just how is your son these days, General?" Cousin Lizzie asked, braving the quiet.

"John Jr. is doing quite well, thank you for asking, Lizzie. He and his wife and their children are most comfortable at Stones River Farm near Nashville. They were here for dinner not a week ago."

Olivia had almost forgotten the general had a son by his first wife. No fault to Elizabeth, however. She'd mentioned him often in her letters, but Olivia had never met him.

"Selene received a letter from someone special today," Elizabeth announced in a lyrical voice, and Olivia peered up.

Selene continued eating her dessert, a tiny smile her only response.

"Indeed," the general replied. "But doesn't she routinely receive such letters? I've chased off at least four admirers this month alone. None of them worthy."

Elizabeth shook her head. "You are far too severe on her gentleman callers."

Sipping his coffee, the general waved the comment away. "Who might this someone special be? Don't tell me, let me guess. Might he be ... a butcher?"

His comment drew laughter.

"Or baker?"

"Father," Selene said, her tone playfully scolding.

"Or perhaps a candlestick maker?" he finished.

Olivia watched the scene unfold, grateful for the shift in topic and enjoying the syllabub, but noticing that Mary wasn't taking part in the playful exchange.

"Dear husband." Elizabeth laughed. "Surely you can guess the author of said letter."

"Yes, I could," he answered, his smile faint. "But I want my daughter to tell me. I want to hear her say the gentleman's name."

Hearing a pinch of seriousness in the general's voice, Olivia feigned interest in the cream pooling at the bottom of her bowl while still sneaking looks.

A gradual blush crept into Selene's cheeks. She gently laid her spoon aside and looked down the table at her father. "His name is General William Hicks Jackson, as you well know, Father." A smile bloomed on the young woman's face, as telling as any declaration could be.

"Ah, yes." General Harding scooped a bite of syllabub into his mouth and, judging by his expression, savored the taste. "I believe I've heard of this gentleman before. But I wanted to know how my daughter felt about him." His gaze grew endearing. "One can always tell how a woman truly feels about a man when she speaks his name. She either does it with affection, stemming from pride. Or with hesitance ... born of shame."

The table fell silent, and Olivia went still, her lungs expunged of air. She kept her focus on her bowl, needing to take a breath but not daring to for fear she would gasp.

"And I can tell," the general continued, "that you are most proud of your General William Hicks Jackson."

Parting her lips, Olivia drew in a slow, silent breath, her lungs and eyes burning.

Selene chuckled. "He's not *my* general, Father."

"Not yet, perhaps," the general countered. "But I have a hunch he'd certainly like to be. And why should he not, with you as the prize? Of course"—his laughter was curt and telling—"in order for that to happen, he'll have to win me over first."

Finally breathing again, Olivia glanced down the table and found Selene's smile ever bright and hopeful, while Mary discreetly brushed something from her cheek.

Following dessert, General Harding rose from his seat at the head of the table and conversation fell to a hush. "Before we depart the table this evening, I'd like to make a toast, ladies ... if you could somehow bring yourselves to cease jabbering to each other for two minutes straight."

Elizabeth and the others laughed at the feigned sternness in his tone, but Olivia thought of Charles again and couldn't.

The general raised his water glass. "To Miss Lizzie Hoover, the fair daughter of my first cousin, who has most graciously agreed to coordinate this busy household and keep it operating as it should." He looked at the opposite end of the table. "You will no doubt help to ease the weight that my dear wife has had resting on her delicate shoulders for far too long."

Elizabeth's pleasant countenance faltered for an instant, shadowed by a frown. Then quickly smoothed.

"I'm grateful to you, Lizzie," the general continued, "for coming here not only to serve as our head housekeeper, but to be a part of our family as well. Cheers, everyone!"

Crystal stemware *tinked* together amidst the harmony of laughter and whispered welcomes, and Olivia smiled until it almost hurt.

"And now ..." The general turned. "A second toast."

Her face grew warm.

"To Olivia, the daughter of my wife's dearest friend in the world—"

And wife of a traitor to the Confederacy whose last name I cannot bring myself to utter, Olivia heard him say in her mind, half certain she read it in his eyes.

"God rest her dear soul," the general added softly. "Olivia, we welcome you to Belle Meade ... and offer our condolences for your loss and for all you've been through in recent days."

Olivia's grip tightened on her glass. *Thank you*, she mouthed.

"And looking toward what I hope will be a brighter future, I trust you'll find yourself settled in most quickly here and that you'll soon come to enjoy the benefits of living in such a lovely—and lively—setting." Smiling, he lifted his glass, though not nearly as heartily as he'd done the first time. "Cheers!"

Crystal stemware *tinked* again, and they all sipped their water, the sound of servants in the next room drifting toward them.

Elizabeth reached over and squeezed Olivia's arm. "Livvy, we're all so glad you're here." Elizabeth's gaze swept the table, and the other females smiled and nodded. All except for Mary, who dipped her head, her gaze averted much like her father's.

Olivia tried not to look as uncomfortable as she felt. "Thank you, Aunt Elizabeth, and to you as well, General Harding"—she looked back at him—"for the kindness and generosity of your invitation to live here. It's something I'll never take for granted ... I promise."

Following dinner, she could hardly wait to escape and get back to her room. Weary, disappointed, and feeling defeated in a way she couldn't define, she thanked Elizabeth again for the meal, then excused herself.

"Livvy?" Aunt Elizabeth motioned to Selene, Mary, and Cousin Lizzie, who had their heads together. "The girls are planning a foray into town next week. Perhaps you'd like to join them."

The last thing Olivia wanted to do was face anyone in town again, especially after what had happened earlier that day. She caught the none-too-subtle objection in Mary's expression and read a hint of it in Selene's, and their feelings about being seen with her in public became all too clear.

She forced a smile. "Thank you for the invitation, but ... I can't think of anything I need from town at present."

Swift relief showed in Mary's features. And Selene's.

"That's understandable," Selene offered gently, apologetic. "Since you only just arrived."

"Yes, exactly." Olivia nodded, not blaming the girls for their feelings but still having to hold back the hurt.

She'd barely reached the foyer when she heard General Harding say her name. She turned, pushing a smile back into place. "Yes, General?"

"Could I have a word with you in my office, Olivia? I promise it won't take long."

Chapter SEVEN

M y office is through here, Olivia." General Harding led her through the study, and Olivia followed, scanning her surroundings.

On one wall stood three handsome mahogany cases filled to overflowing with silver cups, pitchers, and trophies. She couldn't begin to count them. A hundred, at least. And all for the general's beloved racehorses.

General Harding opened a door that led to an outside porch. "Mrs. Harding has been after me to have an internal entry to my office installed, so she doesn't have to come outside to see me." He opened yet another door and motioned to Olivia to enter. "But I believe it's best this way. Helps to keep traffic down and my mind focused when I'm in here."

He gestured to a chair off to the side of the mahogany secretary, and Olivia took a seat, followed by a very deep breath. The head of a buffalo loomed on the wall beside her, staring down with angry, onyx eyes. Beside it was that of a deer, and Olivia wondered, as she had before, what made people want to hang such things on their walls as decor.

"As I said a moment ago, Olivia"—General Harding closed the door behind him with a solid click—"I'll keep this brief. I realize you're tired and eager to get settled for the night."

"No," she lied. "I'm fine."

"My original thought was to delay this conversation until tomorrow." He settled into the large leather chair opposite hers. "Then I decided that tonight would be more opportune for us both. Best to get some things right out in the open from the beginning, don't you agree?"

Wanting to shake her head no, she nodded. "Of course, sir."

"First and foremost, I want you to know that—"

A knock sounded on the door. With an annoyed look, the general excused himself, opened the door, and stepped outside. Olivia overheard the general's voice as well as another man's. She couldn't make out what they were saying, but the tone of the exchange was terse. A moment later, the general returned.

"My apologies." He took his seat again. "That was one of my foremen. A man applied for work today. *Vagrant* would best describe him." He sighed, shaking his head. "A stubborn sort with far too much confidence for his own good. I declined to hire him, and he left angry and disgruntled. My foreman wanted to assure me he escorted the man off the property."

Ridley Cooper. Olivia looked out the window. It had to be. But she couldn't see anything or anyone. It was too dark. She turned back and, for absolutely no reason, found herself feeling sorry for the man—rough around the edges though he was—and half wishing the general would have given him a chance.

"I can read a man's character upon first meeting," General Harding continued, "and while this one showed talent, he's also no good." His gaze met hers and held. "I knew the same thing about your husband the first time I met him. Talented ... but no good."

Olivia tensed, the syllabub in her stomach doing a lopsided somersault. No surprise that he wanted to speak with her about Charles ... Still, she dreaded hearing whatever it was he wanted to say.

"We'll speak of this but once, Olivia, and then I never care to hear the man's name uttered in my presence—or house—again. While I firmly believe that a man who is a traitor deserves a traitor's death, what happened to Charles Aberdeen is abominable. The manner in which those men carried out their mission against him, and then paraded his—"

The general's lips firmed behind his beard. He stared at her, his grey eyes unflinching, disgust clearly written in his features, and Olivia silently begged—pleaded—for him to move on.

As if reluctantly granting her wish, he let out his breath. "What they did was beyond the pale. And it's deeply unfortunate that you must bear the sting of embarrassment not only for him, but also for yourself, having been his wife. In my inviting you into this home, you must know that I'm also inviting a certain measure of this shame and reproach upon myself and my family. Upon the reputation of Belle Meade."

Olivia inwardly flinched, but held his gaze. None of this was anything she didn't already know. But hearing him speak so plainly about it, about her life, cut deeply.

"However, I'm most willing to do it, owing largely to my wife. She holds great affection for you, Olivia, as she did your mother. Elizabeth grieved Rebecca's passing like that of a dearest sister."

"Thank you, sir," Olivia whispered. "I hold like affection for your wife as well."

He opened his mouth to say something, then paused, apparently changing his mind. He laughed softly. "I noticed your ... *hesitance* earlier this evening as Selene was sharing with us about General Jackson."

Olivia thought back and answered honestly. "I don't know what you mean, sir."

He smiled. "One of the most important decisions in a father's life, Olivia, is who his daughter will marry. That decision cannot be taken lightly, nor made in haste. It must be acted upon with lengthy consideration and only after careful study of the man's character. To do any less would show a lack of regard for the institution of marriage ... and for the daughter. Would you not agree?"

Thinking of Selene and their conversation at dinner, Olivia nodded. But when the general said nothing else, another possibility occurred to her, and Olivia bristled. "With all respect, General Harding, I believe that when my father made the match for me with Charles, he did so with great regard. Nor was his decision made in haste. He honestly believed that—"

"Olivia." The general held up a hand, concern lining his features. "I in no way meant any disrespect to your father or his memory. On the contrary, my dear. My intention, clumsy though I now realize it was, was to honor his daughter by assuring her that I'll show the very same consideration in choosing *her* next marriage partner as I will show in choosing the partners of my own daughters."

Olivia could only stare as the full weight of his meaning slowly settled around her. "M-my next marriage partner?"

"Yes." He leaned forward, his smile patient, even fatherly. "As head of this household and ... your benefactor, I pledge to find you a husband who is an honorable and upright man. One who will take care of you in the manner that your father would've wished. Understandably, we're not speaking of an imminent betrothal. We need to let time pass, observe the customary mourning period. But I would wager that since the marriage between you and your late husband was not"—he paused—"one of the heart, let's say, you might indeed find yourself open to another relationship sooner than you may think, *if* the opportunity presents itself."

"But I ..." Thoughts were coming so fast, elbowing their way through surprise and confusion, and Olivia struggled to filter them. They weren't thoughts General Harding would welcome either. As soon as she gave them voice, she knew she would regret it. Because he *was*—strictly speaking—what he said he was. Her benefactor. She simply hadn't thought the situation through in that light.

But the way he'd said *if* the opportunity presents itself made her wonder if he already had a man in mind. No, that wasn't possible. Charles had only been gone a week. Still ...

The syllabub curdled in her stomach.

"It's not likely," he continued, "that the gentleman will be anyone from Nashville. Understandably ... your situation being as public as it is. But you're a lovely woman, Olivia. Intelligent and not too old. You're from a good family. There's no reason why we shouldn't be able to make a good match for you. You'll make some man an excellent wife."

"But General Harding, I ..." How did she voice her resistance to this in a manner that wouldn't offend him? Or even worse, turn him against her? It wasn't as if she had other options available to her. "I-I feel that I need to say something to you, and this isn't easy for me. I—"

He held up a hand. "You don't have to thank me, dear. It's my duty and obligation in an instance such as this, as I told Elizabeth. But it's also my pleasure. When the time and circumstances are right, I'm sure we'll both know."

Sensing his sincerity and the genuineness of his intention and already having known remarriage was likely in her future, Olivia gauged the wisdom of her response and finally acquiesced. "I'm sure you're right, General. In time ... we'll know."

She rose, eager to be out of this office and back in her room.

"I'm sorry, Olivia, but there's one more thing I need to discuss with you."

Biting back a sigh, she reclaimed her seat, silently plotting ways to make herself as unappealing as possible to each and every one of his unmarried colleagues. Which wouldn't be difficult. Especially when placed next to Selene.

The leather chair creaked as General Harding shifted his weight. "Elizabeth certainly has enjoyed exchanging letters with you through these many months. They've been a source of encouragement for her. At her core, my wife is happiest when she's serving others."

"I'm the one who's grateful to her, sir. Your wife is ..." Olivia smiled, thinking of how much Elizabeth meant to her. "She is the kindest and most generous woman I know."

"Yes," he said. "She does indeed possess those qualities in abundance." He ran a hand along the desk's edge, his expression pensive, and she realized he wasn't eager to address whatever it was he wanted to say. "I'm sure you're wondering why I promised the head housekeeping position to you, then gave it to Lizzie."

"The thought did cross my mind, yes, sir. Aunt Elizabeth assured me there will be plenty for me to do, but ... I wish to have a purpose. To be helpful. If I'm going to live here, I must contribute in some way."

"She told me you said that, and that displays a very commendable trait." Again that thoughtful consideration. "Are you aware, Olivia, that my wife has been under a physician's care for quite some time now?"

She felt a frown. "I knew Aunt Elizabeth struggled with fatigue on occasion, but ... no, sir, I didn't know that."

"The doctor's diagnosis is a 'greatly weakened constitution,' likely brought on by the stress she bore throughout my incarceration during—"

"The war," she finished for him, remembering the anxious tone of Aunt Elizabeth's letters during that time. "She carried such a burden during your absence, sir. Not only for Belle Meade, but for your welfare." Recalling a portion of a letter, she smiled. "She was deeply concerned that you wouldn't have the clothing you needed and that you would get chilled and suffer poor health." What she didn't say was that the clothing Elizabeth had questioned as being warm enough had been his long johns.

His smile was brief. "She exercised a great amount of concern for me. More so than was necessary, as I assured her in my letters. Many times."

"But of course she was concerned, sir. You're her husband. She loves you very much."

"Yes . . ." He looked away. "And I care for her as well."

His matter-of-fact response and lack of emotion took her by surprise. Then she reminded herself to whom she was speaking—General William Giles Harding, a military commander accustomed to war and leading men into battle. A man probably none too comfortable sharing his feelings. Much less his feelings for his wife. With a near stranger.

"You're a compassionate person, Olivia. Which is an admirable—and somewhat rare—quality to possess these days."

Surprised yet again, she could only whisper, "Thank you, sir."

"You took care of your own mother, did you not, while she was ill? Before she passed?"

Olivia studied him, feeling something shift in the room. And inside her. She swallowed back the haunting sense of regret and remorse that always accompanied the memory of her mother's passing. "Yes, sir, I did."

He nodded, then leaned forward. "Which leads me to the reason I'm most grateful you've come to live with us. Your presence is unmistakably providential, Olivia, and holds far greater import than managing the household's activities. Because . . ." His voice wavered. Only for an instant. But it was enough for her to know she didn't want to hear whatever it was he was about to say. "Because I need you to help my sweet Elizabeth to die."

Chapter EIGHT

*R*idley wiped his forehead with his shirt sleeve, his back muscles screaming and hunger gnawing at his stomach. Not to mention the pounding in his head. It was dark out, the sun long having set, but still the air in the stable thrummed with heat.

For the past few hours, at Green's orders, he'd mucked stalls until he'd lost count of how many loads of manure and urine-soaked hay he'd hauled out, only to haul fresh hay back in. He'd narrowly missed being kicked by the wounded mare he'd seen earlier that day. A stable hand had brought her in about an hour ago and stuck her in the last stall, which had struck him as odd, seeing as this stable housed stallions. The gash on the horse's leg was bad, and she was downright skittish. Wouldn't let anyone come near her. Not that he blamed her.

But he'd done everything Robert Green — or Uncle Bob, as he'd heard men refer to him — had asked him to do and more, sensing the man was testing to see if he was serious about learning. So Ridley wasn't about to complain. He'd gotten what he'd come for. Or would, soon enough.

Sighing, he hung the pitchfork and rubbed at a walnut-sized knot on the back of his head. Sore didn't begin to describe it. It's what he got for egging that man on earlier, but it had been worth it. He drank his fill from a fresh barrel of water, then eyed the barrel of feed next to it. There was a day when he would've eaten it without question and would've been grateful for it. It was remarkable, what a man would eat to stay alive.

Wiping his mouth, he straightened and braced himself as jagged-edged memories rose inside him. Every evening they came, uninvited guests. They brought with them the dark, bone-numbing cold of Andersonville. Days on end without food. Nights spent sleeping in shallow trenches six inches deep in water, so full of filth and vermin he'd wake up feeling more like a corpse than a man.

He walked to the door of the stable and stepped outside into the night, then reached into his pocket and pulled out the seashell. The day he'd entered Andersonville, the corporal on duty ordered all the prisoners to empty their pockets of valuables. He had, except for this shell, knowing it would mean nothing to anyone else. Still, he'd expected them to find it when they patted him down. Either they didn't feel it or didn't care … but he sure did.

With his thumb, he rubbed the smooth inside of the shell, and with the nail of his forefinger, he ticked off the twenty-eight tiny ridges on the outside. He turned the shell over in his palm, always feeling a little homesick when he stared at it, yet feeling the comfort of home as well.

The pale sheen of a full moon lit the yard in a silvery half light, and he drew in a deep breath, the faces of men he'd known in prison passing before him. Soldiers he'd served with, who — after only a few months — were hardly recognizable as men anymore, much less the soldiers they'd once been.

A breeze kicked up and a sudden cool hit his cheeks. He quickly wiped them dry, hearing steps coming up behind him. He slipped the shell back into his pocket.

"Well done, Lieutenant." Robert Green held up a lantern. "You hungry?"

Ridley cleared his throat and shrugged. "I could eat."

Green laughed. " 'I could eat,' " he parroted back. "I bet you could. Come on with me."

Ridley grabbed his pack. "What about the other lanterns?"

"Leave 'em. We got a man who'll see to that."

Ridley followed, not knowing where they were going.

He figured four weeks, six at most, and he'd have learned what he needed to know and would be on his way west. No later than the end of June for sure, which was when the last group of wagons left Missouri for the Colorado Territory. The letter in his pack from a trail guide outlined the details. They had to make it across Kansas before the first snowfall. He'd filed his application for 160 acres of land under the Homestead Act three years earlier, during the war. It had been accepted with the agreement that he improve the land within five years—easily done if he left this summer—then he'd file for deed of title. He had the money from the sale of the house and farm, what little it had brought. But it was a fair start compared to most. Add some to that amount by working here—if that worked out—and he'd have enough since it was just him alone. Then he'd be gone.

On the far side of the meadow he made out a cluster of cabins, ones he'd seen earlier that day. "Is that where the stable hands bunk?"

"Some of 'em. Others come and go from town. The servants and their families live over there too. But ain't no way I'm puttin' you in with them, Lieutenant." Green humphed. "Not with what done happened 'tween you and Grady today. No, sir."

"But I was provoked. I was just defending myself."

Robert Green stopped short. "You look me straight in the eye and tell me you didn't take pleasure in poppin' him a good one."

Whether it was Green's surprisingly parental tone or that he was dead on right, Ridley couldn't keep from smiling.

"Mmm-hmm ..." Green eyed him. "We got us a good share of Rebel boys workin' here, and seems to me it ain't too wise for you to be mixin' with that crowd. So you ain't stayin' with the other workers, Lieutenant. Not knowin' what I know 'bout you." He took off walking again.

Ridley easily caught up. "I'm obliged to you for thinking about me."

Green huffed. "It's me I's thinkin' about. You get yourself found out and *I'm* the one who be in trouble."

While Ridley knew that was true, he also sensed the man was actually being kind but didn't want a fuss made over it. "Where're we going?" he finally asked.

"Home." Green motioned ahead to a cabin set off from the others.

"That's your place?"

"Yes, sir, it is. Old Mr. Harding, the general's father, built it hisself. Well, half of it anyways. That part"—Green pointed to one side—"used to be Dunham's Station, a place to trade along the route."

Sure enough, as they got closer, Ridley made out what actually appeared to be two tiny cabins, joined by a dogtrot.

"When Old Mr. Harding bought it some sixty years back," Green continued, "he added the other side for his family and they lived here 'til they built the big house."

At mention of the big house, Ridley looked back to see the windows on the main floor of the home glowing a warm yellow. They looked so welcoming, he could almost imagine walking up the front steps, knocking on the door all proper like, and being invited inside. *Almost.* He wondered which room Olivia Aberdeen was in right now and whether or not she'd eaten dinner or knew what her responsibilities in the home would be yet.

He still couldn't imagine her being a head housekeeper. Didn't fit, for some reason. Then again, he never would've imagined he would have apprenticed himself to a Negro.

Green strode through the night with ease, the full moon lighting their way, and Ridley recalled what the man had said about him and his parents being "a present" to the Hardings when Green was just a little boy. "You been here all your life, is that right?"

"Sure 'nough. Since I's two." Green gestured ahead. "And this cabin be where the general was born. So the place got special meanin' to him. And me too, I guess."

Ridley contrasted the modest cabin with the comparative wealth and beauty of Belle Meade. "General Harding certainly has made his way in the world, hasn't he, Mr. Green?"

"Yes, sir, he sure done that." Green took the stairs to the porch and paused on the open breezeway connecting the cabins, frowning. "But somethin' you got to do, sir. You gotta stop callin' me Mr. Green. No white man in a hundred miles of here does that. Most folks don't even know my last name. Everybody 'round here just calls me Uncle Bob."

Ridley smiled. "All right then. *Uncle Bob.* You best stop calling me lieutenant too. Most folks back home called me by my last name. You can too, if you want."

Green shook his head. "Think I like your Christian name better, sir. *Ridley.* It's a good name. A strong name. 'Sides ..." He chuckled. "I once had me a dog by the name of Cooper."

Ridley laughed as Green reached to open the door.

Green stilled and looked back in the direction of the big house. "Lawd, what is that?"

Ridley turned in time to see a ball of flame streaking through the dark. It arched upward, upward, then crashed in a flurry of sparks against the stallions' stable.

"What in tarnation is—"

Ridley was off the porch and running. The distance that would have taken five minutes to cover at Robert Green's pace, he covered in one. As he drew closer, he spotted a shadow headed for the woods.

But it was either the shadow or the stable.

The torch lay burning against the wall and he kicked it away, quickly determining the arsonist had failed in his original intent — to reach the open door at the top. Instead, the fingers of flame slowly licked and curled their way up the dry wood. Ridley shed his outer shirt and began beating the flames, but they were too many and too spread out. He raced inside the stable, hearing a volley of gunfire signal behind him and, seconds later, the peal of a bell.

The stallions, frenzied by acrid smoke, reared as Ridley opened the double doors to the stables, then bolted past him. He came to Jack Malone's stable and the newly arrived stallion pawed the ground in protest, then leaped forward, nearly taking Ridley down as he tore out of the stall. At the far end of the stable, a man — a stable hand Ridley had met earlier in the day — began flinging open the remaining doors. Ridley grabbed an armful of blankets when he heard the crack of a whip.

"Get outta here, you stupid — "

Ridley saw which stall the man was in and reached the doorway in time to see the tapered end of the whip slash the haunch of the wounded mare. Cornered, the mare reared and fell into the wall. The man raised his arm a second time, but Ridley grabbed him. "Green told me no whips!"

The man jerked away. "It don't matter with her. She's bein' put down tomorrow anyway."

The mare gained her feet and pawed the ground with her good leg, her eyes stark with fear and confusion. It was a look Ridley had seen before.

The man raised the whip again, and Ridley started to charge him. The mare let out a high-pitched scream, then charged from the stall into the night.

Ridley grabbed the horse blankets and raced back outside. The lower half of the stable wall was engulfed in flames, which steadily crept higher. A dozen men — Bob Green among them — fought its progress with shirts and quilts and whatever else they could lay hands on. Ridley threw them blankets and set to work. Together, they fought from all angles, confining the flame, working to smother its life.

Without warning, water rained down, and Ridley turned to see men and women—dark-skinned and light—formed into a line. The human chain passed buckets of water between them with practiced efficiency, sending bucketful after bucketful sailing overhead, dousing both the wall and the soot-covered men.

Finally, in the haze of smoke and hacking coughs, someone called out, "I think we got it!"

A minute later, "The inside is clear too, Uncle Bob!"

Then a collective sigh wove its way through the group.

Fully spent, Ridley leaned over, hands on his thighs, to catch his breath. His eyes and lungs burned, and the pounding at the back of his head had grown worse.

"That's the man right there, General! The one who set the fire!"

Ridley looked up and saw Grady Matthews—the man responsible for the ache in his head—striding toward him, his chin bandaged. But it was who was with him, rifle in hand, that brought him upright.

Uncle Bob had been right about his meeting with General Harding coming soon enough. But Ridley could already tell it wasn't going to be the introduction he'd hoped for.

Chapter
NINE

Who can tell me what happened here?" Harding's voice carried over the crowd, pushing aside the sudden silence.

Ridley quelled the urge to answer, having learned the hard way that sometimes it was best to keep his mouth shut. Especially when a man with a gun was staring him down.

"I can, General." Bob Green worked his way to Ridley's side. "And it weren't this man's fault, sir. He was with me when the fire started. We saw it from my cabin, and he went runnin'. Got here first and started puttin' out the flames. Got the horses out too, sir."

"You arrived here first?" Harding asked, his focus shifting back to Ridley.

"Yes, sir." Ridley nodded, noting suspicion in the general's tone.

Closer up, General William Giles Harding was taller than he'd imagined. In fact, the man was pretty much his match in stature and weight. He'd always heard Harding had a presence, a commanding quality that inspired men to follow. And while Ridley would have to concede that point, he also knew he rubbed men like Harding the wrong way. He didn't know why exactly, but they had the same effect on him.

"And just who might you be?" Harding continued.

"This here's Mr. Ridley—"

"Thank you, Uncle Bob," Harding interrupted. "But I'd rather hear it from him."

Ridley felt Green look over at him and could almost hear the man thinking, *Come on now, Ridley. Don't you go messin' things up from the start.* Ridley took a step toward Harding. "I'm Ridley Cooper, sir. I arrived here this afternoon, hoping to get a job."

"And just where are you from, Mr. Cooper?"

"South Carolina, sir."

"That's a long way from Nashville. How did you come to hear about Belle Meade?"

If he'd had a dollar to spare, Ridley would've bet it Bob Green was piling up prayers about now. He gave a relaxed laugh, confident it would appeal to a man like Harding. "Beg your pardon, General, but it's more like who *hasn't* heard of Belle Meade."

The comment drew laughter and nods from those gathered, but only the faintest of smiles from General Harding.

"I asked Uncle Bob about a job this afternoon," Ridley continued. "He told me I'd need to speak to you about it. Of course he didn't tell me that until *after* I'd already mucked out every stall there was and nearly got trampled by Jack Malone."

That drew even more laughter, along with a widening, more genuine smile from General Harding. Ridley felt the tension drain. Movement behind the general drew Ridley's eye, and he spotted the silhouettes of five women standing on the front porch. He was cloaked by darkness and hidden in the crowd, but the soft glow of lantern light coming from the house backlit the women's forms, and he thought he recognized Olivia Aberdeen standing particularly close to Mrs. Harding. A second later, his hunch was confirmed when the women turned to go inside. He'd recognize Olivia Aberdeen's bustle anywhere.

"I did see who set the fire though, sir," he said, returning his attention to the matter at hand. "The man ran off into the woods." He pointed. "Right over there."

Harding briefly glanced in that direction. "And you didn't see fit to give chase, Mr. Cooper? You just let a man like that run off, so he can come back any night and try the same thing again?" He shook his head. "I thought you boys from South Carolina were made of stiffer mettle than that."

A ripple of expectancy moved through the crowd, but Ridley's smile came easily. "I thought about chasing him, General Harding. Then figured that catching a fool like that"—he purposefully glanced at Grady—"wasn't worth risking a thoroughbred like Jack Malone. Much less a stable full of them, sir."

Wordless, General Harding studied him for a moment, and Ridley began to wonder if he'd overstepped his bounds. Wouldn't be the first time.

Then Harding stepped forward. "I couldn't agree more, Mr. Cooper." He reached out a hand.

Ridley accepted, finding the general's grip firm and unyielding. He heard Bob Green sigh beside him and figured the man was satisfied in how things had turned out.

And he was pretty sure he had himself a job.

Olivia awakened before sunup from a fitful night's rest. She curled in the bed, the general's request playing like a sad, dissonant chord over and over in her mind. *I need you to help my sweet Elizabeth to die.*

She shivered, even though the room wasn't cold. She'd come up here last night and cried tears she didn't know she had left. General Harding was mistaken, that's all. He had to be. Aunt Elizabeth couldn't be that sick. Yes, she had appeared a little fatigued. But seriously ill?

Olivia rolled onto her back, unable to believe it. Unwilling. She could name a dozen situations where doctors predicted one thing, only to see the opposite. Doctors weren't infallible. She knew that well enough.

The first hint of pink filtered through the lace curtains on the east-facing window, and she pushed back the bedcovers and padded softly across the carpeted floor. She nudged the window up further, wanting to smell the newness of morning, then knelt and peered at the grounds just a floor below. It was so peaceful ...

The estate and meadow beyond lay shrouded in low-hanging fog, feathery wisps clinging to tree branches and hovering in the low places where the meadow sagged. Outside her window, wisteria—thick and hearty—wove its way through a trellis. She breathed deeply, loving the aroma of the fragrant purple flowers.

From this vantage point, she had a full view of the beautiful meadow for which Belle Meade was named and of the old Harding cabin. The one the general's father built, as Elizabeth had once written. A curl of smoke rose from its chimney. Set against the misty morning, the scene looked more like a portrait on canvas than reality. She could see someone moving about inside the cabin and wondered who lived there now.

A bell tolled, echoing across the meadow. *One, two, three, four ...*

Minutes later, servants appeared on the grounds below, their workday begun.

Elizabeth will not die.

The thought came so vividly, she felt the certainty of it as surely as her own heart beating solid and strong in her chest. "Elizabeth hasn't been told," the general had explained last night. "The doctor counseled that would be best, at least for now. After thorough consideration, I agree. She could live for several months yet, or ... only a matter of weeks," he'd finished softly, displaying remarkable stoicism. "I see no reason to upset her nerves and cause her undue stress with this revelation. And I must insist, Olivia, that you keep our confidence as well."

That's when she'd started to cry. "Do Selene and Mary know?"

He had shaken his head. "Again, I request that you allow me to share that news with my daughters when the time is right." He'd risen from his desk then and accompanied her to the door, his hand resting on the latch. "Elizabeth needs someone to help care for her. Not all the time yet, certainly. But that time will come. And"—his voice lowered—"according to what your dear mother shared with Elizabeth before she passed, your tender care greatly eased her own journey home. That's what I'm asking of you, Olivia ... please. To ease Elizabeth's journey home."

Now, with knees aching from kneeling at the window, Olivia stood and pressed her palm flat against the pane. She would help Elizabeth in every way she could. But to gain strength, to get better. Not to die. Having cared for her mother, she knew something about nurturing the sick. When the doctor had first diagnosed her mother, he'd told the family she didn't have long to live. Olivia looked at the framed drawing of her mother she'd placed on the bureau. Her mother had died just one day shy of Olivia's fifteenth birthday—five years *after* the doctor's diagnosis.

Olivia sighed. Doctors didn't always know best.

As agreed, she would keep her promise to the general not to tell. But it wasn't right ... a husband keeping such a thing from his wife. Equally in the wrong was the doctor who instigated the deception.

She was weary of a world where men wielded such power. If the tables were turned, men wouldn't stand for it. So as women—her breath fogged the pane—why should they? The unspoken question hung in the silence like a forbidden whisper. But unlike the vapor on the window that quickly vanished and was gone, Olivia's question lingered.

She'd gone from her father's home to Charles's house, and now—with only a brief respite—would be married off again to a man of the general's choosing. She sighed, watching a mockingbird light on a nearby branch. What was it like to be free? To have choices as men did? And the ability to pursue them. To be able to choose marriage? Or not.

The questions felt so preposterous, she was tempted to smile.

But didn't.

Through the misty haze of a half-risen sun, she spotted one of the general's thoroughbreds in a corral by the stable and was grateful no one had been hurt in the fire last evening. General Harding said the damage to the building was minimal compared to what it could have been and that while he had no idea who had started the blaze, he was determined to find out.

Hearing the distinct *clink* of pots and pans from the kitchen directly beneath her, Olivia set about getting dressed. She glanced at her trunk and thought of Mr. Cooper, wondering where he'd sheltered for the night after the general had sent him away. Ridley Cooper had carried her trunk all that way without complaint. And the shell he carried … Such sentimentality for a man who seemed so wild and untamed.

A servant had hung her gowns—including yesterday's dress, now clean and mended—in the wardrobe. Having brought only two with her to Belle Meade—one black, one grey—made choosing easy. She'd been forbidden by Charles's brother to take any other dresses with her, and she'd complied. Except for one. She reached past the two mourning ensembles to the rich russet-red fabric. She pulled out the dress and held it to her face. She breathed in, but the scent of her mother's perfume had long since faded.

Holding the dress against herself, she looked in the full-length mirror. She'd never be able to wear the gown. She was taller than her mother had been, so the dress was several inches short. Plus it was sleeveless, not a fashion recommended for a woman with a scar extending halfway up her arm.

Other than the richness of the fabric, the dress was simple. No lace or fancy piping. But she remembered her mother in this dress as clearly as if she'd seen her in it yesterday, and leaving it behind was something she simply hadn't been able to do.

With a sigh, she returned the dress to the wardrobe. After using the chamber pot, she dipped a fresh cloth into the tepid water in the basin on the washstand before running it over her skin, relishing the coolness. By the time she dressed, the aroma of sausage, eggs, and biscuits filled every corner of her room; and Olivia quickly decided she was going to like living above the kitchen. No matter that her room wasn't located in the same wing as the family bedrooms. Not only did her quarters come with a lovely view of the sunrise and this aromatic preview of breakfast, but an open-air porch just outside her door connected this wing to the main house.

Lizzie Hoover's room was next to hers, she'd learned; but she hadn't seen Cousin Lizzie since dinner last night, nor had there been a light beneath Lizzie's door when Olivia had retired. Perhaps Lizzie and Mary had stayed up visiting.

Mary Harding. Now there was a story waiting to be told, but it was one Olivia already knew. She'd learned a great deal about the girl simply from watching her at dinner. Noting Mary's furtive glances at her father, watching him as he watched Selene tell a story. Listening to Mary tell a story of her own right after, her expression hungry for her father's same laughter and approval. Mary's smile dimming bit by bit throughout the evening when his reactions were always slightly less enthusiastic for her than for her older sister.

Olivia smoothed a wrinkle from the corner of her bed. Perhaps there were advantages to having been an only child. She'd never worried about being her father's favorite. She knew from the time she could talk that business was her father's priority. But she'd had her mother's love. And that had been enough.

Most of the time.

Olivia stepped onto the porch and reached to close the bedroom door behind her, but stopped and crossed back to shut the window first. Flicking the lock into place, she glanced out the window and paused, seeing a cloaked figure emerge from the woods, cut across the meadow and head in the direction of the house. Olivia observed for a moment, quickly deciding it must be a woman. The person moved with too much grace to be masculine. But what was a woman doing out in the woods this time of morning?

As the woman drew closer, Olivia concealed herself to one side of the window, nudging the curtain back. The woman carried a sack of some sort. Judging by how she maneuvered it, it looked heavy. Olivia squinted, trying to see if she could tell what—

The woman stopped and looked directly up at Olivia's window.

Olivia jumped back, heart in her throat. She winced and gritted her teeth, praying the woman hadn't seen her, but she knew better. The woman—older, in her fifties, perhaps—had looked up with purpose, as if wanting Olivia to know she'd been spotted.

Regardless of whether or not the woman had seen her face, Olivia knew she wouldn't forget the woman's skin, which was the subtle brown of heavily creamed coffee, and her dark hair—hair more like a white person's than a Negro's. Beautiful too. Curly and wild about her head, as if the cloak's hood could scarcely contain it.

Not daring to move for at least a full minute, Olivia finally relaxed. She'd only been looking out the window, after all. It wasn't as if she'd done anything wrong. Summoning courage, she peeked back around the curtain.

But the woman was gone.

Chapter TEN

"I ain't never had a white man stay as a guest with me before." Green closed the cabin door behind them, the pinkish hue of dawn swiftly giving way to golden yellow. "You don't reckon we're breakin' any laws by you stayin' here, do you?"

Green's chuckle drew a smile from Ridley. "I imagine in some people's books we are. But I don't particularly care what those people think." Ridley paused at the edge of the porch and stretched, still a little weary, somewhat sore, and definitely hungry. The jerky stew Bob Green had served him last night—a fair portion for one man, but slim for two—had warmed his belly but hadn't come close to filling it. Still, Green had shared what he had, and Ridley was grateful. "We fought a war." Ridley shrugged. "And they lost. They don't get to make the rules anymore."

"That's just the kinda smart talk that gets your face all messed up. Like it is now and like it was when I first met you—"

Ridley touched the purpling bruise on his cheek.

"—and that kinda talk is somethin' you can't do. Not workin' here at Belle Meade anyway. I know the war's over, but these people ... they still ain't readin' from the same book as you."

They cut a path toward the main house.

Ridley looked over at him. "You know I wouldn't say that to just anyone else. I can be discreet." He smiled. "When I try, Uncle Bob."

Green just looked at him. "But that's just it. You don't have to *say* anything. You say it without even openin' your mouth. It's in the way you carry yourself. The way you treat folks. The way you treat *me*, more like a white man than what I am. Everybody tells a story, Ridley, whether they want to or not. Oh, some folks is good at hidin' it. But all you got to do is listen, just listen ... and you'll hear it."

Letting that settle inside him, Ridley focused ahead and felt a smile coming as he watched what might have resembled a horse in another lifetime slowly plod toward them. The gelding's sway back and drooping lower lip revealed its age, as did the balding patches in its coat. "Looks like one of your lead stallions is trying to make a run for it."

Uncle Bob laughed. "That's just Old Gray. He been here at Belle Meade for years. He ain't dead, but he been workin' on it for a while."

"Looks like he's working extra hard at it today."

"Aw, come on now." Uncle Bob walked the short distance to the fence and gave the gelding a good rub behind the ears. "Old Gray been a good friend. He still pretty strong. He just don't move too fast no more. But he still got some good days in him."

As they walked on, Ridley studied the side of the stable damaged by the flames. "Who do you think started that fire last night?"

Green shrugged. "Somebody jealous over General Harding havin' the best thoroughbred farm in all of Dixie. There be plenty of them folks to go 'round. Ain't the first time somethin' like this happened. Probably not the last."

They took the steps up to the side porch, and Green knocked on a door. It opened and a tiny slip of a woman grinned big, then waved them inside.

"I was startin' to think you wasn't coming this mornin', Uncle Bob. You're later than usual. And you brought somebody with you too." She patted Ridley's arm. "I *love* havin' men in my kitchen."

"Mornin', Susanna." Green settled himself at a small table in the corner and motioned Ridley to do likewise. Two other women working at the stove turned and greeted them. Ridley nodded in their direction, and they both smiled back, then looked at each other and grinned.

"Susanna, this here's Mr. Ridley Cooper. He—"

"I know who he is," she said, glancing at the other women. "We all do. You the man who almost got hisself blamed for the fire last night."

Ridley nodded. "Yes, ma'am. That's me. But I didn't do it."

"We know." She smiled. "That's why I said *almost*. Don't you worry. None of us pay Grady Matthews no nevermind." She motioned. "You need something for that?"

Ridley touched the bruise on his cheek. "No, ma'am, I'm fine. Thank you."

"Mr. Cooper'll be workin' with me for a while," Green continued. "And this woman here is Susanna Carter." Green inhaled deeply, eyeing the scrambled eggs with sausage and biscuits she was serving up. "Best cook in the whole of Dixie and wife to Big Ike. So you best watch your step around her, or Big Ike'll make sure you do."

Susanna playfully shushed him.

"And helpin' her over there is Chloe Harris and Betsy Lee. They got husbands who work here too."

Susanna set a full plate before each of them, and Ridley could only stare, unable to remember the last time he'd eaten so well.

"Everythin' all right, sir?" she asked.

"Everything's fine, ma'am." He glanced up. "More than fine. It looks delicious. Thank you."

"Not as good as my stew last night." Green huffed. "But it'll do."

Ridley grinned and scooped a forkful of eggs, then saw Green watching him and set his fork back on his plate.

"For this fine eatin', Lawd, we thank you. And for these women who get up long before the sun ..."

Bob Green didn't bow his head, didn't even close his eyes, yet he spoke the words with such respect, nobody listening could have doubted his sincerity or who he was addressing—and that Green believed with everything in him God was listening. Susanna and the other two women had paused from their work.

"... cookin' and carin' for this family like they do, and for me too, I thank you, sir."

Without ceremony, Green took a bite of a warm biscuit and looked like he was about to pray all over again. Ridley took a quick bite before it was too late and continued eating for five minutes straight. He only stopped for sips of coffee, before using the last of his second biscuit to sop up every last bit of butter and goodness on his plate.

Susanna motioned. "You want more? There's plenty."

He eyed the eggs in the pan. "No, ma'am. I'm good. Thank you."

She just laughed, grabbed his plate, and piled it high again.

"You know anything new?" Green asked her.

"I do," Susanna answered, stirring a pan on the stove. "But it ain't good."

Green paused, looking at each of the women. "Anybody we know?"

Betsy nodded. "You 'member Bud and Luvenia and their two boys? Over at the Foley place?"

Green nodded, frowning.

Susanna pulled the pan off the burner. "Them boys started goin' to school. A freedmen school, for us folks." She looked at Ridley, who nodded. "Bud and Luvenia's boys got beat up day afore yesterday. White men come into the classroom, dragged everybody out. They took a stick to some of the kids, but they 'bout beat the teacher to death. He was a Negro come down from New York City. Just to open the school, the paper said. He's supposed to live, but they won't be openin' the school again. Not that they could find anybody to teach even if they did."

A hush fell over the kitchen. Ridley set his fork on his plate, keenly aware of the tension in the air and the color of his own skin and of all the battles yet to be fought despite a war having been won.

A moment passed and Green drained his coffee cup. Susanna filled it again. "Thank you, ma'am," he said softly. "So ..." Green looked up, the tone of his voice clearly marking a shift in the conversation. "How're things here in the house? How's the missus?"

When Susanna didn't answer, Ridley looked up, sipping his coffee, and caught the tail end of a look she'd tossed Green.

Green paused, then looked pointedly over at him and back to the women. "It's all right." He nodded. "He's with us."

Only then did Ridley realize what Susanna had been asking. And he felt more than a little honored by the acceptance.

"She ain't feelin' too good this mornin'." Susanna was petite but she wiped down the tabletop with a vengeance. "She got the weariness again. Took breakfast in her room." She exhaled. "She ain't hardly ate a bite. She just too good is what it is. She done give and give all these years. Now she 'bout give out."

The other women nodded, as did Bob Green. Ridley couldn't help but think of Olivia Aberdeen and knew she would be concerned about her friend.

"The widow who come yesterday." Green sipped his coffee. "What's she like?"

Ridley's interest ticked up a notch, though he tried not to show it.

"She seem nice enough." Chloe joined them at the table, buttered biscuit in hand. "I went to turn down her bed last night, but she was already in there. Thought I heard her cryin'."

Susanna sighed. "Can't blame her after all she been through."

"All she been through?" Betsy turned from where she was kneading a lump of dough. "Here she been, livin' high and mighty. And all the time knowin' that her man was a—"

"How you know she knew?" Susanna frowned. "You don't know that for sure. 'Sides, if Missus Harding took her in—which she did—then that widow must have some good in her. I ain't sayin' that maybe she ain't done somethin' she shouldn't. I *am* sayin' it ain't right how a woman gotta pay for her man's wrongs. And we all know that's the way of it."

Chloe gave a soft *mmm-hmm.* And even Betsy nodded.

But Ridley waited, wanting someone to say more about Mrs. Aberdeen. About her late husband. What he was or—more rightly—had been.

"Jedediah told my Richard," Chloe continued, " 'bout pickin' her up in town yesterday. People starin' real ugly like." Her voice lowered. "There was this one white woman, he said, looked straight at her"—she made a face—"and *spit!* Right there in front of everybody."

Ridley felt as though they had to be talking about someone else. It couldn't be Olivia Aberdeen. But she had arrived yesterday, and Jedediah had brought her. So it had to be her.

"Sure hope she don't get too much in your way, Susanna," Betsy said over her shoulder. "Helpin' with runnin' the house and all."

"Oh, the widow ain't helpin' Susanna with the house." Chloe rose from the table. "Not no more. That other woman, she gonna be doin' that."

Green looked up. "What other woman?"

Ridley frowned. So Olivia Aberdeen *wasn't* going to be the Hardings' head housekeeper after all.

Susanna laid aside the dish she'd been drying. "The daughter of the general's first cousin. Miss Lizzie Hoover. She ain't never married. Her parents both gone now, so the general took her in."

"She gonna be livin' here for good then," Green said, more a statement than a question.

Susanna nodded. "I think she work out fine. She done asked me last night to help her learn what to do. I told her I'd teach her right. Show her how Missus Harding likes things done."

"So what's that widow gonna do?" Green asked.

Ridley looked back at Susanna.

"Don't rightly know." She gathered their empty plates. "But Missus Harding is right partial to her, I could tell right off. So *all* of us is gonna be kind," she said, looking pointedly at the other women. "We gonna make her feel welcome."

Chloe and Betsy both nodded. Betsy more reluctantly.

Ridley drained his coffee cup, eager to leave so he could ask Bob Green privately what they were referring to.

"Jedediah told my Richard somethin' else too ..."

When Chloe didn't continue, Ridley looked up to find her looking directly at him. "What's that?"

Chloe's smile bordered on suspicious. "Jedediah say you walked her the rest of the way here, after the carriage wheel broke. And that you toted her trunk all that way."

He nodded slowly. "Yes, ma'am. That's right."

The women glanced at each other as if knowing something he didn't.

"He also say that when he got back to that carriage," Chloe went on, a teasing quality sparkling in her dark eyes, "that door still be locked tight as a sugar chest. Which got us to wonderin' ..." She glanced at Susanna and Betsy. "How'd that woman get herself outta there? Her wearin' that big ol' dress and all."

Considering the curious expressions of the women before him, Ridley found himself tempted to smile. But what he'd just learned about Olivia Aberdeen wouldn't let him. Not knowing her well at all — or her situation — he still hurt for her. Recalling her exhausting sense of propriety, he felt honor bound not to divulge how she'd gotten out of that carriage.

On the other hand, these women had welcomed him into their kitchen and their community, just as Bob Green had, and their inquisitive stares were all but burning a hole through him. Even Green wore a mischievous grin.

A picture flashed into Ridley's mind, and he recalled rounding the corner to see Mrs. Aberdeen straddling that window. He didn't think he'd ever get the image of that shapely leg out of his mind, much less how he'd felt his way around the woman's bustle.

Finding his smile again, he met their gazes. "I know you're not going to believe this," he whispered — and would've sworn the women leaned forward, Green along with them. "But you know how those fancy hoop skirts of theirs can sometimes take on a mind of their own?"

They all nodded.

"And you know how small the windows in those carriages are?" He raised his brows and the sudden twinkle in their eyes told him their imaginations were rushing to fill in the blanks. "Well, what I find interesting ... is how the doors on those carriages, if you look at 'em *just* right, will sometimes *pop* right open for no good reason. Then slam shut again" — he snapped his fingers — "just like that!"

Stunned silence layered the room until Ridley grinned and winked. Then laughter broke out.

"Oh, that's *good*," Chloe said, pointing at him.

Susanna's high-pitched laughter carried over the others, and she swatted his arm. "You gonna fit in here just fine, Mr. Cooper!"

Bob Green smiled in approval, pushing back from the table. Even Betsy, shaking her head from across the room, grinned at him.

"Thank you, ladies, for breakfast," Ridley said, following Green out the door.

"Oh, Mr. Cooper?"

He turned to see Betsy standing inside the doorway.

"When you get ready to shave all that hair off your face, you let me know. I can shave the fuzz off a ripe peach with nary a nick."

"Thank you, ma'am." He rubbed his beard. "I'll keep that in mind."

"You do that," she said. " 'Cause I'm guessin' that underneath all them whiskers, you's probably *real* nice lookin'." Her smile turned surprisingly sweet. "For a white man!"

Halfway to the stable, Ridley could still hear their laughter.

Chapter
ELEVEN

*R*idley waited until they reached the mares' stable, then glanced around to make sure they were alone. "Uncle Bob ... what we were talking about back there ..." He gestured. "About the widow," he said, lowering his voice. "And her late husband ..."

Green looked over at him, reaching for a harness.

"What was all that about?"

"You ain't from here, Ridley, so I'm guessin' that's how you ain't heard about it. But it ain't no secret. *Everybody* knows. It was all over the newspapers, or that's what they tell me. I heard 'bout it from Susanna. She reads—and writes too." A spark of pride colored his tone.

As they walked toward the back of the stable, mares sauntered to the stall doors, nickering. Green touched each as he passed.

"Susanna read off to me what the paper said, and the widow's husband ... he done wrong. He was an important man too. Worked for the government. Had hisself a office up in Nashville. Supposed to be headin' up some new plan, Susanna told me. Makin' things better for people. Helpin' 'em get jobs. But instead of doin' that, he lied to 'em and took their money."

Green paused by a stall door, and one glance inside told Ridley what they were here to do. The pretty little bay mare raised her head, then backed away, snorting. Dried blood crusted the gash on her leg.

"And some of them folks ..." Green sighed, shaking his head. "They finally had enough, and they killed him. Right there in town. Not far from that fancy office of his. Shot him, drug his body through the streets, then strung him up for all to see."

"Strung him up?" Ridley got a familiar feeling. "Wrote the words *traitor* and *scalawag* above him?"

Green frowned in question. "That's right."

"I read that article," Ridley explained, "when I first got into town." But he couldn't believe *that* man had been Olivia Aberdeen's husband. "The article had the words"—he glanced behind them, making sure they were still alone—"*Northern Sympathizer* in capital letters at the top. That caught my attention."

"Mmmm …" Green nodded. "I'm guessin' it would."

Ridley read caution in Green's eyes but needed no reminder of how people around here felt about the "other side." Still, he couldn't get the impression he'd formed of Olivia Aberdeen to marry with this new one.

Green opened the stall door and the mare reared. Stopping right where he was, Green indicated for Ridley to do the same. Then he lowered his eyes and, after a minute, the mare calmed. But her attention never wavered. Moving slowly, Green reached for a handful of feed and held it out to her. She looked at it, then at him, then tossed her head.

"You's a pretty girl," Green said softly. "And I's sure sorry 'bout you bein' hurt."

The mare stared at him, then snorted. Her haunches quivered, calling attention to the welts left by the whip.

"Come on, girl." Green inched his hand closer. "Just take a little."

Though he tried repeatedly, whispering things Ridley couldn't always hear, the horse refused to oblige. Finally, Green left the stall and closed the door behind him. He dumped the feed back in the barrel and brushed his hand on his pant leg.

"Last night …" Ridley gestured. "She was in the other stable with the stallions. I didn't think mares were supposed to be in there."

"They ain't. Same fool who put her in there is the one who left those marks on her backside. I sent him on his way last night. I won't abide a whip bein' taken to one of my horses. And the general won't abide a chance meetin', so to speak, between one of his stallions and a mare. Not with what he charges to stud."

Ridley glanced beside him. "How much does he charge?"

"Depends on the stallion. But with Jack Malone …"

Ridley nodded, listening closely.

"A hundred dollars."

"A hundred dollars! To stand with a mare?"

Green smiled. "Well … they's doin' a little more than just standin'."

Ridley laughed, but couldn't imagine that kind of money.

A moment passed.

"She lost a foal last year." Green's voice went soft. "Stillborn. Handsome little black colt. She kept lickin' his head, tryin' to get him to move." He blew out a breath. "She ain't been the same since."

They stood watching her, and she stared back.

"Was she bred here?" Ridley asked.

"Sure was. Triumph was her sire, Exquisite was her dam. General had real high hopes for her. For her foal too. But after that birth ..." He shook his head. "We was just talkin' 'bout breedin' her again, and now this. General already said to put her down, but I know she still got somethin' left in her—if her leg'll heal. Used to be, she could outrun the wind." Green held out his hand and made a clucking noise with his tongue. The mare didn't move. "She still a fine lady, she just don't know it anymore. Do you, Miss Birdie?"

"Birdie?"

"It's short for Seabird. That's her name."

"There you are, Uncle Bob!"

They both turned. General Harding strode toward them. Just seeing the man again made Ridley tense.

"Mornin', General Harding," Green said.

Ridley nodded. "Morning, sir."

The general gestured to the stall. "You're here to take care of Seabird, I assume. She's been a good horse, Uncle Bob. But it's her time."

"Actually, sir—" Green ducked his head. "I been rethinkin' that. She's a fine mare, and I figure she still got some good years left in her. With your say so, I wanna spend time workin' with her, seein' if we can't get her back. Her chances for foalin' again would be good. And with Jack Malone here, I thought she might—"

The general shook his head. "I'm afraid I overestimated her, Uncle Bob. We both did. Seabird doesn't have the stamina or strength we thought. Besides, you're not going to have time to work with her. Not with what I have planned." Harding shot Ridley a glance, obviously enjoying the moment. "I've given this a great deal of consideration, and next summer—June to be exact—Belle Meade will host its first annual yearling sale."

For a moment Green said nothing. Then he glanced down the long aisle bordered with stables, each one filled with either a mare or a foal or mares about to foal. "A yearlin' sale? We sure got enough stock for that, sir. And I'm bettin' people will come. Lots of 'em will come."

Harding briefly laid a hand on Green's shoulder. "If we work this right, people will come from miles around, Uncle Bob. But we have our work to do in getting these colts and fillies ready for sale."

"Yes, sir, we do," Green said, then glanced behind him.

Ridley trailed his gaze to the mare and remembered how she ran yesterday, even with a busted leg. That horse wasn't short on stamina or strength, and looking at her now, he would have bet she was think-ing the very same thing. He felt the outline of the shell in his pocket. *Seabird*, what a name for this horse ...

He couldn't decide if what he was considering was the wisest or most foolish thing he'd ever done. But whichever it was, he couldn't let it go.

"So let's have no more talk of Seabird, Uncle Bob," the general finished. "Take her out to the meadow. To the high pasture, if you want. But get it done."

"General Harding?"

His focus swung to Ridley. "Yes, Mr. Cooper?"

"What if *I* were to agree to take care of the mare, sir? To work with her. See if she can regain her strength. You've already made an investment in her, give me a chance to prove your investment was sound." Ridley glanced back at the horse who, at the moment, looked decidedly less imbued with the ability to reason. Then he caught Bob Green's hopeful expression and forged ahead. "But if it turns out you're right, sir, and her time *has* passed, I'll put her down myself."

General Harding said nothing at first, and Ridley knew the man was sizing him up. "When I agreed to hire you, Mr. Cooper, it wasn't so you could nurse a horse back to health. I appreciate your concern about my investment, but I know a thing or two about horses. And I'm not a believer in throwing good money after bad."

"Neither am I, sir. But ..." Ridley knew he needed to tread care-fully. He also knew Bob Green believed in that horse. But more than anything, he wanted to prove General William Giles Harding wrong. For so many reasons. "I'm certain Seabird has something left in her. I'll work with her on my own time. After regular hours."

General Harding gave a brief laugh. "Careful, Mr. Cooper. Determi-nation and stubbornness are close cousins."

"As are confidence and arrogance." Ridley smiled. "Sir."

Wordless, Green shifted his weight, looking between them.

Harding's eyes narrowed, his demeanor reflecting more of a challenge. "I've always held that if a man truly believes in something, he should be willing to stand behind his claim. And since I've already made an investment in this horse, as you yourself stated, Mr. Cooper, my only question to you is ..." He drew himself up. "Seeing as you believe the mare still has some life left in her, are you willing to pay the cost of what her recuperation and retraining will require?"

Ridley quickly estimated the expense and wished he'd never started down this road. He didn't have the funds to see this mare back to wholeness. He needed every penny for his venture west. Yet he had no choice. If he backed down now, Harding would win and would consider him weak and foolish. But what bothered him even more was that Bob Green might be disappointed in him.

And *that* was a price he wasn't willing to pay.

"Yes, sir," he answered. "I'll pay the expenses."

"Including the lease for her stall," Harding added. "I'm running a business here, Mr. Cooper. Not a charity."

Ridley bristled, wondering how much additional that would be and knowing Harding was taking advantage. It didn't sit well, but if Seabird came back and was as strong and promising a horse as Bob Green believed ... "Yes, sir. I'll pay the lease for the stall too. But if the mare regains her strength and I can get her back to full health ... then she's mine."

Harding's expression shed a layer of congeniality.

"Because, sir," Ridley continued, "I've always held that if a man truly puts his best into something and gives his all, he deserves to be compensated accordingly. And seeing as you had already decided to put her down ..." Ridley let the silence fill in the words he knew were best left unsaid and waited. He tried to read General Harding's reaction, yet couldn't. But if the man agreed to his terms ...

He'd have a Tennessee thoroughbred to take west with him. A horse of the finest breeding stock, one he'd never have been able to afford otherwise.

Finally, the general smiled, a tight, humorless curve. "Mr. Cooper, if you get that mare back on her feet and running again *and* under control, not skittish and shy as a new bride, I'll not only sign her over to you" — Harding laughed — "I'll invite you to dine at my table."

Ridley couldn't get his hand out fast enough. Dining at this man's table wasn't important to him, but this mare was.

"One more condition," Harding added. He shot a look first at Bob

Green, then at Seabird. "Seeing as you're using my facilities and my head hostler, if you ever get that lady to race again, and she wins a purse, I get fifty percent. No cap on earnings. For her lifetime."

"Twenty," Ridley countered.

"Forty." Harding smiled.

"Twenty-five *and*"—it took Ridley everything he had not to grin— "when you want her to serve as dam to one of your sires, I'll forego the first fee."

Harding laughed out loud. "You'll forego a fee? A fee for a *dam*? That's rich, Mr. Cooper. But ..." He laughed again. "I like a man with a sense of humor and a touch of stallion in him." Harding extended his hand and Ridley gripped it tight. "We have ourselves a deal."

Chapter
TWELVE

You're certain you feel well enough, Aunt Elizabeth?" Olivia peered out a window in the front hallway. The weather couldn't have been more perfect, especially after it had rained for the past two days. Olivia was positive a brief walk in the sunshine and fresh air would do Elizabeth a world of good. "We'll be sure not to go too far. Because remember, this morning the general did encourage you to stay in bed and get some—"

"I am more than certain I'm well enough, Livvy. As for the general …" Elizabeth waved and made a *pfft* sound. "I know he means well, but if he had his way, all I would do is rest! Besides," she whispered, "once he leaves after breakfast, he stays gone until dinner time. So he'll never know." She winked and reached for a set of pruning shears and a basket on a nearby table. "You arrived at Belle Meade four days ago, and I want the pleasure of walking the grounds with you, my dear. What with it having rained and me being abed, we need to make up for lost time! And with the girls gone into town for the day, we ought to do something fun as well!"

Needing no further persuasion, Olivia grinned. "Then let's get to walking!"

Olivia held open the front door then hurried to link arms with Elizabeth as she descended the stairs, once again reminded that doctors' prognoses were not always the final word. Whatever "weakened constitution" Elizabeth had been plagued with, she seemed worlds better today. With loving care, nutritious food, and a moderate amount of rest, Olivia planned on making that a recurring theme. Just as she had with her mother.

They cut a leisurely path across the front lawn in the direction of the old cabin, the sun wonderfully warm and air redolent with the scent of honeysuckle and jasmine. Servants and workmen dotted the grounds, busy at their tasks. Despite the gentle rains, the ground was barely spongy, and Olivia enjoyed the chance to be outside. Yet she couldn't help but keep an eye out for General Harding astride his black stallion.

"How do you like your room, Livvy?"

Olivia glanced beside her. "I like it very much, Aunt. Thank you. I think the view may be my favorite part." For the past two mornings, just as she'd done the first, she'd risen to watch the sunrise, then dressed and hurried through breakfast to be available to Elizabeth. Not that she'd done much. Elizabeth mainly rested.

Yesterday, the general and their daughters, Cousin Lizzie included, had attended church services in town. But Olivia volunteered to stay home with Elizabeth, knowing that would be best. For everyone. The widow of Charles Winthrop Aberdeen wouldn't be welcome at any church Olivia knew of, and being seen with her in public would only hurt the Hardings. The general and the girls understood that. Only Elizabeth seemed shy of acknowledging the truth. That knowledge, coupled with the fact that chancing another carriage ride like the last wasn't high on her list, Olivia accepted that her Sundays would be spent at Belle Meade.

Though Elizabeth had been abed, the past two days still held accomplishment. Olivia had managed to write several letters on her behalf, with Elizabeth dictating from bed. And she'd read to her as well — articles from *American Turf Register and Sporting Magazine*, a publication on horses, among other things, that the general kept on his bedside table. Elizabeth seemed to enjoy the stories, and Olivia had to admit they were entertaining.

"Well, I'm glad you like the room." Elizabeth patted her arm. "It's always been a favorite of mine for the view alone."

"I love the porch too." Olivia glanced up as they passed beneath it. "I sat out there last night with a blanket and rocked while I listened to the rain."

"Are you having trouble sleeping, my dear?"

"Mmm, only a little. The rain worked like a tonic."

"That's good." Elizabeth smiled. "It does the same for me."

Worked like a tonic was stretching the truth, Olivia knew, because she'd lain awake each night, waiting for sleep to come. But she didn't want to sound ungrateful. After all, she had a safe place to live and her needs provided for. She'd come to Belle Meade with the hope of finding a fresh start, a haven. And, in a sense, she'd gotten that.

Just not in the way she'd expected.

As they rounded the side of the house, she glimpsed the old Harding cabin and saw a Negro man coming out the door. "Does he live there now?" she asked, gesturing, noting that the man walked with a slight limp.

Elizabeth looked back and smiled. "Oh, yes, that's Uncle Bob. He's been here at Belle Meade forever it seems. Long before I came. He's the head hostler and — according to my husband — has a way with horses like no man he's ever seen."

Olivia watched him from the corner of her eye. Something about the man inspired trust. Perhaps it was the way he carried himself, with humility yet pride, in the best sense of the word. Or maybe it was the manner in which he surveyed the estate with obvious appreciation, as if drinking in the views. But to have to work around horses all day . . .

Olivia inwardly shuddered.

"Now, back there" — Elizabeth motioned — "is the smokehouse, which smells so delicious after the hog killing each December. Though I'm certain the hogs would disagree." She giggled. "Then there's the blacksmith shop. Over here, back toward the front, is the dairy. Beyond it are the servants' and workmen's cabins. And of course the paddocks out front where the mares are trained — oh, perhaps we can go to the stables after our walk and see the foals! I love watching them play."

As wonderful as it was to see Elizabeth so exuberant, Olivia recalled the wounded mare that nearly took a bite of her face, and she quickly decided a visit to the stables wasn't high on her list. So she nodded, then pointed. "What's that over there?"

Elizabeth looked. "That's the greenhouse. I'd love to show it to you!"

For the next half hour, Olivia drank in every imaginable color on nature's palette, along with every heady scent. Elizabeth knew every flower and greening shrub by name, and nearly all of them, it seemed, were in bloom.

"Most of these" — Elizabeth indicated a table laden with flowers and herbs — "came from Carnton, my childhood home. My mother, God rest her soul, planted her garden with the help of her friend, Rachel Jackson."

Olivia felt her brow furrow. "*The* Rachel Jackson?" she whispered. "The first lady?"

Elizabeth nodded. "Rachel and my mother were friends. Rachel was kind enough to furnish my mother with slips and seedlings from her own garden at the Hermitage. So these plants are all very special to me."

"As well they should be." Olivia had known that Elizabeth's father, Randall McGavock, had once been mayor of Nashville. So it shouldn't have surprised her to discover Elizabeth's family had been closely acquainted with that of the late President Andrew Jackson. Still, it served as a reminder of the caliber of people who had opened their home to her.

Yards of roses, clematis, coral honeysuckle, and fragrant jasmine covered the length of a white paling fence separating the back of the house from the garden. Elizabeth took snippets of flowering vines and rose blossoms and laid them in her basket. A gravel walkway that divided the long beds nesting both vegetables and flowers extended from the smokehouse all the way to what appeared to be a cave nestled in the side of the hill.

"Our gardener, Mr. Hunsaker, lives there."

Olivia turned to see Elizabeth pointing to a quaint little house that seemed precisely what a gardener would call home.

"The general brought Mr. Hunsaker all the way from Switzerland. He's likely out in the orchard today." They walked together, arm in arm, on around the house. "One day soon, I promise to show you the cashmere goats and the deer park, which are located just past the yards housing the beef and dairy cattle. Selene will insist you see the Shetland ponies as well. And perhaps we'll catch sight of a buffalo while we're out. Though we won't dare venture a closer look as one of them nearly—" Elizabeth inhaled sharply. "Is that the carriage you were in on your way here?"

Olivia trailed her gaze and saw the conveyance—or what was left of it—sitting abandoned beside one of the stables. "Yes, ma'am, it is," she answered, finding it sobering to view the damage from this perspective—also finding it odd that seeing the carriage again would make her think of *him*.

Mr. Ridley Adam Cooper.

Where was he now and what was he doing? Remembering something he'd said—*I may not get what I've come for*—she felt a little sad to know whatever his purpose in traveling to Belle Meade had been, he'd left empty-handed.

"Oh, Livvy." Elizabeth shook her head. "The general told me the accident involved a broken wheel, but I never dreamed it was so serious. How frightening that must have been for you." Elizabeth looked back at her. "And yet you haven't said a word about it."

Without wanting to, Olivia recalled what it felt like to be falling toward that open door, the ground rushing up to meet her. She relayed the experience to Elizabeth, watching her eyes go wide. Olivia's own eyes watered at the memory. "It *was* frightening." She gave a breathy laugh. "I have no idea, Aunt Elizabeth, how I didn't fall out." Even now, she shuddered to think what might have happened to her if she had.

"Oh, my dear." Elizabeth covered Olivia's hands with her own. "I have to believe that God somehow closed that door for you. And that he kept you safe for a reason."

Olivia nodded, though not fully convinced. Because why would God choose to close that door to keep her safe, yet allow her to live with a man who — for five *long* years — had treated her with such disregard and lack of feeling? None of which she'd shared in letters to Aunt Elizabeth. Though she'd sometimes wondered from Elizabeth's responses if she'd managed to read between the lines.

"Livvy."

Olivia refocused.

Elizabeth's eyes glistened. "Your mother was my dearest friend in all the world. And while I would never seek to take her place in your life, I do hope you'll confide in me, if you need to. Because ... I have a feeling that there's much you need to share. And I'll have you know I'm a *very* good listener."

The sincerity — and safety — in Elizabeth's voice coaxed Olivia's guard down and emotion tightened her throat. "I'm so grateful you invited me here," she whispered, barely able to force out the words. "I had nowhere to go. No one ... *No one* has spoken to me in town since ... the incident. And all of our friends" — her voice caught — "or what few we had ... blame me too. But Aunt Elizabeth, I didn't know. I promise, I didn't. I knew he wasn't a good man, but I didn't know the extent of what he was doing. If I had — "

"If you had, Olivia, what would you have done? Turned your own husband in to the authorities? Who most likely, with this current government, would have simply slapped his wrists and sent him back home? To you? Just imagine what he might have done then, being the kind of man he was." A shadow eclipsed Elizabeth's features.

Olivia knew she should say something. Right then. She'd wondered how to tell Elizabeth the truth about her and Charles's relationship—or lack thereof—and how cruel he had been at times. Not only when delivering a well-placed slap across her cheek or gripping her arm so tightly it left a mark, but the emotional hitting he'd done. The marks on her cheek had faded, as had the bruises on her arms. But the things he'd said—as well as all the things he hadn't—had left a far deeper wound. And now was the moment for her to tell Elizabeth. To say it out loud. And yet ... the words wouldn't come.

"It's not commonly spoken of, Livvy." Elizabeth lowered her gaze. "At least not in our circle. But I know for a fact there are husbands—even among the higher stations in life—who often resort to ... violence. It's disgraceful." She shook her head. "Both for the men *and* women. And it would pain me beyond words to think of that ever having happened to you." Elizabeth took hold of her hands. "So don't for one moment blame yourself for not turning him in to the authorities. Not for a minute! Promise me that. All right, my dear?"

Seeing the urgency in Elizabeth's expression, hearing the taint in her tone at the mere mention of the subject, Olivia could only nod. "I promise," she whispered, swallowing back the truth, as she'd done a hundred times before, not wanting to say anything that would bring Elizabeth pain or further disgrace herself in this dear woman's eyes.

Elizabeth smiled and held out her arm. "Walk with me?"

Olivia slipped her hand through. Gravel crunched beneath their boots as they strolled the garden path. Elizabeth continued to provide colorful and interesting commentary about Belle Meade, but Olivia could only half listen. Two questions kept weaving their way in and out of her train of thought. How was it she could feel such shame over something she hadn't done herself, but that had been done *to* her? Never had she considered herself deserving of Charles's outbursts of anger. Only unable to escape them. And the second question—one that haunted her almost as much as the first: would she ever be rid of this heaviness within? She prayed she would. It only seemed fair, considering. But based on personal experience, she'd learned that God didn't always answer prayers in a way that seemed fair.

"... and that, my sweet Livvy, is a brief tour of Belle Meade."

Olivia exhaled, returning fully to the moment. "I must admit, Aunt

Elizabeth, I had no idea the extent of businesses the general was involved with here. I thought Belle Meade mainly consisted of the horse farm."

"That's what we're known for." Elizabeth took a deep breath, seeming to relish being outdoors. "But my husband is quite an enterprising man, if I may boast on his behalf."

Olivia nodded, then paused. "What is *that*?" She pointed to a post sticking up from the ground, a glass jar mounted on one side.

Elizabeth chuckled. "It's a contraption the general designed years ago to measure rainfall. He says he grew tired of farm hands returning from the fields saying the ground was too wet to plow. So ..." She touched the side of the glazier's jar. "He had the servants construct this. And when it rains, he checks it and knows."

Olivia nodded. "Clever."

"That's my husband."

They both laughed.

"Oh, Livvy, look!"

Olivia lifted her gaze. Two foals, one a reddish brown, the other black and white, chased each other around the paddock, kicking their spindly back legs as if trying them on for size. Beyond them in the meadow were two mares keeping watch, each identical in color to one of the foals. Their mothers, Olivia presumed. The foals raced round and round, stopping only briefly to prance and stomp and survey the meadow as if they were rulers in a kingdom.

And despite her dislike of the animals, Olivia smiled. Until the black and white foal leaned over and nipped his friend on the neck. She exhaled. "He's biting the reddish one!"

Elizabeth laughed. "They're only playing." She leaned close. "And a horse that color isn't called reddish, dear. It's called chestnut."

"Chestnut," Olivia repeated, tucking it away in her memory.

"Oh my ..."

"What?" Olivia asked, watching the *chestnut* foal nip the other one back. *Good for you ...*

"Livvy—"

Olivia turned in time to see Elizabeth's eyes close and managed to grab hold of her just as she sank to the ground. Olivia went down with her. "Aunt Elizabeth! Are you all right?"

"I can't ... breathe," Elizabeth whispered, fingering her collar.

Olivia unfastened the top two buttons of Elizabeth's shirtwaist, not liking the paleness of her complexion. "We need to get you back to the house." She tried to coax Elizabeth into standing but failed. She looked around for a servant. Not a one in sight.

Elizabeth went limp in her arms.

"Aunt Elizabeth?" Olivia patted her aunt's cheeks. "Stay with me!" No response.

Panicking, she screamed for help. But no one came. Her heart sank. She screamed again. "Somebody help me!"

After what seemed like an eternity, a man came running from the stable. "What happened?"

"I don't know." She fanned Elizabeth's face, watching for any sign of her coming to. "We were just standing here, talking, and then ..." Olivia looked up, and when she saw the man's face, all the words in her head seemed to muddle at the back of her throat.

But when she glimpsed the rider on the black stallion cresting the hill, remarkably, her speech returned. "Please!" she begged him. "Help me get Mrs. Harding inside the house! Quickly!"

Chapter THIRTEEN

As Ridley Cooper lifted Elizabeth into his arms, Olivia ran ahead, working to wrap her mind around seeing him again. And here. At Belle Meade. She'd thought him long gone. Never slowing, she lifted her skirts and raced up the front steps to open the door, then looked back to find Mr. Cooper close behind her—and the general's stallion flying down the hill.

Olivia pointed. "Upstairs, please. To her bedroom." Calling for Susanna, she led Mr. Cooper up the winding cantilevered staircase, moving as quickly as she could, Mr. Cooper staying right on her heels. Winded, she turned left down a short hall. "This way. Through here."

Taking care, he maneuvered through the doorway and gently laid Elizabeth on the bed. Her head fell limp to one side. Olivia pushed the servants' call button on the wall and poured fresh water from the pitcher into the basin, then doused a cloth. Wringing it out, she turned back only to find Mr. Cooper with his finger pressed to Elizabeth's neck.

"What are you doing?" she asked.

"Checking her pulse."

"You're a *doctor*?" She came alongside him, hearing both the disbelief in her own voice and his sharp exhale.

"Not hardly, ma'am." He glanced up, a shade of humor in his eyes. "But a man I knew during the war was. He taught me a few things while we were in"—he stopped and focused back on Elizabeth—"while we served together. Her pulse seems fine." He leaned down. "So does her breathing."

Olivia laid the cloth across Elizabeth's forehead and eased down onto the bed. "I don't know what happened. She was fine one minute. Then the next, she said she couldn't breathe."

"Best I can tell, ma'am, she just fainted. Could've been the heat, or maybe too much sun. Give her a minute. She'll come around."

Hoping he was right, Olivia grabbed a magazine from the bedside table and fanned Elizabeth's face for a moment, then leaned down. "Aunt Elizabeth," she whispered, taking the cloth from her forehead and pressing the cool against her cheek. "If you can hear me, please wake up."

Not a twinge.

Olivia's heart dropped. This was her fault. Their "brief walk" had turned out to be much longer than she'd planned, and apparently Elizabeth's health was far more fragile than she'd thought. What if the doctors were right?

Even thinking that what General Harding had told her might be true threatened to peel back another precious layer of hope.

Mr. Cooper shifted his weight beside her, and Olivia lifted her head.

"Thank you, Mr. Cooper, for coming to our aid. I very much appreciate your help."

His smile stayed mostly hidden behind that unruly growth of beard, but an unmistakable kindness moved into his eyes. "You're most welcome, Mrs. Aberdeen."

Looking at him, so many thoughts came to mind. Seeing the way he looked at her now — fully in the eyes, like they knew each other well instead of being near strangers — revealed a lack in decorum and gentility in his breeding, a forwardness that did more than flirt with the boundaries of propriety. Her face grew overly warm.

"Livvy?"

Olivia turned back, feeling a trickle of relief at hearing the voice and at being released from his gaze. "Aunt Elizabeth."

Elizabeth's eyes fluttered open. "What happened?"

"Apparently you fainted." Olivia took hold of her hand. "And it's my fault. I'm sorry. I let you walk too far."

"Oh no, dear." Elizabeth took a breath, shaking her head. "It's no fault of yours. I'm sorry to be such a bother."

Steps sounded on the staircase — too light to be the general's — and seconds later Susanna rounded the corner, tea service in hand. "Gracious!" She stopped short at the foot of the bed. "What's goin' on in here? I thought y'all was just ringin' for tea, ma'am."

Olivia rose from the bedside. "Mrs. Harding and I went out for a walk, Susanna, and ..." She briefly bowed her head. "I'm so sorry. I must have tired her out because she fainted dead away."

Susanna plunked the tea service down on a side table, and Olivia jumped, keenly aware of Ridley Cooper's quiet attention. She'd only had brief interactions with Belle Meade's head cook, but she had an inkling that, once riled, this little woman could be formidable.

Hands on hips, Susanna shook her head, looking between Olivia and Elizabeth. "How many times am I gonna have to say this? No ... more ... faintin', Missus Harding!"

Mrs. Harding? Realizing Elizabeth was the target of Susanna's wrath and not her, Olivia let out a breath. She glanced at Ridley Cooper, then looked between the two women. "Are you saying she's done this before?"

"Done this before?" Susanna huffed. "Lawd, Missus Aberdeen. This woman done put the fear of God in all of us so many times I can't keep count. She got up from a chair last week and fainted dead away right there. Thank the Lawd Betsy was there to catch her." She smoothed a loving brown hand over Elizabeth's forehead. "It just be tired blood, is what I'm guessin'. She get stronger, in time. She just gets to thinkin' she can do more than she can. We got to look out for her is all." Susanna winked at Olivia. "Slow her down some. But she gonna be fine."

Elizabeth got a sheepish look. "I'm sorry, Livvy. I should have told you, but I didn't want you to worry. Not with everything else you've had pressing on you."

Olivia leaned down. "You about scared me to death," she whispered, smiling, though more on the outside than in. "How long have these ... spells been occurring?"

Elizabeth shrugged. "Not too terribly long."

Susanna cleared her throat.

Elizabeth sighed. "About three years now, I'd say. Off and on."

Three years. Olivia smoothed a frown before it fully formed. That was a long time to struggle with "tired blood."

"Just what're *you* doin' up here, sir?"

Hearing Susanna, Olivia looked up to see the head cook eying Ridley Cooper with suspicion, and she hurried to intervene. "This is Mr. Cooper, Susanna. He's ..." she faltered. "He's an acquaintance of mine." She caught the slight smile he gave her but ignored it. "He found us in the yard and was kind enough to carry Mrs. Harding inside."

"Is that right, Mr. Cooper? An acquaintance?" Susanna's dark eyebrows arched in question. "You make it a habit of rescuin' women, do you, sir?"

Mr. Cooper smiled, but said nothing, and Olivia got the impression maybe he and Susanna had met before.

Heavy footfalls thundered up the stairwell, and Olivia—knowing to whom they belonged—braced herself. Not only to explain to the general about having taken Elizabeth for a walk, but to explain Ridley Cooper being in his bedchamber.

True to form, the general strode into the room looking every inch the military commander that he was. He glanced at Elizabeth first, anxiety lining his features, then at Olivia, his concern quickly melting to censure. "So it *was* my wife I saw being carried into the house, Mrs. Aberdeen."

Olivia nodded, hearing accusation in his tone. "Yes, sir, it was. But I can expl—"

"General . . ."

All eyes turned to the bed.

"My dear, Olivia is not to blame." Elizabeth smiled as Susanna propped a pillow behind her head. "It took every ounce of charm I could muster to persuade her to allow me outside." Elizabeth's voice, though soft, possessed an insistence that demanded attention. "I was eager to show her your handiwork, my love, and then simply got carried away." Her laughter came out feather light. "Apparently I stayed too long in the sun. Please forgive me for worrying you. For worrying all of you." Her gaze swept the room. "And to you, Mr. Cooper, my thanks for your assistance."

General Harding turned, as though only now realizing Ridley Cooper was in the room. "Mr. *Cooper?*" He frowned. "I'm to understand that *you* carried my wife into the house?"

It was all Olivia could do not to intervene again on Mr. Cooper's behalf. But knowing the general as she did and knowing how angry he was going to be—and already was—with her, she didn't dare.

"Yes, sir," Mr. Cooper said. "That's right."

Stoic, the general faced him square on and Olivia cringed, bracing for another confrontation.

"Then may I offer my thanks, Mr. Cooper." The general extended his hand. Olivia's jaw went slack. "It appears as though you're going to be a welcome addition here at Belle Meade."

"Thank you, sir." Ridley Cooper gripped his hand.

Olivia could only stare. *Welcome addition?* How had this man—termed a *vagrant* by Harding the other night in his office—managed to become a welcome addition?

Her surprise must have played openly across her face because as soon as the general turned, Ridley Cooper cut his eyes in her direction and smiled, almost as if to say, *So much for what you said about the general not hiring.*

She recalled what she'd said to him that day in the carriage and her stomach knotted. He had every right to toss those words right back in her face. Just as Charles would have done. She looked away, grateful Mr. Cooper didn't know the truth about her personal circumstances. She hoped, too, that he hadn't learned about her not being given the position of head housekeeper. Although the chances of him already knowing were good. News like that always traveled swiftly through the servants and hired help.

Once he knew those things, she'd be smaller in his eyes, she knew. And for reasons she couldn't explain, she didn't want Ridley Cooper to think about her that way.

General Harding crossed to where she stood, his gaze unflinching. "If you'll kindly step aside, Mrs. Aberdeen, I'd like to see to my wife's health."

Olivia Aberdeen left the bedroom quickly. She'd seemed nervous from the moment General Harding had entered the room. Intent on speaking with her, Ridley followed her into the hallway, then heard the general call his name.

He paused long enough to see Mrs. Aberdeen descending the stairs. "Yes, General?" He stepped back inside the room.

"How's our little mare coming along, Mr. Cooper?"

The question took him by surprise. Not that the man's interest in the horse was unexpected, but his timing certainly was. General Harding had just made a point to tell Mrs. Aberdeen—in a rather biting tone—that he wished to see to his wife's health. Yet now, not a minute later, he was discussing business?

Ridley read similar surprise in Mrs. Harding's face, except her expression also held shades of disappointment. "It's only been a couple of days, General, so it's too early to tell. First order of business is to get her leg healed. I've been salving her wounds and changing bandages a couple of times a day. We won't know anything on that count for at least a week."

"And you're keeping track of your expenses?"

Ridley tasted a bitterness in his mouth. "I told you I would. Our agreement hasn't changed."

Harding held his gaze. "And if, by chance, I'd like to—"

"Anytime you want to see the ledger, the book is in Uncle Bob's cabinet. Where it always is, sir." Ridley heard a door close somewhere downstairs. "Now if you'll excuse me, General, I need to get back to work." For a brief second, he thought Harding was going to make objections, but the general just nodded and turned away. "Ladies," Ridley added, nodding to Mrs. Harding and Susanna. He took the staircase down, frustration dogging each step.

He didn't appreciate his word being questioned. Especially by a man like Harding. A man who had built his estate on the back-breaking work of others. A man who wouldn't possess what he did right now, especially in terms of thoroughbreds, if not for the loyalty and integrity of a man he'd once held as a slave.

Descending the winding staircase afforded Ridley a better view of the foyer than he'd gotten on his way up. And—he whistled low—this place was something to behold. Portraits of thoroughbreds claimed nearly every inch of wall space. Some included a groomsman holding the lead rope, others pictured only the horse. A bronze and crystal gasolier hung from the ceiling, and the finest of furniture decorated the spacious area below. All of it screamed *wealth*.

But the mansion wasn't what he wanted to see right now. He paused at the base of the stairs, wondering which way she'd gone.

Mrs. Aberdeen had seemed embarrassed when she'd left a moment earlier, and he knew why. Harding obviously blamed her for what had happened to Elizabeth, and General William Giles Harding could be an intimidating man. What he couldn't figure out was why the general had seemed so intent on pinning the blame on her when the outcome clearly wasn't her fault.

The foyer opened to four different rooms, and he briefly peered inside each one as he crossed to the front entryway. All proved empty of people, but full of things. He turned to leave when a portrait in one of the rooms caught his attention. He stepped closer.

It was of the general, he was certain. But the likeness had been captured several years earlier. Twenty, at least. With not a trace of a beard. Striking, what difference a beard could make in a man's appearance. A companion portrait of Mrs. Harding hung beside it. Her likeness, too, exuded a youthfulness that her countenance—though still attractive—no longer claimed. And the portraits had been hand colored, no less. Beautifully so.

He closed the front door behind him and scanned the yard. No sign of Mrs. Aberdeen. She hadn't had time to get too far, *if* she'd even come this way. He felt for her, knowing what he did about her situation. Widowed, with a late husband who'd been murdered and hung for treason, and now apparently bearing the shame of his actions.

He searched to the right of the house, wanting to see if she was all right. To see how she was getting settled in after such a rocky arrival. At least that's what he told himself. But in light of what had just happened upstairs, there was something else he wanted her to know.

Whatever her position was at Belle Meade, it was clear she and Elizabeth Harding had a very close relationship. Equally clear was that she and General Harding did not. He'd felt an almost palpable tension between them today.

He took the steps down to the yard and started toward the stable when he spotted her. Off to the left. Walking hurriedly in the direction of the old cabin. *Perfect.*

Chapter FOURTEEN

Ridley caught up with her easily and—judging by the rigid set of her jaw—she was still upset. He couldn't blame her. "Mind if I join you, Mrs. Aberdeen?"

Her glance was fleeting. "Not at all, Mr. Cooper." Her smile, too bright and brief to be genuine, was still pretty.

Everything about her said she preferred to be alone—the stiffness in her shoulders and evenness of her stride, as though she were counting the steps until he took his leave.

"I won't take but a minute of your time, ma'am. I only wanted to see how you're getting along. How your first few days here have been."

"I'm getting along very well, Mr. Cooper. Thank you for inquiring." Her voice might have sounded convincing to anyone who hadn't just witnessed the scene in the bedroom.

"Well ..." He nodded. "That's good to hear."

They walked on in silence, passing the cabin, and he sneaked another look at her, silently adding *pleasantly evasive* to the mental list already containing the words *prim* and *proper*. Did she have any idea how easy she was to read? And that her politeness—while well intentioned, he felt certain—didn't fool him in the least?

The slope of the ground curved and formed a path along the side of the creek, and they followed it. How many times in recent months had he bedded down by a creek similar to this while making his way from the coast to Nashville? The sluicing of water over smooth rock produced a tranquil tune, providing an excellent companion to the long nights of silence.

But the silence coming from the woman beside him all but drowned it out.

Deciding to honor her obvious desire to be alone, Ridley came directly to the point. "About what was said, Mrs. Aberdeen. Back there with the general. Just to make sure everything's clear between us, I—"

"Yes, Mr. Cooper." She stopped and turned, her eyes flashing. "I'm aware you were hired by the general, so ..." She stood a little straighter. "Congratulations to you, sir."

He eyed her, a tad confused. "I beg your pardon?"

She looked at him as though he were a simpleton. "I saw the way you looked at me back there, when the general referred to you as a *welcome addition*." A tinge of bitterness punctuated the words, helped along by the hurt in her eyes. "You gained employment here at Belle Meade, even after I expressly told you that General Harding wasn't hiring. That being the case ..." She briefly looked away, firming that delicate jaw of hers again. "I was wrong. And you were right." She looked back, a polite—if false—smile curving her mouth. "There, I said it. Have I rendered the satisfaction you require, Mr. Cooper?"

Ridley stared, partly fascinated by how she'd managed to get all of that from a simple look but mostly wanting to shake the woman for getting it so wrong. If she only knew what he'd truly been thinking in that moment.

Not that he wanted to share it with her.

"So it's your understanding, Mrs. Aberdeen, that I've tracked you down to demand an apology?"

"Well, you *were* able to obtain a job, were you not?"

Something inside told him not to answer, but he didn't listen. "I was."

"And did I not assure you within minutes of our first meeting that your chances of that happening were slim?"

"Those weren't your exact words, as I recall them, ma'am. But that was the gist of it."

"So?" She looked up at him, defiant, as if she'd just proven something worthy of condemnation on his part.

He couldn't help but smile. "If the day ever comes, Mrs. Aberdeen, don't ever try to defend yourself in court, ma'am. It won't go well for you."

Her mouth slipped open. "I just offered you an apology, Mr. Cooper."

"One I didn't ask for, Mrs. Aberdeen. Nor one I require."

She let out a breath and turned toward the creek.

Anger rolled off her in waves, and he felt a fair amount of frustration himself. She crossed her arms, wrapping them around herself, and he noticed her left hand absent of a wedding band. Rings were expensive, he knew, and not every married woman had one. Even fewer married men. He would've bet good money, though, that she'd been given one.

Recalling what he knew about her late husband from Uncle Bob and the others, he wondered if she'd chosen to take it off, wanting to forego the unpleasant reminder.

He sighed and rubbed the back of his neck, wishing he could take back the comment about her defending herself in court. That had been a careless thing to say. But how in God's green earth did the woman conclude he wanted an apology? It was with good reason he'd never married. Or even come close. He didn't understand the fairer sex. And never would.

He glanced in the direction of the stable, knowing he'd best get back to work. Feeling a need to test the silence before he spoke, he cleared his throat. "I'm sorry for disturbing you, Mrs. Aberdeen. I could tell you wanted to be alone. And ... I should have respected that."

She continued to stare at the water moving past them.

"Good day to you, ma'am." Feeling a heaviness within, he started back, struggling to remember why it was he'd sought her out in the first place. Not that it mattered now.

"Mr. Cooper?"

He paused and turned, not ten feet away. She stood exactly as he'd left her, facing the creek.

"I didn't ..."

Her voice trailed off, and for a second he thought the melody from the creek had washed away her words. Then she turned to face him.

"I didn't get the position of head housekeeper."

The words *I know* were nearly out of his mouth before he caught them. It didn't feel quite right. Not with the way she was looking at him. "I'm sure you'll find other ways to help, ma'am. I bet a lady like you knows how to do many things."

She smiled and bowed her head. "Earlier, *before* I interrupted you ... You said you wanted to make sure everything was clear between us." She lifted her gaze. "What were you going to say?"

He took a step back in her direction and stopped. "I was going to tell you that I thought you handled yourself well with General Harding, ma'am. With the whole situation."

She gave a soft sigh. "Thank you, Mr. Cooper."

"You're welcome, Mrs. Aberdeen."

"One more question?"

Hearing subtle longing in her voice, he nodded, waiting.

"That first day, when I was in the carriage, you said you may not get what you've come for. What is it that you've come here for, Mr. Cooper?"

For not wanting to talk a minute ago, the woman certainly was chatty now. "I want to learn more about horses, how to work with them, how to train them. And I figured ... what better place than here? The best thoroughbred farm in the country. Uncle Bob has agreed to teach me, with the general's permission, of course. Have you met Uncle Bob yet?"

She shook her head.

"You'll like him. And he'll like you."

Her mouth curved in a smile, but he sensed she was contemplating something.

"You said you wouldn't be here long. That you were only passing through."

He nodded. "Yes, ma'am. That's still my plan." Watching her tuck a strand of hair behind her ear, he added *good memory* to the mental tally he was keeping on her. "Once I'm done, I'm headed to the Colorado Territory."

Her eyes widened. "The Colorado Territory? But there's nothing out there. It's wild. There are no cities and hardly any people. There's only ..." She huffed a disbelieving laugh. "Indians and bears and ... freezing cold. Why in heaven's name would you want to go there?"

Tempted to laugh at her response, the simplicity of the answer within him wouldn't allow it. "Because it's a world away from here."

"From Nashville?"

"From the South."

She frowned as though unable to comprehend him thinking such a thing. "But ... what will you do there?"

He'd already told Bob Green about his plans and saw no harm in telling her. That part of his life wasn't a secret. "I want to start my own ranch. Cattle, which is what my father did, so I know all about that.

But I want to have horses too. Thoroughbreds." It felt good to say it aloud, to know he was finally on his way to making it come true. Or at least closer to it. "You might say it's become a dream of mine. Not just the horses, but seeing the land. While it's still wild, as you say, and unsettled, it's a whole new world ready for the making, and I aim to be part of it. I've heard it's beautiful too. The mountains so high they disappear into the clouds, the air so fresh and cold. And the snow ..." He smiled, remembering how an article he'd read had described it. "They say it'll almost blind you, it's so pure and white. And the sun shines most all the time, even in the winter."

She said nothing, and Ridley realized he'd been going on like some old woman. "I'm sorry. I got carried away."

"On the contrary, Mr. Cooper." The perplexed look on her face slowly gave way to a smile. "I envy you."

He recalled what she'd said about never wanting to leave Tennessee. "You envy me my dream, Mrs. Aberdeen?"

Her smile faded. "I envy you having one."

"Now take it *slow* this time, Ridley." Uncle Bob spoke in a hushed tone, adjusting his weathered black derby on his head. Sweat from the afternoon sun moistened his face. "Like I done told you ... don't rush it. Give her time."

Ridley wiped the perspiration from his brow, heeding Green's advice—or trying to—just as he'd been doing every afternoon for the past two weeks. They'd managed to meet regularly enough, but never for very long. Work in the stables always kept coming. At this rate, he wondered if his plan to be here only a month—six weeks at most—had been too shortsighted.

Taking a deep breath, he eyed the mare and lowered his head a little, like Uncle Bob had instructed. A friendly act, he'd called it. Then, keeping eye contact with her, he inched forward, still believing he could do this. But his patience was wearing thin. He was beginning to think that learning this "gift" was going to take much longer than planned.

Seabird took a cautious step backward, the corral fence behind her. Her ears pricked like they had when Uncle Bob put the harness on her. Uncle Bob was the only one she would let come close so far. Nobody else.

"Real gentle like," Uncle Bob urged behind him. "So she knows you don't mean to hurt her."

Resisting the unexpected urge to say, *I heard you the first twenty-seven times*, Ridley slowly brought his hand up, determined to make this horse trust him. To show her that if she'd just let him—

The mare pawed the ground and snorted.

"Come on, girl," he whispered, tired of her mulishness. He'd only treated her well, so she had no reason to distrust him. "It's all right. I just want to—" He reached for the harness and the horse reared, a hoof slicing the air inches from his face. He ducked to one side, then backed away, biting back a harsh word. His last thread of patience snapped. "Did you see that?!"

Uncle Bob raised his eyebrows, as if surprised at the outburst. "Mmm-hmm ... I saw it." He took a long drink of water from his tin cup. "Thought I told you to take it slow."

Ridley stared hard. "I *did* take it slow." His jaw hurt he was clenching it so tightly. "She's just plain mean, that's what it is. Mean and ornery."

The mare blew out a breath that resembled a snorting laugh, and Ridley eyed her.

Uncle Bob sighed. "Take five minutes to cool down."

"I'm fine. I don't need—"

"I *said* ... take five minutes to cool down."

Ridley strode to a bucket of fresh water he'd brought out earlier, downed a few ladles, then tilted his head back and doused himself with the rest, aware of Uncle Bob doing the same a few feet away. Ridley heaved a sigh, not welcoming this challenge like he'd thought he would, nor this short fuse on his patience. It reminded him of former years and a part of himself he thought he'd left behind.

Not a breath of wind stirred. He wondered what the weather was like in the Colorado Territory and wished he was already there. But, surprisingly, thinking of being there made him think of somebody he would miss a little if he were.

He looked toward the house, figuring she was inside tending to Mrs. Harding. He'd only seen her a handful of times in recent days, but he found himself watching for her, hoping to run into her, which didn't happen often since he mainly worked in the stables and that was the very last place Olivia Aberdeen wanted to be.

She'd informed him she would be serving as a companion to Mrs.

Harding, at least for the time being. Forced enthusiasm had colored her tone when she'd told him about her new position, and he wondered if that's what had prejudiced his opinion about it. Being a companion to a lady was an admirable occupation for a young woman. But he sensed Olivia Aberdeen wanted more out of life than that. Whether she knew what that was yet or not. What she'd said the other day had returned to him, again and again: *I envy you having one.*

A dream, she meant.

He hung the empty bucket back on the fence post, thinking of the advertisement he'd torn from the paper a day earlier. He might be chasing a wild hare, but it was an opportunity he'd thought she might like. He didn't know if her duties with Mrs. Harding would allow it, but it was worth a shot.

Hearing steps behind him, he turned.

Uncle Bob's gaze was firm. "You ain't earned her trust yet, Ridley. That's the reason she reared up on you. You can't do nothin' 'til you earn her trust."

Glancing back at the mare, Ridley exhaled a spent breath, wishing he could be rid of his frustration so easily. "I've fed her. I've watered her. I've helped you change her poultices—while managing to dodge her hooves." He leveled a stare. "I've done everything you've told me to do, Uncle Bob. But she still isn't warming up to me. Or haven't you noticed?"

Uncle Bob looked at him a long moment. "I told you from the start … this ain't gonna be easy. I told you it was gonna take some time too. And you said to me, 'Time is somethin' I—'"

"I know what I said to you, Uncle Bob. I was there, remember?"

"I ain't sure you was. Cause this man I's seein' now," he said, pointing at Ridley's chest, "ain't the man who asked me to teach him. All this man before me wants is to get what he come for and then hightail it outta here, headin' west." Uncle Bob narrowed his eyes. "You tell me that ain't right."

Ridley ran a hand over his beard, an ache starting at the back of his head. And in the pit of his gut.

"Hey! Uncle Bob!"

Ridley turned, and—seeing who it was—his mood went from bad to worse. Grady Matthews stalked toward them. With the exception of Grady Matthews and two or three of the men Grady consorted with, Ridley got along with everyone. More than got along, actually. But Grady flat rubbed him the wrong way.

As the man got closer, Seabird trotted to the opposite side of the corral. Open dislike showed in Grady's face, which didn't bother Ridley a bit. For reasons right or wrong, he returned the sentiment.

Grady gestured. "Uncle Bob, Mr. Ruel just arrived with his mare. We need to know where you want to put her. He's also wantin' to know when she's gonna get covered."

"Put her in number seven. And tell him his mare ain't meetin' Jack Malone 'til the general has his hundred dollars in hand and I know for sure she's healthy. I'll be there directly."

Grady nodded and shot a look at Seabird then back at Ridley. "Me and some of the boys are takin' bets she splits your skull before you're done."

Ridley forced a smile. One good punch. *Just one.* "How's that jaw doing, Grady?"

The man's smile vanished, which only encouraged Ridley's.

"Grady." Uncle Bob stepped forward. "Mr. Ruel's waitin'."

With a final glare, Grady stalked off.

One look at Uncle Bob and Ridley's smile flattened out. He didn't care for the shadowed look in the man's eyes. Made him feel like a recalcitrant youth.

Ridley grabbed a rope and started walking. "I'll see if I can coax her back over here. If not, maybe we should think about using another horse."

"Leave her! We done for today."

Bob Green's clipped response brought him around. "We're done? But you said—"

"I said we's *done!*"

Ridley stared for a second, then trailed Uncle Bob to the gate. "What are you upset about?"

"The problem ain't the horse, Ridley. You's the problem, sir."

Ridley could only stare. Grady Matthews could've punched him square in the jaw and he could've taken it standing. But hearing Bob Green speak those words about him threatened to buckle his confidence. Not that he was about to show it.

"What do you mean I'm the problem? I'm doing everything you've told me to do."

"No you ain't. You ain't listenin' to me. Oh, you say you is. But I can see inside that head o' yours. You's talkin' up a storm in there. And that horse, she hears it too."

The muscles in the back of Ridley's neck started to tighten up, making his head hurt worse.

"She ain't only listenin' to what you sayin' here." Uncle Bob touched his own mouth. "She listenin' to what you sayin' here." He pointed his index and middle finger at Ridley's eyes, then laid a hand over the vicinity of his heart. "And here. But you ..." Uncle Bob exhaled. "You's just *so* busy talkin'. Just like with Grady there."

Ridley held up a hand. "He's the one who—"

"You was talkin' on the inside 'fore he even got close. I ain't sayin' he's in the right. He ain't. But the truth of it is ..." Uncle Bob glanced around, then looked back, his brow furrowed. "You's better than that, sir," he said, his voice dropping to a whisper. "I know you is. That's the only reason I said yes when you asked me to teach you. Men like Grady"—he shook his head—"they could barely find their way out of a feed sack. But you ..." He looked at Ridley with eyes so intent, so kind. "You's different, sir. I knew it that night on the mountain," he whispered. "And I know it now. Don't go provin' me wrong."

Ridley said nothing as Uncle Bob walked away, unable to describe what he was feeling.

Even as he lay in bed that night, in the upper loft of one side of the cabin, staring out the window at a thumbnail moon, he still couldn't define it. And the statement Uncle Bob had made before retiring didn't help: *You got to want this, Ridley. You gotta want it more than anything.*

Sleep a long distance off, he made his way noiselessly down the ladder into the lower room of the cabin and into the dogtrot, careful not to wake Uncle Bob, whose soft snores came from a corner bunk.

Once outside, Ridley eased down onto the porch steps and stretched his legs out, willing some of the restlessness in him to calm. The night air was still warm, but a whisper of wind against his bare chest provided a welcome respite. He rubbed a hand over his beard and listened as the chirrup of crickets and the rustle of a breeze through the grass played a familiar, even comforting, melody.

It reminded him of the recent Sunday morning when he'd heard songs in the distance, coming from a gathering down near the servants' cabins. Uncle Bob had asked him to go along, saying Susanna, Betsy, and the others would be there. But he'd declined. Still, he'd enjoyed listening to the songs from afar. Some of them comforting in melody, even though he couldn't make out the words. Other songs he'd recognized from younger, more innocent years.

He glanced toward the big house, as Uncle Bob called it, and noticed the solitary glow of lamplight coming from a window above the kitchen. Apparently someone else couldn't sleep either. He wondered which bedroom belonged to Mrs. Aberdeen and if she ever had trouble sleeping at night.

The light from the second story bedroom went dark, and somehow the night around him felt emptier. Lonelier. And the dream of the Colorado Territory another world away.

What if he couldn't learn what he needed to learn by the time the end of June came around? He had the chance to own a thoroughbred in Seabird, if he could get her well and running and tamed again, which was an opportunity worth taking. He also needed what Uncle Bob could teach him too.

So many threads to tie together in so short a space of time, and he'd been living with this dream forever it seemed. Feeling an unexpected pang in his chest, he searched the night sky, a knot forming at the base of his throat. For the longest time, he'd known with the fullest certainty God had forgotten about him. Had forgotten about them all. That he'd just up and left this big mess of a world behind. Ridley swallowed, remembering the endless string of months at Andersonville — his belly empty for days on end, his flesh cold as a corpse's when winter came.

Then on his way to Belle Meade, as he'd been coming through Atlanta, witnessing Sherman's destructive path, he'd heard a street preacher. The man had said something that had not only stuck with him, but had somehow worked its way deep inside: *God never leans over the balcony of heaven and gasps.*

The idea had struck him as funny at the time, but the more he'd thought about it, the more he liked the idea — that nothing ever surprised the Almighty — and he hoped it was true. Because if it was, then maybe it meant God was still watching and maybe there was a reason behind some of the things that happened. Not all, probably. God couldn't be expected to take all the blame. Men had made a fairly good mess of things, after all.

You's different, sir. I knew it that night on the mountain ... And I know it now. Don't go provin' me wrong.

What Uncle Bob had said drifted toward him in the dark, and

Ridley sighed. He leaned forward, elbows resting on his knees, and he knew in that moment what he'd felt when Bob Green had spoken those words.

Humbled. And it was a different feeling for him.

A part of him had been ashamed, while a greater part of him had wanted — and still did — a chance to prove himself. To show Uncle Bob he wasn't wasting his time. Ridley ran his tongue along the inside of his cheek. There used to be a day when a man wouldn't have spoken to him like Uncle Bob had and stayed standing. But somehow it was different hearing it from Bob Green. An iron grip worked its way around his throat, and Ridley slowly realized part of the reason why he'd come all this way — walked over five hundred miles from the South Carolina coast to get back to this place.

He not only wanted to learn what Bob Green had to teach him, he wanted Bob Green to be proud of him. Something his own father — with his dying breath — had made clear he hadn't been.

Chapter
FIFTEEN

With June all but upon them, May was making its last stand a warm one. Sitting with Elizabeth in the shade of the front porch, Olivia stifled a yawn. As was becoming habit, she'd stayed up much later the previous night than she should have, unable to sleep. A comment the general had made in passing at dinner had been the culprit last night. A remark about hosting a dinner party for some of his older, unmarried colleagues.

At least she *thought* he'd made the remark in passing. That's what had kept her awake. She wasn't sure.

"If I'm not mistaken, Livvy, this last letter brings me current on my correspondence." Elizabeth's tone held contentment. "Thank you, dear."

"My pleasure, Aunt." Olivia fanned the last page of the letter, making certain the ink was dry before she folded the pages and slipped them into the envelope. She counted the remaining pieces of stationery in Elizabeth's writing basket. "Aunt Elizabeth, you only have nine sheets left. I'll order more, if you'd like."

"Thank you, dear. You're so organized, Livvy." Elizabeth peered over at her. "And so attentive to details. I was telling the general that just yesterday."

Questioning the catlike smile curving Elizabeth's mouth, Olivia gave a tiny shrug. "I am my mother's daughter."

Elizabeth's expression softened. "Yes, you are, dear. And though I don't think I've told you this," Elizabeth said, eyes crinkling at the corners, "sometimes when I look at you, I see Rebecca. In years past."

Olivia smiled, warmed by the thought. *And* by seeing who had just exited the stable and was headed toward a corral: Mr. Ridley Cooper.

Carrying a rope and some gear, he opened the gate to the corral, moving with such confidence and authority, an unassuming fluidity about his actions. She hoped the horse training was going well, but from what little she'd glimpsed, she had her doubts. Unless standing and staring at a horse and having it stand and stare back at you was considered forward progress.

She felt a slight regret for having spoken the way she had to him at the creek that day, especially since she'd been mistaken about his intent. She wasn't accustomed to speaking her mind, much less so plainly, but Ridley Cooper seemed to bring that out in her.

And she had to admit—even if it wasn't all that ladylike—it had felt rather good.

Watching him, she thought again of how far away the Colorado Territory was. She'd checked a map to be sure and *four* of her fingers had fit in the distance spanning from here to there. Even on the map, it looked so different from Tennessee. Only a year ago, or maybe it was two now, she remembered reading in the newspaper about Indian wars in the Colorado Territory. The savages had attacked a town and, in turn, the settlers had retaliated. The descriptions in the newspaper had been graphic.

And yet, that's where Ridley Cooper wanted to go.

He wanted to start a ranch out there. Without question, he'd see his dream to fruition. She could tell by the fire in his eyes when he'd spoken about it. Despite her reservations about him and how he tended to rub her the wrong way, he impressed her as a man who, when he saw something, went after it. And got it. Much like another man she knew at Belle Meade.

Like a stubborn tide, a recurring thought rose again, one she'd pushed aside multiple times in recent days: she had no dream for her life. Not like Ridley Cooper did. And knowing that only stirred the unsettling restlessness inside her.

Her focus shifted to the man following Mr. Cooper: Uncle Bob. He was leading a horse. Presumably the mare that had been injured in the carriage accident, if the horse's bandaged leg was any indication. Olivia felt a shiver, glad to have some distance between her and that animal.

She felt a keen prick at her next thought. As soon as Ridley Cooper learned what he needed to from Uncle Bob, he'd be gone. She had to admit, doubtful as she'd been about Mr. Cooper on their first meeting, she'd found herself almost looking forward to the times they saw each other lately. And she enjoyed the chance to watch him from afar.

"Would you read more from that book to me, Livvy? The one we started yesterday?"

Her attention nudged back to her aunt, Olivia nodded, still keeping an eye on Ridley Cooper. "Certainly, Aunt Elizabeth."

Leaning forward in the rocker, she retrieved the book, frowning at the cover the same way she had the first time she saw it. The image on the front was a picture of a rope looped in a very peculiar fashion — a knot in the making, she guessed — and below it the very simple and un-enticing title: *The Horse*, by William Youatt and John Stuart Skinner.

She'd thought *American Turf Register and Sporting Magazine* had been an odd choice for Elizabeth. But this? "You're certain you wouldn't prefer a novel, Aunt Elizabeth? I could check your library, see what's there. Perhaps something you haven't read yet."

"No, no." Elizabeth laughed. "This one's fine, dear. The general has read it many times. It's a favorite of his."

Olivia nodded. *Of course it is.* She settled back in her chair. "And you're certain you're not too warm? Or wouldn't like more tea?"

"No, thank you. I'm fine. But this new chaise is splendid." Elizabeth stretched her legs out on the overlong chair and arranged her skirt over her ankles. "I'm glad the general paid me no mind when I told him I thought this was needless."

Olivia only smiled, not about to admit that after Elizabeth's objection, the general *had* dismissed the idea of purchasing the chair. He'd placed the order only after Olivia had gone to him privately and insisted the chaise would be of benefit.

Following Elizabeth's fainting spell, the family doctor had ordered a week's bed rest. This past week he'd approved Elizabeth to rise and move about the house for a couple of hours each day, which included coming outside to sit.

Olivia opened to the page holding the marker. Yesterday Elizabeth had requested she read the preface, so they hadn't gotten far. "Chapter One," Olivia read now, ready to infuse enthusiasm into the text that she was certain it would lack. " 'The Horse in England and America, as He Has Been, and as He Is.' " *Truly?* She stifled a sigh. A novel would have been so much better. " 'Of all the beasts of the field, which, as we are told, the Lord formed out of the earth and brought unto Adam to see what he would call them, none has more engaged the attention of the historian and the philosopher—none has figured more in poetry and romance—than the horse …'"

She glanced up as she read, watching Mr. Cooper who, none too surprisingly, was standing in the middle of the corral looking at the horse. Not wanting to give Elizabeth the impression she was disinterested in the book, she alternated reading a line or two with watching the events in the corral. Each time she looked up it was to find the horse and Mr. Cooper still staring at each other, Uncle Bob off to one side.

Mr. Cooper would take a few steps forward, then stop. The horse would take a few steps back and stop. It was like a dance. Only … not.

After reading two more paragraphs, Olivia looked up to see Mr. Cooper kneeling down, his hand outstretched to the horse. The mare just stood, staring at him. She smiled, the scene so comical. But it was also sweet, in a sense. Until she remembered how close that horse had come to biting her. She hoped Mr. Cooper knew what he was doing.

She read a few more lines, ending a particularly long paragraph with a flourish, then looked over to catch Elizabeth's reaction, only to find her aunt's eyes closed, her head resting against the cushion.

Marking their place in the book, Olivia rose from her chair, slipped the book in the basket, and decided to get a closer look at Ridley Cooper and that mare.

Wanting to appear as if she were simply out on a stroll instead of coming to see him, Olivia took an indirect path to the corral, around a rose garden on the north side of the house. As she drew closer, she slipped behind a dogwood tree, welcoming its partial privacy. She heard Uncle Bob speaking, his voice soft.

"There you go, Ridley. That's better."

She looked to see what the head horse trainer was referring to, but again, all she saw was Mr. Cooper kneeling, holding out his hand, a good six feet from the horse that looked ready to bolt at any second. And then …

The horse took a step toward him. Just one, so tentative. The mare shook her head from side to side and whinnied, then looked at Mr. Cooper straight on.

"It's all right, girl," he whispered. "I'm not gonna hurt you."

Olivia couldn't see his face, but she heard a smile in his voice. She also sensed fear in the horse's stance, in the way it pawed the ground. The horse looked over in Bob Green's direction, and although Olivia knew it was silly, she would've sworn the mare was looking at Uncle Bob to see what *he* thought about Ridley Cooper.

The horse inched forward. Closer, closer ...

Only three feet separated man and beast now. Olivia silently cheered the animal on. She didn't like horses. But even more, she disliked seeing someone—some*thing*—so afraid.

"That's it," Mr. Cooper spoke softly. "You can do it, girl ..."

Ever so slowly, he rose, hand still outstretched. The mare's ears pricked. Then it lunged forward—only a foot—snorting and pawing the ground. Olivia's breath clamped tight in her throat. If she'd been Ridley Cooper, she would've run screaming for her life.

But he didn't move.

He stood motionless, his head slightly lowered—his hand still outstretched—his attention anchored on the mare. As quickly as the horse had lunged, it quieted, and they just stood staring at each other.

Something about the scene brought a warmth to Olivia's eyes, and when Mr. Cooper inched his hand closer, part of her wanted to say, "No, don't. Not yet."

But it was too late.

The mare bolted and ran full out to the other side of the corral. Olivia's heart squeezed tight. Especially when she saw Mr. Cooper bow his head.

She stepped out from the tree, and Uncle Bob turned. She'd only met the man once, in the kitchen one morning when he and Mr. Cooper were having breakfast, and he'd seemed as nice in person as she'd imagined him to be at first glance.

Uncle Bob tipped his black derby. "Afternoon, Missus Aberdeen."

Ridley Cooper turned and saw her and gave a shy laugh. "Did you see all that?"

Olivia debated, then nodded. "You almost had her convinced."

He dragged a hand through his hair. "Unfortunately, almost doesn't count for anything."

Uncle Bob briefly gripped his shoulder. "It's a whole lot closer than where you were, Ridley. For both of you." Tipping his hat to Olivia again, Uncle Bob headed in the direction of the mare.

Mr. Cooper approached the fence. "What brings you out here, Mrs. Aberdeen? I thought you considered corrals and stables off limits."

"I do. That's why I'm still staying a good ten feet on this side."

He gestured. "You can come closer. It's all right."

Hearing the teasing in his voice, she shook her head. "I'm fine right where I am, thank you."

He gave her that smile, the one she was becoming more familiar with. As familiar as she could be considering that the beard hid half his face. But as wild and wooly as Ridley Cooper appeared to be, she was beginning to think that beneath his rough exterior there might actually reside a caring man. Even if he did lack the manners and upbringing of a gentleman.

"I'm glad you came out here." He rested his forearms on the top rail. "I ... ah, wanted to give you something."

She studied him, aware of how he was watching her, similar to how he'd watched the mare. "And just what would this *something* be, Mr. Cooper?"

He reached into his shirt pocket, then hesitated. "I'm not fully sure why I did this, Mrs. Aberdeen." He rubbed a hand over his beard. "I guess it was because of what you said the other day." His voice lowered. "About envying my having a dream."

Her curiosity more than piqued, Olivia glanced at his shirt pocket.

"I know you said you're going to serve as Mrs. Harding's companion, and I'm sure that'll work out fine." He nodded as though trying to assure her it would. "But when I saw this advertisement" — he withdrew a piece of newsprint from his pocket — "I thought the position might suit you. And that maybe you could do both."

Seeing the mare was a safe distance away, she closed the gap, took the clipping from him, and began to read.

"The notice says twenty hours a week," he continued, "but there at the bottom it says the hours are negotiable. Mornings or afternoons. If it's something you're even interested in."

Olivia nodded, feeling him watching her. She acted as though she were reading the verbiage again, when really she was buying time, thinking of what to say. She was touched he'd thought of her. More than touched, actually. But she knew something he didn't. No family in Nashville would ever allow her to teach their children. Not in a school and certainly not in a tutoring position such as this.

"You may not believe this, Mr. Cooper, but ... teaching is something

I wanted to do when I was younger. But when my father arranged ..."
She caught herself and glanced away, reaching for a pleasantness she
didn't feel. "When I married, of course, I put those plans aside."

He didn't nod like people usually did in the ebb and flow of conversation, whether they agreed with what you were saying or not.
He didn't say anything. He simply watched her with those hazel-blue
eyes, and she found it unnerving to be so closely regarded.

She folded the clipping down the middle, watching the crease
become more prominent with each pass of her thumb and forefinger.
"And then of course there's the business of getting to and from town,
and I'd—"

"Have to ride a horse," he said matter-of-factly.

She looked up, knowing better than to be startled by his directness. "I was going to say that I don't wish to inconvenience the Hardings. But yes, that is a consideration too, and—"

"I could take you, either on horseback or by carriage. I don't mind.
I've already spoken with Uncle Bob, and he seems to think we could
work it out. We'd still need to run everything by the general to be
sure. But"—his eyes narrowed playfully—"if those three boys who
need tutoring also need to learn how to climb out a window, there's
nobody better to teach them than you."

Olivia tried to laugh, knowing he'd intended to be humorous, but
she couldn't. A bitter taste tinged her mouth. "You addressed this
issue with someone else *before* addressing it with me, Mr. Cooper?"

He stood a little straighter. His humor faded. "I wouldn't call asking
Uncle Bob if I could borrow a buggy to take you into town 'addressing
the issue with someone else,' Mrs. Aberdeen. I was merely seeing if
this would be a plausible opportunity before I presented it to you."

Olivia felt a heat building within. Charles had controlled *everything* for her from the very beginning—choosing what committees
she would serve on and with whom, arranging her schedule, including who she could and couldn't see, and when. Even demanding to
approve her choice of gown for formal events they'd attended. She
reminded herself this man wasn't Charles, but despite that ...

Like morning dew beneath an August sun, every trace of gratitude
within her evaporated. She looked at the advertisement clutched in
her hand and saw it through different eyes. It hurt her cheeks to smile.
"Thank you for thinking of me, Mr. Cooper, but I'm afraid this opportunity isn't one I can pursue at this juncture." She held it out.

But he didn't take it. He just studied her with a patience that wore hers thin. "Don't you ever find that exhausting, Mrs. Aberdeen?"

"Don't I ever find *what* exhausting, Mr. Cooper?"

"Being so proper all the time. Always having to say the right thing. Do the right thing."

She wished now that she'd never come down here. "I wasn't attempting to be *proper*, Mr. Cooper. I was simply trying to express my gratitude for your kindness in—"

"Well, you're obviously not feeling too grateful right now, that's fairly plain to see. The problem is, ma'am, I don't know why. But I'd sure like to."

Chapter
SIXTEEN

*T*he flush of Mrs. Aberdeen's cheeks told him she was upset. But for the life of him, Ridley didn't know why. He wasn't about to take the advertisement back though. Not without her telling him the truth, which he sensed simmered just below that prim and proper exterior.

"You're mistaken, Mr. Cooper." Her voice teetered on the edge of calm. "I *am* grateful to you, sir. But for reasons I'd rather not discuss, I simply cannot apply for this position."

She gave him a polite smile that made him want to climb over the fence. "Why can't we at least discuss your reasons?"

"Because I told you just now that I'd prefer not to. It's my prerogative, as a lady, to—"

"Is it because I spoke with Uncle Bob about the position first? Is that what has you all riled up?"

"I'm not riled up, Mr. Cooper."

"Surely it's not the comment about teaching the boys to climb through a window."

Her jaw clenched tight. "As I said, I'd prefer not to discuss my reasons, Mr. Cooper."

"Fine, Mrs. Aberdeen. But would you be kind enough to at least tell me what I said that upset you?"

"I'm not upset." Her mouth formed a tight curve.

"Please." He held up a hand. "Don't smile at me like that. It doesn't have the desired effect, I assure you."

Her politeness flattened. "And just what, may I ask, do you think is the *effect* I desire?"

Finally, something he knew the answer to. Only, she wasn't going to like it. "Your desire, Olivia Aberdeen, is that everything appear the way it *should* be, ma'am, instead of how it actually is."

Her mouth slipped open. "You have no right to—"

"For instance," he continued before she could protest, knowing she wouldn't like being interrupted. Maybe if he got this woman angry enough, she'd let down that blasted guard of hers and he'd get a glimpse of who she really was. "When you're asked a question, you respond in the way you think a 'lady' should, instead of honestly speaking your mind, which I believe you're quite capable of doing, by the way. And," he added, when she opened her mouth again, "you refuse to accept my assistance when climbing through a window, yet you'll willingly climb through that same window yourself, as long as you think no one is watching."

Her eyes flashed, and he saw the sharp tip of truth hit its mark. He also knew if looks were fire, he'd be burned to a crisp right now.

"As I was saying, Mr. Cooper—"

"I'm not done yet, *Olivia*."

Her eyes widened.

"I don't know why you didn't get the position of head housekeeper here, but from what I've seen in you, ma'am, you're smart and you've got spunk, which counts for a lot these days. And if I were over there right now …" He glanced at the fence separating them, hoping she'd hear the 'olive branch' in his tone. "I'd help you close that polite little mouth of yours." He smiled when she clamped her pretty mouth shut. "That is, *if* I wasn't afraid of losing a finger."

The hurt that slipped into her eyes told him the peace offering had floated right past her, and he felt bad now for trying to egg her on.

She moistened her lips. "I'm pleased you find my predicament so amusing."

"No, ma'am." Ridley looked at her straight on. "I never said that. All I said was—"

"Let me be clear on a few things, Mr. Cooper."

Ridley felt his own eyes widen and closed his mouth with pleasure.

"You have no right to speak to me in so casual a manner, sir." Her voice, barely higher than a whisper, was tight with anger. "Our lack of acquaintanceship does not afford you the liberty to tell me what you think I should or should not do. To even suggest that you *think* you know what is best for me is beyond the definition of absurdity. And arrogance." Her chest rose and fell in quick succession. "I am *more* than capable of determining the course of my life, and I do not require your assistance in that regard." She lifted her chin. "Nor do I desire it."

Proud of her in ways he couldn't describe and intrigued by her all the more, Ridley took a step back from the fence to give her room. He had some idea about the kind of man her late husband had been from what Green had told him, and he'd pretty much drawn his own sketch from there. So even though it was only him and Olivia Aberdeen standing here, he couldn't shake the feeling she was fighting with someone else.

"Furthermore," she continued, thrusting the folded newsprint toward him again, "I will thank you to take this advertisement and … and …"

Seeing her struggling for the right words, he smiled. "Put it with the horse droppings?"

She blinked, and her cheeks flushed a deeper crimson. She looked down as though just now realizing all she'd said, and from where he stood, Ridley found himself praying she wouldn't back down. Not now. Not after having come this far. On the brink of saying something, he held back when she lifted her head.

"You may *put it* wherever you like, Mr. Cooper."

As she strode back toward the house, triumph in her gait, Ridley watched the sway of her shapely hips and wasn't nearly so bothered by the fact that he was going to be at Belle Meade a little longer than he'd planned.

Something else occurred to him too.

Although he respected a widow's time to grieve, what if a particular widow didn't necessarily need that time? What if her situation were different? He contemplated that, along with the bustle sashaying a right pretty little path away from him, and wondered … What would keep a man from testing those waters, stirring things up a little, just to see if there was interest there?

He wouldn't be here too much longer, he knew. But try as he might, he couldn't resist the challenge.

Later that night, he picked his way in the darkness toward the servants' cabins. Fourth cabin on the left was what Uncle Bob had said. Ridley found it easily and knocked on the door.

Betsy answered, a child in her arms and one clinging to her skirt. The soft glow of lamplight haloed her form. "What you doin' here, Mr. Cooper? Uncle Bob be needin' somethin'?"

"Evening, Betsy." Ridley smiled and fingered his beard. "You once told me you can shave the fuzz off a ripe peach with nary a nick. Does that still hold true, ma'am?"

A sassy sparkle lit her eyes. "I think you's about to find out!"

Minutes later, with her husband, Julius, and their four children seated at the table watching, Ridley straddled the straight back chair Betsy offered. "It's not often I let a woman with scissors, much less a razor, this close to my throat."

Julius laughed. "Just be glad she ain't mad at you, sir. Ain't many things I's scared of, but my wife with her dander up and somethin' sharp in her grip ..." He feigned a shiver. "Lawd, have mercy."

The children snickered, their dark eyes wide.

Betsy threw them all looks. "You men hush up. And you young 'uns stop that gigglin'." She grabbed a handful of Ridley's hair. "You gonna let me shape this mess up too?"

Ridley grinned. "Do whatever you can to make me look presentable, Betsy."

Looking like she'd been handed keys to a candy shop, she stepped back and eyed him, then started clipping. His hair first and then his beard. She looked over at her family. "This man right here, I know he ain't lookin' like much right now." She made a face. "But when I be done with him, he gonna be one handsome devil. You see soon enough."

Ridley timed his response between clips, trying to speak without moving his mouth. "I'll just be grateful ... to have some blood left ... when you're through." He winked at the youngest girl, who started giggling again.

Betsy put down the scissors, and Ridley ran a hand over his trimmed beard. He reached for the cracked hand mirror on the table, but Betsy swatted his arm.

"You look when I be sayin' you can look," she huffed, mixing the shaving soap in a cup. " 'Til then, you just sit tight and do what I say."

"Mean as a snake, that woman," Julius whispered from the other side of the table.

Ridley shot him a close-mouthed smile as Betsy brushed the minty lather over his face and throat, working it in as she went. The woman knew what she was doing, that was for sure. She tilted his chin back and, after throwing the children a last desperate look, Ridley closed his eyes, enjoying their laughter.

A while later, Betsy handed him a warm towel and he scrubbed his face and neck, the heat soothing against his skin. He ran a hand over his smooth jaw, hardly recognizing his own face. As promised, he'd felt not a single nick as she'd pulled that razor across his skin.

He looked up at her. "I've never had a better shave, Betsy. Thank you, ma'am."

A slow smile, smooth as honey, spread across her face. "Mmm-hmm. I knew you had some good looks 'neath there, Mr. Cooper, but you's almost as good lookin' a man as my Julius here." She winked at her husband, then looked back at Ridley. "I ain't gonna ask whether you got your sights set on a woman yet or not. But if you do …" She shook her head. "Heaven help her. I hope she gets a runnin' start." She pulled the mirror from behind her back and held it up. "But even then I ain't sure she stands a chance."

Chapter
SEVENTEEN

Ridley glared at Seabird, summoning patience he didn't have and doubted he ever would. He could live forty lifetimes and not have the patience of Uncle Bob. Which likely meant he'd never have the gift. Maybe it was something you were born with anyway. He didn't know. He only knew time was running short.

It was already June, and he felt no more equipped to work with horses the way Bob Green did than he had the first day he'd arrived. It wasn't Uncle Bob's fault, Ridley knew. But he was giving his best. What else could he do? It didn't help that he hadn't shared with Uncle Bob his plans to leave at the end of this month, but it felt wrong telling him. Like being invited to a fancy banquet in your honor and then informing the host to hurry because you had another appointment.

Ridley ran a hand over his smooth jaw, still getting accustomed to the beard being gone. And still waiting to run into Olivia Aberdeen again. Belle Meade was a big place, but he had a feeling she was going out of her way not to see him. Something he was determined to change.

"Try it again, Ridley." Uncle Bob's voice, ever patient, held a touch of weariness.

Ridley shook his head. "It's no good. I think she's past working with today. Let's go get some dinner."

"She's testin' you. Try it again."

Ridley knew he wasn't imagining this new thread of resistance in the mare. It was almost as if she were reading him at times, anticipating what he was going to do and counteracting him just for spite. "I'm just saying that I think she's made up her mind to—"

"And all I's sayin', sir, is to try it again. I gotta tell ya, Ridley ... Gettin' this mare to cozy up to you is just the start. If you think she's givin' you a time, you just wait 'til you start handlin' something like Jack Malone. Lawd, you ain't met stubborn 'til you's workin' with a stallion. This mare here, she was a good-tempered little girl some time back. But losin' that foal, then the accident with the carriage, then gettin' whipped by that fool of a ranch hand I fired ..." Uncle Bob gave a disgusted grunt. "She's just a little shy now, that's all."

Just a little shy my—Ridley cut the thought short, knowing little good would come from it. He gripped the rope in his hand, weary of playing student. An ever-failing one at that. But thinking of the Colorado Territory and what awaited him—if he ever got there—buoyed him on. What a boon it would be if he could take this mare with him.

Her leg was healing and she was moving better, though not running full out yet. But the skittish little thing still refused to let anybody come near, except Uncle Bob.

Rolling his shoulders to loosen tight muscles, Ridley made a slow approach toward Seabird again, forcing a pleasantness to his expression he didn't feel. The horse tossed its head, sidestepped a foot or two, and pawed the ground.

"What is it you thinkin' 'bout right now, Ridley?"

Ridley briefly narrowed his eyes, wanting to say, *I'm thinkin' about what a complete waste of time this is.* But he didn't. "I'm thinking I wish she wasn't so stubborn."

Uncle Bob sighed. "How come it's always her fault, sir? Why can't it be *your* fault? Leastways some of the time."

"Because all I want to do is put this lead rope on her." Concentrating again on Seabird, Ridley summoned his best Uncle Bob voice, as he thought of it. Low and smooth, gentle as a whisper. "I'm not going to hurt her. I'm not the one who hurt her. I have no intention of hurting her," he continued, inching forward and choosing phrases Uncle Bob had used in instructing him in past weeks. "I'm tellin' her right now, with my eyes, with my voice, just like you said, that she can trust me ..."

Seabird whinnied. Her flanks quivered. She took a step back.

"... and that I only have her best in mind, and that I'll take care of her." Seabird's ears pricked as his voice grew a shade firmer, and Ridley knew from experience what was coming next. "If she'll only *listen* instead of running away!"

The mare darted to the right, passing him in a flash, and didn't stop until she reached the far side of the corral.

Ridley heard a heavy sigh behind him but paid no attention. He'd heard the same thing a thousand times in recent weeks and had since chosen to ignore it.

"You ever been with a woman, sir?"

The unexpected question caught him off guard. "What did you say?"

"You heard me, sir. I'm askin' if you ever been with a woman."

Ridley started to answer, then held back. "What does *that* have to do with *this*?"

" 'Cause I's just wonderin' if that right there"—he motioned to where Seabird had been standing—"is how you treat a woman when you with her, that's all."

Ridley stared, not knowing where Uncle Bob was going with this. And not sure he wanted to know.

The older man laughed. "I ain't never had me a wife. Hope to someday though." He smiled. "But my guess is I already know more than you on this count."

Ridley laughed, not exactly feeling his masculinity being questioned so much as jokingly prodded. "And just how do you figure that, old man?"

Uncle Bob grinned and gestured to the mare. "The right answer to my question, the one I was askin' you before is, 'I's tryin' to figure out what *she's* thinkin'.' "

Ridley waited, knowing this man well enough to know more was coming.

"That's part of the secret of learnin' all this, Ridley." Uncle Bob's smile faded. "You gotta stop thinkin' 'bout yourself so much, and start thinkin' 'bout them. Try to see things how they see 'em. What do you think they see when they look at you and me?"

Ridley shrugged. "In your case, someone a lot smaller than they are."

Smiling only a little, Uncle Bob shook his head. "No, sir ... That's just it. They see someone who can do 'em harm. Someone who's after 'em. They is the prey, sir. Not us. Which, when you think 'bout how things work, makes no sense at all. They got the power to trample our bones to dust." Uncle Bob's expression went soft, like his voice. "And here they give us the right—the *honor*, sir—of ridin' 'em. Of sharin' their strength. Of harnessin' it. Of havin' a better life with them helpin' us than we'd ever have left to our lonesome."

Uncle Bob grew quiet and looked out across the meadow. Ridley felt he should say something, but everything he thought of saying seemed to pale by comparison. So he left the silence alone.

Later that night, after dinner, the two of them sat out on the porch in the dark. Uncle Bob smoked his pipe, the rich aroma reminding Ridley of his grandfather. Powerful, how scent could pull you back across a lifetime of living in scarcely a blink.

"A lot of folks'll tell you," Uncle Bob said, speaking around the pipe, "about training a horse."

Ridley had to smile, hearing him pick up the conversation where they'd left it earlier. Reminded him of some old married couples. But there was something comforting in knowing someone well enough where you could do that.

"They say you gotta show 'em who the master is and who it ain't. That you got to be stern. Rope 'em and beat 'em, show 'em how it's done." Uncle Bob took a long pull from his pipe, the tobacco crackling and popping as it burned. "But the truth of it is, sir, if a man gotta have a stick or a whip in his hand to make him feel strong, or if he gotta beat somethin' to make it do his biddin' . . ." He shook his head, the creak of his rocker keeping odd time with the crickets' chirruping. "He ain't no master. And he ain't got no strength either. Not the strength that counts. Not with blood horses," he added softly. "And not with any other livin' creature on God's green earth."

Ridley searched the vast array of stars dotting the night sky, letting the truth of Uncle Bob's wisdom settle into the blanket of darkness around them, burrowing deep within. And for the first time since realizing he wanted to come to Belle Meade to find Bob Green, he got a sense that maybe he was here to learn about more than just horses.

But the truth went deeper than he'd thought, because memories best left untouched began to stir. Images he'd hoped would fade with years returned with the clarity of yesterday. He was nine years old again, standing at his father's side, watching a young Negro boy not much older than himself being bid on by men who wouldn't even look the boy in the eye. But it was the auction he'd seen four years later—the baby boy being ripped from his mother's arms, the young woman being stripped naked and poked and prodded like livestock, ogled by every white man in the crowd—that had sickened him so he'd barely been able to reach the alleyway before his stomach had emptied itself. He'd been so ashamed to be there. To be *white*. The world had looked different to him ever since.

Ridley straightened, then took a deep breath, filling his lungs, not so much pushing the memories aside as willing them to be at rest. He looked toward the main house, and his thoughts—as they always seemed to do these days when given wing—took a favorable turn and landed on one person. He found himself thinking about her at the oddest times, day and night. And his imagination needed little prompting where she was concerned.

But the question at the forefront of his mind right now, spurred on by Betsy's reaction when she'd shaved his beard a week ago ...

If circumstances forced him to forego heading west this summer, and he had to winter here until the next, was there an inkling of a chance that a spunky little blue-eyed, prim and proper, spitfire of a young Southern woman would ever consider giving a man like him a second glance?

"Which one do you think would be best for the front parlor, Livvy?" Elizabeth fingered swatches of drapery fabric, holding them at various angles. "I can't seem to decide."

Scarcely able to tell a difference in the swatches, Olivia leaned closer. She didn't want to hurt Elizabeth's feelings, but her heart simply wasn't in this. All morning long they'd been sorting through sample after sample of drapery and wallpaper swatches.

Yet all she could think about was the teaching position Mr. Cooper had told her about the other day and how thoroughly she'd berated him for it. Justifiably so, in one sense. The man had no right to offer her advice on personal matters. Especially when his opinion in the matter was unsought. And yet ...

Having had time to reflect on their exchange, she knew she'd overreacted. But the last thing she wanted was to have to offer Ridley Cooper another apology.

She cringed, knowing it was probably the right thing to—

Don't you ever find that exhausting, Mrs. Aberdeen? Always having to say the right thing. Do the right thing ...

Recalling his forwardness, Olivia squashed the emerging apology before it had time to form. And did so gladly. Rudeness such as that didn't deserve common courtesy. But she had given a lot of thought to that advertisement. Even if she did apply for the position, the answer would be a swift and emphatic no. Because she'd been the wife of Charles Winthrop Aberdeen, and everyone in Nashville knew it.

Just this morning, Elizabeth had received an invitation from the Nashville Ladies Auxiliary for a special tea to welcome new members. The invitation had included Selene and Mary and even Lizzie Hoover. But not her. Regardless of the fact that she'd been a member of the club for the past four years—before Charles's true nature had been made public—Olivia knew there would be no invitation forthcoming for Mrs. Charles Winthrop Aberdeen.

And the question that had begun to plague her was if there would ever come a time when people's memories would fade. When they would allow her to have a future again. Or would she always be atoning for her late husband's sins?

"Or perhaps you think I should simply string up some old feed sacks. I hear they're all the rage in Paris."

Olivia blinked, her aunt's words finally registering with her. She'd allowed her mind to wander. "Oh, Aunt Elizabeth, I'm sorry. I ... My mind is simply elsewhere today." She reached for the swatches but her aunt set them aside.

"Livvy." Smiling, Elizabeth reached over and squeezed her hand. "You know I'm simply having fun with you. But I can tell something is bothering you. Whatever it is, dear, you can share it with me. And if it's the invitation from the auxiliary, then let me repeat ... I have no intention of going. And neither will Selene or Mary or Lizzie."

"I admit ..." Olivia sighed. "The invitation does have something to do with how I'm feeling. But I don't want to keep you all from going." She looked up, insistent. "Honestly, I don't want you—or the others— to be penalized because of me."

Elizabeth gave her a look that said they would discuss it later, followed by one that urged her to continue.

"There is something I'd like to ask you, Aunt Elizabeth." She bowed her head. "But I'm afraid there's no way to say this without appearing ungrateful to you and the general."

Elizabeth gently lifted Olivia's chin. "In a thousand lifetimes, Livvy, I could never consider you ungrateful."

Olivia tried to smile, but a weight bore down in her chest that made it impossible. "Do you think ... there will ever come a time when ..." The heaviness moved into her throat. "... when people will forget about what Charles did? Or, more rightly, that ... they'll forget he was my husband?"

The shadow eclipsing Elizabeth's expression answered first, and Olivia lowered her head.

"Livvy," Elizabeth whispered, covering her hand, "look at me."

With effort, Olivia did as asked.

Elizabeth's voice, while tender, held the distinctive clarity of truth. "I do believe in time some people will begin to accept you again. Others, I fear, will likely never do so."

Olivia searched her gaze. "Others," she repeated softly, understanding who Elizabeth meant. "The families who lost sons and husbands to the war, then lost their homes and fortunes as well. *Everything*," she whispered, feeling a familiar ache inside. "Aided by the hand of my late husband."

"None of which was your fault, Livvy. Remember that." Elizabeth cradled Olivia's cheek. "They say time heals all wounds, which may be true. But it doesn't take away the scars. Some of those, we must learn to live with."

Staving off tears, Olivia nodded and instinctively covered her left arm. "If it were within my power, Aunt Elizabeth, I would return every last guilty cent that Charles stole. I would make it right. With all of them."

"I know you would."

Confronted by the bleak reality of her own future, Olivia sat straighter on the velvet settee and tried to summon a strength from within herself, as she'd done so many times before. But the strength failed to come, and tears welled in her eyes. "Sometimes I feel so afraid." She took a steadying breath. "Afraid of being with someone wrong again. Someone like Charles. But then I'm equally afraid of being alone." She gave a humorless laugh, ashamed of her fear. And how deep it went.

She squeezed Elizabeth's hand and wondered, selfishly, if the doctors were right. What would life be like without Elizabeth Harding? She remembered only too well what losing her mother had felt like, and she did not wish to walk that path again.

Tears slipped down her cheeks. "In your letters, Aunt Elizabeth, you wrote often about ... believing that God has a plan."

Elizabeth nodded.

"But ..." Olivia's breath caught. "I'm not so sure sometimes."

Elizabeth pulled her close. "Oh, my dear. Just because you're afraid doesn't mean you don't believe. It simply means you're human." Elizabeth drew back slightly, her smile warm with acceptance. "Like the rest of us. Things *will* get better, Livvy. Mark my words. And God does have a plan for your life. It may not be easy, but nothing worth having ever is. He'll show it to you ... in time."

A soft knock drew their attention.

"Sorry to bother you, Missus Harding." Susanna stood in the doorway. "But the general says he's ready to see Missus Aberdeen now, ma'am."

"Very good, Susanna. Thank you."

Olivia dried her eyes, looking to Elizabeth for explanation.

"Now, Livvy. Don't be angry with me."

Elizabeth rose from the settee, and Olivia came with her, offering a steadying arm. Elizabeth looped her arm through but didn't lean on Olivia as she'd been doing. Perhaps the beef liver Susanna prepared for Elizabeth each evening was helping with the "tired blood" after all.

"All I'm guilty of, Livvy dear, is boasting to the general about how organized and wonderfully detailed you are. Last evening he inquired whether I thought you'd be willing to help him in his area, and I told him it was worth speaking to you about. I hope you don't mind."

"Of course not, Aunt Elizabeth." Olivia's perspective brightened at the prospect of doing something other than staring at drapery samples or choosing wallpaper. Plus the opportunity to prove herself to General Harding. "I'd be happy to help in whatever way I can."

"That's exactly what I told him you'd say."

Elizabeth led the way through the foyer and into the study where she paused. Huddled together, Selene, Mary, and Cousin Lizzie stood clustered by the front window, peeking through the drapes, whispering and giggling like schoolgirls.

Elizabeth smiled. "Pray tell, ladies, what are the three of you doing in here?"

Selene glanced back over her shoulder, wearing a mischievous grin. "We're simply admiring something, Mother."

"And exactly what would that *something* be?"

The young woman's grin deepened. "Just one of Father's new stallions."

Mary and Lizzie laughed all the more—until Mary turned. Her gaze connected with Olivia's. The girl's humor cooled considerably, but only until she turned back to the window. Olivia had tried reaching out to Mary to no avail. Elizabeth had encouraged her not to worry. Mary would come around. But Olivia wondered. Still, she felt an odd sort of kinship with the girl and wasn't ready to give up.

Not wishing to keep the general waiting, she hurried on to his office, eager to see how she might help and having absolutely no interest whatsoever in seeing a stallion.

Chapter EIGHTEEN

*B*uttoning a fresh shirt, Ridley strode toward the side porch of the main house where General Harding's office was located, hardly believing what he was about to do. He cast a dark look at Uncle Bob, who followed beside him. "Explain to me again what exactly possessed you to tell the general I could do this? Much less that I wanted to?"

"Don't you worry, Ridley. You can do it. Whatever the general says, you just go 'long with it, sir. I be here to help you."

Ridley paused a distance away from the front corner of the house, aware of a nearby open window and movement behind the curtains. He lowered his voice accordingly. "Uncle Bob, you and I hardly have time to train together as it is. And with all the foals being born and due to be born and all the training to be done with them. Then with Jack Malone and the mares arriving every day for him to service …" Ridley knew Uncle Bob had meant well, but he also knew the man didn't know he was planning on leaving in three weeks. "I simply don't see how you and I are going to—"

"I know it, I know." His voice low, Uncle Bob nodded and pointed to a button Ridley had missed. "But you got to see that the foreman you's replacin'—" He leaned closer. "He was a good man, sir. Fine man. Friend of the general's. But he ain't never listened much to what I told him. And I *know* how to run things in these stables. Better, I mean. I know who's doin' the work and who ain't. Who treats these horses the way they should and who ain't. And them that ain't need to be gone, sir. I don't give a lick what side they fought for or who they done fought with. And somethin' else …" His brow lowered. "The colored men ain't gettin' paid nearly what Grady and them other white men are. That ain't sittin' too well. But ain't no other white foreman gonna do nothin' 'bout that 'round here. 'Ceptin' you. You get my meanin'?"

Ridley sighed. "Yes, I get your meaning." Frustrated, he ran a hand over his jaw, feeling the hint of stubble. He'd shaved yesterday and again this morning, in continued hope of seeing Mrs. Aberdeen. But after their run-in over a week ago, she was sure making herself scarce.

Last night, relaxing with Uncle Bob on the front porch of the cabin, he'd caught sight of her on the second-story porch of the main house, sitting with Mrs. Harding just as the sun set. Soon after, he'd glimpsed her entering the room over the kitchen, the one with the latticework beneath the window. Her bedroom, he guessed, which had made him smile, wondering if she knew what a handy ladder that lattice would make. How many times had he and his brothers shinnied down and back up the chimney wall of their childhood home? Probably more times than they'd used the front door.

He doubted Olivia Aberdeen had done much shinnying up or down anything in her lifetime. But that was certainly something he'd like to teach her, if given half the chance.

"Sir, is you havin' second thoughts about this?"

"No," Ridley answered, pulling his attention back. "More like fourth and fifth."

"If you's worried how the other men are gonna see this … you gettin' to be foreman after bein' here only a short time … don't you worry none about that. All the men like you, sir. All 'cept Grady and his clan, and nobody pays them no mind anyway."

Appreciating that more than Uncle Bob knew, Ridley glanced at the general's office door, still trying to figure a way out of this without having to admit he hoped to be leaving soon.

"Why can't you just talk to the general yourself, Uncle Bob? Instead of talking to a foreman? Harding listens to you. I've seen him. He respects you."

"Yes, sir, he does. Him bein' willin' to see you now be proof of that. General Harding's a good man. But he hires foremen to run things 'round here, Ridley. Men he fought with in the war. What's it gonna look like if I go runnin' my mouth behind that foreman's back to the general, whinin' every time that man ain't doin' somethin' I think we need to be doin'?" Uncle Bob shook his head. "A black man tellin' a white man what to do?" he scoffed. "You know that ain't done, Ridley. Not more than once, anyhow."

Ridley had to smile. "Not unless it's you telling me what to do, huh?"

Uncle Bob nudged him. "That's different. You's a white man, all right. But you ain't the same, sir. And God's honest truth?" Looking down, Uncle Bob bit his lower lip, causing the whiskers on his chin to bunch out. "You's more like a friend to me than any white man ever been. 'Cept maybe the general. He been mighty good to me. But ..." He shrugged, not finishing.

Ridley eyed Uncle Bob, having gotten to know this man fairly well in recent weeks. "You're not just saying that so I'll go on inside, are you?"

"No, sir. I promise I ain't." Then one side of his mouth tipped up. "But it sure is good timin', ain't it?"

Ridley gave him a look. But then saw no way around admitting the truth. "I need to confess something, Uncle Bob. Something that I should have told you from the very start. And no matter how I say it, it's not going to come out right."

"Yes, sir?" Uncle Bob looked at him, waiting.

"When I first came here, I ..." Ridley thought again of being invited to a fancy banquet only to insult the host by leaving quickly, and he hoped Bob Green wouldn't be insulted by what he was about to say. "My plans have always been to be here for only a month or two. To learn what I need to from you and then move on. I'm not interested in this foreman's job or in staying here in the—"

Uncle Bob laughed. "Is you kiddin' with me?"

Ridley stared, then shook his head.

Uncle Bob's laughter died, but his smile didn't. "You standin' here tellin' me that you came here with the idea that you was gonna know in a month or two what took me a lifetime of learnin'?"

Ridley heard the humor in his voice but the truth undergirding the question was far louder and even more convicting. As the reality of his situation settled over him, Ridley shrugged. "I wasn't thinking of it that way. I was just eager to—"

"You eager to get on with life, leave the war and all of that behind. I know that, sir. I see it in you every day. I see you rubbing that little shell you keep in your pocket." Uncle Bob smiled. "But things worth havin' take time. You gonna learn it, I know you will. But you's *far* from ready right now, sir."

He gave Ridley a droll look, which Ridley returned.

"Did I tell you 'bout the pay, sir?"

Ridley shook his head.

Uncle Bob's eyes lit. "From what I hear, it's enough to cover what the general's chargin' you to lease a stall *and* all the other money you payin' for Seabird, with some to spare for that place you's wantin' out west."

Ridley turned and walked on, his decision made—and also made for him. As he passed the corner of the house, he glimpsed the second-story porch and the bedroom above the kitchen, and thought of that lattice again. And felt a smile. Staying here a little longer might hold other advantages too.

"Just remember," Uncle Bob whispered behind him, "whatever he asks, you and me can do it. Together."

Ridley raised a hand in silent response, hoping the man was certain about this. Because he certainly wasn't.

The last thing he needed was more time spent in General Harding's company, and becoming a foreman would only increase that. If that man started peppering him with questions about the war, it could end badly for him.

And for Uncle Bob.

Olivia listened, growing more excited as General Harding laid out his plan.

"So you see, Olivia"—he leaned forward, the supple leather of his chair gently complaining—"it would be of great advantage to have someone with such attention to details to oversee the ordering for the entire farming operation. Someone whose sole responsibility would be to make certain adequate supplies are always on hand. The gentleman who resigned, a foreman, as I told you … This was originally under his oversight, but it was becoming burdensome in addition to his other duties. And frankly, he allowed a few of our staple items to become depleted, and we had to do without for a few days until the next shipment arrived, which is unacceptable. So when Elizabeth *raved* about your talents …" he said the word as though not altogether convinced, "I thought this would be a good fit for you. And you *did* communicate a desire to be of assistance." His expression held question. "I'm assuming that hasn't changed?"

"No, sir. Not in the least." She smiled. "I'd be pleased to handle the ordering for you." She knew she could do this—keep track of ledgers and books and accounts. And he'd said he would pay her. Two dollars a week. That might not be much by some people's standards, but she'd never earned her own money before. It was a liberating feeling, and it would allow her to buy a handful of necessities, to not always have to depend on the Hardings' charity.

"Very well, then." He glanced out the front window. "I've seen the way you've organized my wife's life, including her desk and correspondence and the upstairs attic. No doubt my business affairs will benefit immensely from that same watchful supervision. Which I trust has not been exaggerated."

Eager to prove herself, and not wanting to let Elizabeth down, Olivia determined to earn his approval. Not an easy task, she knew. "You mentioned wanting to receive a monthly report, General. I'd be happy to provide a weekly summary as well, if you'd like."

He shook his head. "I have enough reports to review as it is. Monthly will suffice. Besides ..." He handed her a ledger that proved to be heavier than it looked. "Belle Meade is a large estate, Olivia. It will take a good deal of time to inventory everything in both of the—"

A knock sounded on the door.

"Excuse me, please."

"Of course." Curious, Olivia opened the ledger and began perusing the columns. The leftmost column contained the list of inventoried items, followed to the right by the breakout of monthly expenditures for each item. Her eyes widened as she read the dollar amounts, then grew even larger when she reached the totals at the bottom of the page. *Good gracious* ... She'd had no idea how much it cost to run a plantation such as this.

She thumbed several pages, seeing nearly every line and column filled, and her confidence slipped a few notches. Still, she could do this.

"Yes, come in," she heard the general say behind her, and was a bit perturbed with him for allowing their meeting to be interrupted. She had so many questions to ask.

"Thank you, General."

Hearing a male voice, she glanced behind her to see a man in the doorway, the sun at his back. She returned her gaze to the ledger.

"I believe the two of you are already acquainted," the general said.

Olivia turned around again. "I'm sorry, General, but I don't believe this gentleman and I have had the—"

"Mrs. Aberdeen," the man said, stepping into the office. "It's good to see you again, ma'am."

Recognizing the voice but unable to reconcile it with the somewhat familiar—and more than somewhat *handsome*—face, Olivia shifted in her chair to get a better look. And her grip on the ledger went lax. The heavy volume slipped from her hand and landed on the floor with a thud, but she scarcely noticed. *"Ridley Cooper?"* she whispered, absently touching her own smooth cheek.

He smiled at her. *Oh* ... did he smile. She felt it all the way to her toes and in other places she had no idea a smile could reach, much less *warm*.

"Actually, ma'am ..." His gaze briefly dropped to her mouth before settling again on her eyes. "I think *Mr.* Cooper would be more appropriate. But I'm comfortable with the informal, if you are."

Her face flaming, Olivia glanced at the general for his reaction, but he'd turned his back, searching through some files on a table behind him. She bent to retrieve the ledger dumped spine-open at her feet, but Ridley Cooper beat her to it.

"Here you go," he whispered, their faces coming close as they both straightened.

The wry tilt of his mouth—a mouth she could see very, very well now—made her own go dry. She took the ledger from him, aware she was staring. But unable to stop.

The general turned back and gestured. "Shall we all take a seat?"

Olivia felt behind her to confirm the chair was still there then eased down, welcoming its support. Mr. Cooper claimed the chair next to her, and she sneaked another look at him, unable to believe the transformation. *Heart-stopping* was a word that came to mind. But considering how hers was racing at the moment, that description didn't quite seem fitting.

"Excellent timing, Mr. Cooper. Thank you for joining us."

The sound of General Harding's voice pulled her back.

"Mrs. Aberdeen and I were just discussing her taking over the responsibility of ordering the inventory for the farm."

Mr. Cooper nodded. "Uncle Bob indicated you'd found someone to handle that from here on out. But"—he glanced over at her—"I didn't realize that *someone* was Mrs. Aberdeen."

Ridley Cooper's expression said he knew he'd caught her off guard and was enjoying her stunned reaction. Who would have thought shaving a beard could make this much difference? Yet it wasn't only the beard that was gone. He'd cut his hair too. Hair, thick and dark, that possessed more curl than she remembered, and an invitation to touch—much the same as his smooth jawline. She wanted badly to accept that invitation, but of course did not.

Yet one thing hadn't changed: those eyes ... staring into hers right now.

"Uncle Bob speaks very highly of you, Mr. Cooper ..."

Ridley turned back to the general. As did she.

"... and since I, in turn, think mighty highly of him ..." General Harding offered a tilt of his head.

"Thank you, sir. I appreciate that."

The two men continued speaking and, after a moment, Olivia looked between them, feeling as though she were no longer in the room. Slightly miffed, she hadn't missed the fact that the general had told Uncle Bob she'd be overseeing the ordering before he'd even asked her. What if she'd said no to the general's request? What would he have done then?

But she wouldn't have said no—couldn't have—under the circumstances. Still ...

"I don't typically promote someone to foreman so quickly within the ranks, Mr. Cooper."

She frowned.

"But considering Uncle Bob's personal recommendation *and* having observed your work myself in recent weeks, as well as seeing how well the men respect you, I'm willing to make an exception."

"Thank you, General. Uncle Bob's been very generous with his knowledge and with his understanding of the workings here at Belle Meade."

Olivia stared, disbelieving, as the conversation continued without her, as it had before. Ridley Cooper was being promoted? To a foreman? She scarcely restrained an exasperated sigh. Apparently his intention of staying at Belle Meade for only a short period of time had changed, and the appeal of the Colorado Territory had faded by comparison. Which was no wonder. She hadn't understood his desire to go to begin with. But still ...

Why did everything come so easily for men? And for Ridley Cooper, in particular, it seemed. Opportunities abounded. Here. Out west. Choices were his for the taking. And meanwhile, for her ...

The ledger grew heavy in her lap, and she shifted in her seat, consoling herself with the reminder that she did have this new opportunity.

Two dollars per week. And she was determined to make the best of it, despite these two men.

Finally, the general rose from his chair, as did Mr. Cooper. She followed suit, eager to leave, but Ridley Cooper blocked her exit by shaking hands with the general.

"Mr. Cooper, I believe we're in agreement on everything. I'll get a standard contract for the position to you this afternoon. Look it over tonight, then return it to me with your signature in the morning."

"I'll do that." Mr. Cooper moved toward the door.

"Oh," the general said. "Mrs. Aberdeen?"

Surprised he remembered she was still there, Olivia turned. "Yes, General?"

"If you'll plan a time to meet with Mr. Cooper, I'm certain he'll be happy to orient you with where the supplies are kept in the stables. He'll also show you where the tack and—"

"The stables?" Olivia searched his expression. "I don't under-stand." She laid a hand on the ledger atop the desk. "I'll be keeping the ledger for ordering supplies."

"*Yes*." General Harding's tone hinted less at kindness and more at condescension. "And just where do you think the supplies for the horses and other animals are kept, Mrs. Aberdeen? In the kitchen pantry?" He laughed.

But she didn't. And neither did Mr. Cooper, she noticed. It felt as though a curtain she hadn't known was there had been ripped away.

Parched, she tugged at her high collar. "I simply didn't ..." The room had grown warm and prickles of perspiration dotted her spine. "I didn't realize I would be working around ... horses." Even saying the word took effort.

Again, General Harding laughed. "I declare, Mrs. Aberdeen, you *do* know you're living on a stud farm, don't you?"

Olivia forced a laugh, if only to expel a tiny measure of embar-rassment—and dread—burning a hole inside her. She could feel Mr. Cooper looking at her and made it a point not to look back. It only made the situation worse knowing he knew she was afraid of those animals. And made it all the more difficult to pretend to the general that she wasn't.

General Harding opened the office door, and Mr. Cooper exited first.

"Also, Mrs. Aberdeen, regarding those monthly reports ..."

Olivia paused inside the doorway, wondering how on earth she was going to do this. Just thinking about being around those animals made her stomach twist in knots.

"Submit them to Mr. Cooper first, if you would. Then he can review the figures before passing the reports along to me."

She swallowed, her mouth tasting like metal. First the horses, and now working alongside Ridley Cooper? She could already imagine him teasing her about her fear. Like Charles had done. "S-surely, General"—she broke out in a cold sweat—"Mr. Cooper will be busy enough. I-I'm certain I can manage on my own."

General Harding looked down at her. "I appreciate your confidence, Mrs. Aberdeen. But it's only right that he review the documents first, since you'll be reporting to him."

Mr. Cooper paused on the porch steps. "She's reporting to *me*, sir?"

Witnessing his surprise—learning this was news to him as well—helped counterbalance her own. But only a little. Just the other day, she'd told him she could determine the course of her own life, make her own decisions ... And now this. She couldn't even submit a report without his approval.

The irony was beyond rich. And she was certain he'd lap it up.

"Yes, that's right, Mr. Cooper. Mrs. Aberdeen will report to you." The general stepped out onto the porch, smugness creeping into his smile. "Unless you think that aspect of your promotion will prove too challenging."

"No, sir, not at all," he answered quickly. "I'm certain Mrs. Aberdeen and I will get along just fine."

Sensing the general awaiting her response as well, Olivia summoned the practiced smile she knew by heart. To her astonishment, however, it wouldn't come. She managed a nod. "Yes, General. I'm certain we'll get along *just* fine."

Chapter
NINETEEN

M rs. Aberdeen! Wait!" Not about to let the opportunity to speak with her get away, Ridley marveled at how swiftly she covered ground in that bell-shaped skirt. Maybe it wouldn't be so hard to teach the woman how to shinny up and down a lattice after all.

"Mrs. Aberdeen ..." He caught up with her. "Do you have a few minutes to speak with me, ma'am?"

A dark eyebrow arched. "I see we're back to Mrs. Aberdeen. It's not Olivia anymore?"

Although privately appreciating her sharp wit, he refused to be drawn off course. "Do you have time to speak with me, please?"

"That depends, Mr. Cooper." Never breaking stride, she tossed him a look that could have split stone. "Are you asking that as my superior? Or as an acquaintance?"

"That depends." He smiled. "Which answer will get you to slow down?"

"Neither at the moment."

She veered off to the right and headed for the front porch, obviously an evasive maneuver. He adjusted accordingly.

"Two minutes, that's all I'm asking."

"I really can't right now. I need to see to Mrs. Harding."

She gathered her skirt and started up the front steps. Ridley took them by twos, beating her to the top. The door to the house was open, the day being warm, and she tried to sidestep him. But he anticipated the move and cut her off.

"I'm a persistent man, Mrs. Aberdeen. Avoiding me isn't going to make me go away. Besides, looks like we'll be working together. You're going to have to see me eventually."

Briefly closing her eyes, she sighed. "So it would seem," she said beneath her breath.

He gestured to the line of rocking chairs. "Would you be more comfortable sitting?"

"I thought you said this would only take two minutes."

His chivalry rusty from disuse, Ridley opted for the more straightforward — and familiar — approach. "I just wanted to tell you, ma'am, that having you report to me wasn't my idea. I was as surprised by it as you were. I hope you realize that."

"I do. But I hope you realize, Mr. Cooper, that either way, I don't like it."

He nodded, feeling the opposite, but knowing better than to admit it. "Fair enough. But I'm going to do my best to make it work. And I hope you will too. Doing well here at Belle Meade means a great deal to me. And ... to my future." He tried to phrase it in such a way that she would understand he meant his plans to go west. However delayed those plans were for the time being.

She met his gaze. "Yes, well, I have a future too, Mr. Cooper. And my succeeding in this position means a great deal to me as well. For many reasons."

He could imagine what some of those reasons were. But he would've liked to have known more. Maybe in time she'd open up to him.

"So," he said. If she'd been a man, he would've offered his hand to shake on the deal. As it was, all he could do was stare at her. "We've reached a truce then? I help you, and you'll help me?"

She nodded succinctly, then stood a mite taller. "But one thing I would appreciate agreement on before we go any further ..."

Seeing the reprisal of anxiety in her expression, similar to what he'd seen back in the general's office, he could guess what she was going to say next.

"No one else here knows about my ..." She peered around him to the open front door. "About how I don't care for ... you know," she whispered, and he nodded. "And I would greatly appreciate it if you would keep that information to yourself." She bowed her head, her shoulders lifting in a shrug. "Please," she added.

Ridley studied her. This woman never ceased to fascinate him. Here, he'd expected her to enlist his help in keeping the inventory, so she could avoid being around the horses. Instead, she was more concerned about what people would think if they discovered her fear. *Still wanting everything to appear the way it should be ...*

He'd pegged her well. "You have my word on it."

She stepped around him to go inside.

"Before you go, ma'am—"

She turned back, and Ridley—remembering her reaction at first seeing him in the office and the repeated glances she'd stolen his way—made a point of dragging a hand over his clean-shaven jaw. Just the thought that Olivia Aberdeen might find him somewhat attractive felt like a hard-won victory. Because every time he was with this woman, his attraction to her only deepened. "You haven't said anything about it yet, ma'am."

"Said anything about what, Mr. Cooper?" Her brow furrowed.

A nice touch, he'd grant her that. But unconvincing. "About me shaving off my beard." He smiled when he saw a flicker in her eyes— that she knew *he* knew she'd noticed—but then those pretty blue eyes went predictably vacant again.

"I'm sorry." She shook her head. "I must not have been paying close enough attention. But, now that you mention it ..." She stepped back and looked at him. "It looks ... nice."

"*Nice?*" he repeated. Not exactly the word he'd have chosen from her.

She pursed her lips as though trying not to smile. Or maybe she was fighting the urge to say what she truly thought. "Good day, Mr. Cooper."

Before he could say anything else, she skirted past him into the sanctuary of the house. But he didn't mind. That hint of a smile—but mainly those repeated glances back in the office—were enough.

At least for now.

Standing a good distance from the entrance to the mares' stable, Olivia gripped the ledger against her chest, feeling her breakfast of hotcakes and sausage debating on whether or not to stay down. She offered a vote, but her stomach clenched tighter, threatening to overrule it.

Nearly a week had passed since she'd met with General Harding about overseeing the farm's inventory. Since then, she'd visited every operation on the plantation—the cattle, pigs, and cashmere goats; the dairy; and the Shetland ponies, which she had to admit were quite charming little creatures. At least from where she'd stood watching them, a safe distance behind the fence. And, without exception, she'd managed to inventory each of the businesses without trauma.

She'd chosen to walk between locations instead of taking the general's suggestion of riding a horse, heaven help her. But covering the distance between destinations—sometimes up to three or four miles each way—had proven more of a challenge than she'd originally thought. It had been worth it though, when considering the alternative. Well, mostly worth it.

The blisters on the soles of her feet and backs of her heels made walking and standing—even now— –excruciating. She'd barely managed to get her boots on this morning. She was capable of walking the distance. That wasn't the issue. She merely needed more appropriate boots. Either that or the use of a carriage and a servant, which she didn't feel at liberty to request after General Harding had suggested she ride.

Twice in recent days the general had asked if she'd begun inventory in the stables yet, and twice she'd told him it was next on her list. She simply hadn't told him it was last.

Smoothing sweaty palms over her skirt, she continued toward the open stable door, each step painful. The horses weren't the only thing she was nervous about seeing again. The last time she'd spoken with Ridley Cooper had been following the meeting with General Harding, and she'd noticed a definite change in the man that afternoon. In the way he'd spoken to her—even more forthright than usual, almost daring. She'd seen him from afar a handful of times since then and would've sworn she'd caught a difference in the way he looked at her too. And she wondered if the conclusion she'd jumped to was correct...

Now that Ridley Cooper was her supervisor, so to speak, did he feel as if he had the upper hand? *Well* ... She raised her chin a notch. If he thought for one minute that she was going to kowtow to him because General Harding mandated that he review her reports, he would find himself sadly mistaken.

And yet—her chin lowered a touch—it was a delicate balance, because she did need his help inventorying the stables.

When she reached the entrance to the stable, the pungent smell of horse sweat and hay hit her in the face, and her stomach twisted. Choking back both breakfast and fear, she pictured sweet Aunt Elizabeth recommending her to the general for this task specifically, and she forced one foot in front of the other.

Chapter
TWENTY

Shielded from sunlight, the air in the stable felt instantly cooler, yet closer. Olivia told herself there was as much air in here as outside. But it didn't feel true.

She wouldn't have thought it possible, but the stable appeared even larger from this perspective than when viewed from the mansion. Rows of stalls lined both sides, each containing a pair—or two—of ominous black eyes peering her way, following her progress.

A tickle started in her nose, resulting in a sneeze, and she tugged her handkerchief from her sleeve. She looked up to see a gentleman approaching, although upon closer examination—as he took the liberty of examining *her* more closely—she decided the term *gentleman* wasn't quite accurate.

"Good morning, sir. I'm looking for a Mr.—"

"Then you've come to the right place, ma'am. Because I'm a mister, for sure." He leaned in, sniffing loudly, and Olivia took a backward step. "You sure smell pretty. Gonna make these other ladies in here mighty jealous."

With his tongue, he poked at the bulge between his lower cheek and gum, then puckered. Anticipating what was forthcoming, Olivia looked away. But when he swallowed instead, she brought a hand to her midsection, convinced that breakfast was finally about to revolt. He was a big man, broad through the chest and powerful looking. And she wanted no part of him.

She took a needed breath. "I'm looking for Mr. Ridley Cooper. If you would be so kind as to direct me to where he—"

"Whatever he can do for you, ma'am ..." He smiled, the gesture not an improvement. "I'll do you one better. Now tell me, did you come down here to ride? Or do you want a tour of the place? Tell me your pleasure and I'll serve it right up."

He braced an arm against the stall beside her, and the air thinned around her face.

"Excuse me, sir, I think I'll—"

"Matthews!"

She looked past him to see Mr. Cooper striding toward them, thunder in his eyes.

"Matthews, you're needed outside. In the second corral. *Now.*"

Matthews straightened and threw Mr. Cooper a none-too-friendly look, then aimed a stained-tooth smile at Olivia as he departed.

Mr. Cooper glanced out the door, then back at her. "Morning, Mrs. Aberdeen. You all right? You look a little pale, ma'am."

Hearing the subtle query within a query, she swallowed, her stomach's rebellion quieting. "I'm fine, Mr. Cooper." She indicated the ledger in her grip, eager to prove she could do this. "I'm ready to get to work, if you don't mind showing me where everything is kept."

He hesitated, watching her, then motioned. "I'd be happy to."

He led the way between the stalls, and she worked to keep up with him, wincing every few steps. She kept her focus straight ahead and stayed dead center in the middle of the aisle, wary of the horses peering from their stalls, not wanting to get too close.

Mr. Cooper looked back. "Am I moving too fast for you?"

"Not at all." Her feet throbbed and she clenched her jaw, trying not to think about it. It would be hours before she could return to her room and take off her boots.

"You know …" He slowed his steps. "I half expected you to come earlier in the week. Thought you might choose to go ahead and get the worst part out of the way first."

She heard the teasing in his voice and started to make a verbal list of all the inventorying she'd completed. But when she saw his expression, she read only kindly meant humor and decided a smile would suffice.

Without warning, a chestnut mare appeared in a stall to the right, nickering and tossing her head. Olivia jumped back, nearly losing her balance. A strong hand came around her waist and held her steady.

"It's all right." Mr. Cooper laughed softly. "It's just Gem. She's trying to give you a proper welcome, that's all."

Olivia glared at the mare, none too convinced about the proper welcome, but only too aware of Mr. Cooper's hand lingering on the small of her back. "Jim doesn't sound like a proper name for a mare."

He frowned, but only for a second. "Oh … No, it's Gem, as in jewel. Uncle Bob named her that, because he says he saw a diamond in the rough when she was first born. This girl's pretty proud of herself, and with reason." He moved to stroke the horse's forehead. "She came in first at the track on Tuesday. This lady can fly!"

Seeing Mr. Cooper's ease with Gem reminded her of another mare. "How is the horse you've been working with? The one that was hurt in the carriage accident?"

He glanced down the aisle, and Olivia followed his gaze to where the mare in question stood staring at them.

"Seabird's coming along. She still doesn't quite trust me yet though."

Olivia saw evidence of that lingering distrust as they passed Seabird's stall. The mare backed away, eyeing them both.

Much to Olivia's relief, they reached a narrow corridor away from the stalls.

Mr. Cooper paused. "How is Mrs. Harding feeling these days?"

"I wish I could say she's much better, but she's not. At least she doesn't seem to be getting any worse."

"Did I see the doctor here again yesterday?"

She nodded. "He continues to prescribe rest, which General Harding has asked me to encourage."

He continued down the short hallway. "You don't agree with that?"

Realizing she'd allowed her opinion to color her tone, Olivia chose her words carefully. "It's not that I disagree with her resting. I simply think that exercise is also good. Within reason, of course," she added, thinking back to the day when Elizabeth fainted on the lawn. An episode that hadn't occurred since.

Mr. Cooper led her into a room with high windows lining one of the walls, and she stopped inside the doorway and stared. Shelves from floor to ceiling, and each stuffed with boxes and crates of all sizes. On a far wall hulked a row of tall wooden cabinets, each with numerous drawers. Inventorying this would take at least two full days, maybe three. She recalled the dollar amounts she'd read in the ledger …

All of this, for racehorses.

"It's something, isn't it?" he asked quietly. "These animals have a better life than most people I know."

She laughed. "I was thinking something very similar."

"Well" — he made a sweeping gesture — "where would you like to get started? The shelves on this side hold gear like bridles and lead reins, along with halters and harnesses. On that side, in drawers, are brushes and combs and ..."

He rattled off the inventory in the room as if he'd worked here for a year instead of a month. But seeing a chair in the corner, and with her feet feeling as if she'd just marched through cut glass, she quickly made up her mind to start with the drawers.

Sometime later, the bell in the tower by the servants' cabins announced lunch, and with seven drawers inventoried and at least twice that many remaining, Olivia sat forward in her chair to stretch. Her neck and shoulder muscles burned, and her chemise was damp with perspiration. Another warm June day.

She rose from the chair, then grimaced and fell back into the seat. Her eyes watered, the pain in her feet was so intense. For a moment, all she could do was squeeze her eyes tight and wait for the throbbing to subside. Perhaps it had been the blood rushing to her feet that caused the pain, but they pulsed with heat. She wished she could remove her boots, but didn't dare. But perhaps if she loosened the laces a little ...

She worked on the left boot, then the right. It wasn't immediate relief, but it helped. Noting how tight the boots felt, she doubted she could've gotten them off if she'd tried.

"I hope you're hungry." Mr. Cooper walked through the doorway holding a basket. "Susanna and the other ladies fixed us a good lunch."

Olivia looked to make sure her skirt covered her boots. "How kind of them." She touched the back of her hand to her forehead and felt moisture. She was sure she looked a sight.

He gestured. "Care to take a break and join me outside?"

Eager to trade the warmth of this room for fresh air, she hesitated, uncertain she could stand, much less walk. As nonchalantly as possible, she put pressure on the soles of her feet. Hot needles of pain fanned in all directions.

Tucking her chin, she breathed through gritted teeth as embarrassment warmed her further. She gradually looked up. "Would you mind terribly if we ate in here instead?"

He stepped closer. "Are you all right?"

"I'm fine." But even as she said it, her body broke out in a damp sweat.

He set the basket aside. "Tell me what's wrong."

She shook her head. "I'm fine. I simply need to—"

"Remember?" He looked at her pointedly. "That doesn't work with me."

She clenched her jaw, not appreciating his supervisory tone. "My feet are just a little sore, that's all."

He frowned. "From what?"

"From *walking*." She hoped he caught the slight sarcasm in her tone.

He looked down at her feet, and she could see his mind turning. "Where did you walk?"

She looked away. "Around the estate."

"How far around the estate?"

"A ways."

"How far is *a ways*?"

Feeling like a foolish child and resenting him for it, she exhaled. "I walked to the other places to do the inventory this week, and I—"

"You *walked* to all those places? To the cattle farm too? And the sheep?"

Incredulity darkened his tone, and she sought to match it in her own. "Is that not what I just said?" Knowing he knew her fear only made having to admit this worse. "How did you *think* I would get there, Mr. Cooper?"

"I assumed you would have called one of the servants to drive you in a buggy. That would have been the logical thing."

His use of the word *logical* triggered something deep within. "I didn't feel at liberty to do that. Not after the general had suggested I *ride*."

He exhaled, disbelief hardening his features.

In all her life, Olivia had never wanted to leave a room more. The countless times Charles had lectured and berated her for doing something "wrong" or for failing to meet his expectations ... Yet she'd sat there and taken it—his smug, pitying looks—wishing she'd had the courage to leave. And now she had the courage, but not the means.

A shadow eclipsed Mr. Cooper's expression, followed by a flood of understanding, chased by regret, and finally the worst of all ... pity.

"*Don't* look at me like that, Ridley Cooper."

He moved closer. "Why didn't you ask me to take you? I would've taken you."

"I didn't need for you to take me. I got there myself."

"Yes." He gave a brief laugh. "I can see that."

Something snapped inside her. She bent and quickly retied the laces on her boots and stood. Unprepared for the lightheaded feeling that flooded her, she used the cabinet to steady herself, raising a hand of warning when Mr. Cooper drew closer.

"Sit back down, Olivia."

She strode past him, anger and bruised pride giving her strength she didn't know she had. At the end of the hallway, she paused for a few seconds and leaned against the wall for support. She swallowed a groan, feeling the seams of her boots about to split open.

Hearing him behind her, she pushed on, stone-silent tears slipping down her cheeks. Thankfully, the lunch hour saw the stable emptied of workers. But not horses. She kept to the center, like before.

"Olivia, please come back. I want to talk to you."

She didn't turn around. "You've already said quite enough, Mr. Cooper. Now leave me alone."

She was halfway down the line of stalls when the lightheaded feeling returned in force. But it was the floor beneath her turning to white hot coals that finally proved too much.

Chapter
TWENTY-ONE

Ridley caught Olivia as she sank down. "It's all right," he whispered, lifting her in his arms. "I've got you." For lack of a better option, he carried her into a freshly-hayed stall and laid her down, mindful of her feet.

She looked up at him, her chin trembling. Whether from anger or crying, he wasn't sure. Maybe both.

Her face was drained of color, her breathing heavy, but despite the evidence of tears, her eyes were fierce. "I don't want your pity!"

"Good. I'm not offering it."

She raised up on her elbows. "And I'd prefer not to have your help."

Hearing her injured tone, but mostly wounded pride, he laughed. "Well, I'm afraid you're stuck with that—unless you want to be in here when Juliet gets back from being exercised. She's due to foal any day so things could get pretty exciting."

Olivia Aberdeen fixed him with a glare, then gave her head a tiny shake. Just as he had the day they'd first met, he glimpsed what remained of the obstinate little girl still tucked somewhere inside.

Seeing her hastily tied boots, he knelt at her feet. But she quickly yanked her skirt down over her ankles, her expression relaying her intent.

He sat back on his haunches. "Tell me you're not serious."

She shook her head. "It's not proper."

"But it's just your feet!"

"I'd ..." She glanced to the side. "I'd just feel better if you didn't."

He sighed. "So how am I supposed to help you?"

"What if ..." Her gaze edged back. "What if you went to get Susanna? Maybe she could—"

"She and Betsy and the other ladies are all busy feeding the workers. Who will be back anytime."

She winced, rubbing her lower leg.

"Just let me have a quick peek. I promise I won't look at anything I shouldn't. Unlike the first time we met." He couldn't resist.

Seeing her eyebrows shoot up, he smiled to let her know he was only joking. Mostly.

Biting her lower lip, she finally nodded.

He further loosened the laces to make the boots easier to slide off, but as he nudged the left shoe away from her stocking heel, she gasped and fell back, gripping handfuls of hay.

"I'm sorry," he whispered, hurting for her. He hurt even worse when he saw the blood-soaked stocking.

She tried to sit up, but he put a hand to her shoulder.

"Just lie still, until I get the other one."

Dread filling her eyes, she lay back.

The right boot was even harder to remove than the left, and by the time he was done, silent tears slipped from the corners of her eyes. They tore at him, as did his own thoughtlessness at not anticipating that she'd choose to walk all that way instead of asking for a buggy. Seeing the bloodied blisters on her feet caused other images to surface too—ones he'd already spent a lifetime burying since the end of the war.

Knowing what he needed to do next, he ached for her. "All right ... That's behind us."

She wiped her eyes, hesitant to look at him. "Is it bad?"

Muted laughter and the conversation of stable hands returning from lunch drifted in, and Ridley grabbed her boots. "Change of plans." Before she could protest, he handed her the boots, lifted her in his arms, and headed for the rear of the stable. As they left, she glanced back in the direction of the voices, understanding.

At the rear door, he spotted Jedediah and four others walking past. He waited for them to move from the line of sight before cutting across the meadow to a wooded path leading down to the creek. It didn't bother him in the least to be seen with her like this. But he knew it would bother her.

"Are you all right?" he asked, once they reached the shade of the trees.

She nodded. "They still hurt, but having the boots off feels like heaven by comparison." She looked downward. "Thank you, Mr. Cooper. For your discretion, among other things."

Gone was any trace of wounded pride, and he smiled — sorry for why she was in his arms, but not about her being there. "I'm nothing if not discreet. But ..." He glanced at her, liking this perspective. "Don't you think we can finally move past the Mr. Cooper, *Olivia*?"

She pursed her lips. An adorable act that challenged his former contentedness at merely holding her.

"Think about it, my dear," he continued, mimicking the refined speech of what — he was certain — she would consider a proper Southern gentleman. "With all we've been through together, don't you think we've at least achieved the modicum of acquaintanceship that would allow us the intimate privilege of addressing one another by our Christian names?"

Surprise lit her expression. "That was actually quite lovely. The way you said it, I mean."

He stopped short. "Don't make me drop you, Olivia."

Her arms tightened around his neck. "Very well ... *Ridley*. But I must admit, I'm impressed you know the word *modicum*."

He feigned losing hold of her, and she squealed, gripping him tighter. Her eyes, the purest cornflower blue, were dark-rimmed and perceptive, and the slow-coming, shy but receptive smile subtly mirrored in her expression was all woman.

Ridley was fine until her gaze slid to his mouth and lingered. Then all he could think about was how her lips would feel against his and how sweet her kiss would taste. He hoped Betsy was right about the woman he'd set his sights on not standing a chance, even if given a running start. Because he wasn't about to give Olivia Aberdeen any kind of advantage — fair or not.

"Where are we going?" she whispered.

Reaching for patience nature hadn't given him, Ridley continued walking. "Just up ahead, to the creek. Then to see Rachel. She'll know what to do for you."

A little frown formed on the bridge of her nose. "Who's Rachel?"

He chose not to answer that particular question, knowing some things were best experienced firsthand.

Olivia looked ahead at the cabin nestled at the edge of the woods, not that far from the mansion, then back at Ridley. Glad he was with her and grateful for his strong back, she still wrestled with embarrassment over what he'd just done for her at the creek. "I'm sorry you've had to carry me all this way."

"I'm not, so don't you be."

She'd never been carried in a man's arms like this. She'd expected to be on her wedding night, but Charles had simply led her into the bedroom and closed the door. Remembering what followed made her stomach knot tight. But she didn't want to think about Charles right now.

Or ever again.

"Thank you for what you did," she whispered.

His grip on her tightened. "For a minute there, I thought you were going to faint on me."

"For a minute there, I thought I was too. I'm sure I would have ... if you hadn't kept talking."

One side of his mouth edged up. "You were surprised I knew that many words, I could tell."

She made sure he saw her smirk. "Perhaps I felt a *modicum* of surprise, yes."

They laughed, the banter easing her embarrassment. While the creek water had stung the open blisters, it had helped loosen her stockings, stuck with dried blood to her feet. But the stinging paled in comparison to what followed. With Ridley's back turned, she'd removed her stockings as far as her ankles. Then, with a tenderness she'd not imagined a man capable of possessing, he'd gently coerced the fabric free from the open wounds. Much to her shame, but with her gratitude.

She sneaked looks at him, wondering how much he knew about her circumstances—about *her*—and if one of the servants had told him about Charles, about what had happened. Because certainly, they knew. Yet no sooner had the thought surfaced, than she banished it. She did not want to think about that now.

As they drew closer to the cabin, her earlier concerns returned. "Are you certain she won't mind us showing up unannounced?"

He nodded. "Rachel's not that kind of person. Not only won't she mind you coming ..." He gave her a funny smile. "She probably already knows we're on our way."

She looked back at him. "You mean … she has the second sight?" She'd heard of people who got glimpses of the future before it happened.

"I wouldn't say that. But the woman does know things. And she's gifted at healing too. She doctors all the servants and the stable hands. She's the one who's been making the poultices for Seabird's leg. That healed up with hardly a scar."

The cabin was similar to the ones on the other side of the mansion, only larger. With apparently little regard given to their order, clay pots of all shapes and sizes dotted the front and side yards, their borders overflowing with herbs. Olivia recognized milk thistle and primrose, but none of the others.

Before she and Ridley even reached the front porch, the door opened, and a woman stood waiting inside, in the shadows. Almost as if she'd been expecting them.

"You bringing me a patient today, Mr. Cooper." It wasn't a question.

"Afternoon, Rachel." Ridley nodded. "Yes, ma'am, I am. Rachel Norris, may I present — "

"I know who this is. Me and Missus Olivia Aberdeen, we go back a ways, you might say. We met each other before."

Olivia squinted, wishing she could see the woman better, certain Rachel Norris was mistaken. As if complying with her unspoken request, the woman slowly stepped into the sunlight.

"You and me got a glimpse of each other awhile back, ma'am. I'm sure you 'member. Though we ain't had the pleasure of meetin' face to face yet."

Seeing the woman's dark brown curls and skin the color of well-creamed coffee, Olivia felt a memory shake loose. Then with jarring recollection, she knew where she'd seen this woman before. From her bedroom, that first morning at Belle Meade. Rachel Norris had been wearing a cloak then, her hair wild and free. What Olivia hadn't seen at that distance, however, was the woman's startling blue eyes. Eyes that told an all-too-familiar story in a single glance. Eyes gently wreathed by time that seemed to be reading every one of her thoughts at that moment.

Olivia bowed her head, her face growing warm. "I … hope we're not bothering you, ma'am," she offered, feeling Ridley move his shoulder. Only then did she realize she was digging her nails into him.

"Why would you be sayin' such a thing now, Missus Aberdeen? When Mr. Cooper already told you, you weren't." Rachel stepped to one side and gestured for them to enter.

Certain now that she didn't want to go inside, Olivia had little choice when Ridley entered. But at least he was with her, and would stay, she felt sure.

A pungent aroma layered the cabin, at once sweet and savory. And overpowering. But no wonder, with dried clumps of herbs hanging from every rafter along with onions, beets, and corn—various fruits as well.

Olivia sneaked a look at their hostess as they passed. Rachel Norris wore a dress of dark green and brown, colors of the earth. Her curls were swept to the side today, held together by a thin leather strip. The woman was older than Olivia would have guessed from first sighting. Midway through her fifties, maybe even sixty. Despite her years, she was still beautiful, in an exotic sort of way, and graceful in the manner of a fox. Which Olivia thought seemed appropriate as she looked around, feeling as though she'd entered a den.

Rachel pointed to a worn settee by the cold hearth, and Ridley crossed the room, gently depositing Olivia there. She sat, boots in her lap, the soles of her feet tender on the plank-wood floor.

Rachel eyed her—namely, her bare feet—and Olivia arranged her skirt to cover them.

"You either a strong-headed woman, Missus Aberdeen, or you's a fool. Which is it?"

Ridley laughed, then quickly cleared his throat. But Olivia could only stare, wishing her mouth wasn't as dry as cotton. "I assure you, ma'am. I am *not* a fool."

Rachel looked at her with those penetrating eyes. "I didn't take you for one, Missus Aberdeen. Just wanted to hear it from *you*. Are you hungry? Either of you? I've got some soup simmering on the stove."

Olivia nodded, skeptical about what might be in it but half starved. "Yes, please. That would be nice."

Ridley motioned toward the door. "None for me, Rachel. Thank you. I need to get back to work. But I'll return for you shortly, Mrs. Aberdeen." He looked back at Rachel. "How long do you think—"

"Two hours, sir," Rachel said. Then looked at Olivia again. "Make it three." She walked him to the door.

Olivia leaned forward on the settee, trying none too discreetly to capture his attention, but he didn't look at her. Not until the very last second, just as the door closed.

Then he winked. And smiled.

A while later, lying on the settee as Rachel Norris had instructed, her bare feet propped on pillows and her appetite sated, Olivia observed the woman from behind. Rachel worked methodically, grinding pungent herbs with a mortar and pestle, then mixing them with liquids from dark glass bottles to create a mysterious concoction.

The soup, on the other hand, had been filling and surprisingly tasty—though Olivia guessed Rachel Norris was a woman who held nutrition in higher regard than appeal to the palate. Still, she'd been thankful for the woman's generosity and had told her as much.

Minutes passed, and Olivia watched in silence until she couldn't take the suspense any longer. She forced a sweetness to her voice, hoping to draw conversation from the woman. "I'm lying over here wondering what it is you're doing over there. And if that's what you're going to put on my feet."

No response. The woman didn't even turn around.

"Because if it is ..." Olivia laughed, but it sounded coerced, even to her. "I think I'd like to know what's in the mixture."

Rachel Norris kept stirring.

Olivia leaned and peered to the side, trying to get Rachel's attention, and nearly fell off the settee, but caught herself just in time.

Perhaps the woman was deaf and could only read lips. Olivia didn't think so, but in her mind she went back over their first moments in the cabin, trying to remember if Rachel had been facing them whenever she'd responded. Finally, unable to draw any positive conclusion, Olivia gave up that thread of thought.

She didn't think Rachel Norris was deaf. Rude, perhaps ...

Hanging directly over Olivia's head was a particularly large clump of dried onions, and she stared at it, wondering how long it had been there and if—

She squinted, certain she'd seen the clump move.

Tense, she waited, watching for it to happen again and relishing how much she was going to enjoy giving Ridley Cooper a piece of her mind for bringing her here.

Finally, her nerves a jumble, she sat up, mindful of her feet. "As I'm thinking this through ... maybe a better course of action would be for me to seek out a doctor's advice first. *Before* I bother you by seeking treatment. Then if his remedies don't provide improvement, I could come and see you again." But if she ever got out of this cabin, she knew she wasn't coming back.

She waited. Still no response.

She tried putting weight on her feet, then questioned that choice. Her feet weren't as sore as they had been earlier with her boots on, but walking would be painful. She'd have to go barefoot in the dirt too, and that meant cleaning the blisters all over again. That thought alone was deterrent enough. But still, she'd had her fill of the silence.

Olivia raised her chin and cleared her throat with intent.

Not a peep.

"I know you can hear me, Miss Norris. And I would appreciate—"

"It's *Missus* Norris, ma'am." Rachel turned around, bowl in hand. "I was married. Years ago. My husband be dead now. Like yours," she added in a softer voice.

Olivia moved her mouth to speak but nothing came out at first. "So ..." She worked to couch the truth gently. "You *have* been listening to me this entire time, and yet you didn't respond."

Rachel set the bowl on a side table and pulled up a chair. "That's 'cause you wasn't askin' me anything, ma'am. You's just over here *wonderin'* this, *thinkin'* about that ... plannin' out loud what you's gonna do. You carried the conversation all by your lonesome. Pretty good at it too."

As she had the first time she'd seen this woman, all Olivia could do was stare.

"Besides ..." Rachel scooted her chair closer and reached for the bowl. "You didn't really want me to say nothin'. Your voice can be real sweet, ma'am, just like your words." A warm smile hinted at the corners of Rachel's mouth while more than warming the striking blue of her eyes. "But really, Missus Aberdeen, I hear what you ain't sayin' *between* all them words. You just wanna be gone from here. Away from me and outta my cabin."

"Why ..." Olivia exhaled a humorless laugh, flustered at the woman's directness and embarrassed now at having been so transparent. "That's simply not true, Mrs. Norris. I'm happy to be here and appreciate what you're—"

Rachel cocked her head and looked at her with such kind yet indisputable challenge that Olivia felt the words of the well-meant but false courtesy die on her lips. She didn't like how Rachel Norris saw through her so easily … like someone else she knew.

"Somethin' I learned long ago, ma'am, is the more the words, the less the meanin'. But I can understand you feelin' the way you do, I guess. You's a white woman, after all. You's used to different things, different ways. But I'd still like to help you, if you're willin'." Rachel motioned. "Now you go on and lay back down there, ma'am. I need to get this slathered on there good and thick. Give it time to seep into them wounds real good 'fore Mr. Cooper get back."

Not knowing exactly why, Olivia did as the woman asked. And as Rachel Norris smoothed the unpleasant-smelling cream over the soles and heels of her feet, Olivia thought of what Rachel had said to her and knew why Ridley Cooper liked this woman so much.

She didn't know what was in the mixture but after an hour and then two, she no longer cared. The pain moved from a steady thrum to a distant echo, until finally it was all but gone.

Later that night, Olivia lay in bed beneath a thin sheet, turning first this way, then that, welcoming even a whisper of breeze from outside. Finally, she rose and padded across to the open window, wearing stockings per Rachel's instructions, along with another application of that awful-smelling — but wonder-working — mixture containing who-knew-what.

She wondered again about Rachel Norris and her place in everything here at Belle Meade. Per Ridley, Rachel doctored the servants and the stable hands and even the horses, which explained what she did here. But the woman's cabin was considerably nicer than the other servants' quarters and was set apart from the others too. It simply made Olivia question if there was some other relationship to the family that—

A knock on the door brought Olivia around. Who would be awake at this hour? She opened the door a fraction and glimpsed Mary standing a few feet away outside Cousin Lizzie's bedroom.

Lizzie's door opened and indistinct bits of conversation and laughter punctuated the quiet. Then Mary turned and headed for the stairs.

"Mary," Olivia whispered once Lizzie's door was closed. She wasn't sure what she was going to say to the girl, but she'd been looking for opportunities to speak with her in the hope of smoothing whatever rift was between them.

Mary paused, oil lamp in hand, and the light cast a golden sphere about her, revealing the dull expression the girl seemed to adopt whenever they spoke.

"Good evening, Mrs. Aberdeen. Is there something you need?"

Always the same starched politeness and thinly veiled dislike.

Olivia stepped onto the porch, welcoming the breeze. "You're up awfully late tonight, Mary." She smiled, doubting the offering of friendship would be returned. Which it wasn't. "Having trouble sleeping too?"

"I needed to give something to Cousin Lizzie, Mrs. Aberdeen. Which I did. Now ... good night, ma'am." She turned to leave.

"Mary—"

The girl stopped, her stiff manner saying she would've preferred not to. But proper breeding—which Olivia knew only too well—wouldn't allow it.

"Please, Mary, as I've said before, I welcome you calling me Olivia. I'm not *that* much older than you, after all."

Mary nodded, but said nothing.

Realizing this was going to be an uphill battle, Olivia chanced another step closer, searching for the right words. "While this might not be the best time ... I've been wanting to tell you that I'm very grateful to you and your family for welcoming me to Belle Meade."

Mary made no move to respond, and Olivia felt a need to fill the silence. After all, she'd initiated the conversation.

"Ever since my own mother died, your mother's friendship has been a source of encouragement for me. I don't know what I would have done without her. But of course, being her daughter, you already understand what a wonderful woman she is."

Mary's lips took a surprising upward turn. "Oh, of course, I do. Since *I'm* her daughter, as you said."

The girl's tone seemed at odds with her smile, but Olivia forged ahead, eager to mend the tension between them. "I've wanted to compliment you on your piano playing the other evening. Your hands move over those keys with so little effort, it seems. You're quite gifted, Mary."

"Not as gifted as Selene."

As soon as she said it, Mary bit her lower lip, and Olivia felt a stab of pain for the girl, already having witnessed the preferential attention the older daughter garnered at the younger's expense.

Olivia managed a smile. "I don't believe that's true for one minute. Selene's older. She's simply had more opportunity to practice, that's all. Besides, you have your own gifts. I've seen you sit and work for hours on a piece of lace until every stitch and loop is perfect."

Mary's expression softened slightly, as though she wanted to open up but couldn't.

Olivia glanced down at the girl's lace collar. "Your work is exquisite, Mary. As your mother and I were walking the other day, I commented to her about it, and she was swift to agree. So I know she feels the very same."

Even in the flicker of lamplight, Olivia could see Mary's features go shuttered again. So the girl's sweet smile was especially surprising.

"How *kind* of you to share my mother's opinion with me." Mary glanced toward the stairs. "It's late, so I'm certain you'll understand that I need to take my leave. I bid you good evening, Olivia."

Mary was already to the stairs before Olivia could respond. "Good night, Mary," she whispered, knowing she'd said something to upset the girl. But having no idea what.

Back in her room, Olivia sat by the window, drinking in the quiet and saying a prayer for Mary Harding.

Moonlight bathed the meadow, and the corrals below were silvery still and quiet. The wisteria on the lattice had nearly finished blooming, but she still caught whiffs of the heady fragrance. The old Harding cabin was dark, which wasn't a surprise. It was late, and Ridley woke with the sun, as he'd told her.

Barely had the thought fully formed when she saw someone step off the porch. Knowing only Ridley and Uncle Bob lived there, she easily distinguished which of them it was. Uncertain at first if he could see her—or if he even knew which bedroom was hers—she received an answer when Ridley raised an arm in greeting.

She smiled and stuck an arm out the window and waved back, careful not to lean out too far. Feeling like they were doing something they shouldn't, she did it again. Just because she could.

Chapter
TWENTY-TWO

*T*oday's the day you're mine, girl," Ridley said softly, smiling at the sideways look Seabird gave him from across the corral and aware of the crowd they'd gathered. Jedediah and a handful of other stable hands watched from the gate, as did Jimmy—the young boy he'd met on his first day—wearing the same old worn cap pulled low to his ears.

Perhaps it was due to the afternoon temperature, which held steady at stifling instead of racing well past an all-out swelter, but Ridley had a hopefulness in him today. He sensed Seabird's resistance waning, and he aimed to take full advantage.

The past week had seen him so busy with the stud farm and foaling he hadn't spent the time he'd wanted to with Seabird—or Olivia, for that matter. But today he was committed to doing just that. On both counts.

"She lookin' at you different, sir," Uncle Bob whispered behind him. "That's good ... Mighty good."

Ridley pulled a piece of cut-up apple from his pocket and held it out. Seabird's nostrils twitched.

"Come on, girl." He inched forward, palm open, offering extended. "It's here for the taking. Just come and get it."

Seabird tossed her head and whinnied, then took a step. Followed by another. Ridley smiled, having grown to know this horse's looks and moods almost better than his own. She was a pretty thing and fleet footed. Her leg had healed better than even Uncle Bob expected, though she'd still never be the racer Gem was. When General Harding had observed her earlier in the week, Ridley had seen his regret. But a deal was a deal, Ridley had taken pleasure in reminding him.

Seabird stopped no more than a foot away, and Ridley, palm extended, felt something akin to gratitude welling up inside. He slowly closed the distance, partly relieved, but mostly excited that, finally, he'd convinced this mare that she could—

Seabird bolted. In a flash, the mare was across the corral, clearing the fence with a foot to spare. If Ridley hadn't seen it, he wouldn't have believed it. At full gallop, giving the wind something to envy, she headed for deeper pasture, never slowing.

A chorus of whoops and laughter rose behind him from the stable hands, and if Ridley hadn't been so shocked, he might have joined them. "Did you just see that, Uncle Bob?"

"I did, sir . . . But I still ain't believin' it. She ain't never run like that. And she ain't never been a jumper either."

Jimmy ran toward him. "Good Lawd a' Mighty, Mr. Ridley! I ain't never seen a horse do that. Standin' still as a tree, she was." The boy struck a comical pose. "Then off she go like a cannon!" He laughed, falling into step with Ridley. "Want me to saddle up a mount for you, sir? So you can go fetch her?"

As he always did, Ridley tugged the curved bill of Jimmy's cap an inch lower, earning a grin. "Thanks, but I think I'll walk." He shot a look at Uncle Bob, who just nodded, silently confirming what Ridley already knew.

Seabird had met him on his turf, with his rules. Now he needed to show her the same courtesy.

He found her in the lower pasture, about a mile out, maybe more. Just standing there, waiting on him. At least that's what it felt like. He got within twenty feet of her, and Seabird didn't move. Just looked at him.

He started to move closer, then stopped. He couldn't say why. He only knew not to. Not yet.

He stood there for a while, the sun on his face. Then he knelt until his knees started aching, and then he finally sat. Just watching her. Admiring her beauty and the speed she'd displayed and realizing for the first time what a privilege these animals gave to men. To be carried upon their backs. To benefit from their strength. They carried kings and paupers alike. Rich and poor. Into battle and into market. They pulled cannons during war and ploughs before and after. What was it Uncle Bob had said about them that night on the mountain? Something about how God had made a wondrous thing when he'd made these creatures.

And it was true.

The sun slowly sank beyond the hillside, casting an orange glow across the meadow and turning the field grass to a lustered gold. The chirrup of crickets accompanied the first pinprick of light in the darkening sky, and that's when Ridley heard the rustle of the grass. He looked back.

Seabird walked toward him, a steady, measured gait, and stopped just inches away. Ridley slowly extended his hand, the piece of apple cupped inside. She made quick work of it, then drew closer and nudged his head. He laughed, slowly rising. "Just like a woman," he whispered. "Always wanting more."

He leaned in and touched his forehead to hers and gave her a gentle rub. "Thank you, Miss Birdie," he whispered, remembering what Uncle Bob had called her once. "Thank you for all you give."

Elizabeth took a sip from the china cup. "Mmmm ... This is delicious, Livvy. What is it?"

Working at sounding nonchalant, Olivia leaned forward in the porch rocker and poured herself a small taste. "It's a blend of tea I wanted you to try."

Elizabeth laughed. "Well, I know it's tea, dear. I meant ... do you know what's in it? I detect a hint of orange." She took another sip, her eyes narrowing. "And clove, perhaps. But also something else I can't quite identify. It leaves a strong, though not unpleasant, aftertaste."

Olivia smiled, feeling a flutter of triumph. "There *is* some orange peel in there, I believe. And cloves, as you've said." She took a sip, remembering how she'd questioned the very same thing. "But I think what you're tasting might be gingerroot."

Elizabeth nodded enthusiastically. "Yes! I imagine you're right. I love ginger!"

Smiling, Olivia imagined how pleased Rachel would be when she told her about Elizabeth's response.

After personally experiencing the benefits of Rachel's herbs herself, Olivia hadn't wasted any time in sharing with Rachel the specifics about Elizabeth's condition. Though not the doctor's prognosis. She felt certain the herbs could be of help to Elizabeth as well. And over the past several days, Rachel had gathered the necessary ingredients and worked to perfect what she'd since named "Missus Harding's Special Blend."

The first dozen or so batches of dried herbs and fruit—while no doubt beneficial to the body—had *not* been pleasant to the palate. So Rachel had mixed and remixed, then brewed and brewed again. Olivia's job had been not only to taste but to determine how it settled on the stomach. Finally, Rachel came upon a combination she deemed "nature's perfect ingredients," which Olivia then deemed as delightfully tasteful and—over the course of the past two weeks— also *friendly* to one's digestion.

Olivia sneaked a look at Elizabeth. She'd made the decision to introduce the tea to her quietly, knowing some people weren't open to trying what many termed "Negro remedies." She didn't consider Aunt Elizabeth to be among them, but she wasn't as certain about the general and didn't want to take that risk. Not when she truly believed Rachel's herbs could be a factor in Elizabeth regaining her strength.

Olivia sipped her tea, slowly rocking back and forth. Then on a whim, she stuck out her leg, smiling and angling her foot this way and that until Elizabeth took notice. "Thank you again, Aunt Elizabeth, for the loan of your boots. They fit perfectly."

Elizabeth grinned. "I'm so glad. They were always a little snug for me so I rarely wore them." She frowned. "But really, Livvy ... Next time, ask Susanna or Jedediah to call for a wagon if both of the carriages are gone. There's no need for you to walk all that way."

Olivia simply smiled and let the comment go by.

Elizabeth stretched her legs out on the chaise. "The general is speaking very highly of you these days, my dear."

"Is he?" Olivia glanced beside her, pleased at the news.

"He said the inventory report you prepared was the most detailed he's received from an employee, especially for the stable supplies, which reflects most positively on you and your talents, dear." She smiled. "And likewise on me for recommending he hire you."

Olivia laughed. "Thank you, Aunt Elizabeth. I'm so glad he approves." If the woman only knew *why* the report for the stables had been so extraordinarily detailed ...

Olivia looked toward the corrals, then the mares' stable, and as she did with growing frequency these days, she wondered if he was working there or perhaps with the stallions today. Ridley Cooper was the reason she'd spent nearly a full week doing what should have taken her no more than three days. He was her "reward" for braving the stables, and—contrary to lording it over her as she'd first thought he might do—he, too, had complimented her on the thorough manner in which she inventoried all the items.

The more time she spent with him, the more she wanted to spend. He made her laugh. Not only at things he did, but also at herself. Though she felt guilty about it at times. She *was* in mourning, after all. Yet if not for the dull gray and black dresses she wore day in and day out and the reminder of her social standing—or lack thereof—she could almost forget about being in mourning when she was around him.

Almost.

Two days ago she'd seen him in the kitchen, and he'd said there was a favor he wanted to ask of her. Then they'd been interrupted by one of the stable hands needing Ridley's assistance, and she hadn't seen him since. Partly for that reason, she'd decided to begin with inventorying the horse tack this month. She wanted to know what favor he wanted. But she also dreaded the long walks to the other destinations. Not that she was about to complain. She'd made six dollars in the past three weeks. *Six.* And she still had three dollars and sixteen cents left of her earnings. And this after sending her measurements with Selene to the Hardings' personal dressmaker. Per Olivia's request, the seamstress was sewing her a simple shirtwaist and skirt in appropriate mourning colors. Something more practical for everyday. Olivia had never known earning a wage could be so rewarding.

"Would you please pour me another cup, Livvy? If there's enough?"

"Oh, there's plenty." Olivia refilled her aunt's cup, praying the herbs would strengthen her the way Rachel thought they would.

Despite the warmth of late June, Elizabeth cupped her hands around the delicate fine china. "I enjoyed attending church services yesterday with the general and the girls, even though I had to be in that horrid wheelchair." She threw a look back over her shoulder. "It was wonderful to see everyone again." She reached for Olivia's hand. "But I certainly missed you being there, Livvy. I was glad to learn, upon returning home, how *swiftly* your headache improved."

Olivia didn't miss the knowing look Elizabeth gave her and could tell her aunt knew the truth about her staying behind from church.

Conceding the point with a gentle shrug, Olivia looked out across the meadow. "I used the time to read. And to think. Like I do every Sunday morning." What she couldn't say, but what was true, was that she missed the singing most of all. The hymns. The purity of the voices and harmonies rising to the rafters.

"I understand your not coming with us, Livvy. Considering how many people know you at McKendree Church. But I do so wish you could go to church somewhere. I think you'd find it an encouragement now. Perhaps you could go someplace where no one knows who you are?"

Olivia couldn't help but smile. "Well, that's an encouraging prospect, Aunt. Choose a church based upon no one knowing me and with the intent of hiding who I am."

"Oh, my dear ..." Elizabeth's expression turned pained. "Forgive me. How thoughtless ... I didn't mean for it to come out that way. I only meant to say—"

"No, no." Olivia gently squeezed her arm, feeling badly now for having made light. "Forgive me for joking. I completely understand what you intended, Aunt Elizabeth. And I love you for it. But I think we both know that my going to church anywhere in Nashville is not advisable. Perhaps in time ... But for now, I'm fine."

Elizabeth smiled and gave a semblance of a nod.

Moments passed in easy solitude between them, as they often did. Then Elizabeth gently cleared her throat. "Livvy, I ... I promised the general I would speak to you about something, dear."

Finding that prelude none too comforting, Olivia turned.

"The general and I will be hosting a dinner party sometime next month for a number of his ... *colleagues* from out of town with whom he fought in the war. Now before you say anything"—Elizabeth rushed her words, as though sensing the resistance building in Olivia—"I want you to know from the very outset that both the general and I realize you're still in mourning and that you're not interested in *any* way in marriage right now. Which is as it should be. This would only be a dinner party where you would meet and visit with our guests."

"All of whom will be older and unmarried, I assume?" Olivia asked, remembering the general's comment awhile back, while also honing in on the phrase *out of town*.

"But, Livvy dear, we can't help but think that if the right gentleman were to come along—in time—you might be willing to consider his proposal. Someone kind and gentle. Someone with whom you got along. Someone who was nothing like … your late husband."

Although Olivia loathed the idea of remarriage, she knew it was inevitable. After all, despite what Aunt Elizabeth had said to the contrary, she couldn't—and didn't—expect to live at Belle Meade forever. And honestly, why would she want to? While she was carving out some friendships here, she wasn't welcomed by anyone in Nashville. And there would come a time—a time Olivia was loathe to even consider—when Elizabeth would no longer be here, and her own time of being here at Belle Meade would end.

She had no idea where she'd go then. Charleston and Savannah were lovely cities, she'd heard. As were Mobile and Chattanooga. But she had a feeling once Elizabeth was gone, which she prayed again would be a long way off, almost anywhere in the South would be preferable to Nashville.

Olivia did her best to remove defensiveness from her tone. "I'm so grateful to you and the general for all you're doing for me, Aunt Elizabeth. And, of course, I'll attend the dinner. But please, *please* communicate to General Harding that I'm in no way interested in pursuing anything with any of these gentlemen. I'm simply not ready."

"I completely agree with you, my dear. It's far too soon. The general will be certain to tell them you're in mourning. And they'll see your manner of dress of course, so there'll be no misunderstanding, I promise."

Having no choice, Olivia nodded, determined not to dwell on this for now. After all, she had at least one year—if not two—before she would have to consider any man's offer.

If an offer even came.

A while later, Olivia finished a chapter in a novel she was reading aloud to Elizabeth when she looked up to see Ridley striding toward the house, sun on his face, his dark hair disheveled. His sleeves were rolled up to reveal muscular forearms, and his work trousers were caked eight inches deep in dust and dirt.

He stopped a few feet from the porch, and even though she knew his smile wasn't aimed only at her, it felt like it was.

"Afternoon, ladies. Mrs. Harding, I hope you're feeling better today."

"I am. Thank you, Mr. Cooper." Elizabeth gestured. "Might I interest you in a glass of lemonade or perhaps a cup of hot tea? Though I doubt the latter will hold as much appeal today."

"No, thank you, ma'am. But I appreciate it."

"According to my husband" — Elizabeth smiled — "you have recently bested him in a gentleman's agreement, Mr. Cooper."

Olivia looked from Ridley to Elizabeth, then back again, not having heard about this. Ridley looked down briefly. "I would hardly call it besting him, Mrs. Harding. Your husband and I did have an agreement though. I fulfilled my end of the bargain, and he did his. But he managed to gain a fair amount in the process, I assure you."

"He usually does." Elizabeth regarded the man in the yard below, her expression hinting at pride. "But from what he tells me, one of his prize thoroughbreds now belongs to you."

Olivia stared. Ridley Cooper owned one of General Harding's thoroughbreds? It had to be the mare she'd seen him working with so often.

"Yes, ma'am." He nodded, pleasure in his eyes. "And I'm grateful to have her. But I'm sorry . . . I didn't mean to interrupt you ladies. I just came to see if Mrs. Aberdeen," Ridley continued, hazel eyes moving to Olivia, "is coming to inventory today."

Olivia sensed a subtle hope in his tone, but wondered if it was her wishful thinking. "I am, Mr. Cooper. In fact, I was on my way there now." She narrowed her eyes, enjoying her higher vantage point. "Is there a problem?"

"No, ma'am. No problem. I just came across something else you might want to inventory. If you're coming now, I'll walk with you."

Olivia could tell by his behavior there was something he wasn't telling her. But it didn't matter. She wanted to go. "I need to get the ledger, and I'll be right there."

She went upstairs to get the book and returned minutes later to find Ridley standing on the porch steps speaking to Elizabeth. Catching bits and pieces of what he was saying, Olivia padded softly to the open front door and paused to the side, not wanting to interrupt just yet.

"Yes, ma'am, I was. I was assigned in Nashville. For most of the war, anyway."

"Did you have opportunity to meet the general?"

"No, ma'am, but ... I knew who he was."

"Of course you did." Warmth softened Elizabeth's voice. "I'm guessing every Confederate soldier in Nashville knew who he was. My husband is the type of man people seem to notice." Wifely pride colored her tone. "You *do* know he was incarcerated, do you not?"

"Yes, ma'am." Ridley's voice grew quiet. "I knew about that."

"The Federals took him from me and delivered him to a Northern penitentiary. Fort Mackinac. Have you heard of it?"

"Yes, ma'am ... I have."

Elizabeth sighed. "It was an awful, awful time for us all. I feared he would freeze to death up there. As it was, when he stepped from the train upon returning home I scarcely recognized him. He seemed so ... changed."

"I'm sure it was a difficult time for you, Mrs. Harding."

The silence lengthened.

Feeling guilty about having listened for so long, Olivia made a shuffling sound against the carpet and then bustled through the doorway, ledger clutched to her chest.

Ridley lifted his gaze, looking almost relieved to see her.

He was quiet as they walked to the barn, but when he bypassed the door and continued on around to the side, Olivia's curiosity heightened.

"I thought you said you came across something I needed to inventory."

He paused at the corner of the building, his reticence from moments earlier all but gone. "I said something you 'might' want to inventory. Big difference. And I need for you to close your eyes."

"Why?"

He smiled. "Just give me your hand and close your eyes, Olivia."

"There's not a horse around the corner, is there?" She'd gotten the occasional feeling he wanted to help her get over her fear of horses, and she wasn't the least bit interested.

Hand outstretched, he gave her a look that said she should know better. "No, there isn't. I wouldn't do that to you. I promise."

The way he said it, the way he looked at her, she knew it was true. Still, she was hesitant to put her hand in his. But that had nothing to do with horses.

Chapter
TWENTY-THREE

Ridley led her around the corner, watching to make sure she didn't peek. Her hand was so tiny in his, and she clung so tightly. None too certain he'd be able to talk her into trying this, he was determined to give it his best. Especially when remembering the blisters on her feet from last month. "Okay, stop here."

She did, her eyes still closed, holding the ledger against her chest.

"And now, m'lady ..." He gave her hand a little squeeze. "Your chariot awaits!"

She opened her eyes. And blinked.

Judging from her expression, Ridley guessed she either didn't make the connection to what it was or—more likely—didn't like it.

"It's so *small*." She released his hand. "But ... what's it for?"

"It's a horse cart." He placed a hand on one of the wheels. "Something to get you back and forth between the businesses on the plantation."

She eyed him, then the cart again. "This is very generous of you. But a small cart or a regular carriage ... It still has to have a *horse* to pull it, correct?"

"Don't make up your mind just yet." Ridley gestured, and Jimmy walked from the stable on cue, cap tucked low over his ears, smiling for all he was worth—and leading a Shetland pony behind him.

Ridley heard a bubble of laughter escape from Olivia before she clamped a hand over her mouth. A glint of possibility lit her eyes. As if he'd rehearsed it, the miniature pony looked over at her, a bushy tuft of golden-brown hair hanging down in his eyes, his short stubby legs working to keep up with Jimmy's pace.

Olivia's sigh held humor. "He's adorable. But he's still a horse."

"Actually, he's more like a ... *quarter* horse." Ridley waited, seeing if she'd catch it.

She cut her eyes at him and slowly ... her mouth tipped upward.

He shrugged. "At least it made you smile. Have you met Jimmy yet?" He gestured. "This young man helped me build this for you. We couldn't run Belle Meade without him. Jimmy, this is Mrs. Aberdeen."

The boy doffed his worn cap, ducking his head as he did. "I know who you is, ma'am. I seen you walkin' before. *A lot*. You must like to walk."

Olivia slid Ridley another look, and he gave her a quick wink, hoping she knew her secret was still safe with him. Her tiny smile made him think she understood.

"Yes, Jimmy, I *do* like to walk. For the most part, anyway."

"Mr. Ridley here, he done fixed you up a real nice little ridin' cart, ma'am."

"I didn't do it alone, Jimmy. Remember, you helped me."

The young boy smiled. "Yes, sir. I did." Jimmy pulled on the pony's lead rope. "I get Copper all hitched up for you, Missus Aberdeen, then you can take him for a turn."

Olivia's laugh came feather soft. "That's not necessary, Jimmy. I ... ahh ... don't need to go anywhere right now."

Jimmy's smile slid away. "But don't you wanna try it out, ma'am? Least see how it rides?"

Ridley knew if he'd asked her that, she'd have turned him down flat. But Jimmy asking? That was different. He'd chosen his young apprentice wisely.

Olivia's lips started moving before the words were formed. "Well ... I ..." Then she stopped, and the prettiest smile spread across her face. "Why don't you show me instead, Jimmy? First, I mean. Then maybe I could do it after you."

Ridley inwardly shook his head. Oh, she was good.

Jimmy set to work—oblivious to the woman's ploy—and had the little pony hitched to the cart in no time. The boy climbed in, reins in hand. "Are ya sure you don't wanna go with me, Missus Aberdeen? This gonna be fun!"

"Oh, I'm quite sure." She gave a little wave. "I want to see you first."

With a smile, Jimmy gave the reins a slap and little Copper took off at a nice easy pace, just like they'd practiced, his stubby little legs stomping.

"Now see there." Ridley sidled up to Olivia. "Doesn't that look like fun? Nothing to be afraid of. Just a nice smooth ride."

She nodded, watching Jimmy and Copper's every move. Jimmy completed half a circuit around the meadow and headed on back, just as Ridley had instructed, when a couple of mares came galloping up from the lower pasture. Copper saw them, and his short legs started churning. The Shetland pony was no match for the mares' speed, but he gave it his all.

"Whoa, boy!" Jimmy yelled, pulling back on the reins at first, the cart bumping and bouncing beneath him. Then the boy started laughing. "Get 'em, Copper," he yelled, slapping the reins. "We can catch 'em, boy!"

Ridley watched as his brilliant idea unraveled before his eyes— even while part of him wanted to laugh.

Jimmy finally brought the cart to a standstill beside them, laughing nearly as hard as Copper was breathing. "I told you, Missus Aberdeen. It was gonna be fun!"

Olivia's smile blossomed. "And you were right, Jimmy! It *looked* like fun! But I think I'll wait on taking that ride for now. For Copper's sake," she added quickly. "He appears to be a tad winded at the moment." She turned to Ridley and laid a hand on his arm. "Thank you, Mr. Cooper, for thinking of me," she said, her voice lowering. She leaned in, smiling, and whispered, "But not … on … your … life." And with that, she turned and walked into the stable.

Ridley started to follow, to get her to reconsider. Then he decided to bide his time and give her some room. After all, he had a backup plan.

Later the following afternoon, Olivia finished her day's work in the tack room, discovering the inventorying process much easier the second time around—and also discovering Ridley Cooper to be a kinder, more thoughtful man than she'd previously believed. A continuing theme, it seemed.

Still, after seeing how little Copper had behaved while pulling that cart yesterday, there was no way she was putting herself in that situation. But she did appreciate what Ridley, along with young Jimmy, had done for her. She'd find a way to thank them both.

She picked up the nearly empty glass of iced lemonade Ridley had brought her earlier and drank the last of it, the lemony pulp tasting both tangy and sweet. The glass still felt cool in her hand, though the ice was long melted—not unlike her harsh opinion of Ridley following their first meeting. She'd been disappointed that he hadn't lingered after delivering the drink and that he hadn't been back since.

Her stomach alerted her that it was nearing dinner time, so she finished reviewing the last drawer, made her notes, and closed the ledger. On her way out of the stables, she kept to the exact middle of the aisle, walking with purpose, her gaze focused straight ahead, not daring to return the looks of dark eyes following her progress. They were beautiful creatures, all of them. But their sheer strength and unpredictability literally stole her breath.

Once outside, she inhaled deeply, appreciating the fresh air and the late-day sunlight. She was growing more accustomed to being in the stables, but that didn't mean she liked them any better.

She'd started for the house when she spotted Jimmy—at least she thought it was him—sitting cross-legged on a barrel by the stable, his face mostly hidden by his cap.

She approached, but he didn't look up, apparently lost in the magazine in his lap. "Jimmy?" she tried softly. And then again more loudly, when he didn't answer.

He lifted his head. "Missus Aberdeen!" His smile was immediate. "How you doin', ma'am?"

As she had yesterday, she felt an instant liking for the boy. "I'm doing very well, thank you. How are you?"

"I's good." He tipped his cap to her. "Just lookin' through this paper the general give me." He held it up.

"*American Turf Register and Sporting Magazine*," she said, smiling. And not hard to believe, it was an issue she'd already read to Elizabeth. "So that's what you're reading."

No sooner had she said it, than she realized she'd likely misspoken. The flicker in the boy's expression and his gentle half shrug confirmed it.

"Well, I ain't 'zactly readin', but …" He hopped off the barrel, appearing unaware of her faux pas. "If you got a minute, please, ma'am … Maybe you could help me find somethin' in it?"

Still a bit embarrassed over her misstep, Olivia nodded. "I'd be happy to, Jimmy."

"The general said somethin's in here 'bout Jack Malone comin' to Belle Meade, and I want to see it." His smile brightened. "I can usually pick out the plantation's name by them double sticks, but I just ain't seein' 'em this time."

Double sticks. It gradually registered with her what he meant, and Olivia motioned toward a nearby tree stump. "I'd be happy to help you, Jimmy. Let's sit over here." She sat, balancing the ledger on her lap and liking the way the boy plopped right down beside her. She guessed him to be eight or nine, though something about him seemed older.

"I happen to have read this issue before." She flipped through the pages until she located the article. "I know exactly where it is. Here." She held the magazine between them and read slowly, moving her finger beneath the words as she did. "And see, here's the name of the—"

"There's them double sticks," he said, tapping the two *L*s in the word *Belle.* "You read good, ma'am. And smooth too. Like my mama's gravy." He made a face like he was tasting it.

Olivia laughed. "Jimmy, how old are you?"

"I's nine, ma'am. Gonna be ten soon."

She studied him, aware of an idea pushing to the forefront of her thoughts—also pushing against propriety and everything she'd always known or been told about Negroes. But looking into this boy's eyes, seeing an eagerness she recognized, she couldn't help but question the validity of what she thought she knew.

Though no one else was around to hear, she still lowered her voice. "Would you like to learn how to read, Jimmy? Better, I mean. More than just ... the double sticks?"

His eyes flickered with hope. "I's s'posed to start learnin' to read a ways back. At a free school, my mama called it. But it done closed down 'fore I could get there."

Olivia nodded. "A freedmen's school, since you're a *free* young man now."

He grinned. "Yes, ma'am. That be it."

She knew something about these schools, though not much. Charles had always taken the newspaper with him to work, most times before she could read it. Part of his attempt to control her, she knew. Which he'd done quite well, looking back on it. But she'd read each *Harper's Weekly* from cover to cover when it arrived. She'd pilfered money from the food budget over time to pay the four dollar yearly subscription in advance.

She finished reading the article on General Harding's purchase of Jack Malone, then closed the magazine, her decision measured and made. "Why don't you ask your mother if it's all right with her if I teach you how to read. And if she says yes then we'll start this week."

Jimmy looked up at her. "Really, Missus Aberdeen?"

Olivia felt a funny tickle in her chest. "Really, Jimmy."

His grin nearly stretched from ear to ear. Then just as quickly faded. "I'm sorry you didn't like your cart, ma'am."

"Oh, no, don't think I didn't like it. I liked it very much, Jimmy. I just ... Well, I wasn't in the frame of mind to ride yesterday, that's all."

"So, you still be willin' to try it sometime then?"

If she didn't know better, she'd have thought Ridley had put him up to asking her that, and she glanced around just to make sure he wasn't standing nearby somewhere, listening.

Unable to say no to this little boy, Olivia felt the word coming and was helpless to stop it. "Yes," she said, her insides twisting just thinking about it. "I'll try the cart ... sometime."

Then she hurried on her way before he could pin her down as to *'zactly* when.

Chapter
TWENTY-FOUR

W hat do you mean she's *missing*, Jimmy?" Ridley strode through the stable to Seabird's stall. Empty, sure enough. He felt the tension in him building. What else could go wrong this week? The past few days had been nothing but frustrating. First, a colt had been stillborn. Two more mares were due to foal any day but showed no signs of starting yet. Then he'd had to fire a man for stealing. If it weren't for Olivia's careful record keeping, he might not have found out about the man's thieving for some time.

And on top of everything else, he'd received an invitation to dine with the Hardings on Saturday night two weeks hence, and there was no way he could refuse. Even Rachel, when he'd mentioned it to her yesterday, had said he had to go. And he found himself dreading it, for several reasons. He'd seen how the Hardings dressed, and he didn't even own a suit. Didn't want to waste the money on buying one either, not with saving to go west. He'd told Rachel as much, and she'd said just to wear his best. But that frustration seemed like nothing compared to his current predicament.

He sighed and, seeing the worry in Jimmy's eyes, tried to rein in his anger. "How long has she been gone?"

"I took her to the corral this morning like you told me, sir." Jimmy worried the outside seam of his baggy trousers. "Then I come back inside to get a bucket of water for her, and Mr. Grady asked me to—"

"Mr. Grady?" Just the name set Ridley's teeth on edge.

"Yes, sir. He had me run something up to the general's office for him. Important papers, he said. And when I come back—"

"Seabird was gone," Ridley finished for him.

"Yes, sir. I'm sorry, sir."

Ridley retraced a path back outside, Jimmy close behind. Ridley stood and searched the meadow and the mares' corrals, then the lower pasture as far as he could see, remembering how Seabird had cleared the corral fence a couple of weeks ago. Finally, when the mare was his, she went missing ...

Yet she couldn't have gone far. Even the day she'd jumped the fence, she'd only wandered a mile or so. He'd find her. And while he knew Grady Matthews was foolhardy, he wasn't cruel. At least not to animals. Uncle Bob wouldn't have kept the man around if he was.

Ridley saddled a mare and headed in the direction Seabird had run the other day. But she wasn't in the lower pasture. He circled the meadow and came up back behind the servants' cabins, then on around the west side of the house. But still, no sign of her.

He rode on to the stallion stable and adjoining corrals, remembering the man who had put Seabird in a stall in there on his first night. Uncle Bob always made a point of saying horses remembered things, but surely the mare wouldn't have gone there.

Ridley dismounted and checked inside, but none of the stable hands had seen her. He walked to the back where they kept studs before they were taken to the breeding shed. He spotted Uncle Bob in a stall working with Vandal, a lead stallion. Two other men assisted him, one of them Grady Matthews.

Ridley nodded to the other hand, while watching Grady for the slightest difference in the man's behavior. "Uncle Bob, Seabird's missing. None of you have seen her, have you?"

Grady laughed beneath his breath. "Don't tell us you went and lost your prize mare already, Cooper."

"Hush up, Grady." Uncle Bob gave the man a warning glance, then turned back to Ridley. "She ain't in her stall?"

"No. Or the corrals or lower pasture." Ridley explained what had happened. "It's not Jimmy's fault." He cast a glance at Grady, almost certain he'd caught a glint of culpability in the man's eyes, but he couldn't be certain and knew better than to accuse without proof.

Uncle Bob handed the lead rope to Grady. "We be finished with Vandal in a few minutes, then we help you look for her."

The stallion, impatient, tried to rear up as they led him away, but Grady held him steady.

Uncle Bob looked back. "We all know Miss Birdie can jump a fence, Ridley. But she ain't no rogue mare. Ever how she got out, she ain't goin' far."

Ridley nodded, agreeing. Still, something about it just didn't sit right. Seabird had motivation to jump the fence that day. She'd wanted to get away from him then. But today ...

He walked on outside and looked out over the meadow, searching for her again.

"Well, this is a nice surprise."

He turned and felt the first bright spot in days.

Olivia frowned. "I was about to ask if you were having a good day, but I already see the answer to that question on your face."

Ridley rubbed his stubbled jaw. "I'm sorry." He tried to smile. "It's just been a rough week. And Seabird's missing."

"Your mare?"

"Jimmy put her in the corral, but when he came back a few minutes later, she was gone. It's not his fault," he rushed to add, having seen her and Jimmy talking and laughing together this week. He gathered she was fond of the boy. So was he.

"I'm sorry, Ridley." Her gaze swept the meadow.

The very fact that she was looking for the mare—that she cared enough to—eased his burden a little. She was so pretty. The way her dark hair was pinned up in the back and sort of ... rolled up on the sides. A few curls hung down here and there, and he wished he had the liberty of touching them. Of touching her.

"Ridley," she said, still looking out over the pasture. Her eyes narrowed. "Isn't that your mare?"

Turning, he spotted Seabird trotting up the meadow inside the fence, and he felt a weight lift. "Yes, it is. She must have decided just to take a little run around the—"

Then he saw another horse—Jack Malone—galloping up behind her. The stallion nipped Seabird's withers, and she bucked at him. Unwilling to be put off so easily, Jack Malone caught Seabird by the mane and tried to edge her off to the side, pinning her in by the fence, but Seabird reared.

Recognizing the telling behavior, Ridley felt the weight that had lifted just moments earlier come crashing back down.

"You're telling me that you knew the mare was not only capable of jumping the fence but that you saw her do it?"

Ridley met General Harding's stare. The anger simmering in the man's voice belied his calm expression, and the close quarters of the general's office swiftly grew more so.

"And yet you still chose to leave her alone in the corral."

"General, every thoroughbred at Belle Meade is capable of jumping a—"

"A simple yes or no response will suffice, Mr. Cooper. You left her alone in the corral."

Ridley took a deep breath. "Yes, sir. I did."

News of what had happened spread quickly, so he'd had no choice but to inform General Harding. Uncle Bob's examination of Seabird had removed any doubt about what had happened in the pasture. Jimmy had hovered close around Seabird's stall, watching Ridley with guilt-ridden eyes. But it wasn't the boy's fault. It wasn't anybody's fault, it seemed. Although Ridley still wondered about Grady Matthews.

General Harding gave a heavy sigh and crossed to his desk chair. But he didn't sit down. "You're certain Jack Malone covered her?"

Ridley nodded. "But what we don't know yet is whether—"

"She'll be with foal," Harding finished in a clipped tone, irritation edging through. "Which we will know soon enough, Mr. Cooper. I'll have her checked in a month, and if she *is* with foal, you'll have two choices. Either the foal will be mine upon birth—*if* it lives." Ridley almost winced at the harsh reminder. But the possibility Seabird might lose another foal had already crossed his mind. *If* indeed the covering had taken. "Or you'll pay me the one hundred dollar stud fee. And the fee will be payable *in full* upon confirmation that the covering took. Though I have a good mind to demand payment right now, like I do with everyone else." Harding gripped the back of his chair and took a deliberate breath, then let it out slowly. "If you cannot pay the fee then, Mr. Cooper, you'll legally assign the foal to me. Is that clear?"

Ridley knew the options were fair, under the circumstances. "Perfectly clear, sir."

Harding studied him for a moment. "If I didn't know better, I'd think you were intentionally trying to make a fool of me, Mr. Cooper."

Caught off guard, Ridley faced him square on. "No, sir. That's not the case at all. What would give you cause to think that?"

"Well …" Harding eased down into his chair, his laugh not the least humorous. "The fact that you're here so short a time and not only have you made foreman, but you now own one of my thoroughbreds.

A horse I'd ordered to be put down, mind you. But that apparently has been miraculously healed and now goes sailing across fences to mate with my champion stud that, incidentally, I have publicly advertised as having no open bookings until this fall."

The grounds for the man's frustration were becoming clearer. Ridley remained silent, letting the general's words and their steam hover in the air like mist until they finally drifted downward and dissipated in the quiet. Whatever Ridley said next—and he needed to say something—he needed to tread carefully. Remaining at Belle Meade was even more important now than it had been before. And for reasons other than what had initially drawn him here.

"General Harding, I assure you, sir … None of this transpired with the intent of bringing embarrassment upon you." Ridley worked gently to refute the general's statements without causing further offense. "I'm grateful for the opportunity you gave me to be a foreman here at Belle Meade and also for the deal we struck together for Seabird, which again"—he saw a glimmer of what he hoped was respect in Harding's gaze—"is something I greatly appreciate. I learned a lot from Uncle Bob through working with Seabird. And I would never have been able to afford a horse like that on my own. But the truth remains, General. What happened today was not by my design. Uncle Bob told me you'd planned on breeding Seabird again this spring. But after the accident with the carriage and seeing how skittish she was, I had already decided to wait another year to breed her, thinking that would be best. *Knowing* it would."

"And yet, Mr. Cooper … here we are."

"Yes, sir, General." Ridley looked across the desk at him. "Here we are."

For a long moment, General Harding didn't say anything. Then he leaned back in the chair and motioned for Ridley to sit. Ridley did as indicated, though not wanting to. He didn't welcome further discussion on this topic or any other. Not with William Giles Harding. Though he'd come to respect General Harding to an extent, familiarity between them was dangerous territory.

"I sense a likeness between us, Mr. Cooper. You strike me as a man of integrity. And honor. One not afraid to work hard for what he wants. Those are traits I admire."

"Thank you, sir. They're ones I hold in highest regard as well."

Harding steepled his hands beneath his chin. "Yet it strikes me how very little I know about you. And I make it my business to know everyone who works here at Belle Meade."

Ridley felt a ripple of warning. "That's understandable, sir."

"I place great trust in Uncle Bob as head hostler and have never been given reason to question that trust. So I'm wondering ... What did you do in so short a time to cause him to speak so highly of you?"

Wanting to be anywhere but in that office right now, Ridley forced himself to try to relax and to think of something truthful to say. "I'm not sure that I know exactly. Other than ... Uncle Bob is a unique man. I think he tends to bring out the best in a person, sir. I think he's done so with me, at least. He demands a lot, that's for sure. But he also makes a person want to try harder, to do better. And that's a unique quality in a man."

Harding regarded him. "I agree wholeheartedly. But he doesn't always have that effect on people, Mr. Cooper. I think it depends on the man. The night of the fire, the night Uncle Bob first spoke up about you ... That was your first day here at Belle Meade, was it not?"

Quickly seeing where the general was going with this line of questioning, Ridley worked to stay two steps ahead. "That's right ... Except I think you mean the night of the fire *after* the afternoon when Uncle Bob asked me to muck out every stall between here and Mississippi." Ridley laughed softly. "Then to cart in at least forty bales of fresh hay. Almost a full day's work without even the promise of getting a job." He smiled, finding it came genuinely when he remembered everything Uncle Bob had asked him to do that day. "I didn't even know if there was a job open. All I knew was that I'd heard about Belle Meade and about General Harding's thoroughbreds, and I'd come a long way to work here. And to learn, if given the chance."

Satisfaction slowly spread across Harding's face. "Don't feel too badly, Mr. Cooper. Uncle Bob uses that ploy to weed out the men from the boys, so to speak."

"Does it always work like it did with me?"

"Only with men worth their salt, Mr. Cooper." General Harding leaned forward. "I hear you've set your sights on the Colorado Territory." The general laughed. "Don't look so surprised, Mr. Cooper. Uncle Bob mentioned it. And don't worry, your job isn't in danger. My last foreman was only going to stay a few months before he headed to Missouri. And that was seven years ago."

Ridley managed a laugh, surprised Uncle Bob had revealed his plans. But then, they weren't a secret.

Harding glanced at the clock on the mantle. "A few of the men who served under me in the war have already gone out there. I hear it's beautiful country."

Tensing a little, Ridley nodded. "That's what I hear too, sir. I'm looking forward to seeing it."

"My only concern is the yearling sale in June of next year, Mr. Cooper. I'd like a commitment from you that you'll stay through that event before leaving. There's a great deal of work to be done, and I would appreciate your facilitation. And who knows?" He shrugged. "Seven years from now, you may find yourself still here."

Ridley managed a smile, knowing that wouldn't be the case. He had just two years to claim and develop his land out west. He'd have to leave next June at the latest or risk losing his land forever. But another year at Belle Meade meant more time to learn from Uncle Bob. "You can count on me staying through the yearling sale, sir. Next June. But after that, I'll be on my way."

Harding rose and held out his hand. "We'll see about that when the time comes. But until then, I appreciate your commitment. A man is nothing without his word. And in my book, a handshake is as binding a contract as any words dried on paper."

Ridley matched the general's strong grip, feeling a nudge of guilt over Harding not knowing the whole truth about him. Perhaps, in time, Harding's bitterness toward the Federals would ease. But looking at that beard — and certain it had grown an inch just since they'd been in the office — Ridley doubted that would be the case.

He followed Harding to the door.

"Something else I'd appreciate, Mr. Cooper, are your ideas on how you think we might draw interested buyers. This being Belle Meade's first yearling sale, I want to make it a successful one. I considered holding it this summer, but not every Southern gentleman's bank book is what it was before the war. The demand for fine horse flesh is on the rise, however, and I believe that by next year, there will be a strong market for my thoroughbreds."

"Yes, sir. I agree. I'll be sure to give that some thought."

"Very good." Harding reached to open the door. "My wife tells me you were assigned to Nashville for the war, Mr. Cooper."

Ridley winced and was grateful Harding's back was to him. "Yes, sir. That's right. For the majority of the time."

Harding opened the door. "Who was your immediate command-ing officer? I met some of the men from South Carolina. Perhaps I knew him."

Ridley paused inside the doorway, feeling more like he was bal-ancing on the edge of a cliff. Against a stiff wind. What were the odds the general would recognize the name of a Union officer? From Pennsylvania. And with so common a name. "Samuels," he answered truthfully, determining in that moment—and respecting this man and himself enough—not to lie. Yet he also had an obligation to Uncle Bob to keep *their* secret safe, which he would, regardless of whether or not his came to light. "My commanding officer's name was Robert Samuels."

Harding repeated the name, frowning. "Can't say that name rings a bell. But there were so many of us. Still …" The general sighed, staring out across the meadow. "After all was said and done, it wasn't enough, was it, Mr. Cooper?"

Ridley looked at him, eye to eye—thankful the man hadn't asked what regiment he'd been in—and shook his head. "No, sir, General Harding. It wasn't."

Chapter TWENTY-FIVE

Now it's your turn, Jimmy. And try to write it exactly like I showed you this time."

Ridley stood outside the door of the tack room, making no secret of his presence, but doubting Olivia had noticed him. For the past two weeks, he'd observed her teaching and found his gut instincts about her talents proven correct. He enjoyed watching and listening to the spirited exchange between teacher and pupil.

Or pupils, he silently amended, noting Jimmy's younger sister snuggled against Olivia.

"But, Missus Aberdeen"—Jimmy's eyes grew bigger—"I can't do it 'zactly like you done, ma'am. You got yo'self a heap more practice at it than me."

"Just do the best you can, Jimmy. That's all I'm asking."

"Miss 'Livia?" Jimmy's little sister, Jolene—two or three years younger than Jimmy, Ridley guessed—tugged on Olivia's skirt. The girl was nearly as tall as her brother and claimed the same lithe build. Ridley smiled at the way Jolene took hold of Olivia's hand whenever the little girl asked a question.

"Yes, Jolene." Olivia leaned down. "What is it, sweetie?"

"When's it gonna be my turn to have the slate, Miss 'Livia?"

"After me, Jo-Jo." Jimmy shot his sister a glance. "You already done had it twice. And these is my lessons. I'm pert near to bein' a man. That means I get to learn first, over a girl. Right, Missus Aberdeen?"

"Actually, Jimmy …"

Ridley grinned, hoping Jimmy was ready for the response that statement was certain to garner.

Olivia slipped an arm around his and Jolene's thin shoulders. "I think both you and your sister should have the right to study and learn if you so desire. Boy or girl, it makes no difference."

Jolene lifted her chin a couple of notches just as Jimmy lowered his.

"Now, Jimmy ..." Olivia pointed to the slate. "Write that row of letters there as best you can."

Hunkered over the slate, Jimmy did, then held it up.

"*Very* good!" Olivia smiled. "Now, Jolene, it's your turn."

Little Jolene took more time than her brother, but finally held up the slate, hopeful.

"*Very* good as well!" Olivia beamed, slipping her hand into her pocket. "And for all your hard work in recent days ..." She placed something into each of their hands.

"A sugar stick!" Jimmy crunched down on the candy.

Jolene gave hers a delicate lick. "Thank you, Missus Aberdeen, for givin' this to us."

"Oh, I didn't give it to you, Jolene. You both *earned* it. There's a difference."

Ridley grinned at the life lesson. Olivia was gifted at teaching. She had a way of breaking things into bite-sized pieces Jimmy—and now Jolene—could grasp. And she was so patient with them. He wondered though ...

Did she grasp what a daring thing it was she was doing? For years, it had been illegal to undertake a slave's education, and yet here she was—a white woman—teaching the children of former slaves at one of the largest plantations in Tennessee. When he thought of it that way, he couldn't help but admire her, while also being glad it was only two students and not a freedmen's school. That would be an entirely different situation, with far greater risks than he would ever encourage her to pursue.

Listening to her answer a question from Jimmy, Ridley wondered if General Harding knew about her teaching. He quickly guessed he didn't and could wager the man wouldn't approve of her actions.

"Ridley, got a minute to help me with somethin' outside?"

Recognizing Uncle Bob's voice, Ridley started to turn, but Olivia glanced up right then. She smiled and mouthed *hello*. Ridley winked and nodded, proud of her in a way he couldn't define and wishing it were just the two of them having dinner together tonight instead of him joining the entire Harding family. It wasn't being with the Harding women that he dreaded. They seemed nice enough. It was spending time in General Harding's company—especially since the incident with Seabird—that wore on him.

In recent days, when visiting the stables, the general had struck up conversations with him that always led to war talk. The man had reminisced at length about his own experiences, while Ridley only commented when forced to. And even then, he'd kept to generalities. He'd caught Harding looking at him pensively a couple of times, as though the man knew he wasn't being as talkative as he might.

Ridley joined Uncle Bob outside and started to grab one end of a hefty crate of supplies.

"Mr. Cooper!"

Ridley glanced up to see Jedediah, along with a handful of other workers with him. "Jedediah. Gentlemen." He nodded to the rest. "Everything all right?"

"Oh yes, sir." Jedediah smiled, then glanced at the other men with him. "Everythin' be fine."

Ridley didn't know the other stable hands as well as he did Jedediah, but he'd worked with them on several occasions. One of the men—Bartholomew, an ox of a man, one of the hardest workers Ridley had ever seen—met his gaze then lifted his chin slightly. Ridley sensed that his part in the gathering either wasn't his cup o' tea, or maybe he wasn't here of his own volition.

"Mr. Cooper," Jedediah continued, "we been gettin' some extra pay in our pouches, sir, and … we just come by to say thank you. We know it was you who done it. Who got it for us. Got us the same pay as the white workers."

All the men nodded—even Bartholomew—but none of them looked Ridley in the eye, and it became clearer to him in that moment what they were feeling. It was something he understood only too well. In a blink, he was back at Andersonville, filthy bowl outstretched, hunger clawing the back of his stomach even as pride choked his throat. It was a humiliating thing for a man to have to act beholden to someone for something that should be rightfully his.

"I appreciate that, Jedediah. Gentlemen." Ridley looked at each of them, seeing a part of his past he'd never forget. "But I didn't *get* you anything. A man deserves a fair wage for a fair day's labor. Keep doing the work, and you'll keep getting paid."

A glint sparked Jedediah's eyes. Bartholomew stood a little taller, as did the others. "Yes, sir, Mr. Cooper," they said one after the other before walking away, heads higher than when they'd come.

Uncle Bob looked over at him but said nothing, which suited Ridley fine. Ridley hefted the other end of the crate, and together they carried it inside to the hallway.

"That's mighty good of her," Uncle Bob said, nodding toward the tack room as they lowered the crate. "What she doin' with them young 'uns."

Ridley straightened, his sense of pride in her returning. "Yes, it is. She seems to enjoy it. And she's good at it too."

Uncle Bob looked at him, then nodded.

"What?" Ridley asked, catching a curious flicker in the man's expression.

"I didn't say nothin'."

"No. But you *want* to. I know you do. Might as well go ahead and get it out. You'll end up telling me on the front porch tonight anyway."

Uncle Bob looked up and down the hallway. "I's just wonderin' if you ready for this fancy dinner tonight. Ready for whatever talk might come up."

Ridley eyed him, matching the man's whisper. "Do you know something I don't?"

Uncle Bob hesitated. "I got word they's gonna be some other people there."

"Other people?"

"Folks from out of town. A couple and two other gentlemen. Two men who fought with General Harding."

"War buddies," Ridley whispered, more to himself than to Uncle Bob. "I've tap danced my way around things so far. I guess I'll just do it again."

"I know you did, sir. I heard you in here the other day. I's surprised you got any sole left on the tips of them boots."

They both smiled, but not for long.

"This may sound selfish, but I'm not sorry I came here. What you're teaching me, what I've learned ..." Ridley looked away. "What I *am* sorry about, though, is that I've put you in a predicament that might bring you harm."

Uncle Bob's brief exhale tugged his attention back.

"Sir, there're times in life when you know—as sure as the sun's gonna come up in the east and go to bed in the west—that what you're doin' is what the Maker wants you to do. I feel that way every day here at Belle Meade. Always have. And I feel it when I'm workin' with you. Never in all my years would I'a guessed a man like you would be here, and that I'd be teachin' you. But you's here for a reason, sir. I know that with everythin' in me. So no matter what comes, sir ..." He shook his head. "Don't you ever say you's sorry. 'Cause I sure ain't."

"What're you men doin' talkin' all low and serious like that? You ain't careful, I'm gonna start me some rumors."

They looked up to see Rachel Norris walking toward them down the corridor. She carried her customary herbal pouch, as Ridley had come to think of it. "Afternoon, Rachel."

She smiled, exchanging a brief hug with Uncle Bob. She was older than Uncle Bob by several years, Ridley guessed, though he wasn't good at measuring such things. He knew they'd known each other for a long time.

Uncle Bob reached for the pouch. "You bring me some fresh makin's for poultices?"

Rachel swatted his hand. "This be for Missus Aberdeen. She was supposed to come by for it directly. But with it bein' such a fine day out, I thought I'd bring it myself."

Ridley glanced at the pouch, hoping Olivia wasn't feeling poorly. But surely not. She looked in full health to him. At the far end of the stable, a ranch hand entered with a mare and Uncle Bob excused himself.

Ridley gestured down the hall. "Mrs. Aberdeen is working in the—"

Jimmy and Jolene appeared in the doorway of the tack room, followed by Olivia.

"Rachel!" The children yelled in unison and ran straight for her.

The older woman embraced them, then produced two wrapped pieces of candy from her pocket. Ridley recognized Rachel's homemade caramels, as did the children, judging by their grins. Rachel gave them another hug before they scampered off unwrapping their sweets. "I heard you been teachin' Jimmy and his sister, Missus Aberdeen. Awfully kind of you."

Olivia beamed, looking equal parts woman and girl. "Believe me, it's my pleasure." She glanced at the herb bag. "Is that what I think it is?"

"It is." Rachel handed it to her.

Ridley looked between them. "Why do I get the feeling you two are up to something?"

Olivia looked at him, her expression hinting at guilt.

But Rachel eyed him. "Tell us your secrets first, Mr. Cooper. Then we'll tell you ours."

"That's right," Olivia chimed in, borrowing confidence.

Ridley held his hands up in mock truce. "I know when I'm beaten."

Olivia smiled at him, then looked at Rachel. "Thank you so much for this. I was nearly out. It's working wonders! Just like you said it would."

His curiosity definitely roused, Ridley didn't dare push for more information. Not with Rachel here. But he quickly decided the herbs couldn't be for anything personal for Olivia. She hadn't blushed in the least when referring to using them. Maybe later tonight—if they had some time alone, like he intended—he could make sure she was all right.

Olivia tucked the pouch behind the ledger in her arms, hiding it. "I'll see you at dinner?"

The question was aimed at him. He nodded. "I'll be there."

He watched her go, then realized—too late—that Rachel was watching him watch.

She just smiled. "I'm good at keepin' secrets, Mr. Cooper."

He tilted his head in acknowledgment. "As am I, Mrs. Norris."

She raised an eyebrow as though impressed, her blue eyes seeming even more so. "You ready for dinner at General Harding's table?"

"As I'll ever be, I guess."

"What you plannin' on wearin'?"

"I have my best shirt clean. Same for my trousers."

She looked at him thoughtfully. "They need pressin'?"

"I did my ironing last night too. Nearly burned my collar *and* my thumb in the process."

"Well, at least you didn't burn down the old Harding cabin. That's sayin' somethin'." She grinned. "By the way, I been meanin' to ask you. How'd you like our church?"

It was his turn to grin. "It was … *different*. But good."

He'd only been to the Negro church once, tired of Uncle Bob asking him to go. But he was glad he'd visited, even if he'd felt a little awkward. And not because he'd been the only white person there. His discomfort, if he could call it that, had stemmed from feeling like he was the only person there who didn't really *know* the Almighty. Not like the rest of them, anyway. But watching them worship, listening to them sing, made him want to. More than he ever had before.

"I'll be back this Sunday," he said, giving Rachel a look. "Long as you promise I don't have to preach."

"No." She waved the comment away. "We don't make you preach 'til your third time."

Later, after bathing in the creek, Ridley made his way back to get ready for dinner. His hair was still damp but would dry quickly enough in the summer sun. It was nearly to his collar again, but—he ran a hand over his jaw—at least he was clean-shaven. When he crested the hill, he spotted Rachel sitting in Uncle Bob's rocker on the porch. She stood as he neared.

"Evening, Mrs. Norris."

"Evening, Mr. Cooper. I hope you don't mind." She motioned toward the door. "I left somethin' inside for you. Thought maybe you could use it tonight."

He followed her into the cabin and saw a suit hanging from the mantle.

"It belonged to my husband," she said, her voice unusually soft. "It's a few years old, but I cleaned and pressed it. You're a touch taller than he was though, so I let out the pants. But other than that, my Noland was right about your size. There's a shirt too." She pointed. "And a tie." She gave a little sigh, like a memory had squeezed her heart. "Noland told me toward the end, he said, 'Rachel, don't you go buryin' me in that suit, woman. I ain't never felt right in it, and I ain't spendin' my days in the hereafter tuggin' at no collar.'" The smile on her mouth trembled. Her eyes watered. "I gave 'bout everythin' else away, but not these. Not 'til now."

Ridley fingered the sleeve of the suit. It reminded him of one he'd owned before the war. Another lifetime ago. This woman's gift was far too generous, yet to refuse it would be nothing short of an insult. "Thank you, Mrs. Norris. I don't quite know what to say." He looked back at her. "If it fits, ma'am, I'll wear it with pride."

Smiling, Rachel reached for the door behind her. "I'll wait outside, if you don't mind. I'd like to see it on you."

Ridley soon found her estimation on the fit to be near perfect. The coat was a tad snug through the shoulders, but everything else felt tailored to him. Wearing the shoes he'd polished with saddle oil last night, he stepped outside.

And the look on Rachel's face said everything.

Chapter
TWENTY-SIX

*O*livia couldn't keep from staring at him. It didn't help that Ridley was seated right across from her, sandwiched between Mary and Cousin Lizzie—both of whom seemed positively giddy. And with good reason. They were seated beside a most appealing man.

Ridley Cooper was—without question—beyond handsome this evening. She loved the circumstances under which he'd been invited to dinner, a gentleman's agreement with the general regarding a mare. And Ridley had bested him, just as Elizabeth had said. Ridley seemed so at ease in this setting too. Observing him like this—a proper gentleman if ever she'd seen one—she had a hard time imagining him in the wilds of the Colorado Territory.

He hadn't said another word to her about leaving, and she assumed that since he'd taken the job as foreman, he'd decided to stay. Which made perfect sense. And the probability of that gave her more enjoyment than it should have.

The suit he wore wasn't the latest in fashion, but what it lacked in that regard, he more than made up for in how he wore it. She'd always heard that the clothes made the man. But the man sitting across the table from her was disproving that adage. In every way.

She didn't know what she'd expected him to wear tonight. She hadn't really thought about it. She'd only ever seen him in his work clothes. But she hadn't expected him to look like this. Like a dessert so luscious one wouldn't want to ruin it by taking a bite. Yet at the same time, all one wanted to do was gobble it up. The comparison made her smile. Until Ridley caught her attention. And the way he looked at her from beneath slightly hooded eyes temporarily caused all the air to be expelled from her lungs. She reached for her glass of lemonade just for a taste of something cool.

"So tell me, Mrs. Aberdeen ..."

With effort, Olivia dragged her focus from Ridley's and placed it on the older gentleman seated to her right: decorated Confederate General Percival Meeks. She couldn't forget the name because General Harding had made a point to use the title at least three times during dinner. That and Percival Meeks truly resembled the image his name conjured.

A much older man, though kind and gentle from best she could tell, General Meeks was somewhat challenged in girth. Quite the opposite in every way from the younger and lower-ranking colonel seated on her left. Yet having observed the general during the meal thus far, she'd decided it wasn't his advancement in years that had contributed to that condition, but rather his sustained—and enthusiastic—contribution to the weight saddling his middle. A man of grand proportions, as her mother might have said. He was also balding. Though that, in and of itself, didn't bother her. She'd seen many a handsome man of that description.

But the way General Meeks wore what remained of his hair made for an interesting study atop his large, round head. His hair had thinned on the top, and he shaved all but the sides where it still grew in thick behind his ears and around the base of his skull, giving him the appearance of an aging athlete wearing a somewhat sagging—and hairy—laurel.

"How do you like living at Belle Meade, Mrs. Aberdeen? The general told me you've only been here since May. And ..." General Meeks leaned a little closer, offering a compassionate smile, the skin on the crown of his head bunched up in a puddle of wrinkles. "He told me you were recently widowed," he whispered, his eyes conveying genuine kindness. "I'm truly sorry for your loss, ma'am."

Knowing where General Harding stood on her remarrying and aware that these two colleagues of his weren't from Nashville, Olivia safely assumed this was *all* General Harding had told him about her widowhood. "Thank you, General Meeks. I very much enjoy living here and appreciate your condolences."

"My own dear Sarah passed some seven years ago now. It's hard to believe it's been that long. Time passes so quickly in some ways and yet—"

"So slowly in others," she finished for him, grateful to see Susanna and Chloe carrying in the dessert trays. She hoped it was something that would melt quickly. Dinner would be over faster that way.

"General Meeks." General Harding's voice carried over the lively table conversation. "What opinion do you hold of these changing times, sir? Do you believe the market for thoroughbreds is improving or do you hold that . . ."

Momentarily relieved of Percival Meeks' attention, Olivia sipped from her water glass and enjoyed the lilt of Aunt Elizabeth's laughter from the foot of the table. No one would have guessed how ill she'd been a few weeks back. Even General Harding had commented recently on the improvement in her health, which Olivia felt certain could be attributed — at least in part — to Rachel's special blend of tea. The doctor's prescription for additional rest was certainly a contributing factor, as was Susanna's insistence that Elizabeth eat a daily portion of liver to fortify that "tired blood" of hers.

Elizabeth wouldn't be running a footrace any time soon, but at least she was well enough to host a dinner party. Although Olivia imagined the dear woman would be abed tomorrow because of it.

Setting her glass back on the table, Olivia found her focus drawn yet again across the table. To Ridley. He was speaking, but — she looked closer — no sound came from his lips. Then she realized . . .

He was mouthing something to her.

She frowned the tiniest bit, trying to communicate she hadn't understood. Then growing nervous someone might see them, she swept the table with her gaze. But no one was watching. She looked back again to find his lips tipped in a half smile. And he mouthed it again — only four little words — but they lit a warmth inside her, like someone had struck a match within her chest.

Cousin Lizzie chose that moment to ask him a question, and Ridley answered without missing a beat. So Olivia waited, watching, knowing full well she was dancing very close to the edge of what some might consider inappropriate behavior for a widow. But still, seconds later, when Ridley sought her gaze again, she simply smiled and nodded.

"Here you are, Missus Aberdeen." Susanna appeared by her chair. "Some o' my Tennessee blackberry cobbler."

"Thank you, Susanna. It looks delicious." Olivia eyed the steam rising from the bowl. So much for something that melted quickly. "And it's still warm."

"Why, o' course, ma'am. It's best warm from the oven with cream poured right over."

Susanna placed a bowl before Colonel Burcham. "Here you are, Colonel. I hope you enjoy my—"

"I don't eat blackberries," he said in a clipped tone, then slowly looked up. He smiled at Susanna, but it wasn't friendly. "I'm surprised you didn't make note of that the last time I was here."

Conversation around the table dropped to a low hum, and Susanna swiftly removed the bowl she'd set before him. "I'm so sorry, Colonel. I—"

Elizabeth leaned forward. "My deepest apologies, Colonel Burcham. I reviewed the dinner menu beforehand, so I fear the oversight was mine. Susanna ..." Elizabeth's smile would have seemed natural to anyone who didn't know her well. "Why don't you get the Colonel a slice of your pumpkin bread with the honey-cinnamon butter you make. Colonel, you do like pumpkin, if memory serves."

"Yes, ma'am, I do. And I thank *you* for remembering." He cast a dark look at Susanna's back as she hurried from the room.

Dinner conversation resumed with an awkward limp, but Olivia— tenser than she'd have thought over such an exchange—didn't miss the glance Elizabeth shot General Harding over the rim of her coffee cup. Nor did she miss the disapproval on Ridley's face.

Colonel Bryant Burcham, a man built for war—tall and broad shouldered, with rugged features that might have otherwise held appeal—scoffed beneath his breath. "It's not the same as it used to be."

Olivia knew the comment was meant to engage her in conversation, but she was so angry, she couldn't respond. Her hands shook with the force of it, yet she didn't understand why. She was offended for Susanna, most certainly. But this was something more.

The Colonel looked over at her. "This never would have happened before. But now—"

Olivia forced herself to meet his gaze.

"They've lost their motivation, Mrs. Aberdeen. That's the simple truth of it. They're lazy creatures at heart. They require a firm hand, much like those thoroughbreds out there. They're happier that way."

Something white-hot sparked inside her, and Olivia realized what it was she was feeling. The tone the Colonel had taken with Susanna—such condescension, superiority—was how Charles had often spoken to her. And that tight smile Colonel Burcham had given ... How often had Charles smiled at her that same way?

Olivia shivered at the memory.

She glanced at Chloe, who was still pouring coffee at the far end of the table, and knew by the way Chloe kept her eyes down that the woman had heard what he'd said. As apparently had Ridley, judging by his darkened features.

Olivia unclenched her hands knotted in her lap, reaching for calm she didn't feel and searching for a way to redirect the conversation. "Colonel, where are you from originally? I don't believe you've told me."

"No, I haven't." His smile was friendly this time, but not at all appealing.

As he took the bait of conversation, Olivia smiled on cue and responded to his questions with brief answers before turning the questions back around. All the while, she felt General Harding watching her. She glanced toward his end of the table and soon wished she hadn't. The subtle tilt of his head, the way he glanced at the gentlemen beside her—one thing became abundantly clear in that moment ...

Regardless of her own desire to wait as long as possible to remarry, the general obviously desired that it happen sooner, which meant it would. And she felt an unseen clock begin to tick. She counted back over the weeks since Charles had died and felt another tiny shard of her heart break off. A little more than nine months remained before her year of mourning would be spent.

She glanced at the men seated on either side of her—both of them looking at her in turn—and she suddenly felt like a prized filly on the auction block. Never mind that she was still in mourning. If she were going to have any part in choosing her next husband, it would be an uphill battle against whatever designs General Harding already had in the works.

Susanna returned with the Colonel's dessert, and Olivia busied herself with her own, keeping up with the various conversations around the table—Mary and Lizzie taking turns with Ridley; Mr. and Mrs. Foster, a couple visiting from Mobile, Alabama, engaged with General Harding and General Meeks. Down the table Selene sat with her own General William Hicks Jackson, the very man Selene spoke of so often and so fondly.

Aunt Elizabeth had confided that General Harding expected General Jackson to ask for Selene's hand. Though, supposedly, the general had made it clear later would be better than sooner. Watching Selene's expression now, Olivia doubted the young woman would agree.

General Jackson, a former Confederate officer, was eleven years Selene's senior and quite a horseman himself, Elizabeth said. From what Olivia observed, he seemed to truly care about Selene, which made her glad.

If not also a wee bit envious, in a melancholy way.

Following dessert, the men retired to the study and the women to the parlor, where Olivia spent the next hour visiting with the other ladies.

"Selene, dearest?" Mrs. Foster asked. "Why don't you regale us with some songs before my husband and I must take our leave. The last time we were here you sang so beautifully."

"Yes, dear," Elizabeth chimed in. "And please include my favorite."

Cousin Lizzie invited the men to join them, and Selene played the piano and serenaded them in accomplished fashion, singing one song after another.

Sensing someone watching her, Olivia discreetly glanced to the side, hoping to find Ridley the guilty party. Which he was, though not alone. General Percival Meeks, who sat in their line of sight, tilted his head to her in silent acknowledgement.

Olivia smiled, aware of Ridley watching General Meeks now. Thinking of what Ridley had mouthed to her earlier, she was especially eager for this portion of the evening to draw to a close. She shifted her attention back to Selene and couldn't help but notice Mary, who sat off to the side, studying her older sister.

Selene finished the song and everyone clapped, Mary included. But longing shadowed the young woman's features.

"Well done, dear daughter," the general said, clapping longer than anyone else. "Splendid, as always. And now, for the finale . . ."

Olivia found herself hoping—*praying*—he would call upon Mary to play. Olivia sneaked a look across the room and would've sworn the young woman was praying the very same thing.

"You know which song I would like for you to sing, Selene."

Olivia's heart fell and only grew more tender as Selene's slender fingers moved effortlessly over the ivory keys, breathing life into the song the general requested. The familiar tune filled the parlor as it had so many other parlors throughout the South in recent years.

When Selene reached the refrain, she turned back and—with a look—invited everyone to join her. "O . . . I wish I was in Dixie . . ."

Olivia sang along softly, sneaking glimpses about the room and half expecting to find Mary struggling with her emotions. But it wasn't Mary who caught her eye.

It was Ridley, who wasn't singing at all.

Well past midnight, the evening finally drew to a close, and Olivia was relieved when General Meeks and Colonel Burcham took their leave, followed shortly by General William Hicks Jackson, Selene's beau. Mr. and Mrs. Foster excused themselves to the guest quarters upstairs, and Selene, Mary, and Cousin Lizzie did likewise to their separate bedrooms. Which left only her, the Hardings, and Ridley in the foyer by the open front door.

Olivia quickly realized that, considering Ridley's silent invitation to her during dinner— *Walk with me later?*—which she had accepted and still wanted to keep, this had the potential to be a most awkward situation.

"Mr. Cooper." General Harding extended his hand. "It was a pleasure to have you at our table this evening. Despite how the invitation came to fruition."

Ridley shook his hand. "Thank you, General. And thank you, Mrs. Harding, for a delicious meal. One of the finest I've had, ma'am. And just for the record . . ." His smile held a touch of conspiracy. "I thought the blackberry cobbler was exceptional."

Elizabeth's fatigued expression softened with pleasure. "Thank you, Mr. Cooper." She shook her head. "I can't believe I forgot that detail about the colonel. I've already told Susanna to make note in the menu book, so we won't forget again. I'm just sorry it happened and over a dessert, of all things."

"Colonel Burcham is a fine man, my dear. And a trusted friend." General Harding's tone leaned toward correction. "He's simply accustomed to his orders being obeyed."

"But the war is over, sir—"

Olivia's eyes widened at Ridley's comment and again when she saw he wasn't finished.

"I believe we need to accept that and move on with our lives. And let others move on with theirs. Wouldn't you agree, General?"

A breeze wafted through the open front door as if nature itself sought to lessen the tension thickening the air.

"Yes, Mr. Cooper, I would agree ... to a certain extent. But not everything needs to change, nor should it. Some things are the way they are for a reason."

Ridley's smile came across as a little too pleasant. "And some things are the way they are, sir ... simply because we've never changed them."

Olivia wished she could gently tug on the sleeve of Ridley's coat, just to warn him not to overstate his case. Though remembering the dark look on his face earlier and knowing how he always spoke his mind so freely, she doubted a mere touch would make any difference. She would likely have to rip his sleeve off to gain his attention.

"Well ..." Elizabeth looped her arm through the crook of her husband's. "It's very late and we're all tired. Dear?" She glanced up at the general. "Would you be so kind as to assist me up the stairs?"

General Harding didn't move. "You're young yet, Mr. Cooper. And idealistic. You believe you know best how life should be. I know that because not long ago, I knew a young man very much like you. Knew him quite well, in fact." Harding stroked his beard, which brushed the top button of his vest. "But as that young man grew up, as he built a home and family, established a plantation, and then a stud farm ... When he fought a war that threatened to take all of that from him, he learned a thing or two about life you have yet to learn, son."

Sensing Ridley about to respond, Olivia intervened.

"Mr. Cooper?" She caught a flicker of gratitude in Elizabeth's eyes. "I'm ... in need of your help. I'll be at the stable first thing in the morning, and ... I could use your assistance in the tack room. With a new shipment of supplies. If you don't mind."

Knowing she hadn't fooled anyone, least of all the men, Olivia urged Ridley with a look to please let this go. For the moment anyway. Yet she couldn't help but feel a sadness, too, that their walk would have to wait for another time.

His gaze leveled at Harding, Ridley finally nodded and looked over at her. "Of course, Mrs. Aberdeen. I would be delighted. Mr. and Mrs. Harding ..." He bowed slightly. "Again, thank you both for a pleasant evening." He got as far as the porch when he turned back. "And, Mrs. Aberdeen, I'll look forward to seeing you first thing in the morning. If not ... *later.*"

Olivia searched his expression, wondering if she'd imagined the slight change in his tone there at the last. But before she could react, General Harding firmly closed the door.

Chapter
TWENTY-SEVEN

*R*idley didn't know which frustrated him more—General Harding's stubborn arrogance or the fact that he hadn't gotten the time alone with Olivia he'd been looking forward to.

He opened the cabin door, surprised to see Uncle Bob still up.

Uncle Bob looked him over, then whistled low. "Lawd, sir ... You look 'bout fancy enough to have yourself put on paper money."

Ridley smiled briefly, removing his coat and tie. "It was Rachel." He fingered the lapel of the suit coat before hanging it neatly on the back of a chair. "It belonged to her husband. She brought it over here earlier ... Had already tailored it to fit me."

"Well, she done good. You look like a young Mister Harding hisself. Or one of his fancy, rich friends."

Ridley scoffed.

Uncle Bob's grin faded. "I aimed for that to come out in a good way, sir." His eyes narrowed. "Did the evenin' not go well for ya?"

Ridley sat down in one of the chairs, then immediately stood again. "The evening went fine. Right until the end." He described the exchange he'd had with General Harding in the foyer. Uncle Bob's expression went from interested to wary to disbelief and back again.

"You done said that to him? The part about things bein' the way they is 'cause we ain't never changed 'em? Right out to his face? And with Missus Harding there?"

Ridley nodded. "And Mrs. Aberdeen too. I knew I shouldn't but ... I just couldn't *not*."

Then Uncle Bob laughed. And laughed again.

Ridley glared. "It's not funny. Come morning, I might not have a job."

"Oh, sir ..." Uncle Bob rose from his chair, hesitating a second to massage his back like he sometimes did before straightening. "Your job is just fine. Mr. Harding likes a man with a strong spirit. One who speaks his mind. 'Course he likes to be respected too. But all men do. He ain't no different in that way from you and me." Uncle Bob eyed him.

"I know."

"Do you? 'Cause I ain't really sure you do. You and him ..." Uncle Bob glanced out the front window toward the main house. "You's a lot alike, sir. Oh, not in some ways, I know. But I been knowin' that man for nigh onto forty years now. I know him pretty well. And I been livin' and workin' with you day in and day out." Smiling, Uncle Bob patted him on the shoulder. "Trust me, sir. You's a lot alike. That's why you got this job. You had the gumption to stand up to him. He respects you, Ridley. I see that clear as day. Now ... I'm headin' on to bed. These bones o' mine are tired. I see you in the mornin'."

"Goodnight, Uncle Bob. And ... thank you." A little tired, Ridley wasn't ready to go to bed yet.

He strode outside to the porch and started to sit on the steps like he often did. But when he looked toward the main house and saw a faint golden wash of light coming from the second-story room above the kitchen, it was all he needed.

Ridley stood in the pitch dark at the bottom of the lattice and stared up at Olivia's open window, glad he'd changed out of the suit, but wondering now if this was as good an idea as it had seemed when first he'd thought of it. Yet, recalling how she'd smiled and nodded at his mouthed invitation over dinner, he quickly decided it was.

He gripped the lattice and climbed a ways up, wanting to test its strength, and he was impressed. No flimsy trelliswork for General William Giles Harding. This lattice would support Big Ike and four of his friends. It would seem that everything the general built, he built to last.

He climbed back down, then whispered up, "Olivia!"

Nothing.

He tried again, a little louder this time, mindful of another second-story window open a little farther down. He wasn't sure whose room it was, but guessed it belonged to somebody, because although the room was dark, the window was open.

He heard movement above him and saw a shadow pass. "Olivia!"

The shadow stilled. A silhouette leaned out, backlit by subtle lamplight. Olivia peered down. *"Ridley?"*

"Yes ... it's me."

"What are you doing down there?"

He laughed softly. "Wondering if you're ready for that walk."

Her head tilted to one side. "I'm almost ready for bed. Besides ... isn't it too late?"

"It's only too late if you want it to be."

Seconds ticked past, and he wondered if she was going to send him packing. Then he heard her giggle.

"I'll be down in five minutes," she said softly and ducked back inside.

"Wait!" he called up in a harsh whisper, guessing at her intention.

She poked her head back through.

He motioned. "I want you to come down this way."

"*This* way?"

"Sure ... By climbing the lattice. I've tested it, and it's strong enough. It'll be fun. I'll help you."

"Thank you. But I think I'll take the stairs."

"Where's your adventuresome spirit, Olivia Aberdeen?"

"I wasn't born with one, Ridley Cooper!"

She disappeared before he could say he knew that wasn't true. Climbing out a carriage window, working in the stables even though she was scared spitless of horses, teaching the children of former slaves ...

The woman was braver than she thought.

Staring up, he heard the murmur of voices from above and suddenly wondered what he would do if General Harding's head poked through that window. But surely the general wasn't—

The sound of a door closing. Followed by footsteps.

Olivia reappeared in the window. "The Hardings left their bedroom door open for ventilation," she whispered. "And the general heard me when the porch creaked." She glanced back behind her. "He called out to see who it was. I told him I'd just taken a step outside for some air, then turned around and hurried back in here."

Ridley heard the disappointment in her voice, which told him two things: she wanted to go with him, but she had no intention of climbing down the lattice.

So he started up.

"Ridley! What are you doing?"

"I'm coming up to help you down."

"No," she whispered. "You can't. What if ... What if someone comes in here? What if they see us?"

"No one's going to see us." He kept climbing, knowing the real reason for her protests—and silently appreciating the workmanship of whoever had built this lattice.

He reached the window and smiled. "Good evening, Mrs. Aberdeen."

She laughed, looking down at him. "You're out of your mind, Ridley Cooper, if you think I'm climbing out this window."

He didn't have to feign disappointment. "I'll be with you the entire way down. And back up again. You won't fall, I promise."

"You know you can't promise that. We *both* might fall!"

"I've been climbing trees since I was three years old, Olivia. Trust me. I won't let you fall."

If she hadn't hesitated in that moment, he'd have thought all was lost. But she *did* hesitate, which told him he'd almost won her over.

"Just put one leg out first. I'll make sure your foot is where it needs to be. Then we'll—"

"I've got on a skirt, Ridley. How am I supposed to climb down in a skirt?"

"Easy. Just bend over, grab the back hem, pull it up, and tuck it into the front of your waistband. And make sure it's in there good and tight."

She gave a sharp exhale. "I'm not about to do that!" she whispered. "Can you imagine how that would look? You'd be able to see my—" She closed her mouth. "Well, never mind that, I—"

"Lest you forget, Olivia ..." He didn't even try not to smile. "I've seen your ... unmentionables before. And believe me, this will show far less than that did. Besides," he added quickly, anticipating her rebuttal, "my mother used to do this all the time when she climbed trees with me and my brothers. And she was as fine a lady as they came. And ... she never fell once."

Olivia said nothing, and he could see her thoughts hard at work. If she disagreed with him about the skirt issue, she'd be calling his mother's propriety into question. And as a woman of propriety herself, she would never do that.

"Your mother climbed trees?" she asked softly, the lamplight revealing a smile.

"She did. And she was every bit a lady. Just like you."

Her smile faded a little. "Is ... she still living?"

The soft manner in which she asked told him she already guessed his answer.

"No ... she passed several years ago."

"Do you still miss her?"

Her question touched that place deep inside him that would always hold his mother's memory. "Every day," he whispered.

She nodded. "I still miss mine too."

Making sure he had a good grip, he reached for her hand. "Trust me, Olivia. I won't let you fall."

Chapter
TWENTY-EIGHT

With the back hem of her skirt—minus crinoline and hoop— tucked snuggly into her waistband, Olivia maneuvered one leg out the window. Ridley was right, this *wardrobe alteration* revealed far less than she'd imagined, and the dim light of the single oil lamp aided her determined modesty. But when she caught a glimpse of the ground far below, as well as a mental image of what she was doing, she started to climb back inside.

Ridley's grip tightened on her arm. "Don't look down. Just concentrate on where you're going to put your other foot. I won't let go of you, I promise."

"What if I fall?" she whispered, suddenly out of breath.

"You're not going to fall. Climbing's just like walking, except you're going up or down. With walking, it's one step at a time. With climbing, it's one hold at a time. Now ease your other leg out ... I've got you."

She started to do as he said, then stopped. "I don't think I want to do this, Ridley. I don't think I can."

The distant croak of bullfrogs and cadence of neighboring crickets filled a sudden silence.

"It's all right if you don't want to, Olivia." Ridley's voice blended with the darkness, soft and deep. "And I won't fault you if that's what you decide. But before you climb back in, I want you to know that you *can* do this. You're *able* even if you choose not to. There's a world of difference between the two."

Olivia looked at him from her perch in the window and even in the dim light saw not a trace of coercion in his features, nor did she hear it in his voice. He was simply speaking the truth as he saw it. Like he always did.

Despite the warm night air, her chin shook. She knew in that moment if she didn't do this now, she never would. And she wanted to. Despite being almost paralyzed with fear, she wanted to.

Gripping the windowsill until her fingers ached, she maneuvered her other leg out.

"When you find your foothold," he said, keeping a firm hand at her waist, "test it to make sure it's the lattice and not part of the vine."

She nodded, working to push away the thought of falling. But the more she tried to push it away, the more it came. So she focused her attention on what it would feel like when she found a secure hold on the lattice —

And she did!

She pushed down with the ball of her foot, making sure she was on the lattice, like he'd said. She gave a laugh. "I'm out of the window!"

"Yes, you are!" Again, Ridley's arm came securely about her waist.

She stared back inside her room. What a difference there was in being out here versus being in there. Not but a few inches in relation to distance. But an entire world away — as Ridley had said — in perspective.

She glanced behind her over the darkened meadow, her eyes adjusting to the moon's silvery cast.

"Just pause here for a second." He reached around her and gripped the lattice on the other side, effectively bracing her against the wall. "Take a minute and gain your bearings."

She took some deep breaths. "I can't believe I'm doing this."

"Feels great, doesn't it? Trying something you've never done before?"

"No." She shook her head. "Not really. Not yet, anyway. But I think it might … if I don't die in the process." She giggled in spite of herself.

"Get a feel for where your hands and feet are in relation to each other. And in just a second, we'll move down a rung. Whoever built this lattice built it exactly like a ladder. So just imagine yourself climbing down a —"

"I've never been on a ladder."

"All right then." He exhaled. Or had he laughed? "That's something else we'll remedy soon enough. But for now … you're doing very well. I'm proud of you, Olivia."

Appreciating the encouragement, she wondered if he could feel her trembling.

"Now ... I'm going to take a step down. And once I'm done, I want you to do the same."

"What if I step on your foot when I go?"

"You won't."

"But what if I do?"

"Then I'll plunge to my certain death without having lived a full and meaningful life. But I don't want you feeling badly if that happens."

Olivia affected a sober tone. "Not to worry ... I won't. After all, this was your idea."

Laughing, he moved down a rung, just below and beside her. "All right, your turn."

Releasing hold of the lattice with her left hand proved to be one of the hardest things she'd ever done. The simple act of letting go seemed counter to logic. But feeling Ridley beside her, feeling his hold on her arm, she let loose.

Then she did it again and again, taking turns with him as they climbed lower, until finally her boot touched solid ground. She hadn't slipped once. Relief—and *exhilaration*—poured through her. She peered up at her bedroom window, so high above them, hardly believing she'd done it. And so thrilled that she had.

"Now, that wasn't so bad, was it?"

"It was terrifying!" She gave him a little shove in the chest. "But exciting too!" She untucked her skirt from her waistband and shook some fullness back into it.

He bowed at the waist and offered his arm, pale moonlight illuminating his handsome face. "And now, m'lady ... Would you care to accompany me on a walk?"

Surprised at her own willingness to tuck her hand so easily through the crook of his arm, she did just that, enjoying the feel of the earth beneath her boots—something she doubted she'd ever take for granted again.

They strolled around front of the darkened house, then by the gardens, keeping their voices low. The Belle Meade she knew by day seemed another world this time of night. Usually the grounds were bustling with activity, servants, and animals. But under the July moon, all was hushed. Only the occasional nicker of a thoroughbred drifted toward them from the stables. A quiet peace settled over the rolling waves of earth that gradually crescendoed to the hills surrounding the meadow, and Olivia drank it in. No wonder General Harding's father had chosen this spot so many years ago.

The darkness shifted up ahead, and Olivia stopped cold. "Ridley!" she whispered, tugging on his forearm. "I saw someone! Up by the smokehouse!"

He covered her hand. "I saw him too. That was Big Ike Carter."

"Susanna's husband?"

He nodded.

"What's he doing out here at this time of night?"

"He's keeping watch."

She looked at him, not understanding.

"Since the night of the fire, men have been patrolling the grounds at night. General Harding's orders. At first, every man just took a turn at it. But that was hard ... working the night shift, then your regular job the next day too. Someone suggested breaking the time into two shifts, and letting the men sign up to do it if they wanted. For pay. General Harding agreed. The men don't earn much, but it's enough to give them an incentive. And it's worked out well so far. Big Ike's taking the first shift tonight."

She frowned. "I've never seen any of these ... *sentries* out after dark before."

"Good." He resumed walking, and she did likewise. "That means we're doing our job."

"So you take part in it as well?"

"I did at first. But since we started compensating the men, I haven't. I make a good enough wage already. Most of the men—the former slaves—don't."

She didn't have to think long before she realized something. "You're the one who suggested the idea to the general, aren't you?"

He stared ahead, then finally nodded. "I believe a man should be paid a fair wage for honest work. No matter who that man is."

She studied his profile, something else occurring to her. "Were your parents abolitionists, Ridley?"

"No. But they never owned slaves. Never had enough money to. Which suited me fine."

She turned these thoughts over, and as she and Ridley passed the smokehouse, she barely made out Big Ike's mountainous form in the shadows at the far end. He tipped his hat in silent acknowledgement, and Ridley gave an almost imperceptible nod.

"So," she continued, her curiosity roused, "as a Southern man, you fought in the war, all the while holding that slavery was wrong."

"I wasn't the only Southern man to do that," he said quietly.

"No, I'm sure you weren't. But you're the only one I know."

He opened his mouth as if to respond, then apparently changed his mind.

This was nice, strolling beside him. She enjoyed the feel of her hand tucked in his arm.

"You're enjoying teaching Jimmy and Jolene."

It wasn't a question, and she nodded. "Very much."

"I'm glad. They seem to like it too." He nudged her. "I told you you'd make a good teacher."

She grinned. "Yes, you did." Spotting something ahead, she squinted to see it better, then gestured. "What happened to the other wheels?"

Ridley stopped by the carriage, the one she'd arrived in on her first day at Belle Meade. "We stripped them a while back. Took off everything that was still salvageable. We'll chop the rest and use it for kindling for the smokehouse."

Huddled in the dark, the dismembered carriage looked sad and squatty with its wheels gone, the good door too. Olivia walked around to the damaged side and peered in. The seats were absent as well. She ran a hand along the side that had been crushed by the impact, marveling again that she hadn't fallen out.

"Careful of splinters." Ridley came alongside her. "It's pretty chewed up on this side."

Briefly closing her eyes, she could still see the ground rushing up to meet her. "I remember the door flying open," she said softly. "I still don't know how I managed not to fall out."

She remembered the day Elizabeth had seen the extent of the damage and how shocked she'd been. "Aunt Elizabeth believes God closed the door for me. That he kept me safe for a reason. I've nearly come to believe she's right."

Ridley's silence proved even louder than the night's.

Finally, she turned to him. "You don't agree?"

"I didn't say that."

"Your silence suggested it."

He walked back around to the other side, pausing where the door had been.

She peered through to him. "Do you not believe in God, Ridley?"

"Oh, I believe in him, all right. It's not that. It's just ..."

She sensed his tension from where she stood.

"I just think that crediting those kinds of things to the Almighty ..." He shook his head. "Well, it may not always be the whole truth of the matter."

She frowned. "You don't think God could have shut the door, if he'd wanted to?"

"Of course, I do. I'm not saying he couldn't have—or didn't—work to keep you safe in this carriage that day. But knowing you like I've come to, my guess is that you were doing a pretty good job of trying to save yourself."

"Well, of course I was. But I *saw* that door come open, Ridley. I *felt* myself falling out."

"I don't doubt that. But too many times in my life, I've heard people say, 'Well, this happened for a reason, so it must be God's will.' When in my mind, I look at the situation and think maybe he's just expecting them to get off their sorry—" He glanced away. "To stop sitting around waiting on him to do everything, and to get to work themselves to change things."

Olivia studied his profile in the moonlight, recalling what he'd said to the general earlier that evening. "Some things are the way they are because we've never changed them."

He didn't say anything for a moment. Then he nodded. "That's right."

"General Harding obviously doesn't believe that. Not in the same way you do, at least. But you knew that before you said it."

"I did."

"And yet you said it to him anyway."

"Because it needed to be said. I don't think it's fair to try to chalk up the way we choose to do some things as being according to some ... *divine* plan. Same thing when certain things happen, like this." He patted the side of the carriage. "Because a lot of what happens in this life is just dead wrong."

Pain etched his voice, as did a harshness, both of which Olivia understood—and shared. How many times had she questioned God's fairness? It hadn't been fair that Charles treated her the way he had. Yet God had seemingly looked the other way. Just like he had during the war and when the North had finally, and profoundly, proved victorious.

Looking at Ridley now, she could almost see an invisible weight bearing down on him, and she wondered if the years of fighting were to blame. If the defeat of the Confederacy had done to him what it had to so many other Southern sons. Perhaps that was why he'd seemed so eager to leave the South at first. Yet she hadn't heard any of that kind of talk from him in a while.

He walked back to where she stood. "I'm sorry, Olivia." Frustration darkened his tone. "This isn't what I had in mind when I asked you to walk with me tonight."

Funny, she was thinking the same thing. "That's all right. I ..." She shrugged. "Maybe I shouldn't have brought up the subject of—"

"No ... I want us to be able to talk about things. Even things we don't agree about. Especially those things."

She nodded and bowed her head. But with a finger beneath her chin, he gently urged her gaze upward. He tugged a curl at her temple, like he might have done with little Jolene. And though it wasn't an intimate gesture, something about it didn't feel like that of a mere friend either.

"Whether God closed that door," he whispered, "or you did, or whether it was the two of you colluding together ..." Warmth deepened his voice. "I'm grateful you're still here, Olivia Aberdeen."

His simple admittance ignited a spark in her and made her feel appreciated, wanted.

He offered his arm for a second time. "Would you allow me the honor of escorting you back to your window, m'lady?"

Of course was on the tip of her tongue, but Olivia felt a spontaneity she couldn't explain and shook her head. "No, I won't, Mr. Cooper."

He grew very still.

"You promised me a walk, and so far, all you've given me is a mere stroll and a conversation-turned-near-argument. So, no." She tucked her hand through the crook of his elbow, feeling emboldened and liking it. "I'm not ready to go back to my window just yet. I'd very much like that walk you promised instead."

Ridley had to smile. The woman was adorable. There was no other way to describe her. Well, that wasn't quite true. Her features soft with moonlight, her lips turned in a pouty little I've-got-you-now smile, there were other words that came to mind. But adorable was the safest.

Appreciating her challenge, he wasn't about to let her off the hook easily. "That's fairly impertinent talk, don't you think? Coming from a woman who still needs my help climbing back up to that window."

"Impertinent?" She laughed. "You, who speak your mind about everything, regardless of whether the other person agrees with you or not, are calling *me* impertinent?"

Knowing she had him there, he ducked his head. "Well said, Mrs. Aberdeen. All right, you win this round."

"And your vocabulary, Mr. Cooper. First the word *modicum*. And now *impertinent*." Her tone said she was more than enjoying the opportunity to tease him for a change. "Careful, or I'm liable to start believing I don't know you as well as I think I do."

He had to laugh again, though more thoughtfully this time as he considered just how true her last statement was. Wishing it wasn't, he covered her hand on his arm. "Shall we walk?"

The day's heat made for a sultry midnight stroll, but she didn't seem to mind and neither did he. He was just grateful for the time alone with her, and that she'd trusted him enough to climb down. Not once had she slipped either. His mother would've been proud.

They strolled the grounds in comfortable silence, conversation coming easily, and he sneaked looks at her, knowing whatever this ... *friendship* was between them, it had taken a definite turn. A turn that part of him welcomed, while another didn't. When he'd first set sights on this lady, his plans had been to be at Belle Meade for only a few weeks. But now ... With months stretching before him, and getting to know her as he was, his interest in her had deepened in ways he'd never expected.

She was a captivating woman and had proven to be so much more than he'd thought upon first impression. Unfortunately, he doubted her opinion of him would be the same if she knew the truth. Not that it mattered in the end. Their paths might have intersected for a few months at Belle Meade, but their futures were as distant from each other as the east was from the west.

Regardless of what her late husband had done, he was confident that, with time, she would be accepted by Nashville society again. Because of the woman she was, for starters. But also because wealthy widowers looking for wives—especially wives who were young and beautiful and still of child bearing age—had shorter, more forgiving memories than most. Dinner with General Harding's military colleagues had proven that point.

The question in his mind was whether or not Olivia reciprocated their interest. Or would, if the right Confederate general came calling after her period of mourning.

Pushing that bothersome thought to the far edge, he chose a path that looped around the mares' stable, choosing to focus on the present. The occasional neigh coming from the stables revealed their clandestine stroll was no secret to the horses.

"Ridley, I've been meaning … to ask you something."

Noting her reluctance, he glanced her way. She wasn't looking at him.

"Has the … *situation* with Seabird been confirmed yet?"

He smiled at her skirting around the question, understanding her hesitance now. "Not yet. Within a couple of weeks we should know for sure though. Whether or not she's with foal."

She nodded, and he could almost see her making a mental note of how he'd phrased it. She questioned him often while inventorying the various items in the stables, either asking what something was called or what it was used for. She had an insatiable appetite for learning and never asked the same question twice.

Her hand tightened on his arm. "What will you do if she *is* with foal?"

"I haven't made that decision yet. But my options are pretty clear. Either I pay General Harding the stud fee that's owed him—in full— or sign over Seabird's foal. And her foal isn't something I think I want to give up, if there's any way around it."

She kept pace with him, but he sensed something brewing in her reticence. So he gave her the silence he thought she needed.

"Ridley?"

Seconds passed.

"Yes, Olivia?" he whispered, feeling her grip on his arm tighten again. An unconscious gesture, he was sure. But telling, all the same.

"I … I wanted to let you know that I thought it was very good of you to go straight to General Harding and tell him like you did. About Seabird. To be so honest with him. Aunt Elizabeth told me you went that very day."

He shrugged. "Well, if Seabird's with foal, that's hardly something I'll be able to hide over time."

"I know, but … other than the two of us, no one else saw the horses together that day. Another man might have tried to lie his way out of it. Or would have tried to figure a way around having to pay the fee. But you didn't."

He started to respond with a simple thank-you, but that didn't feel right—not in light of the secrets he still held from her. And not with the trace of melancholy in her voice that hinted that her comment went to something deeper. He wondered if she was referring to a man in her not-too-distant past. A man he'd read about in the newspaper even before coming to Belle Meade. Her late husband ... hanged for being a cheat and a traitor. They'd never discussed him. She hadn't broached the subject. So, out of respect, he hadn't either.

"But you were honest," she continued. "And forthcoming. Even when you knew there would be a price to pay. And I think that's most commendable."

She lifted her face to him, and this time he managed a quiet thank you, grateful for the darkness as the underlying truth of what she said struck a nerve. She was paying the price of her late husband's betrayal. But she was also paying the price that Ridley knew he himself should—and *would*—be paying, if people around here knew he'd fought for the Union.

There were moments when he wanted to tell General Harding to his face. Like earlier this evening. But he didn't dare. Not having given Uncle Bob his word that he wouldn't. And not when realizing that everything he stood to gain here, as well as the good he hoped to do for the former slaves—Uncle Bob included—would be swept away like yesterday's garbage.

He glanced down at Olivia's arm looped through his and tried to imagine her in the Colorado Territory. On the one hand, he could. The woman had a strength about her and an independent streak a mile wide, even though she did her best to restrain it—a habit of hers he was working hard to help her break. With a little encouragement, maybe even a little goading, there was no telling what this woman could do. But she'd certainly complicated things for him. In ways she wasn't even aware of, he felt certain.

Feeling her attention, he slid his gaze her way. "What?" He kept his voice low again as they neared the house.

"I was thinking of how expensive that's going to be ... if the general makes you pay the fee. One hundred dollars!"

"I know it." He blew out a breath. "But that's the going rate for Jack Malone to sire a foal. So if Seabird's in the family way, I'll just have to pay it. Having a thoroughbred foal like that, along with a mare like Seabird, is just too good an investment to pass up. I won't find horse-flesh anywhere near their equal in the Colorado Territory."

Her pace slowed. "So ... you *are* still planning on going west?"

Disbelief framed her question, as did disappointment, and Ridley couldn't help but feel bad about it. But also good. Her disappointment gave him hope. "Of course I'm still going. The timing has been delayed, that's all. You ... didn't realize that?"

She stopped beneath her window. "With all that's happened recently, I ..." She lifted a shoulder and let it fall. "I guess I figured maybe Belle Meade had grown on you." She gave a breathy laugh. "At least a little."

"Oh, it has, Olivia. In some very ... *definite* ways."

She nodded absently, apparently having missed his not-so-subtle insinuation. Though tempted to be bolder, he didn't want to risk scaring her off. She could be awfully skittish at times.

"When will you leave?"

"General Harding asked me to stay through the yearling sale to help out, and I gave him my word I would."

"Which is next June. The yearling sale, I mean."

"That's right. Shortly after that I'll head west into the *wild*. How did you phrase it? Where there're only Indians, bears, and freezing cold."

Not responding, she seemed determined to look anywhere but at him.

"I apologize, Olivia, if I did or said anything that led you to think I'd changed my plans about Colorado."

"No." She waved her hand. "You don't have to apologize. I just didn't know, that's all." She reached for the lattice, but he reached for her hand and took it in his. She tried—rather half-heartedly, he thought—to pull away, but he didn't let go.

"Look at me, Olivia," he whispered.

She only gestured. "I need to get back up there before I'm missed."

"You're not going to be missed. No one knows you're gone."

"Still, I think it would be best if I—"

He brought her hand to his mouth and kissed it—*once, twice*—like he'd wanted to do the first time they'd met. Then he lingered, appreciating how her eyes widened, as well as the softness of her skin and how tongue-tied she suddenly seemed to be.

But mostly he liked how she didn't pull away.

"As I said at the beginning, I wasn't originally planning on staying this long." The underside of her wrist was smoother than silk. "Learning all that Uncle Bob had to teach me—that he's still teaching me—has taken longer than I'd expected. But then, I don't really mind." He turned her hand palm up in his and laced his fingers with hers, admiring how well they fit. "Because another interest has caught my attention."

She blinked. Her mouth slipped open the tiniest bit, and there was no question she understood what he was saying this time. Yet, as he'd feared, she gently pulled her hand back. Reluctantly, he let go, knowing better than to push her.

"I'm happy for you, Ridley." Even in the dim light, her smile looked false. "And I know you'll fare well out there. You'll do well at whatever you set your mind to."

Though she hadn't moved physically, she felt miles away, and Ridley couldn't decide whether he wanted to shake her or take her in his arms and kiss her good and long.

"Something you need to understand, Olivia. One night, during the war, on a hillside not far from here … I made a vow that if I got through the war alive—which, at that point, I was none too certain I would—I'd get as far away from all the bloodshed and killing as I could. And I'd go someplace where I could start life fresh again. Without all this … *tradition* and 'this is the way things are' hanging over me." He recalled the painting of the Colorado Territory he'd seen years earlier. "Did you know that Colorado has mountains so high they touch the clouds? Even in the heat of summer, the snow on some of those peaks never melts." His smile came without effort. "I want to see that. I want to breathe the air. I want to make a path where no one's ever walked before. I don't know if that makes any sense, but that's what I want."

"I can understand that," she finally whispered, her hands knotted at her waist. "You wanting those things. But the truth is, Ridley …" She bowed her head briefly before peering back up. "I don't want them."

Her soft admission knifed through him.

"Unlike you, Ridley, I like it here, and—"

"Do you?" He saw her stiffen. "Because I'm not all that convinced you do."

"Nashville is my home. I—"

"Nashville has changed, and home can be many things, Olivia.

Calling a *place* home can sometimes prove to be the loneliest home of all. Particularly when you're treated as an outcast."

She held his gaze, then slowly lowered her head. He couldn't help but think of her late husband again. As dead as that man was, his memory certainly seemed to linger close at times.

She turned and put her hand on the lattice—effectively ending their conversation—and climbed up two rungs.

He took hold of her arm. "You're not ready to go up just yet," he said softly.

"On the contrary, Ridley. I think I am. And I don't need your help to do it either."

He looked pointedly at her skirt. "So I don't guess you need me to remind you to tuck that back in first then."

She peered down, huffed beneath her breath, then climbed down, yanking the back hem of her skirt and shoving it in the waistband— far less ladylike than before. And though he didn't dare let on, he enjoyed every minute.

He shadowed her up the lattice, not about to let her climb on her own just yet. She glanced back at him twice, no doubt shooting him daggers in the dark, which he found equally entertaining. This woman's stubbornness ran a mile deep and another mile wide, and he welcomed the challenge of taming every last inch of it.

Though it occurred to him as he walked back to the cabin that he'd best be careful she didn't end up taming him first.

Chapter
TWENTY-NINE

W ell, General Harding..."

The veterinarian exited Seabird's stall, towel in hand, and Ridley tried to sense which way the man's pronouncement would go. The warm air in the stable grew even more so as all gathered seemed to hold a collective breath, waiting to hear the news.

Word about Doc Fleming's visit today had traveled fast. Most of the stable hands working at Belle Meade had been here when Seabird lost her first promising foal, and they felt a vested interest Ridley hadn't predicted. He was certain the unusual circumstances surrounding Seabird's possible pregnancy were also contributing factors to people's curiosity.

Even Olivia stood with Elizabeth Harding at the far end of the hallway, waiting and watching, though never directly meeting his gaze. But it was the doctor's expression Ridley tried to read.

"The mare appears to be in fullest health, sir," the veterinarian said. "Which is a fortunate thing ... because she is most definitely with foal."

Impromptu cheers and laughter skittered through the crowd, and Ridley accepted a moment or two of congratulatory pats on the back. He couldn't deny, this was the outcome he'd hoped for—had prayed for. Though his prayers had felt somewhat stiff, and his petitions to the Almighty uncomfortably foreign.

Hoping to see Olivia, he glanced down the corridor, eager to catch her reaction to the news. But the hallway was empty. She was gone. Since their midnight stroll over two weeks ago, things had been different between them. She was still friendly and they talked, but she was more distant with him. He sensed she'd been evading him. Only yesterday, as he left the general's office, he'd glimpsed her coming out the front door of the mansion only to see her duck back inside, presumably thinking he hadn't seen her.

But that was all right. He was biding his time.

Even at fifty-six hundred acres, Belle Meade was an awfully small place for a woman who insisted on traveling everywhere by foot. He remembered what Betsy had said the night she'd shaved his beard — that she hoped the woman he'd set his sights on could get a runnin' start. He wanted to tell Olivia Aberdeen that she could run all she wanted. It wouldn't matter. The night they'd walked together and she'd reacted to the news of him going to Colorado like she had, she'd given him reason to hope. And that was all he needed.

Besides, it was time for August inventory, and he'd decided to exercise some of his "supervisory" rights. Just a few questions here and there about what she was doing or if she needed any assistance. He couldn't wait to see her face when he asked. She didn't much like being questioned. Especially by him. Which, of course, just made him want to do it all the more. And if Olivia Aberdeen thought she'd seen the last of that little horse cart he'd built for her, the lady was mistaken.

Uncle Bob, standing a few feet away, caught his attention and motioned. Ridley turned to see Doc Fleming walk back inside the stall, General Harding trailing close behind. He followed. It was his horse, after all. Harding would've done the same had the tables been turned, and Ridley had a question he needed to pose to the horse doctor before giving the general his decision. But before he got to the stall, Grady Matthews stepped in front of him.

"Cooper, me and some of the other men want a word with you ... *sir*." Condescension thickened his tone.

"Not now, Matthews. I'll meet with you later."

Ridley sidestepped him, but Grady matched his move.

"It won't take long, Cooper. We just wanna know why we didn't get a raise too."

"A raise?"

Grady scoffed. "Like the darkies. We always been paid more than them."

Seeing the seriousness in Grady's expression, along with a wealth of pride and ignorance, Ridley wished he could lay the man flat out. Or at least have the pleasure of trying. But if he did, his days as a foreman would be finished. "Matthews, if you don't like the way General

Harding pays his workers, either take it up with him or go work some-where else. Maybe you could find another old war buddy of your father's to latch onto. Until then, get back to work."

Ridley shouldered past him, not missing what Grady murmured beneath his breath. But he ignored it, intent on being included in whatever the doctor had to say.

He entered the stall and, sure enough, upon seeing him, General Harding gave him an accepting—if somewhat annoyed—nod, then addressed the veterinarian. "Dr. Fleming, a word about the mare. You were here when Seabird lost her first foal. What are the odds of that happening again this time?"

The exact question Ridley wanted answered.

Dr. Fleming, an older man with an untamable shock of graying hair, glanced at Seabird. "It's not quite that simple. A number of vari-ables figure into the equation, General. I don't know what you've been doing differently, but this mare's in prime condition, sir. I was here when this little filly took her first steps, and I can tell you, she's never been in better health."

Ridley felt a swell of pride. But he knew better than to think it was due to his own efforts. Anything he'd done, he'd done at Uncle Bob's direction. Yet he couldn't deny the pride he had in Seabird. He caught the mare looking his way, and though he'd never admit it to anyone— except maybe Uncle Bob—he was pretty sure Seabird sensed his emotions in that moment. Maybe even returned them.

"But that said ..." Doc Fleming packed his satchel, caution creep-ing into his tone. "This mare was in good health last time too, and carried to full term. My conjecture about what happened remains unchanged. The trauma of birth was simply too much for the colt. It's rare, given the strength and stamina of these thoroughbreds." He glanced at Ridley. "But it still happens. So while I wish I could give you firm odds, General ..." He sighed, latching the ties on his bag. "I simply can't. The missing variables won't allow it."

General Harding nodded and shook Fleming's hand. Ridley did the same, and the veterinarian took his leave.

Harding's focus turned to Ridley. "Mr. Cooper." The general reached into his suit pocket. "I'll give you fifty dollars right now for the foal and will waive the stud fee, of course."

Murmurs rose from lingering stable hands.

Harding counted out the bills. "Whether the foal lives or dies, the money is yours. I'll also assume all expenses associated with the foaling and for Seabird until the foal is born. But the mare, of course, will remain in your ownership."

Somewhat surprised at the offer, though not shocked, Ridley studied the man, then the cash. He'd already worked the figures backward and forward, and he'd walked in here today knowing what he wanted to do. Paying General Harding the stud fee would take close to half the funds he needed to travel west and start his ranch. But Harding was compensating him well, and Ridley knew he could count on the next several months' salary to replenish his savings.

If anything happened to threaten that income, however, or if he lost his job … All the figuring in the world wouldn't help him then.

Paying the stud fee—buying the unborn foal—meant taking a risk. But as he'd learned only too well, life was full of risks. The trick was knowing when to grab hold of an opportunity and when to let it pass. Everything in him told him to grab hold of this and never let go.

"No, thank you, General. The foal isn't for sale." Ridley reached into the pocket of his trousers and pulled out a neatly folded wad of bills, his fingers brushing the seashell as he did. The silence from the stable hands looking on grew deafening. Young Jimmy stood at the forefront, eyes wide and watchful.

General Harding didn't even glance at the money in Ridley's hand before reaching back into his own pocket. "I'll make it one hundred dollars, Mr. Cooper. So you not only keep your hundred, but you make another. You'd be up two hundred dollars for the day. Not a bad profit."

Ridley didn't move his hand, the wad of bills extended. "*No*, thank you, sir. I'm choosing to keep the—"

"One hundred and fifty dollars, Mr. Cooper. Along with covering the other expenses I've mentioned. That's my top offer." Harding smiled but his expression showed displeasure. "And I won't extend it again."

One hundred and fifty dollars.

Ridley held back his initial response. If he accepted the offer, he'd walk out of here today with two hundred and fifty dollars in his pocket, instead of being down a hundred. That kind of money would go a long way in giving peace of mind and buying a fresh start. But if General Harding was willing to pay that kind of money for a foal unseen—especially knowing the outcome of Seabird's first pregnancy—the man must be counting on something pretty special. Which is exactly what Ridley was betting on. A colt or filly with Jack Malone as its sire and Seabird as its dam ... The hairs on the back of Ridley's neck stood up—the combination of power and speed, the mixture of agility and grace would be unbeatable.

Ridley's fingers tightened on the bills in his hand. "I appreciate your offer, General Harding. It's most generous, sir," he added, mindful of the other employees nearby. "But I choose to keep the foal. Here's the one hundred dollars I owe you for the stud fee. In cash, as you requested." Feeling a subtle sense of triumph, he detected a flicker of surprise in the general's features, as well as displeasure.

Harding took the money, put it and his own away, then leveled a stare. "Raising thoroughbreds isn't for the faint of heart—or wallet—Mr. Cooper. I hope this isn't a decision you end up regretting."

Ridley was about to say he hoped it wasn't too, but the general turned and strode away before he could respond. Ridley watched him go, then looked back at Seabird, hoping this triumph wouldn't prove too costly for him in the end.

"Livvy, I wish you were coming with us, dear."

Olivia tucked Elizabeth's full skirt into the carriage, then stepped back so Jedediah could close the door. "That's so kind of you, Aunt. But I've got more than enough work to do here." Olivia glanced at Susanna sitting opposite Elizabeth in the carriage and caught Susanna's understanding look. "I'm sure you and Susanna will have a wonderful time."

Elizabeth's countenance brightened. "Oh, I'm certain we will. First we're shopping, then meeting Selene and Lizzie for lunch. Mary, too, since she's finishing early with her tutor today. My only regret is that you're not able to take part in the day as well."

Olivia understood what her aunt was saying, but she didn't feel the least bit slighted. Well, maybe the *least* bit. But her being seen in town with Mrs. William Giles Harding wouldn't do her aunt any good, and they both knew it. They'd come to an unspoken understanding on the topic—a delicate trait Olivia had learned from her mother, one of many passed down through generations of Southern women.

After seeing the carriage off, Olivia returned to her room and retrieved her satchel, one Elizabeth had loaned her that the general hadn't used in years. Elizabeth said the satchel had been gathering dust on a shelf and assured her he wouldn't mind. The previous evening, Olivia had taken care to wipe the leather clean of dust, and now she slipped her lesson notes inside, along with a lone worn copy of a McGuffey's Reader, knowing Jimmy and Jolene would be waiting, eager to learn.

With Susanna's assistance, she'd purchased each of the children a slate and supply of chalk, along with two pencils and a few precious sheets of paper. After gaining permission from Jimmy and Jolene's mother, she'd also bought them each a pair of new boots. The expense of the items proved to be more than she'd anticipated, but she'd gladly paid the sum. And would again, even though it had taken most of what she'd saved. "I dickered with the owner, ma'am," Susanna had assured her after returning from the mercantile. "And he came down some on the price. But he asked lots of questions too. Like who was gonna be usin' these things. I told him I's buyin' it all for a white woman, a guest of the Hardings. He said that was all right then, that he'd let me buy it."

When Susanna had recounted the conversation, the mercantile owner's comment had set Olivia's teeth on edge. Just as it did now. Olivia glanced at the clock — only twenty past nine — and she purposefully fiddled about, straightening her desk and then the top of the bureau.

For the past week, around this time every morning, Ridley accompanied Uncle Bob to the stallions' stable. They stayed there until late afternoon, working with Jack Malone, a continuation of Ridley's training, he'd explained. With the bureau in order, she turned to the wardrobe, saw the skirt she'd worn yesterday awaiting a good brushing and kindly obliged.

She checked the time again. Twenty-five past nine.

She wasn't really trying to avoid him. Well, not entirely. She was simply trying to limit their time together. At least that's how she chose to think of it. The issue wasn't that she didn't like Ridley. The issue was ... that she *did*.

She looked out the window across the meadow to the cabin, then gradually drew her gaze back until it rested on the lattice. When he'd kissed her hand that night ... She closed her eyes, remembering. He'd taken her breath away and more. How could one man's kiss — on her *hand*, no less — stir desires within her that sharing another man's bed never had?

Even now, the memory fanned a flame.

She smoothed a hand over the front of her dress and inhaled. Fear flooded every corner of her heart, as it had that night, swiftly followed by anger. Anger at her own foolishness. She'd been down this road before with a man. She knew what would happen if she allowed herself to trust again. Ridley seemed so different from Charles. But Charles had seemed kind and charming too—at the start. Even if she could trust that Ridley was genuinely everything she believed him to be—which she thought he was—he wasn't the kind of man she was looking for.

Feeble, paunchy, and dull. She sighed, tempted to smile as she recalled her mental list of attributes for a second husband.

Ridley Cooper was anything but those things. And knowing he'd only be here at Belle Meade for a short time had given her every reason she needed to pull her hand back and start climbing that lattice.

And yet ...

She'd found herself thinking about those snowy peaks—the ones that outlasted the summer sun—so many times since. What a sight they must be. Not that she would ever see them. Or ever cared to.

Olivia was halfway to the stable when she realized she'd forgotten the satchel. She turned back and was nearing the main house when someone called her name. She turned to see General Harding riding toward her on his stallion. The hooves of the giant black beast pummeled the ground, much like she imagined they would pummel her if given the chance.

She'd grown more accustomed to the mares, although she still didn't like being around them. But the stallions ...

They were a rare breed. As frightening as they were fierce. And so unpredictable. She mustered her last shred of courage and stood her ground—shaking—as the general reined in the terrible beast only feet away.

"Good morning, Olivia." Health flushed his features. "Isn't this the week of inventory?"

Heart still pounding, Olivia nodded as she peered up, unable to focus on anything but the stallion's gigantic teeth as the animal worked at the bit in its mouth. "Yes, sir. I'm headed to the mares' stable now, actually." She gestured. "I forgot something in my room."

He nodded, looking as though he had something on his mind. "May I assume you're still enjoying the work?"

"You may. And I am. Very much."

The stallion snorted, eying her like she was something he'd like to trample. Or chomp. His head was enormous, like the rest of him, and she couldn't imagine riding an animal that size or ever desiring to. The mere thought made her weak in the knees.

"Well, I'm glad. I take it you're in agreement with your increase in pay as well?"

She frowned. "My ... increase in pay?"

"Mr. Cooper is a firm negotiator, Olivia. But I still believe I'm getting the better end of the bargain. He assured me the additional responsibilities won't be too much for you." A hint of smugness communicated doubt. "I hope he didn't steer me wrong."

Feeling as though she'd been thrust mid-stream into a conversation—and one in a foreign language, no less—Olivia wasn't about to disagree. Not with General William Giles Harding. And not about an increase in pay. "No, sir. I'm certain I'll be able to handle the responsibilities quite well." Just like she looked forward to *handling* Ridley Cooper for obligating her further without her permission. Why he'd felt at liberty to speak on her behalf, she couldn't guess. Surely his memory wasn't so dull he'd forgotten her reaction when he'd passed along the teaching advertisement.

Never mind that his instincts had been right about her love for teaching.

The stallion pawed the ground but the general kept him in check. "As I told Mr. Cooper, you're welcome to take one of the mares. Or a stallion, if you feel up to it. It's too far a distance to cover by foot. No matter how fond you may be of walking."

Olivia managed a smile, but only because she was imagining wrapping her hands around Ridley's muscular neck and squeezing tight. What had that man gotten her into? Nothing short of threat of death would motivate her to get back onto a horse. And she'd rather die straightaway than climb onto a stallion again!

Then again, death would be more a promise than a threat in that situation.

"I assume you're aware"—General Harding leaned forward in the saddle—"that the doctor visited Mrs. Harding yesterday afternoon."

Gathering her frayed thoughts, Olivia shook her head. "No, sir. I wasn't."

"Did my wife, by chance, share his report with you?" Subtle challenge layered his tone.

"Not this time. But from the time before, she shared that he was pleased to see her regaining her strength."

"Yes, he said much the same again. But he also confided in me that this ... 'renewed strength' is most definitely temporary. He's seen this before. The weak spells will return." His attention narrowed on her. "I know what you're doing, don't for a moment think otherwise."

Olivia's stomach dropped. *Rachel's tea.* He knew. But how? Elizabeth didn't even know where the tea came from, and she'd been drinking it now for the past two months. The herbs were most definitely having a rejuvenating effect. But what if the general blamed Rachel for masking the "Negro remedy," and Rachel got in trouble?

"General Harding, I can explain. I want you to know that it's not—"

"You're filling my wife's head with foolish ideas of what she'll do once she's well. Traveling with me, seeing her daughters marry ..."

Realizing the mistake she'd nearly made, Olivia felt a flush of hot and cold.

"But we both know that won't be happening for my wife," he continued. "What you're doing is giving her false hope. Which is actually quite cruel."

"No more cruel than withholding what *you* believe to be the truth." Olivia blinked, unable to believe she'd voiced the thought aloud. But seeing General Harding's eyes darken, she knew she had. "General, I didn't—"

"Olivia," he said softly, though it lacked gentleness, much like Charles had sounded whenever he'd used her Christian name. "I realize you're doing what you believe to be best for Mrs. Harding. But I would prefer ..." He paused. "I would *request* that, in the future, you would, as my wife's companion, act in accordance with what the doctor deems best for her well-being. Considering your affection for my wife—and all that you are personally afforded by being here at Belle Meade—I don't believe that's too much to ask. Do you?"

Hearing a thread of warning, Olivia met his gaze and nodded. "I understand, General."

His smile came easily as he adjusted the reins in his grip.

"But I also believe the doctors are wrong, sir. I think Aunt Elizabeth is getting better. And loving her as I do, how can I help but want that for her?"

General Harding looked at her as though she were a child. A simpleton. "Wanting something, Olivia, does not make it so. It's best to accept the world—and our circumstances—for what they are, instead of spending life wishing for something that can never be. But ... I would think you would have learned that by now."

Feeling a prick near the vicinity of her heart, Olivia couldn't respond.

"Have you received correspondence yet from General Percival Meeks?"

She frowned. "General *Meeks*?" she repeated, recalling the older gentleman seated to her right at the recent dinner party. The gentleman who—though kind and good natured—fit her less-than-flattering list of husbandly attributes a little too well. "No, sir. Why?"

"I received a missive from the general in which he sought my permission for the liberty of writing to you, and I granted it. With the understanding," he added quickly, "that it's strictly in pursuit of friendship. However, if something else were to develop along the way ..."

His half smile held possibilities she didn't care to pursue, and she made no pretense of masking her objection. "I am still in mourning, General Harding."

"As I'm well aware, Olivia. However ... General Meeks is a very wealthy man. And a very lonely one." He gripped the stallion's reins. "Which is a favorable combination for any woman. But especially for one in a situation such as yours."

Seething inside, Olivia didn't watch him ride away, but strode back upstairs to her bedroom, grabbed the satchel from the bed— handling it with far less care than before—and stormed toward the mares' stable. Would there ever come a time when a man wasn't in charge of her life? Of *her*?

If she wanted any say at all on this topic, she was going to have to step up her efforts, or General Harding would have her married by Christmas. To Percival Meeks!

Easing her death grip on the handle of the satchel, she slowed her steps and tried to sort her thoughts. *Feeble, paunchy, and dull ...* But also kind and good-natured, she'd already admitted as much. She sighed, feeling an inexplicable moment of reckoning. General Percival Meeks was probably just the type of man she was looking for. Or should be looking for. He was caring. She couldn't imagine him ever hurting her. He was wealthy. She'd be well provided for. And he was Confederate through and through. He didn't live in Nashville, but Chattanooga was supposedly a nice enough city. And he was *safe*. She wasn't at risk of losing her heart ...

Only her dream of what might have been.

Nearing the stable, she spotted Ridley off to the side in a corral, and she paused. Clearly, he was waiting for her. And—upon closer observation—she decided the man had lost his mind. Which worked out rather well at the moment, because she was more than ready to give him a piece of hers.

Chapter
THIRTY

What on earth is he thinking? But looking at the miniature horse cart Ridley stood beside and the not-so-miniature horse whose reins he held in his grip, Olivia could easily guess.

She strode through the open gate, her frustration mounting by the second. Ridley's mischievous smile said he was waiting for her to say something and that he hoped it would be positive.

He would just have to be disappointed.

"Ridley Cooper." She willed a steadiness to her voice. "What gives you the right to speak for me? To obligate me to the general in *whatever* way you've done? I may report to you, but you should have requested my permission first."

His smile faded. His expression turned wary, then apologetic. "Olivia, my inten—"

"*You*, of all people, Ridley"—she lowered her voice even as her temper rose—"who know how I feel about horses." Her throat tightened with emotion, making it impossible to speak. She gestured to the horse that—upon second glance—appeared to be either knocking on death's door or in extremely poor health. Or both. The animal's back was sunken, its gray coat thinned to almost balding in places, and its spindly legs looked near ready to buckle. But it was still a horse, and Ridley was still wrong.

"Olivia, if you'll allow me to explain. My original intent in suggesting to the general—"

"Did you or did you not, assure him that I would accept additional responsibilities without speaking to me first? Fully aware that it would mandate me riding a horse. And knowing that I can't!"

In a blink, Ridley's demeanor went from apologetic to anything but. The transition was jarring, as was his unyielding stare.

"Yes, Olivia." He exhaled. "I'm guilty of assuring the general you would accept additional responsibilities." He laughed, but there was no humor in it. "The first thing I told him was that you would begin reviewing the supply books for the three limestone quarries. All the while knowing it would require you to travel once a month by horse or very small cart"—he indicated the horse cart with a broad wave—"to the quarries on the other side of the plantation."

The way he said it—with a smartness to his tone—made it sound like she'd be going for a picnic! "But that's precisely it, Ridley. You had no right to do that. That was *my* decision to make. You should have told the general to ask me himself whether I wanted to—"

"You're right. It was your decision to make. And I should have asked you first."

She blinked, not having expected to win the argument so easily. Nor for him to have acquiesced so quickly.

"But I knew you'd say no," he continued. "And, to be clear, you weren't to be asked, Olivia. Because the general had requested I find a foreman to do the job. He believes the detailed work will be too taxing for you. But when I realized how much he was offering to pay … And knowing what little you make per week …"

Olivia winced. She was fortunate to be earning a wage at all. And naturally, Ridley's salary was significantly more than hers, being a man and the foreman. Still, his comment rankled.

"I suggested to the general that he give you the opportunity instead."

As his words sank in, so did a glimpse at his original intention. She swallowed, feeling herself grow smaller. She found it difficult to maintain his gaze. Yet looking away would only make things worse. It would be admitting guilt that was already nicking her wounded pride.

"At first," Ridley continued, "General Harding resisted the idea of you doing the job. Then I told him I'd be more than willing to supervise. Make sure you did it right."

The way he said it, she knew he hoped to coax a smile. But even though he'd tried to do something nice, she was still angry at the way he'd gone about it. And she was curious too.

"How much would he have paid me?"

"Eight dollars."

Her eyes widened. "That's double my monthly salary. For one trip?"

He nodded.

She did the math. The two dollars she made per week now, plus eight ... that was sixteen dollars a month. She could hardly fathom making that much. But when she looked at the cart, then at the horse—who suddenly looked surprisingly more alert and agile—all she could think of was how little Copper, the Shetland pony, had bumped and jostled the miniature cart all across the field that day. Her stomach dropped to her feet. She hated for General Harding to win in this situation—or in any other, for that matter—but she didn't need the money that badly.

She shook her head. "I just can't do it, Ridley. I ..." His eyes narrowed. Sensing what he was going to say next, she raced to beat him to it. "I'm *choosing* not to do it." She held up a hand. "All right? Is that better?"

A smile crept back to his face, and the lines in his tanned forehead eased. "Thank you. That's much better." He began unhitching the horse.

She watched him, thinking of what he'd done—and her practically taking his head off for the effort—and the emotion that had made it difficult for her to speak moments earlier worked its way to her eyes. Only this time, it wasn't indignation causing them to burn. He wasn't angry with her, or sullen and punishing like Charles would have been. The difference was glaring. And humbling. And she squeezed her eyes tight until the intensity—and shame—lessened.

"Ridley," she whispered.

He straightened and looked back at her.

"I know you think I'm foolish for being scared of horses, but I—"

"Have I ever once called you foolish, Olivia?"

She studied him, reflecting. Then shook her head and lowered her eyes.

"You're not foolish for being afraid." With a touch, he urged her chin up. "I don't know what happened to make you fear horses so much ... But I have a feeling it's something more than just what happened on the way out here that day."

Hearing his invitation, she debated over telling him, when he moved closer.

"But what *is* foolish, in my estimation"—his mouth tipped, understanding in his gaze—"is when we let fear keep us from reaching for something within our grasp ..." His focus dropped from her eyes to her mouth. "If only we'd try."

She didn't know how, but the distance between them evaporated. He gently cradled her cheek, his hand strong and rough, his breath warm and smelling of mint. And when he leaned in, she jumped, shocked at what he was about to do. But even more so at how much she *wanted* him to do it. *To kiss her.*

But it wasn't proper. There was no understanding between them, no possibility of a future. It wasn't to be done. And it was up to her to—

He placed a feather soft kiss on her cheek, far enough from her mouth to be considered marginally chaste. Yet close enough where she could imagine his lips full on hers. The image was vivid and inviting. He lingered, his hand tracing a path to the curve of her neck. She shivered, and he smiled.

"You're stronger than you think, Olivia," he whispered, drawing back slightly. "I see it in you, even if you don't."

She blinked, too stunned to move and half afraid to. His closeness worked like a magnet, pulling her in and making her want more. A satisfied look moved into his eyes, which contrasted with the subtle, unquenched ache he'd awakened inside her. One she couldn't identify and knew she'd never felt before.

A yearning, she was certain, that General Percival Meeks would never be able to slake.

That afternoon, with Jimmy and Jolene's lesson completed, the supplies in the mares' and stallions' stables inventoried and the order sheet completed, she sought Ridley out, having thought of another question for him. One stemming from something he'd said earlier. She found him in a corral outside the stallions' stable working with Jack Malone, the stud that was going to put Belle Meade on the international map, or so she'd heard General Harding say.

Ridley was tall but the stallion stood a head taller, all powerful sinew and muscle. She watched them for a while, admiring the strength and grace with which the stallion moved—*both* stallions, she thought with a smile. Ridley's skill with the thoroughbred was impressive, and his improvement in recent months undeniable.

Some yards away, Uncle Bob leaned against the fence, overseeing the training at a distance, she guessed, since Ridley would occasionally glance in his direction, and Uncle Bob would either nod in approval or offer further instruction through gestures. The two men communicated with minimal conversation. Which, considering how much time they'd spent together, wasn't surprising. Still, they made an odd pair, the two of them.

It wasn't many a white man who would apprentice himself to a Negro. Even a Negro as obviously talented and respected as Bob Green. But then, as she was slowly coming to learn, Ridley Cooper wasn't like most men.

Deciding her question for him could wait, she grabbed her satchel.

"Mrs. Aberdeen!"

She turned to see Grady Matthews, one of the stable hands, walking toward her, and her guard instantly rose. His gaze swept her up and down as he approached. Not inappropriately so. But still, not in a manner she welcomed.

"Mr. Matthews."

"How are you today, ma'am? You look might pretty."

She nodded a brief thanks. She attempted to avoid the man whenever possible. He'd never acted unseemly toward her. But she always got the feeling that he would if he thought he could get away with it.

"I'm sorry, Mr. Matthews, but you've caught me on my way to—"

"Oh, this won't take long, Mrs. Aberdeen. I was just wonderin' if you could show me where the box of clips for the bridles are. I swear I been lookin' everywhere but I can't find 'em. *Mr. Cooper* wants all the worn pieces replaced."

Not missing his snide tone when he said Ridley's name, Olivia chose to ignore it. She knew Grady Matthews and a handful of other men weren't fond of Ridley. But she chalked it up to jealousy.

She glanced in the direction of the supply room. "They're on the second shelf on the right. In a box marked 'bridle clips.' I know, because we received a new shipment of them last week. I put them in there myself." She smiled a little in an effort to make her response seem less abrupt.

Grady Matthews shook his head. "I just looked, ma'am. They ain't there. Maybe we used 'em all up. I'll tell Mr. Cooper we ran out and need to wait until you get more—"

"We didn't run out, Mr. Matthews. That's the entire purpose behind inventorying. So you won't run out of something when you need it."

Huffing a little, she strode to the supply room, marched to the second shelf on the right and—sure enough—the box wasn't there.

She looked around. "It's impossible that we used that many clips in only a week."

Leaning against the doorway, he gave a befuddled shrug, and it occurred to her how befitting that gesture looked on him. She set out to find the box, only too aware of him watching.

"What's this here?"

She turned to find him looking at the copy of the McGuffey's Reader that had been in the front pocket of the satchel.

"That's a book, Mr. Matthews. Used for teaching someone to read."

"Doesn't have many pictures in it."

"Probably because it's not a picture book."

"Would be a better book though, if it had more pictures."

"Perhaps." Her patience waning, Olivia stood back to survey the highest shelves. "If your purpose isn't to read."

There, she saw it. On the top shelf in the corner. It looked as though someone had simply tossed it up there.

"Are *you* teaching somebody to read, Mrs. Aberdeen?"

Hearing a distinctive difference in Grady Matthews's voice, Olivia turned. Mr. Matthews stood with the book in his hand, all traces of befuddlement gone. And she saw the situation for what it was. And it wasn't about bridle clips at all.

"I found the box, Mr. Matthews." She gestured. "Apparently someone put it back in the wrong place. Perhaps someone who doesn't know how to read."

Seeing his expression darken a shade, she picked up the satchel and reached for the book. But Grady Matthews pulled it back and grabbed hold of her arm instead.

"Some folks don't think it's right for darkies to be learnin' how to read and write, Mrs. Aberdeen. And they feel right strongly about it too. I'm not sayin' I agree with 'em—"

"Of course you're not." Olivia tried to pull away but he didn't let go.

"I *am* sayin' that I think it'd be best for a lady like you to steer clear of all that, ma'am."

"Unhand me, Mr. Matthews!" She spotted Selene in the outer corridor. Selene glanced in as she passed.

"All I'm sayin' is that I think you should be careful to—"

"Olivia!" Selene stuck her head around the corner at the same time Matthews released his hold. "I've finally found you! Oh." Selene made a face. "I hope I'm not interrupting."

Grateful, Olivia smiled at her. "You're not at all. We're just finishing here. Mr. Matthews, if you'll retrieve that box, I'd appreciate it."

Choosing not to allow Grady Matthews's only-too-prevalent opinion to sway her, she took the book from him and walked outside with Selene.

Olivia couldn't remember Selene seeking her out before. And seeing the young woman dressed in her riding habit, she didn't have to guess what she was up to. But the Harding sisters usually rode mares, not stallions. "Are you here to ride?"

"I'm on my way, actually." Selene gestured. "Mary and Cousin Lizzie are having the mares saddled." Her dark brows shot up. "You're welcome to join us, if you'd like."

"Thank you, but I've got plenty of work to do."

Selene's eyes narrowed playfully. "You *always* say that."

Olivia smiled and shrugged, deciding to let the comment pass unchecked. She liked Selene and felt a welcome and an ease with the older sister that she didn't with the younger.

"The reason I'm here, Olivia, is because of Mother." Selene studied her riding gloves.

Olivia glanced toward the mansion. "She hasn't taken ill, I hope."

"No, no. It's nothing like that. Mother's fine. She had a lovely time at lunch, in fact. Several of her friends whom she hasn't seen in a while joined us for lunch. I arranged it as a surprise for her, and she enjoyed it very much. The conversation, the teacakes. All the 'lady's refreshments,' as she refers to them."

Olivia smiled but felt a sting at having been excluded. She understood why. She *agreed* with it. But still, the rejection stung.

"All the visiting wore Mother out though." Selene laughed softly. "So she's resting."

Olivia nodded.

Seconds passed.

"I've been meaning to thank you, Olivia ..." Selene averted her gaze. "For all you've done for Mother since you arrived. The war was hard on her, especially during Father's imprisonment. But she's much improved since you've come."

Olivia warmed beneath the unexpected praise. "Thank you, Selene. But whatever I've given pales in comparison to what you've all given me. So, thank *you*, in return."

Selene smiled, her gloved hands knotted at her waist. "There's one more thing I wanted to speak with you about. Mary and I were discussing it earlier. Since Mother's feeling so much better . . ." She bit the inside of her lip. "We thought perhaps we could do something special for her. Here, at Belle Meade. Something like the luncheon today."

Olivia brightened. "That's a wonderful idea! And you're right, she'd love that. I'm certain Susanna would be willing to make whatever we wanted. The 'lady's refreshments,' as you call them. And though I'm not very good in the kitchen, I'd help in any way I could."

A shadow tainted Selene's expression. "I know you would. And . . . that's what makes this so hard." Seconds passed, and she finally exhaled. "There's no easy way to say this, Olivia, so please forgive me if I come across as rude. I don't mean to, honestly. But . . . we'd like to invite women from town to come. Mother's friends who may not feel comfortable accepting the invitation if they knew that—"

Olivia raised her hand, her face on fire with embarrassment. And comprehension. "Say no more." She forced a smile. "I understand. Simply let me know what your plans are, and I'll be certain to . . . be occupied elsewhere that day."

"Olivia." Selene reached out as though to touch her, then eased her hand back. "If it were up to me, I'd do things differently. But people are still—"

"Please." Olivia shook her head. "You don't need to explain, Selene. I'm fully aware of my"—her smile felt brittle to the point of breaking—"lack of social standing in the community."

"But I know it's not your fault, Olivia. I don't blame you. I want you to know that. I realize you had no choice in whom you married. Which makes me realize how fortunate I am to have a father who's determined to take the time to choose wisely. A father who loves me and . . ." As though just now hearing what she'd said—and insinuated—Selene halted mid-sentence. Color heightened her cheeks. "That didn't come out the way I intended, Olivia. What I meant to say is—"

"It's all right, Selene." Olivia worked for a gracious tone, hearing the inaudible echo of the general's attitude so clearly in his daughter's voice. "Rest assured, I'll help with the luncheon in every way I can." She attempted a sincere smile. "Including making myself scarce that day."

After Selene left, Olivia waited a moment. Then she walked the distance to the mansion, reminded once more that Belle Meade would never be home and wondering whether she would ever feel that sense of belonging to Nashville or to any other place—or anyone—again.

When she reached her room and saw the envelope on her desk, the return address written clear and sharp, she knew she had the answer to her question.

Chapter
THIRTY-ONE

Giving Seabird one last rub behind the ears and trusting Uncle Bob's diagnosis was right, Ridley rose from where he'd knelt beside her in the stall. *"Just give her time."* Uncle Bob's counsel returned. *"She just tired for now. Adjustin' to bein' with foal, that's all."*

Ridley hoped he was right.

Reaching to open the stall door, he heard the plod of hooves behind him and felt a firm nudge on his back. He turned, and Seabird moved closer, nuzzling his chest.

He smiled. "I know what you want, girl. You can't fool me." He covered his shirt pocket where he'd tucked the remaining apple, and the mare sniffed and licked the back of his hand, then started in on his shirt. "All right, all right ..." He quickly produced the treasure.

Today marked the beginning of Seabird's fourth month of being with foal. Three months behind them, eight to go. "You're going to be all right, girl," he whispered, running his hand along the sleek curve of her neck. "So's that foal inside you." *You just have to be ...*

He closed the stall door behind him and headed in the direction of the servants' cabins. Specifically, to the old barn that now served as a church on the first day of the week and a gathering place on all the others.

The calendar nailed to the stable wall announced September, but the heat and humidity hazing mid-morning insisted it was still summer, and he hoped church was meeting outside today. Glancing behind him toward the main house—a habit he'd developed over time and with purpose—he spotted the object of his interest rocking on the second-story porch, just outside her bedroom. He hesitated a full second before retracing his steps.

She was reading a book, he thought. But as he drew closer, he saw the stationery in her hand. She didn't look up as he approached.

"Morning, Olivia," he called up softly, not wanting to startle her.

She lifted her face. Her expression had a faraway, misty-eyed look. "Good morning," she whispered, dabbing her cheeks.

Her voice was hushed, tranquil, like the first spoken words of morning. The image of her lying beside him in bed, her body warm and womanly, tucked against his, crowded out every thought in his head but one . . .

He exhaled, glad she couldn't read his mind. And here he'd come to ask her to church. The irony wasn't lost on him. What was it about this woman that caused him to react this way? He'd wanted to kiss her so badly the other day. But the surprise in her eyes—no, the *trepidation*—had helped him keep his desire in check.

When he kissed Olivia Aberdeen—and he would—he wanted her to want to kiss him back. Without reservation. Without fear. He was willing to wait for that. Or at least try. He just hoped it wouldn't take long.

He stepped closer. "I'm sorry if I'm disturbing you."

She smiled. "You're not." She held up the pages. "I was just reading."

"Letters from a secret admirer?" He said it with a tone she often accused him of having. But the look she gave him made him wish he hadn't. It also made him wish he could read whatever was written on those pages.

She stood, the fading creak of the rocker marking off the seconds. She folded the stationery and slipped it into a book in her lap. "They're letters . . . from my mother to Aunt Elizabeth. Elizabeth and I came across them the other day." Olivia glanced toward her room. "There's a whole bundle of them. I'm reading a new one every day. To make them last."

Ridley felt a tug down deep, knowing what it would mean to him to have something so precious from his mother after all these years. Almost like a visit from the hereafter. Looking up at Olivia, he wished now he hadn't interrupted her. Yet the smile she gave him held welcome, and he decided to act on it.

"Would you care to go to church with me this morning, Mrs. Aberdeen?"

She eyed him. "To church?"

"It doesn't involve a carriage or a horse." He winked. "I promise."

She laughed, moving closer to the porch railing. "And just where is this church?"

He gestured behind him. "Down by the servants' quarters."

Her gaze moved beyond him. "Do you mean ... the Negro church?"

He liked the way she tucked her chin when she tried to act like she wasn't surprised but really was. "Yes, ma'am. Uncle Bob invited me awhile back. I finally went. I've been a few times since."

She leaned forward, elbows resting on the rail. "What's it like?"

"Well, let's see ..." Ridley curbed a grin. "This is the first Sunday of the month so you're in luck. It's the third Sunday you have to worry about." He shook his head. "I had no idea what I was getting into that day."

Her eyes grew round as silver dollars. "Why? What on earth do they ..."

Finally grinning, he enjoyed watching her disbelief give way to that droll look he already knew by heart, accompanied by that spark in her eyes he didn't think he'd ever tire of.

She huffed. "After that, I have a good mind not to go, Mr. Cooper."

"But you will." He smiled up. "Won't you?"

She smirked for a minute. "Will you be preaching?"

"Not hardly."

"All right then." She made a face. "I'll go."

Olivia sneaked a look at Ridley beside her, grateful for his invitation. Spending Sunday mornings alone had grown old, and the past few days—the last three weeks, actually—had seemed especially long. Her twenty-fourth birthday had come and gone days ago without notice, though it hadn't really bothered her.

Aunt Elizabeth had been abed more than usual, needing to rest. For every outing the woman participated in, including the luncheon she'd hosted at Belle Meade, which had gone off without a hitch—and also without *her*, Olivia noted—Elizabeth required a day or two to recuperate. Olivia treasured the extra time together, reading and talking, but it had eaten into her time with Jimmy and Jolene. She'd missed teaching the children. Repetition was so important.

Plus she was feeling that internal clock—the one counting down the days until she would have to remarry—ticking ever faster.

She had yet to respond to General Percival Meeks's two letters. But it was the letter from Colonel Burcham—the first of his missives to arrive—that concerned her most. The Colonel would be visiting Nashville toward the end of the year, around Christmas, he said, and he'd requested permission to call on her. The very thought made her ill. The Colonel was far too much like Charles for comfort, which made Percival Meeks all the more appealing.

"Not walking too fast for you, am I?"

She looked up to see Ridley a step or two ahead and hurried to catch up. "I'm sorry, Ridley. My thoughts were elsewhere for a minute."

"I noticed," he said, one side of his mouth tipping. "Anything I can do to keep that from happening again?"

Hearing the subtle insinuation in his voice, she thought back to the way he'd kissed her on the cheek and couldn't help but smile. "Nothing comes to mind at present, sir. But if I think of anything, I'll be sure to let you know."

"Mmm-hmm. You do that."

His boyish grin made her see him as anything but. How many nights had she lain awake contemplating what might have happened that afternoon if she had turned her head toward him ever so slightly at the last second. Oh, wouldn't that have surprised him! Not that she'd ever do such a thing. She wouldn't.

But it didn't stop her from thinking about it.

She heard singing—and clapping?—before the old barn came into view. The song didn't sound like one she'd heard before, much less in church. If she'd been alone, she would've turned back. But not with Ridley there, the man who feared nothing.

The barn doors stood wide open and, at Ridley's indication, she preceded him, glad they were entering at the back of the gathering instead of the front. She paused just inside to let her eyes adjust.

So many people—sixty or seventy, at least—all crowded in together. A hodgepodge of roughhewn pews, overturned barrels, milking stools, straight-back chairs, and bales of hay served as seating. And every available seat appeared to be taken, as evidenced by the number of people still standing. A couple of them staring. At her.

She suddenly felt very much out of place and also very ... *white*. It occurred to her that—with her past, with what had happened with Charles—she might not be welcome here. Ridley apparently had been, but he worked among them. The men, at least. And they liked him. She could tell by the way they joked with him in the stable.

Oh. Her body flushed hot and cold. Why had she agreed to come here? If they asked her to leave, she didn't know what she'd—

"It's all right," Ridley whispered beside her.

"I know," she answered too quickly, standing straighter, not wanting her fear to show. "I just don't know where to go, that's all."

Then movement caught her eye. She saw Jedediah waving them forward to a pew on the right near the front where two younger men were relinquishing their seats.

Head ducked, Olivia made her way to him. From the corner of her eye, she spotted Rachel, whose face was lifted heavenward, her eyes closed as she sang.

Thank you, Olivia mouthed to both Jedediah and the two men as she scooted in, glad to have Ridley beside her—very close beside her—on the crowded pew. She didn't know the name of the woman seated to her left, but she had seen her before. In the dairy, she thought.

Olivia smiled at her, and the woman smiled back, full and bright, nodding and continuing to sing. She had a pretty voice too—earthy and strong—and she swayed back and forth on the pew, clapping as she sang. Olivia tried her best to appear at ease as the woman rubbed shoulders with her again and again.

She also attempted to make out the words to the song. Something about having a robe, a harp, and ... some wings?

No sooner had she figured out the words to the song than it ended and another began. Started by someone in the back. A woman! But Olivia didn't dare turn to see which one.

This song was also new to her, slower than the first, and sadder sounding. No one clapped along, which made it easier to understand the words.

"Sometimes I feel discouraged," the woman sang beside her, joining in with everyone else. "And think my work's in vain ..." An intangible ache that hadn't been there before layered the woman's voice. "But then the Holy Spirit ... revives my soul again."

"Thank you, Jesus!"

Startled at the shout behind her, Olivia kept her focus straight ahead, wondering what she'd gotten herself into. And if what Ridley had joked about earlier—about what happened in Negro churches— might not be a little true.

"There is a balm," the people sang, their voices blending in a way she wouldn't have expected. "... in Gilead, to make the wounded whole. There is a balm ... in Gilead, to heal the sin-sick soul."

Olivia didn't know what or where Gilead was, but her throat filled with hurt as deeply buried wounds ached for a touch of that balm and the promise it held. Yet even as the steady throb increased, she felt a pinch of shame.

The people gathered in this place had been wounded far more deeply and harshly, and for much longer, than she had ever been. They deserved the balm more. But ... why had she never really examined that thought before now?

The song ended, and she took a steadying breath as Uncle Bob rose, a Bible in his hand, from where he'd been seated at the front. He looked out over the crowd as if searching for someone.

"She ain't come yet, Uncle Bob," a man said from the back. "Big Ike must still be ailin'."

Uncle Bob hesitated, then gave a single nod. "Father God in Heaven ..."

Olivia quickly bowed her head and closed her eyes. In the church where she'd grown up, men always announced they were going to pray, giving the congregation time to bow their heads.

"Lawd Jesus, we come askin' for you to be with our brother Ike who's feelin' poorly."

"Mmm-hmm," the woman beside her murmured. "Heal him, Lawd," she whispered.

Tempted to look beside her, Olivia kept her head lowered and her eyes to herself.

"Lawd, please be with our sister Susanna too," Uncle Bob continued. "As she's carin' for him. Big Ike can be a mite ornery at times ..."

A chorus of *amens* went up, softened by hushed laughter.

Laughter during a prayer? Her head still bowed, Olivia sneaked a look over at Ridley as the prayer continued. Like her, his head was bowed, but his eyes weren't closed. As if sensing her attention, he looked over and gave her a smile, then reached over and briefly squeezed her hand before turning back.

And that made all the difference.

By the time Uncle Bob said amen—along with everyone else, even the women—Olivia felt herself starting to relax.

Seconds passed as Uncle Bob stared at the unopened Bible in his hand. And Olivia began to wonder if he'd forgotten which passage he was supposed to be reading. She'd always thought that would happen to her if women were allowed to read up front. Which they weren't. For which she was grateful.

"I can try, Uncle Bob. If you want me to."

Hearing a familiar voice, Olivia leaned forward and peered down toward the opposite end of the pew. *Jimmy.* Little Jolene sat beside him with their mother.

Uncle Bob smiled big. "Well, come on up here then, son."

Whispers skittered through the crowd as Jimmy made his way forward.

Uncle Bob handed Jimmy the opened Bible. "Susanna has it marked, son. Right there. Startin' with that one."

Only then did Olivia realize the significance of the moment and what Jimmy had volunteered to do. And why *only* the boy—if her guess was correct—had volunteered. Truth's razor-sharp edge cut her to the core, and as Jimmy held the Bible closer to his face, she leaned forward in her seat.

"Let no-o ..." Jimmy sounded out the consonant, his features scrunched up. "N-n-not! Let not!" he finally said, grinning, then nodded as if sure of himself.

Uncle Bob smiled. "That's real good, son."

Jimmy looked down again. "Let not y-y ..."

He doubled his tongue between his teeth, a nervous habit Olivia recognized. She also noticed Uncle Bob looking her way. No ... He wasn't looking at *her.* He was looking at Ridley.

"Let not ... *your*!" Jimmy said, then beamed at his mother, whose face shone with pride. The boy ducked his head again. "Let not your hear-r ..."

Sensing a restlessness in the gathering and experiencing a taste of it herself, Olivia wished she could help Jimmy, but she didn't dare. It wasn't a woman's place in this setting. And certainly it wasn't hers. Not here. And yet ...

She glanced beside her.

Ridley shifted on the pew as if uncomfortable. She tried to give him more room, but there wasn't any more to give. He sat rigid, his shirt stretched taut over his broad shoulders. A muscle tensed in his jaw. And instinctively, she knew.

Uncle Bob was asking him to read. Not directly, of course, but the man was asking all the same. And, for some reason, Ridley seemed hesitant to.

Meanwhile, Jimmy's tongue curled and twirled. "Let not your *heart*!" he announced with a flourish, finally looking up.

"Son, you doin' a fine job!" Uncle Bob's gaze scanned the crowd. "Don't he sound good, folks? Let's thank him."

More clapping. Except this time, Olivia found herself joining in, proud of her pupil, even while realizing they had work to do yet. And she still didn't understand why Ridley wasn't going up there. Then she saw it ... the slightest tremble in his hand before he made a tight fist. And it occurred to her, even as the realization warmed her heart — maybe there was something the ever brave and adventuresome Ridley Cooper was timid about after all.

Chapter
THIRTY-TWO

*P*roud of Jimmy, Ridley watched as the boy reclaimed his seat beside his mother and sister. People continued to clap, some reaching over to pat Jimmy on the shoulder. It was good to see the boy getting recognition for his learning. Ridley glanced down beside him, equally proud of the woman responsible for it.

The clapping faded. He felt Uncle Bob's focused attention and knew what was coming. If Uncle Bob only understood how uncomfortable this was for him. How he'd all but turned his back on anything having to do with God years ago, much less the book that Uncle Bob held out to him now. How many times while at Andersonville—where good God-fearing men had died beside him in the mud, cradled on their sides like babies, their bodies wasted away, covered in filth—he had yearned to believe the words so many of them whispered in their last moments. Words he remembered learning from this book in his childhood. But he couldn't.

Because how could *that* God stand by and watch *that* happen. It made no sense. It still didn't. His eyes burned with the injustice of it.

"Ridley?" Uncle Bob urged him with a look. "Would you do the readin' for us this mornin', sir? Seein' as Susanna ain't able to be here? We'd be much obliged. Ain't·that right, church?"

A flood of affirming *mmm-hmm*s and *yes-sir*s rose from the crowd.

Realizing he had no choice, Ridley moved to stand. But as he did, Olivia discreetly reached between them, gave his hand a squeeze, and flashed a smile that said, *It's all right.* And as he walked toward the front—carrying her smile with him and working to center his thoughts—he hoped the woman knew what she'd just done. Because his patience for that first kiss had just been cut in half.

He took the Bible from Uncle Bob and opened to the place marked with a torn slip of paper. He scanned the pages, found the handful of words Jimmy had read, and lifted his gaze.

All eyes were on him. Which usually wouldn't have bothered him. But standing there, looking out on the flood of eager expressions and knowing he could read every word in this book and yet hadn't in years, because he didn't believe those words, made him feel like a hypocrite. The anticipation in their faces—Olivia's included—shamed him.

He found his place again in the text and cleared his throat. " 'Let not your heart be troubled,' " he started, his voice carrying in the silence. " 'Ye believe in God—' "

"Yes, sir, we *do*!" a woman interjected, and others quickly piled on similar assertions.

Ridley stared at the words, his eyes never leaving the page.

" 'Believe also in me,' " he continued. " 'In my Father's house are many mansions—' "

"Ones even bigger than the big house," a man called out, which earned enthusiastic *mmm-hmms* and *hallelujahs*.

" 'If it were not so,' " Ridley read on. " 'I would have told you. I go to prepare a place for you. And if I go and prepare a place for you, I *will* come again, and receive you unto myself ...' " His emphasis on the word had just slipped out, and he paused for a second, hoping the Lord wouldn't mind. " 'That where I am, there ye may be also.' "

Hearty *amens* rose all over, and Ridley looked to Uncle Bob, seated on the first row, hoping he'd read far enough. But Uncle Bob's single nod told him to keep going. So he did. He read through the end of that chapter then into the next. And the next. As he read, the people responded, and he thought back to what he'd said to Rachel about that very thing. But it felt good ... hearing them agree. Hearing their belief.

Nearing the end of his third chapter, he scanned the next few words and felt a stirring in his chest. The last verse seemed familiar to him, like a road he'd traveled before but had all but forgotten, time and disillusionment having erased the traces of his earlier passing. He cleared his throat again, unaccustomed to reading aloud. " 'These things I have spoken unto you, that in me ye might have peace. In the world ye shall have tribulation ...' " He paused, half expecting someone to respond, knowing what he did about these people.

But the room was silent. Even the breeze seemed to be holding its breath. And gradually, he realized why. Because these people knew what was coming next.

" 'But be of good cheer,' " he concluded, closing the Bible. " 'I have overcome the world.' "

For a handful of heartbeats, stillness hovered over the room. A peace. Then the gathering *erupted* in celebration. There was no other word for it. Whoops and hollers. Shouts and laughter. Ridley would have thought General Harding had given them the month off with wages guaranteed. And all from words dried on a page. Ridley watched in quiet amazement. How could people who had endured such hardship and injustice—far more than he had at Andersonville and for far longer—be capable of such joy? And inexplicable hope?

As he made his way back to the pew, someone started singing and the rest of the gathering joined in, and he knew he'd never forget this moment or this morning. Not when people reached out to touch him and whisper their thanks. Not when he saw the tears in Olivia's eyes and the pride in her smile.

And not when the faint whisper of a distant but undeniable hope began to stir somewhere deep within him too.

A while later, Ridley pushed back from the dinner table, giving Olivia a discreet wink as she did the same. Betsy's invitation for Sunday dinner following church had caught them both by surprise, but he was glad they'd accepted.

He wagered Olivia had never shared a meal with a servant's family in their home like this. But the dinner was delicious, the banter over lunch punctuated with laughter as they'd swapped Belle Meade stories, and Olivia seemed to have genuinely enjoyed herself.

Seeing her return her chair beneath the table, he reached back to do the same.

"Thank you again, Betsy …" Ridley gestured for Olivia to precede him to the door. "For the invitation. And Julius." He extended his hand to Betsy's husband. "Thank you for sharing your table with us."

Julius's grip was iron firm. "Thank *you*, sir, for acceptin'. Good to have you here." Julius included Olivia in his nod. "You too, Missus Aberdeen. You both are welcome anytime."

Olivia returned his smile. "Thank you, Julius. And everything was delicious, Betsy. Those biscuits, especially."

"Oh, that's Susanna's recipe, ma'am. I tell it to you sometime, if you want to know. She won't mind." Betsy winked. "Secret lies in beatin' the livin' daylights out of the dough."

Olivia laughed like it was a joke, but Ridley knew Betsy wasn't jesting. He'd seen the women in the kitchen before, beating the dough before running it through a biscuit brake. He wasn't surprised though that Olivia wasn't familiar with the process. He guessed her upbringing hadn't included much instruction in the kitchen.

"Here you go, ma'am." Betsy presented Olivia with a small cloth-wrapped bundle. "You best take the last of the sweet potato pie with you."

"Oh, no, Betsy. I couldn't. Let Julius or one of the children—"

"Go on, now." Betsy held the bundle out. "I saw you eyein' it. I can make another one for them anytime. After all ..." Betsy's eyebrows rose ever so slightly. "You got to be buildin' your strength, Missus Aberdeen."

Olivia gave a little laugh, her smile vague. "And ... why is that?"

Ridley saw a sparkle—no, make that a *glint*—move into Betsy's eyes, and he read the woman's intention a second too late.

"So you can get yourself a good runnin' start, o' course." Betsy smiled, sweet as molasses, then looked pointedly in Ridley's direction. "She gonna be needin' that. Ain't that right, Mr. Cooper?"

Unable to keep from grinning, Ridley couldn't usher Olivia out the door fast enough. "Thank you both again," he called over his shoulder, holding Olivia's arm as she maneuvered the two front steps.

"What did she mean," Olivia whispered a moment later, "about me needing a ... good running start?"

Ridley shook his head. "You know Betsy. She was just having fun with you." He glanced behind them, and Betsy tossed him a sassy little wave. Julius still stood in the doorway, smiling.

When Ridley turned back, he found Olivia eyeing him.

"So?" Doubt clouded her expression. "You haven't agreed for me to do something else then? Without speaking to me first?"

He attempted a hurt look. "I'm *wounded* that you'd think me capable of such a thing."

Her smile was instant and said he was completely forgiven for his earlier misstep regarding the additional responsibilities at the quarry. No matter how well intentioned his actions had been.

He offered his arm, and she looped hers through it. Recent rains had greened the grasses and trees, and though the temperature was warm, a sense of coming change hovered over the meadow. As if nature knew something they didn't.

"I enjoyed listening to you read this morning, Ridley. You have a gift for it."

"Oh, I'd hardly say that."

She gave his arm a sharp squeeze. "I believe that when someone compliments you, Mr. Cooper"—her tone that of a venerated school-marm—"it is appropriate to say thank you, instead of attempting to dodge the intended kindness. Then afterward, if opportunity allows and etiquette deems it proper, you may offer a more self-deprecating observation. But not before."

He laughed, appreciating this cheeky side of her that was surfacing. "I stand corrected, Mrs. Aberdeen." He made a show of clearing his throat. "Thank you, ma'am, for the compliment. It's most generous of you. However, I admit with the slightest whit of trepidation"—she giggled at him—"that I did feel somewhat inadequate to the task, for many reasons." He nudged her. "That better?"

"Yes, much. But ..." Her steps slowed. "Truthfully though ..." She paused, concern clouding her features. "Why would you say that?"

A breeze stirred a curl at her temple, and Ridley reached up and fingered it. He'd been right. *Just like silk.* She licked her lips, a self-conscious gesture, he knew, but still ... it drew his attention and his desire.

An ancient poplar, its low-hanging limbs spread wide, coupled with a hedge of lavender to provide a semblance of privacy. Sunlight dappled her face, and he read the question again in her eyes.

He sighed. "I'm afraid I don't have an easy answer for that, Olivia."

"I didn't realize I was asking for one, Ridley." A glimmer of a smile lit her expression, then faded. "I could tell, before you went up, that you were nervous. I just wondered why."

If someone had asked him earlier that morning if he would ever want to tell Olivia Aberdeen about his part in the war, about Andersonville, about how the years of fighting and killing had changed him, had changed how he felt about the place he once called home, he'd have said they'd lost their mind. But looking at her now, he sensed such an openness, and part of him did want to tell her. Maybe telling her would ease the pain. Perhaps he'd feel less lonely. He thought of the seashell in his pocket and of how often he took it out at night and held it—counting, reliving, remembering.

The limbs above them shifted with the breeze, and Olivia blinked against a flash of sunlight. Rationality returned to Ridley on a wave. He could no more tell her about fighting for the Union or about being at Andersonville than he could admit it to General Harding. She was a Southern belle through and through, and—in her eyes—he'd be a traitor, a turncoat. Maybe not exactly like her husband, but that's how she'd see him. As would everyone else, once they knew. And his time at Belle Meade would be done, and everything he'd worked for would be lost.

But perhaps he could share a piece of the truth with her. Just a sliver. Enough for her to see a shadow of what he wrestled with inside. Maybe that would be enough.

"During the war," he started, parsing each word as he went, "I did things … experienced things … I can't seem to put behind me. When I close my eyes at night, they're still there. Right in front of me, in the dark. The faces, the scenes, the sounds …" He winced. "The cries."

The compassionate blue of her eyes drew him in.

"I didn't feel close to God at all during those years, Olivia." His laughter came out flat. "Or feel like he was very close to me. Felt more like he'd forgotten me. Along with everyone else. Had just turned his back and left us. It didn't feel right." He tried to smile, hoping to lessen the emotion filling his throat, but couldn't. "Looking back, it still doesn't." He briefly bowed his head, the sliver of truth cutting him more in the sharing than he'd thought it would. He took a steadying breath, then gave it slow release. He searched her expression for the slightest sign of rebuff or judgment. And saw neither. "So when Uncle Bob asked me to stand up there today and read from the Bible …" He shook his head. "I …"

"You felt out of place," she said, her eyes glistening. "Like you didn't belong. Those are feelings I understand quite well." The lines in her brow bespoke painful recollections, and she lowered her head. "I assume you've heard at least something … about my late husband." She peered up, and Ridley nodded. She held his gaze, as if trying to gauge how much he knew. Then she smiled. Or tried to. "I think I've known for a while that you knew about him. I just didn't want to acknowledge it."

"It doesn't matter to me, Olivia. Your late husband did those things. Not you."

"The rest of Nashville doesn't feel that way. That's why I don't go into town, Ridley. That, and ..." She sighed. "I've hated horses since I was a little girl."

"*Hated* them?"

"Have been scared to death of them since I was thrown as a girl. And broke my arm." She covered her left sleeve with her hand. "Then ... last year, my late husband insisted that I ride. A stallion." She briefly closed her eyes. "The horse threw me, then nearly trampled me in the process."

Understanding her fear better, Ridley placed his hand on hers. "Where was the break?"

She seemed hesitant to tell him at first. "Along here." She drew a lengthy line along the top of her arm.

Ridley traced the path slowly, knowing how much that must have hurt. His fingers were rough against the soft lace of her sleeve, and he didn't miss her slight shiver. "I'm sorry that happened to you," he whispered.

"I'm sorry about what happened to you too."

He searched her eyes, reminding himself of his vow to be patient. But when her gaze lowered slightly from his, and her lips parted ...

Ridley drew her against him, the feel of her igniting him even before his mouth claimed hers. Her lips were heaven, and the softness of her mouth ... With one arm, he held her, and with the other, he explored the curve of her back. But it was the way *she* touched *him* ... Responded to him. Her hand on his chest, gripping his shirt, pulling him closer. Ridley deepened the kiss, tasting not just her sweetness, but her desire. She slipped her hand around his neck and wove her fingers into his hair, and like a bolt of lightning, he remembered where they were—

But she broke the kiss first. Quickly. Without warning. And even before he took a breath, he missed her.

"I'm still" —her breath came quickly— "in mourning."

"I know," he whispered. The sharp rise and fall of her chest reflected his own desire and made him want to kiss her all over again.

"And ..." She put a hand up as though warning him. "I don't want to get married again. At least not yet."

He had to laugh. "I know I had a couple glasses of Betsy's cider back there. But ... did you just hear a proposal?"

Her cheeks flushed red. "Well, no. Of course not, but ... we kissed, and ... I didn't want you to think that ..."

He moved closer and her eyes widened. But she didn't move away, he noticed.

"Olivia Aberdeen, I've been wanting to kiss you almost since the first time I laid eyes on you." Her eyes softened, tempting him again. "But that aside, should the time ever come when I'm seeking your hand in marriage ... Believe me, woman, you'll know."

A ghost of a smile touched her mouth, and he steeled himself against what he wanted to do versus what he knew was best. But seeing traces of yearning in her eyes and the fullness of her still-parted lips made it a battle and robbed him of a freedom he'd never known he possessed.

Because he'd never known a woman he didn't want to live the rest of his life without. Until now.

Chapter
THIRTY-THREE

*L*ivvy?" Elizabeth whispered, her voice absent its usual vibrance. "Would you mind staying with me for a while? Instead of going to the stables just yet?"

"Not at all." Olivia laid the stationery box aside and pulled the covers up to Elizabeth's chest. She crossed the bedroom and adjusted the brocade curtains so the morning light wouldn't fall directly across the bed. "Are you certain you feel all right?"

"Oh, I feel fine, dear. I'm simply"—Elizabeth shrugged—"not myself today. I think resting will help. But I appreciate your company." Elizabeth reached for her hand. "Even when we're not conversing."

Elizabeth's fingers were cold, and Olivia covered her aunt's hand with her own. Elizabeth had been active over the past three weeks, more so than Olivia could remember since coming to live here. Her color looked good though. There was a rosy hue to her cheeks. And her strength still seemed to be improving. They'd been on a walk earlier that morning and though reticent—even melancholy, perhaps— Elizabeth had appeared well.

Everyone was entitled to doleful days, as her mother used to call them. Heaven knew her own mother had dealt with such days, and Olivia had certainly borne her own fair share of them too. Though … not so much since being at Belle Meade.

Seeing Elizabeth's eyes slip closed, she gave her aunt's hand a gentle squeeze and tucked it back beneath the covers, then tiptoed to the far window and peered out, wondering if the view had changed since earlier. And hoping it hadn't.

She was pleasantly rewarded.

Ridley and a handful of other men—Ridley now shirtless, along with two others—continued to wage an assault on the defenseless, crippled carriage, their axes and sledgehammers swinging. Ridley's back and shoulder muscles glistened brown in the late-September sun, his body lean and hard, accustomed to work. Although the task the men undertook appeared monumental — and beyond horrendous to her — their occasional banter, punctuated with laughter, drifted through the open second-story window, telling a different story. *Men* ... They were enjoying every minute of it.

Running a finger over her lips, remembering, Olivia sighed. And what a man ...

She kept to the edge of the window, careful not to stand where Ridley would see her if he looked toward the main house. Which he did, she'd noticed, with odd frequency.

Things had changed between them since the kiss. Yet not in a way easily defined. She smiled again recalling his comment about the proposal — after she'd blurted out about not wanting to remarry any time soon.

He hadn't kissed her since. Hadn't even tried. And they'd been alone often enough that he could have. *Disappointed* didn't describe her feelings as much as *confused*. She didn't regret the kiss. But in hindsight, neither did she look upon it as a good idea. No matter how good it was. She was in mourning, after all.

But the way he'd held her so closely, the solidness of his chest against hers, the race of his heart beneath her palm.

She knelt to let the breeze blow directly on her face.

Never, in all the times she'd been with Charles in a wifely way, had she experienced the sense of intimacy she'd had when Ridley had taken her in his arms. It was almost as if Ridley hadn't merely been kissing her, but had been ... *cherishing* her. *Savoring* ... That was an entirely new sensation and exactly what she'd done with him in that moment — and was still doing.

Her face flushed warm again as an ache of desire took her thoughts and emotions in a direction she knew they shouldn't wander. Not for long, anyway. And for good reason. Because in a handful of months, he would be gone. And she would be here. Without him. He'd made it clear the Colorado Territory was his first priority. That, and Seabird having a healthy foal. Which all seemed to be going well so far.

Ridley suddenly straightened and shielded his eyes.

Olivia started to duck, but before she could, he waved right at her.

Shaking her head, she waved back and saw him grin. She felt like a silly school girl. And loved the feeling. Along with knowing he'd wanted to kiss her almost since the first time he'd seen her.

Ridley pointed toward her, then back at himself, and she stared, not knowing what he was trying to say. Then he did it again. Pointed up at her, then back at himself. She shook her head and shrugged. He glanced around him, moved off to the side and away from the other men, then dropped his axe and started doing ... *something*. Grabbing the air above his head and stepping up and down.

Olivia leaned closer to the open window, wondering what on earth the man—

Then it suddenly made sense. And she couldn't keep from giggling. He was mimicking climbing a ladder. But she knew better. *The lattice outside her window.* He pointed to her again, then to himself. And waited.

Olivia stared at him, standing in the sun, watching her watch him, and she recalled the taste of his kiss and, even more, what it felt like to want something more than a kiss from a man.

Reluctantly, knowing she probably shouldn't but that she couldn't *not*, she nodded. Then pointed to herself, then back to him, just to be sure he understood. Smiling, he retrieved his axe and renewed his battle with the carriage with far more stamina than before, it seemed.

Gripping the windowsill, she stood, imagining climbing down that trellis with him again. And—to her surprise—she found the prospect more exciting than terrifying.

The shushed rhythm of soft breaths behind her told her Elizabeth was asleep. Olivia retrieved her satchel and eased into the chair by the desk. She unlatched the main flap and withdrew the stack of teaching materials for the coming week.

Customarily, she didn't work on her lessons around Elizabeth. She'd told herself it was out of politeness—wanting to focus on Elizabeth's needs, since she was, after all, the woman's companion. The truth was she wasn't entirely certain how Elizabeth would feel about her teaching the children of a servant. But ...

Elizabeth was asleep, and she had so much to do. Olivia opened the file.

Jimmy and Jolene were both progressing nicely. Jimmy talked incessantly about the Sunday he read "the Good Book" in front of everyone, and she knew he wanted to do it again. "But better next time," he'd said. "And longer, like Mr. Cooper done." She wanted to help him make that happen. There were other children too — she'd seen them at church — and she wished she could teach them as well. Not that they'd asked or indicated interest. But there was scarcely even time to teach Jimmy and Jolene, what with being companion to Elizabeth and working for the general.

Frowning, she flipped through the teaching materials on the desk. Where were her lesson plans? She'd completed them late last night and slipped them into the satchel before crawling into bed, she was certain of it. She peered inside the main compartment.

Empty. She sighed. Then remembered.

She slipped her hand into the smaller front pocket, pulled out the McGuffey's Reader, and, sure enough, there were the lesson plans, just where she'd —

An envelope, badly creased and wrinkled along one edge, protruded from the pages of the book, as though it had been in the pocket when she'd inserted the book last night. She turned the envelope over, trying to remember if she'd used the front pocket before. The envelope didn't look familiar. It was blank on the outside. No name on the front. No writing whatsoever. And it was yellowed, from time, perhaps, or maybe the leather. She couldn't be certain. But there was something inside.

And the seal was broken.

She glanced over at the bed, then back at the envelope, debating. How private could it be if someone had left it in a satchel, forgotten on a bottom shelf? It could be a letter ... or a list of errands. Or an old family recipe. A recipe Elizabeth would be grateful to have.

Hearing the thread of her thoughts, Olivia knew what she should do. But ... she held the envelope up to the window, her curiosity getting the best of her. She laid the book on the desk and lifted the flap.

The aging stationery crinkled overloud in the quiet. Elizabeth stirred and Olivia froze, her heart skipping a beat. She waited, watching.

Seconds passed.

Elizabeth slept on, and Olivia slowly released her breath, feeling both relieved and a little foolish at being so nervous. Deciding not to risk disturbing Elizabeth again, she took the envelope and the satchel into the private hallway off the master bedroom. She pulled the bedroom door all but closed behind her and peered around the corner to the second-story landing, the floorboards creaking in the quiet. The corridor leading to the other bedrooms was empty.

Satisfied, she lifted the flap and withdrew the stationery. Then unfolded the pages. Letterhead with the Harding family insignia.

> *Dearest Cousin Beatrice,*
>
> *I cannot refrain from saying something appertaining to our eternal destiny; a subject so interesting to me that I am oftentimes so delighted and absorbed in the contemplation as to forget my pains and afflictions, which are very great—often as much as weak human nature can bear. But thanks to God this is not to endure … My Saviour has suffered before me—even more than I …*

The missive continued, but Olivia's patience wouldn't. Curious as to its author, she peeked at the last page.

> *Always, your loving cousin,*
> *Selena*
> *November 26, 1836*

Selena? Or was it Selene? Olivia squinted. The ornate script wasn't clear. But Selene hadn't even been born yet. Olivia studied the name again—along with the date—then went back to reading.

> *If it is our lot to go first, let us depart rejoicing—Surely, B., if I can bid adieu to all earthly ties, it will not be a severe trial to you should it please God to remove you from this vale of tears.*

Olivia raised a brow. Awfully direct, this Selena.

> *True, you have a fond husband and affectionate mother, from whom you would not wish to be separated. I have father, mother, sisters, and brothers, and a father- and mother-in-law, to all of whom I am devotedly attached. I have also a fond husband, who has not obtained the great promise of salvation and from whom I may be eternally separated.*

Olivia paused and reread the last sentence again, sensing the woman's yearning. Charles had not been a fond husband by any stretch and—much as Selena had done with her husband, whoever he was—Olivia had questioned Charles's salvation. Though, given the circumstances, she probably hadn't sincerely questioned it as much as she should have.

Acknowledging the sting of conviction, yet knowing nothing could be done in that regard now, she refocused her attention.

> *I pray God it may not be so, and that he may yet learn to know the truth and feel its consoling and comforting influence in life and its support in death. I would wish to live for his sake, that I might advise and admonish him to make preparations for the future. I, too, have three dear little babies; for them I would wish to live. But as I sense the dawn of eternity pressing ever closer, I would wish for William*

William? Olivia stared at the name, wondering. She scanned the remaining letter, searching for a snippet that might answer the question foremost in her mind. Who was this William? Along with the equally intriguing Sel—

The hushed sound of crying lifted her head. Her first thought went to Elizabeth, and she peered inside the bedroom. But Elizabeth continued to rest peacefully. Olivia closed the door so her aunt wouldn't be disturbed.

"Oh, sweet child ..." A voice drifted toward her from the corridor just feet away. "You know that's not true."

"It *is* true, Susanna. And you know it." Soft, heart-wrenching sobs. "And it's only gotten worse."

"Come here, baby. And hear me good when I say this ... Your mama don't love you any less than she love your sister. It's just that the first girl gets a little more 'tention sometimes. You just as full o' talent and sugar sweetness as Selene. And your mama loves you just the same. Even if she don't say it as often as you might wanna hear it."

Olivia all but forgot the letter in her hand.

A ragged breath followed. "Both she and Father care more about her than me. And about how she'll soon be engaged to the *perfect* General William Hicks Jackson. While I'll end up"—a fresh outburst of sobs—"I'll end up with nobody, because ... because I'm not as pretty as her."

Oh, Mary ... Olivia closed her eyes, her heart breaking for the girl. Since her very first night at Belle Meade, she'd seen the difference in how the daughters were treated. And it wasn't fair. How often had she felt set aside by her own father during her life? Especially at the age of sixteen, as Mary was.

"Now, you look at me, child." Susanna's voice was hushed, but firm as an oak. "You is a lovely thing. But you know what I think about that. What counts more than bein' lovely in your face is the lovely in here. As for your sister ... You know I love her too, but y'all is different from each other. Have been since you first drew breath. And don't you dare go tryin' to be like her again. You be your own young woman. And don't worry none 'bout findin' a man. Just you wait. More 'n likely, he'll find you first. And he be gettin' himself a real treasure, for sure."

More sniffs, followed by a heavy sigh.

"I love you, Susanna."

"Oh, baby, I love you too. Always have ... always will."

A tear slipped down Olivia's cheek. She'd seen Susanna wink at Mary as she served dinner, but she'd never known how close the two really were.

"Tell you what, Miss Mary ..." Susanna's tone lightened. "Why don't let's you and me go and see your mama? She be restin' in her room."

Olivia's eyes widened as she brushed away the tear. If Susanna and Mary caught her standing here, they'd think she'd purposefully been—

"No. I don't want to right now. *She'll* be in there."

Relieved, Olivia also felt the not-so-gentle barb, knowing Mary referred to her.

"No, she won't. She be in the stable doin' work for the general by now. And don't you forget what I done told you 'bout her ..."

Olivia's interest perked up.

"She a good woman, Mary. Better than you know. She been through an awful hard time herself. Got a weight on her shoulders most white women like her couldn't bear. Not and keep their head held high. But she doin' good. And I think you need to give her a chance."

Olivia felt the threat of tears again. Not only due to Susanna's kind words toward her, but for the loving stability and safe haven the woman represented in Mary's life.

"But I don't like her, Susanna," Mary said quietly. "She spends every waking hour with Mama, and I never get a—"

"Now that ain't the truth, Mary. There be plenty of times when I see your mama sittin' all by her lonesome. You could visit with her then ... if you had a mind to."

"But it's not like it could have been ... if Papa had said yes to *me*."

"Mary girl, your folks care too much 'bout your learnin' to let you up and leave school to help take care of your mama. 'Specially when God provided Missus Aberdeen to come when she did. So don't let your own stubborn hurt keep you from lovin' your mama like you should. Lawd ... what I'd give to be able to sit down with my mama again and just hold her hand and rock on the porch. I lost her when I was way younger than you. So don't you waste no more time."

Silence punctuated the gentle reprimand, and Olivia was reminded of the night General Harding had invited her into his office and told her about Elizabeth's condition. She wondered, yet again, whether the general would have agreed to her coming here to live if Elizabeth's health hadn't been compromised. Somehow, she doubted it.

She glanced at the bedroom door, feeling an increasing sense of trespass standing here overhearing a conversation not intended for her. She wished she were back inside the room. Only three or four steps separated her from that wish, but what if the floor creaked and gave her away? They would know she'd been here—*listening*—the entire time.

Maybe they would leave soon and never be the wiser.

"Now, come here, child ... Let Susanna wipe them tears." Susanna laughed softly. "And I done made up my mind ... Your mama *needs* to know about that mark you got in school yesterday. Let's go tell her together. What you think?"

Olivia panicked. She started to take a step, then caught herself. The silence would give her away for sure. She needed to wait for one of them to speak again.

"I got the highest mark the tutor's ever given. And he taught Selene too! He said that ..."

Olivia took a step, and the floorboard creaked. She grimaced when Mary fell silent. Footsteps sounded from the hallway. Realizing there was no turning back, she lunged for the bedroom door, pushed it open, then almost closed again. She waited a frantic second or two, then opened it again and stepped through, her heart pounding.

Mary and Susanna, who had rounded the corner, came to a stop.

"Missus Aberdeen." Susanna's voice held a note of surprise, though her expression didn't. "I thought you was gone already, ma'am."

Olivia pulled the door closed behind her, trying to breathe normally. She kept her voice soft. "Aunt Elizabeth asked me to stay for a while. So I did. Until she fell asleep."

Mary glanced past her. "Is she still sleeping?"

Olivia nodded. Mary lowered her head, then tilted it a little.

"Are those ... Mother's boots?" Mary asked.

Olivia looked down, arranging her skirt to cover her feet. "Yes, they are."

"She ... gave them to you?"

Olivia swallowed, seeing the hurt rising to Mary's eyes. "It was more of a loan, actually. I told her I would only be borrowing them. Until I could buy another pair. Which will be soon!"

Mary stared. "I've always admired those boots. And have told Mother as much ... many times."

Olivia wished she could take the boots off right now and give them to the girl. "As I told your mother, Mary, I'm considering them a loan. In fact, if you'd like them, I'll happily—"

"She gave them to *you*, Mrs. Aberdeen. Not to me."

Mary turned and gave Susanna an almost triumphant I-told-you-so look and left. The soft thud of her boot steps echoed on the staircase, and Olivia's heart ached.

She met Susanna's gaze and sighed. "I'm so sorry, Susanna."

"Sorry for what, ma'am? You ain't done nothin' wrong to her."

Olivia glanced in the direction Mary had gone. "Apparently, I have. And have been doing it for some time. She hasn't liked me from the very start."

"Which should tell you somethin' right off." Susanna's expression held gentle counsel. "The child's just hurtin', Missus Aberdeen. A little more than usual today, I'd say. But she be all right. She's stronger than she looks."

Susanna's remark brought another to Olivia's mind. Something Ridley had said to her. *You're stronger than you think. I see it in you, even if you don't.* She liked that he believed in her and hoped what he believed was true. Because most of the time, she didn't feel strong at all.

But, oddly, thinking back on it, the times she did were when she was with him.

"Somethin' else you need to be knowin', ma'am ..."

Olivia wondered at the bemused look on Susanna's face.

Taking a purposed step, Susanna put her weight on one of the floorboards, and it yielded a telling creak. The same creak—from the same complaining plank—of moments earlier.

Susanna smiled.

Knowing she'd been found out, Olivia felt her face go warm. She winced. "It wasn't my intention to eavesdrop, Susanna. I promise! I was out here in the hallway when I first heard you. Then, after a minute or two, I—"

"I'm only playin' with you, ma'am." Susanna laughed. "You didn't hear nothin' I don't mind you hearin'. 'Specially if you can help the girl along somehow. Though ... I'm sorry for them hurtful things Mary said 'bout you. She don't mean 'em. Not really."

Olivia nodded, not knowing how she could help when Mary obviously disliked her so.

"But I got to say, ma'am ... You put on a good show, waltzin' outta that room and lookin' up like you done. Other than hearin' that creak, I'd have believed you."

Olivia had to grin. The more time she spent in Susanna's company, the more she liked the woman. Same as Rachel and Betsy. Other than Elizabeth—and Ridley, though he hardly fit in the same category— they were the closest things she had to friends.

Susanna gestured. "Was Missus Harding feelin' any better 'fore she went down for her rest?"

"No ... But I think she's feeling fine physically. It's more a case of the melancholies today, for some reason."

Susanna eyed her. "For *some* reason? You mean ... You don't know what today is?"

Feeling as though she should, Olivia shook her head.

Susanna stepped closer. "Today be the day that young Nathaniel died, ma'am," she said softly. "Nigh onto, oh ... twenty-three years ago now."

Olivia had never heard the name. "Was that ... Aunt Elizabeth's son?"

"Yes, ma'am, in a way. But not by birthin'. Nathaniel was the *first* Missus Harding's boy. She had him, and John, Jr., and done lost three others shortly after they were born. But our Missus Harding loved Nathaniel like her own. He was close to reachin' his tenth birthday when he died."

Olivia started to ask the obvious, then hesitated. Tragic though it was, babies died in infancy. But to lose a child of almost ten ...

As if sensing Olivia's unspoken question, Susanna continued.

"Sometimes, back in those years, Mr. John Harding and his wife, the general's folks ... They'd take the kids with 'em into town. Oh, the kids, they loved it. Got all excited at bein' in the city. But one day ... Nathaniel went ridin'." The haze of unpleasant memories clouded Susanna's features. "His horse was gallopin' down Church Street ... and—for no reason, they said—that horse threw him." Susanna closed her eyes. "And that precious, beautiful boy hit a tree. Died right there, they said. 'Bout broke Missus Harding's heart. The general's too. 'Specially after losin' so many other babies."

"So many *others*?" Olivia whispered, not meaning to pry. But maybe if she knew more about what Elizabeth had been through, she'd be better able to help her.

"She and the general done lost six of their own children through the years, Missus Aberdeen. I just figured you knew, with how close you and Missus Harding seem to be."

"I knew they'd lost children. But ... six?" Olivia couldn't imagine laying one child to rest, let alone six.

"It hurt Missus Harding somethin' awful. A part of her just kind o' closed up inside. With some of them sweet babies, she held back from namin' 'em for a few days, wantin' to make sure they was gonna live. Guess it was easier for her somehow."

Olivia considered that for a moment, trying to reconcile why Elizabeth hadn't shared any of this with her. Then again, considering what Susanna had shared, it was no wonder her aunt didn't want to revisit those memories.

"What on *earth* ..."

Olivia followed Susanna's gaze to the general's satchel on a hall chair.

"What's that doin' up here?"

"That's an old satchel that belonged to the—"

"I *know* who it goes to, ma'am. I just wonderin' what it's doin' up here."

"Aunt Elizabeth gave it to me. She said the general didn't use it anymore, and I needed something to carry my papers in, so—"

"Oh no, Missus Aberdeen." Susanna eyed the satchel, then her. "I'm thinkin' that ain't a good idea, ma'am. I know Missus Harding meant well, but has the general seen you with it yet?"

Feeling like someone with their hand caught in the till, Olivia gave a shake of her head.

Susanna let a breath out. "Well, thank you, Jesus, for that. Now, you ain't got to do what I say, o' course. But if I was you, I'd take this real quick and put it back wherever you got it. Just like it was, 'fore he sees you with it. And don't say nothin' to Missus Harding, if you can see to it. I don't want to chance upsettin' her even more."

Remembering the letter in her hand, Olivia looked down at it, then back at Susanna.

Susanna leaned back a little. "What you got there?"

"I found it." Olivia winced. "In the satchel. It's a letter. From a ... *Selena* or *Selene*. But not our Selene. This letter was written thirty years ago."

For a brief second, Susanna looked like she might faint. "Please, Missus Aberdeen ... Put that satchel back. Right now. And put that letter back in there too."

"Put what letter back?" a soft voice said from behind them.

Chapter
THIRTY-FOUR

Seeing Elizabeth standing in the bedroom doorway, Olivia felt the blood in her face pool in her feet. "Aunt Elizabeth ... I-I'm sorry if we awakened you."

"You didn't, Livvy."

Her voice still velveted by sleep, Elizabeth briefly glanced at the letter in Olivia's hand. And all Olivia could think about was the moment she'd decided to open the flap to that envelope, and how she wished she could go back and ... not.

"Is you feelin' any better, Missus Harding?"

"Yes, Susanna. Thank you."

But to Olivia, Elizabeth's tone sounded unchanged from before.

Elizabeth's gaze dropped to Olivia's hand. "So, is one of you going to tell me what letter you were discussing? Or are you simply going to stand here with guilty looks on your faces?"

Susanna opened her mouth as if to speak.

"The fault is mine, Aunt Elizabeth." Olivia fingered the folded stationery, remembering what Susanna said about trying not to tell Elizabeth. But what could she do under the circumstances? "I found a letter in General Harding's old satchel. And ... I read it. Or part of it. I shouldn't have, I know. And I'm so sorry."

Olivia held out the letter. Elizabeth stared at it for a moment, then the pages crinkled as she unfolded them. No sooner did her gaze light on the page, than she folded the letter back.

"This was in the satchel?" she asked, her tone delicate.

"Yes, ma'am." Olivia nodded.

Elizabeth exhaled and along with the expelled air in her lungs seemed to come a weariness and a disappointment. She briefly bowed her head, fingering the letter. Then looked up. "I didn't realize he'd kept one of her letters," she said softly. "I was under the impression he hadn't." A fleeting smile touched her mouth even as tears rose in her eyes. "It's only natural, of course, knowing how much he loved her." Her chin trembled. "I can hardly blame him for that. After all ... he loved her first. Long before he married me."

That evening following dinner, Olivia sat rocking on the second-story porch outside her bedroom, watching the mares graze in the meadow. The spring foals, nearly four months old, frolicked around their mothers, chasing each other, kicking and rearing. Yet, cute as they were, Olivia couldn't get the image of a ten-year-old boy riding down Church Street out of her mind.

"They're beautiful creatures, aren't they?"

Olivia felt a hand on her shoulder and covered it. "Yes, they are."

Already in her dressing gown, ready for bed, Aunt Elizabeth claimed the rocker beside Olivia. For several moments, neither of them spoke.

"Thank you, Livvy ... for not pressing me with questions this afternoon. I feel as though I need to offer an apology for being so emotional about you finding that letter."

"No ... Please don't, Aunt. I'm sorry, again, that I took the liberty of reading it."

Elizabeth gave her hand a squeeze. "You did nothing wrong in my eyes, Livvy." She winked. "If I'd found it, I would have opened it and read it too."

"Yes, but that's your husband's satchel, and Belle Meade is your home."

Elizabeth frowned. "I hope you think of Belle Meade as your home now too, Livvy."

Olivia smiled. "Of course, I do. But ..." Appreciating all that Elizabeth had done for her, Olivia quickly decided it was probably best she not try to explain how Belle Meade being "home" was still different for her. "I regret that my finding that letter made you so sad."

Understanding deepened Elizabeth's features. "The Selena in the letter was William's first wife ... John Jr.'s mother."

Already having made that connection, Olivia nodded.

"I've not spoken to anyone about this, Livvy—other than Susanna, who's been with me since before I married the general. And even then ..." She paused, as if choosing her words carefully. "Susanna's been more of a ... witness to it, not a confidante, per se. But she's been a comfort to me, all the same."

Elizabeth started to speak again, then apparently thought better of it. Olivia sneaked a look beside her. Her aunt stared out across the meadow, her countenance lovely in the golden wash of a late-September sun, but the clench of her jaw indicated her struggle.

"It's hard," Elizabeth whispered, "to follow in someone else's footsteps. Especially when they were so beloved." A moment passed before she spoke again. "When I met William, I thought him the most handsome man I'd ever seen. I still do." She smiled. "He was thirty-two and had two sons who needed a mother. I was twenty-one and in need of a husband. On our wedding day, when I stood at my bedroom window and watched William Giles Harding guiding the sleigh over the snow-covered fields of my childhood, I knew my heart was his. Wholly, without reservation. And that's never changed. But ..."

Seconds passed. When Elizabeth didn't continue, Olivia glanced over to see her fighting back tears. Olivia reached out to her but Elizabeth shook her head.

"His heart has never been completely mine. As I said, I don't fault him. And don't mistake what I'm saying ... I know my husband loves me. But"—Elizabeth drew in a ragged breath—"not the way I love him. And not, I think ... the way he loved her."

Hearing the rawness in her voice, Olivia tried to think of something to say that would help ease the hurt. But she knew from experience that words rarely possessed such power. She risked reaching over again. And this time, Elizabeth grabbed her hand and held tight.

"I feel foolish—and more than a little *selfish*—in telling you all this, Livvy." Elizabeth brushed away a tear. "Because I know your own marriage was far less than what you desired. And deserved. And though you haven't said it outright ... I sense that Charles Aberdeen was ..." Elizabeth hesitated. "A very hurtful and cruel husband."

Olivia felt her aunt's attention but deliberately kept her focus on the meadow, the scene going blurry. She'd often wished she could share that part of her life with Elizabeth, yet hadn't felt at liberty to. And she found it oddly comforting to discover that, somehow, Elizabeth already knew. "Yes," she whispered. "He was."

Elizabeth squeezed Olivia's hand, and they rocked, side by side, the gentle creak of the chairs keeping odd time with the crickets' chirrup. Olivia caught sight of Ridley and Uncle Bob leaving the stable. The men headed for the front pasture. They opened the gate, and Olivia warmed when she saw the number of horses that swarmed to Uncle Bob. But what encouraged a smile was how Seabird immediately trotted toward Ridley. *Please, Lord, let that foal be healthy and strong ... For him. And for his dream.*

Elizabeth leaned slightly forward, and Olivia trailed her gaze to where General Harding stood on the front porch of the old cabin, his head bowed. At first she wondered why he was there. But the cabin was his birthplace, after all, built by his father. After a moment, the general started back toward the mansion, his steps unhurried.

"I didn't know," Elizabeth continued, "until Susanna told me today ... Selena gave the general that satchel, Livvy."

Olivia turned, her eyes widening.

"Susanna said she overheard the general talking to John Jr. about it years ago. She never said anything to me, of course, knowing how I felt about the subject. And I don't blame her. I'm sorry, Livvy ... I never would have given the satchel to you had I known."

Olivia thought of the satchel now tucked in the bottom of her wardrobe. "I tried to return it to his office earlier today, but he was holding a meeting with his foreman. I'll do it first thing in the morning, right after he leaves."

Elizabeth nodded.

"I'm sorry about Nathaniel, Aunt Elizabeth. Susanna told me. I hope you don't mind."

Elizabeth responded with a sad smile. "Not at all. He was an adorable boy. So full of life. I think his death was especially hard on the general because Nathaniel was so like her. Oh, we still had John Jr., and he was a wonderful boy. Perfect in many ways, actually. And he's grown into a fine man. But Nathaniel ... He was so young when she died, and he'd been so close to his mother. He was the spitting image of her too, as William told me. Many times ..."

The words, heavy with meaning, hung in the night air as the sun sank lower behind the hills.

"Both of our daughters are named after her, you know," Elizabeth whispered. "Mary ... Selena ... Harding. William asked me if I would mind. And, of course, I told him no. Which I'd do all over again."

"Because you love him," Olivia whispered.

"With all my heart."

After a moment, Elizabeth rose and moved to the railing. She looked out onto the meadow bathed in the soft, golden glow of twilight. Olivia would have thought her aunt almost serene—if not for the way she gripped the banister tightly.

"Livvy ... Have you ever had a ... premonition of sorts?"

"A premonition?"

Elizabeth looked back, then nodded.

Olivia shrugged. "A premonition about what?"

"About anything. Just a *feeling* that something was going to happen. And then it did."

Olivia thought about it for a moment. "I suppose. Once or twice. Why?"

When Elizabeth didn't answer, Olivia felt a disquiet.

"Have *you* had a premonition, Aunt Elizabeth?"

Elizabeth held her gaze, then looked back out over the meadow. "No." She laughed softly. "Of course not. But I do sometimes feel as if ... a moment I'm living in was one I'd felt coming. If that makes any sense."

It didn't, but Olivia shied away from saying so.

Elizabeth laughed again. "Pay no mind to me, Livvy. I'm a silly old woman."

Olivia stood and joined her at the railing. "You're not that at all, Aunt Elizabeth. You've had a difficult few months. Years, perhaps. But ..." She smiled. "You're getting stronger. And you're feeling better every day, aren't you?"

Elizabeth reached up and brushed a curl from Olivia's forehead. "Yes," she whispered. "I am, dear. Thanks to you."

Later, as Olivia sat by her bedroom window waiting for Ridley, it occurred to her how differently she viewed the Harding family now than when she first arrived. She'd thought of them as having everything, as being so perfect. But perhaps there were no perfect families. Only perfect misperceptions of them.

And perhaps marriages were that way too.

The discovery encouraged her in a way. To know that though

the general and Aunt Elizabeth's marriage wasn't perfect, they'd still made a success of it. Perhaps it wasn't everything the younger Elizabeth had desired at twenty-one. But better than most, certainly. Olivia stared into the dark night. If she knew this, why could she still not let go of that childish dream of finding a man who would love her as she loved him?

When the mantle clock marked half past eleven, then midnight, and there was still no sign of Ridley, she finally changed into her nightgown, blew out the oil lamp, and climbed into bed.

One step closer to relinquishing that dream.

Chapter
THIRTY-FIVE

The next morning, after watching General Harding ride away on his stallion, Olivia waited five more minutes to make sure he didn't ride back over the hill, having forgotten something. Then, with the satchel in hand, she hurried downstairs, crossed the porch to the general's office, and knocked on the door.

As expected, there was no answer.

She opened the door and slipped inside, then closed it behind her.

The room was cool and dark, the window shades mostly drawn. The bison head above the fireplace loomed larger than life, staring down at her with its brooding, onyx eyes. But she returned the stern look this time, refusing to be intimidated. Eager to complete her task, she crossed to the concealed bookshelf to the right of the fireplace where she'd seen Elizabeth get the satchel. Clever—bookshelves hidden behind a door. She'd never seen such a thing.

She scooted around an overstuffed chair to open the door, then knelt in the tight space, relieved when she saw the satchel's home still empty. She peered inside the front pocket, checking again to make sure the letter was in the envelope as before. It was. Remnants of her conversation with Elizabeth came back in snatches, and Olivia ached for her aunt all over again.

She couldn't decide which was more painful: being married to a man you didn't love or being married to a man you loved with all your heart and wishing he loved you the same in return.

She tucked the satchel in its place on the bottom shelf, closed the door, then rose, dusting off her skirt. Three hard raps sounded on the office door, and Olivia froze. But seconds later, when she heard the click of the latch, she dove down behind the chair, grateful the room was dark. Remembering her skirt, she reached behind her and yanked it close just as the door opened.

Someone entered. A man, judging by the weight of his tread. He stepped inside the room and paused. Afraid she'd be heard in the silence, Olivia held her breath. She wished she could see around the chair but didn't dare move.

The telling sound of paper rubbing paper made her think he was reading something. Then she heard a soft thud. Then ... nothing.

Her lungs started to burn. What was he doing? *Did he see her? Oh ... How did she manage to get herself into these—*

Footsteps again. The door opened ... She waited, praying. Then it—blissfully, mercifully—closed. She exhaled, then began to untangle herself from her wad of skirt. Gripping the back of the chair, she managed to stand without the least semblance of grace.

"Lose something back there?" a deep voice said.

Her heart catapulted to her throat. She turned and—seeing who it was—felt a flood of embarrassment, followed by a flash of anger. And hurt. *"Ridley Cooper!"* She pressed a hand to her bodice, willing her lungs to start working again. "What are you *doing* in here?"

"What am *I* doing?" He laughed. "What are *you* doing, is more like it."

Attempting to salvage the remaining shreds of her decorum, she smoothed the sides of her hair and stepped from behind the chair, still tender over his not showing last night. "I was ... returning something."

He eyed her and slowly nodded.

"I was!" Wanting to shift the attention away from herself, she gestured toward him. "Why are *you* here?"

"I'm turning in a report the general asked for." He pointed toward the desk, but never broke eye contact with her.

Olivia crossed the short distance and picked up the pages, pretending to check whether his story was true. She flipped through the report, not really reading it. But very much aware of the wry smile tipping one side of Ridley's mouth. She wanted to ask him where he'd been last night and why he hadn't bothered to come as he'd led her to believe he would. But it felt so ... girlish and simpering. Traits she'd never admired. And besides, if he hadn't cared enough to come, she didn't want to let on that she cared enough to have been hurt by his *not* coming.

"I'm sorry I didn't come last night, Olivia."

"I waited for you until midnight!" The words were out before she could stop them.

His smile deepened, drawing her focus like a magnet.

"One of the mares delivered late last night. It was a difficult birth, and we nearly lost the filly. Uncle Bob and I took turns staying up with them."

"Oh, Ridley, I'm sorry." Even in the dimly lit room, she noticed the signs of fatigue around his eyes. And realizing he had a valid excuse only made her feel all the more girlish and simpering. "Is the mare all right? And the filly?"

"Uncle Bob thinks they will be. And you know Uncle Bob. He knows everything."

She smiled, appreciating the admiration and respect Ridley had for Bob Green. And the way he never shied away from showing it like some of the other foremen did, all of whom were white. A thought occurred to her. "How did you see me over there? I was behind the chair."

"You're right. *You* were. But your, *ah* ... bustle wasn't."

Her face went warm. "Those infernal things. They always get me in trouble with you."

"Which suits me just fine," he whispered, and moved closer. "I've missed you."

She laughed, surprised by the admission. "How can you miss me? We see each other nearly every day. And on Sundays ... at church."

"I know. But ... not like this."

He cradled her cheek, then traced her lips with his forefinger, an intensity in his gaze she'd seen before. And welcomed. But ...

He didn't kiss her.

His hand moved slowly up her arm, over the scar and slight bump hidden beneath her left sleeve, to her shoulder, then to the back of her neck. His hands were strong and sure and moved at a pace that belied the quickening of his breath. And hers.

He tilted her face to meet his. And then ... *oh, finally*, he kissed her. But slowly this time, patiently, unlike the last time. With each lingering touch of his lips, she felt herself being drawn closer. She'd never known a kiss could be so gentle, so ... devoted. It had never been this way with Charles. Not before they were married and certainly not after.

Ridley's hands moved down her back and over the curve of her waist as though he wanted to memorize the feel of her. She wanted to do the same with him but didn't dare.

His arms came around her, and she slipped hers around his neck. Either she was floating, or her feet were no longer touching the floor. Either way, she didn't care. The sting of emotion burned her eyes, and she was certain she'd melt right here in General Harding's office.

The name jarred through her like reverberations through a cracked bell. She pulled back.

"Ridley!" she whispered.

"What?" He moved in to kiss her again.

"We're in General Harding's office!"

He stilled, looked into her eyes, then up at the bison, then back at her. "We should probably leave."

The way he said it so matter-of-factly made her smile. That, and the fact that he didn't move.

She gestured. "You can start by putting me down."

"But that's the part I really don't want to do," he answered. Though with a grin and a quick kiss to her forehead, he did.

Several mornings later, Olivia returned to her room to find a package on her desk. She opened it and immediately tried on the boots. Then sought out Susanna in the kitchen.

"Thank you," she whispered, giving the woman a quick sideways hug. "I appreciate you getting these for me in town."

Susanna patted her hand, smiling. "It's awful nice what you doin', Missus Aberdeen. If you just leave them others with me, I'll—"

"No, I'd rather clean them myself ... if that's all right."

Susanna eyed her. "Yes, ma'am, that be fine. You ever done it before?"

Olivia hesitated, then shook her head.

"That's all right." Susanna gave her a conspiratorial wink. "I teach you. But you gonna have to let 'em dry real good overnight."

The next morning, with black shoe polish still staining her fingertips, Olivia found Aunt Elizabeth reading in the study. A breeze billowed the floor-to-ceiling curtains framing the open window, and Elizabeth looked up as she entered.

"Livvy, what a nice surprise. I thought you'd already be—" Elizabeth's gaze dropped to the boots in Olivia's hands, and she frowned. "Now Livvy ... I told you those were a gift."

"I know you did." Olivia placed the freshly cleaned and polished boots Elizabeth had given her on the floor. "But I ordered a pair with a little lower heel. Better for walking."

She inched her skirt up to show Elizabeth, who wore a dim smile that said she wasn't entirely convinced.

"You're part of our family now, Livvy. You must allow me to give you things on occasion. Doing such gives me great pleasure."

"Thank you, Aunt Elizabeth." Olivia leaned down and kissed her cheek. "I'll be in the stable working for the general if you need me."

"All right, dear. Thank you."

Olivia paused in the doorway to the foyer. "*Oh*, about the boots . . ."

Elizabeth looked up from her book.

"Perhaps someone else could use them. Maybe . . . Mary." Olivia added a shrug for effect, hoping her words didn't sound too rehearsed. "I think she commented once that she liked them. I know I always enjoyed wearing my mother's things growing up."

Elizabeth seemed to think about that for a long moment. "Thank you, Livvy," she said softly. "That's very thoughtful of you. I'll be certain to ask her."

Olivia continued into the foyer, feeling more than a little triumphant and wondering if she'd missed her calling for the stage. Reaching the front door, she heard something behind her and turned. It took a moment for her eyes to adjust to the dimmer light of the front hall, but someone stood before one of the family portraits at the far end.

"Rachel?" she finally asked.

Rachel looked up. "Missus Aberdeen . . ." Sniffing, Rachel briefly looked away, then closed the distance between them. "How you doin' this mornin', ma'am?"

"I'm well. How are *you*?"

"Oh, I'm fine, ma'am."

Though Rachel's voice denied it, Olivia thought she detected a trace of tears in the striking blue eyes.

Rachel pressed her forefinger against her lips. "I just brought a fresh supply of Mrs. Harding's special blend," she whispered. "I put it in the kitchen with Susanna."

"Oh, good!" Olivia whispered back. "I had it on my list to ask you about that this week."

"Well, you can mark it off, ma'am. 'Cause it's all done!"

Olivia returned her smile, resisting the urge to look down the hallway.

"Well ... I best be off." Rachel gave her leather pouch a pat. "Need to gather some more herbs from the woods. Let me know if you need anythin' else."

"All right, I will."

Olivia waited until the door had closed and Rachel's footsteps on the porch faded before she walked to where Rachel had been standing — in front of the portrait of John Harding, the general's father. For a long moment, Olivia stared into his likeness, seeing glimpses of General Harding in the angular features of the man's faces, in the high forehead, and even in the commanding presence the artist had captured.

But it was the striking blue of John Harding's eyes that made Olivia look back at the door ... and wonder.

Later that next week, in the supply room of the mares' stable, Olivia completed her inventory for October in a third of the time it had taken her in June. After five months of this routine, she finally had the supplies in all the various supply rooms across the plantation organized in the same manner. Some of the stable hands were better at returning things to their proper places than others, but the rudimentary pictures she'd drawn on the outside of the boxes and crates were helping the workers who couldn't read a word.

Which, unfortunately, included most of them.

A little warm, she fluffed the bodice of her shirtwaist, grateful for the somewhat cooler temperatures but wishing fall would hurry up and arrive in all its glory. Autumn was her favorite season — the maples fiery red, the cool breezes at night — and she hoped this one would stay for a while instead of bowing so quickly to winter as it had last year.

She reviewed the regular monthly report she'd prepared for General Harding, then the additional notes she'd included on the last page, wondering how he'd accept the suggestions coming from her. She would find out soon enough.

She went in search of Ridley to approve the summary before she submitted it and found him outside in a corral with one of the mares and the tiniest foal she'd ever seen. The filly they'd nearly lost. It had to be. If not for the mare in the corral, Olivia might have opened the gate and stepped inside to get a closer glimpse. As it was, she stayed outside where it was safe.

Still, watching the little creature made her smile. Its spindly legs barely looked strong enough to support its slight weight, much less enable it to run and jump as it was doing. But the way Ridley played with the foal, running this way and that, cutting the foal off at the pass . . .

It was nothing less than charming.

Looking at him now — clean-shaven, a layer of brawn thickening his arm and shoulder muscles after months of hearty food and demanding work, and him appearing so *at home* in these surroundings — it was hard to imagine the "vagrant" she'd first met along the road that day on her way to Belle Meade. A flush of what she guessed could be called *pride* washed through her.

She summoned a formal tone. "Excuse me, sir. I need your assistance with something."

He turned. His smile widened upon seeing her and nearly took her breath away.

"Come on in." He gestured to the gate. "And meet little Dewdrop."

Whether it was the inviting way he said it — like it would give him such pleasure if she consented — or the way the filly suddenly stopped and looked over at her, Olivia wasn't sure. But she wished she could do as Ridley asked. Yet, glancing at the mare who was more than glancing back at her, Olivia shook her head.

"It's all right. I can see from here."

Ridley's smile fell a little. But he nodded. "She's a little charmer, isn't she?"

"She's adorable." But the carefree feeling Olivia had experienced watching the foal a minute earlier was gone. Ridley was disappointed. Not in her, but in her fear of these animals.

He met her at the fence, Dewdrop prancing along behind him. The filly stuck her nose through the opening in the split rails. Ridley's hand came through the space too, and Olivia looked down, knowing what he wanted.

"She's gentle as a kitten, Olivia. I promise."

"No, Ridley. I can't."

"Come on . . . Just once."

Olivia looked beyond him to the mare, who took a couple of steps forward, then paused, staring at her. Then at the foal. Olivia could all but feel the horse's motherly instinct extending like an unseen blanket around her young one.

"The mother is watching us," she whispered.

"I'd be worried if she wasn't. Now give me your hand … before Dewdrop gums your skirt to bits."

Olivia glanced down and, sure enough, the filly had hold of her skirt in its mouth. She tugged the fabric free, careful not to get her hand near the foal's mouth, then backed up a step. "Ridley, I … I just don't want to. I'm …" She hated even thinking the word, much less saying it aloud. To *him*. "I'm scared."

"All right. That's fine." He gave her that smile she loved. "Is that this month's report?"

The ease with which he accepted her decision triggered an unexpected boldness and—clenching her teeth—she held out her hand. He grabbed it quickly.

She looked at the filly. "She doesn't bite, does she?"

"Everything that has teeth bites, Olivia."

She tried to pull her hand back but he kept a firm hold. "Trust me."

Wanting to, but terrified, Olivia willed herself to stop fighting—and shaking—but to no avail. Then Ridley reached out and covered her hand with both of his and—in a gesture that was nothing short of heroic in her eyes—created a cocoon of sorts, her hand safely protected inside. He brought them close to Dewdrop's mouth and Olivia held her breath.

The little foal licked the top of Ridley's hand and nibbled on the sides as if trying to get at a treat hidden within. It was an odd sensation, more … *playful* than fearsome.

"Are you ready?" he asked. "I'll open my hands gradually."

Glancing at the mare, who was still watching them, Olivia nodded. Or tried to. Ridley positioned their hands where both of his were thumbs up, then he slowly opened them, making a slit in the cocoon to reveal her hand within. Dewdrop's tongue brushed against her fingers, and Olivia cringed. Then shivered.

"It feels … rough."

Ridley smiled. "A little. Just wait until she nibbles on your palm."

Olivia stiffened but didn't pull away.

"You ready?"

"No." But she swallowed, determined to see this through. If only just to prove to herself she could do it. "And ... yes."

He withdrew one hand and turned hers palm up in his. Olivia sucked in a breath when Dewdrop began nibbling—no, more like *gumming*—her palm. It didn't hurt at all. In fact, it almost ... tickled.

"Here." Ridley withdrew an apple slice from his pocket and dropped it into her hand. "Her being so young, I'm not sure she'll take it. But I'm guessing if you give her this, she'll be your friend for life."

The apple slice barely touched Olivia's palm before Dewdrop claimed it, munching loudly before coming back for more.

"Now scratch her right here." Ridley pointed to the white spot between the horse's eyes.

Olivia did and couldn't believe it when the precious little filly tried to fit her head further between the rails. Then Olivia saw the mare—*directly* behind Ridley—and drew back.

"It's all right, Olivia. She's one of the gentlest mares we have."

Olivia wasn't so sure.

The mare nuzzled the foal, sniffing and blowing out her breath as if making sure her filly was unharmed. The foal tossed its head, then tried to reach Olivia again. But when the mare stretched its long neck and enormous head over the fence, Olivia stumbled back.

"She only wants to sniff you." Ridley scratched the mare behind the ears and it snorted, sounding oddly satisfied. "Which only seems fair since she *did* allow you to touch her foal."

Olivia shot him a look. "Why do I feel as though I've been tricked?"

"Not tricked. Just maybe a tiny bit"—he shrugged—"coerced." He grinned. "Now come on, give it a try. I'll hold your hand again, if you want. Miserable prospect that is for me."

Olivia tried for an offended look but had to bite her lower lip in order not to smile—until she looked back at the mare. The mare sniffed the air in her direction, and Olivia stared into her huge brown eyes, which held curiosity and, oddly, a measure of uncertainty Olivia understood only too well.

Making a fist of her right hand and trying not to think of it coming back without all five fingers still attached, she took a step forward. Ridley reached out, but she shook her head.

"I want to do it myself."

He laughed softly. "Spoken like a true daughter of the South."

Ignoring him, Olivia closed the distance. And slowly, dread weighing her arm, she reached out her hand, palm up, fingers trembling. Grimacing, not allowing herself to look at those overlarge teeth, she barely contained a squeal as the mare gave her palm a moist and messy lick. Then gummed it as the foal had done earlier. Only harder.

Still ... it didn't hurt.

Ridley laughed out loud. "Good for you!"

Olivia pulled her hand back and took a much-needed breath, still looking at the mare and those big brown eyes that somehow seemed a little ... friendlier than before. As though suddenly bored, the filly turned and set off across the corral. The mare followed, leaving Olivia to stare in bewilderment at her sopping-wet hand. Still holding the report in her other hand, she looked down at her skirt. But couldn't bring herself to—

"Here." Ridley already had the gate open. He closed it behind him. "Allow me." He pulled a rag from his back pocket and wiped her hand clean. "I'm proud of you."

Tempted to brush aside the praise, Olivia heard the sincerity in his voice. Truth was, she was more than a little proud of herself as well. "Thank you, Ridley." She looked up at him. "I'm ... proud of you too." The words just came. She hadn't planned on saying them.

The rag stilled. He studied her, his expression taking on an almost boyish quality. "Proud of me?" He laughed softly. "For what?"

She didn't have to think long to know why. "For all you've accomplished since you've been here. For all you're learning. I saw you working with Jack Malone the other day. And ..." She shook her head, remembering. "I was so glad it wasn't me in the corral with that—"

"Magnificent animal?"

"'Terrifying beast' is what I was going to say."

They both laughed.

"The way you got him to do what you wanted ..."

He held up a hand. "Don't give me too much credit. Uncle Bob was right there helping. I secretly think that horse has it in for me."

He winked, and she smiled, considering how to phrase what she wanted to say next. "You know what you want to do with your life, Ridley. And you're doing it very well."

He took her hand in his and traced funny little circles in the cradle of her palm, which did not-so-funny things to her insides.

"You're doing the same thing," he said softly. "By being a companion to Mrs. Harding. And with your teaching."

She gave a slight shrug. "I appreciate everything Aunt Elizabeth has done for me, so please don't take this the wrong way, but ... being a *companion* to Aunt Elizabeth is something I would have done anyway. She's like a mother to me. And while I love teaching Jimmy and Jolene ..." She glanced away. "It's not like I'm a *real* teacher who—"

"Don't do that." Touching her chin, he gently brought her focus back to him. "Don't dismiss what you're doing, Olivia. You're changing Jimmy's and Jolene's futures. Their lives will never be the same. I can count on one hand—and still have four fingers left—the number of women in your position who would have even noticed those children, much less taken the time to teach them."

His affirmation was like rainfall on parched ground, and she drank it in. Though a part of her still wanted to speak in her own defense. Not against what he was saying but to what she wanted him to understand. That she wanted something *more*. More than the arranged marriage the general insisted on making. She'd already had that. She didn't want it again. If given a choice, she wanted to do something *larger* with her life than get married again. Something important. Something that would last beyond her. And if she *did* choose to remarry, she wanted it to be—

The thought came so clearly and wasn't new to her. She wanted it to be to someone like Ridley. To someone she wanted to be with. At breakfast and throughout the day. On walks at midnight. Sitting beside her at church. Climbing a lattice. She wanted it to be to someone who was a friend—and yet far more.

She covered his hand in hers. "Thank you, Ridley. You always speak your mind. Even when you know the other person might not agree. And speaking my mind is something I've never been encouraged to do. Before meeting you, that is."

"Well, you're definitely getting better at it."

Seeing his grin, she tugged his hand. "What I'm trying to say is you're an honest and forthright man. You always tell the truth. And those are qualities I greatly admire ... for many reasons."

Slowly, his smile faded. He didn't say anything for a minute, just held her gaze. "I assure you, Olivia ... I'm not worthy of such praise."

"Well, I think you are."

He opened his mouth as though to say something else, then

looked away. If she didn't know better, she might have thought she'd said something off-putting. As it was, she simply added *appealing modesty* to his list of admirable qualities.

With feigned stoicism, she presented the report. "For your approval, Mr. Cooper."

He flipped through the pages, scanning as he went. When he came to the last page, he paused. "Have you discussed this with General Harding yet?"

She shook her head. "After noticing some redundancy in ordering, I figured that ..." She frowned, an unwelcome suspicion surfacing. "Are you thinking the suggestions would be better received if they came from you instead?"

"Oh no." He handed the report back to her. "You deserve all the credit for this, Olivia. I just wish I could be there to see the general's face when he reads it."

Chapter
THIRTY-SIX

*I*n the basin in her room, Olivia washed her hands clean of horse, still unable to believe she'd actually touched one of the creatures. Much less *two*. The things Ridley Cooper managed to talk her into doing …

She closed her bedroom door behind her and hurried across the open second-story porch and down the staircase, eager to share her suggestions with the general. Especially after Ridley's comments. A deliciously sweet aroma drifted toward her from the kitchen—Betsy's rhubarb cobbler—and her mouth watered. But that would have to wait.

She rapped twice on the general's office door before hearing voices from inside.

"But General Harding, certainly by now, sir, you must concede that the freedmen are—"

"I am under no obligation to concede anything, Mr. Pagette. Not to you. Not to the Freedmen's Bureau. So you will kindly temper your manner in that regard."

Realizing the general had a guest, Olivia turned to leave.

"Come in!"

Hearing the general's curt response, she hesitated, wanting to go, but not feeling free to. Then she spotted an older gentleman through the window by the fireplace, witnessing her silent debate. Cringing, she opened the door and stepped inside. "My apologies, General. Sir," she nodded to his guest. "I didn't realize you were meeting. I'll come back later."

"Nonsense." General Harding waved her in. "Our business here is concluded. Mr. Pagette, may I present Mrs. Aberdeen, my wife's companion and an employee of Belle Meade. Mrs. Aberdeen, Mr. Pagette from the Bureau of Refugees, Freedmen, and Abandoned Lands."

Noting the office from which the gentleman hailed, Olivia returned his mannerly nod. "Pleasure to meet you, sir."

"Likewise ... Mrs. Aberdeen."

The way he said her last name made her wonder if they'd met before. Of average height and build, the man was pleasant looking, friendly. No distinguishing features. Neither remarkably handsome nor memorably plain, yet she couldn't shake the feeling that she knew him.

"Good day, Mr. Pagette," the general continued. "Before you leave, I invite you to seek refreshment from one of the women in the kitchen. They'll see you're taken care of." He cleared his throat. "Is that this month's report?"

It took Olivia a second to realize the general was addressing her. She glanced at the pages in her hand. "Yes, sir. It is."

"Well, Mrs. Aberdeen, may I see it?"

"Oh ... of course, sir." Handing him the report, Olivia threw an apologetic glance at the older gentleman who remained exactly where he'd been, appearing completely at ease. Which struck her as odd since his exchange with the general had seemed rather terse. Not to mention the general had dismissed him.

"General Harding." Mr. Pagette approached the desk, his manner polite but unyielding. "Perhaps you would allow me to make another request before I go. One that's fairly benign, I assure you."

The general slowly lifted his head. Olivia knew that look. She wished she could tell Mr. Pagette that whatever he was going to ask for, he would do best to save his breath.

"When I first arrived today, General, I was shown a building that would be more than suitable for our purposes. I believe it currently serves as a church for the freedmen. I've already spoken with a few of the families here at Belle Meade, and there is indeed interest. So if you would allow me to prevail upon you, sir, to donate the building for use, then the Freedmen's Bureau would set about to find a—"

"That is out of the question, Mr. Pagette. While I will not seek to prevent you from pursuing such an undertaking elsewhere, I can do nothing to help it along here."

Feeling the tension grow more taut, Olivia looked between the men, wondering what they were discussing. Mr. Pagette sighed, although judging from his expression, it wasn't a sigh of resignation as much as astonishment.

"May I inquire, General Harding ..." The man's tone, still diplomatic, had gained an edge. "As to why you will not seek to help the very people upon whose shoulders the success of your business rests? As does the foundation of the very home in which you and your family reside? And your father before you?"

The question dripped with culpability, and Olivia cringed. Yet she had to admire the man's forthrightness and courage that reminded her of someone else she knew. Confining her gaze to the carpet, she sensed the general's hackles rising.

"Mr. Pagette." General Harding rose from behind his desk. "Your persistence forces me to speak more plainly on this issue than I would wish. It is my belief, sir, that these people, while *most* dear to my family—many of whom I consider to be such—possess the capacity of enduring labor under a sun that would be distressing, if not unsupportable, to any other race. To state it more simply, from their physical and mental organization, I believe they are better adapted to the drudgery of farm work than any other race of people."

Olivia's head came up, pounding.

"My position on this subject," the general continued, his beard flirting with the second button on his vest, "is that they should have the rudiments of education, sir. Enough to protect themselves against the impositions of bad men. But further than that, I *do not* deem necessary."

Seconds passed—how many Olivia didn't know—until she became aware of her breath coming hard. Her face was on fire, like it had been after Charles slapped her. *Education?* For the servants? The Freedmen's Bureau wanted to open a school ... *here at Belle Meade*. She looked first at Mr. Pagette, whose firmed jawline reflected his resolve, then back to General Harding. She wanted to tell the general his suppositions were mistaken. All he had to do was look at Jimmy. And Jolene. And see how they were learning. But she didn't dare.

Mr. Pagette leveled a stare. "Is that your final word on this, General Harding?"

Olivia looked back at the general, silently hoping.

"It is, Mr. Pagette." General Harding crossed to the door. "Again, before you go, sir, I hope you'll seek refreshment from the kitchen. It's quite a long ride back to town."

Mr. Pagette offered his hand. "Thank you for your time, General." He looked Olivia's way. "Mrs. Aberdeen, a pleasure, ma'am."

"All mine," she whispered, still trying to grasp what the general had just said. And done. And what it meant.

The office door closed. General Harding returned to his chair, picked up the report, and began reading it as though nothing had happened. As though he hadn't just decided the futures of over a hundred people.

Including hers. For a second time.

Olivia watched the clock on the wall, wanting to leave the general's office. But he kept on asking question after question, and she couldn't exactly not answer. As excited as she'd been to share her ideas with the general, all she wanted now was to find Mr. Pagette before he left.

"I'm impressed, Olivia." The general looked up from his desk. "And frankly, I wonder why none of the men in charge of ordering in the past have thought about this before."

Olivia glanced out the window. "Thank you, General. With your permission, I'll combine the separate orders from all the different supply areas across the plantation, and we'll start ordering the common items in greater bulk. The prices you see here ..." She gestured to the paper, sneaking another look at the clock on the wall. Twenty-five minutes had passed since Mr. Pagette took his leave. "They are already negotiated with Mr. Burkett, the owner of the feed store. Mr. Burkett came in second lowest on the bidding. All we need is your approval, and we'll move forward."

She hoped the women in the kitchen were stuffing Mr. Pagette full of rhubarb cobbler.

The general looked up. "Do tell me, Olivia, why we aren't going with the lowest price."

"Because, sir, the last two times we've ordered from Mr. Hankler, he's been late in delivery and his product has been inferior. So actually, ordering this way, we'll receive higher quality goods for appoximately the same price. As indicated in the total in this column." She pointed, resisting the urge to tell him she'd already explained this once.

General Harding gave a nod. "Well done, Olivia. Proceed with ordering from Mr. Burkett, and"—he pushed back from his desk, and she took that as her cue to move toward the door—"obtain bids from the other suppliers as you've noted. Then we'll speak again."

"Very good, sir. I'll do that. Thank you."

Smiling, she exited the office, walked as casually as she could past the open front window, then skedaddled across the porch to the kitchen. She found Chloe inside alone. "Chloe, have you seen Mr. Pagette, the general's guest?"

"Yes, Missus Aberdeen. He stopped by, and I give him a cup o' cider and some salt pork on a biscuit. Then he left. Been a while now." Chloe pulled a steaming skillet from the oven.

"Did he say where he was going next?"

"No, ma'am." Chloe shook her head, intent on her work. "He didn't."

Olivia searched the front of the house. No carriage was parked in the drive. Then again, she didn't remember seeing one earlier either. If she didn't find Mr. Pagette before he left, chances of their crossing paths again was slim. It wasn't as if she could inquire to the general about him. And since she never ventured into town . . .

She half walked, half ran to the mares' stable, hearing her mother's voice the entire way. *A lady always walks with grace and purpose, Olivia. She never runs.*

Well, this *lady sometimes does,* Olivia thought. *With purpose too.* Albeit, minus much grace.

She searched the stable. Mr. Pagette wasn't there. Neither was Ridley. But Grady Matthews was.

"Mrs. Aberdeen! Nice to see you again today, ma'am."

She'd seen Mr. Matthews several times since that day in the storage room of the stable. He hadn't mentioned anything further about the teaching. Surely he'd seen her with Jimmy and Jolene. But other than seeking ways to prolong conversations with her and making inquiries that were none of his concern, he hadn't bothered her — or touched her — again.

"Hello, Mr. Matthews. I'm looking for a guest of the general's and thought he might have come in here. Have you seen him, by chance?"

"What's his name?"

"Mr. P—" Olivia almost said it, then caught herself. "That's all right, Mr. Matthews. I don't see him here. I'll look elsewhere."

Leaving before the stable hand could think of another question, Olivia walked back outside and scanned the meadow, then recalled something Mr. Pagette had said back in the office about being shown a building when he first arrived. She covered ground as quickly as she could without running full out and minutes later—winded and overly warm—she rounded the corner leading to the church. And there he was, climbing into a carriage.

"Mr. Pagette!" she called, a stitch in her side slowing her pace.

He gathered the reins and released the brake, not turning.

She called again, louder this time, and he glanced in her direction. She waved and closed the distance between them, fighting to catch her breath.

She stopped a few feet shy of the horse. "I'm ... so glad I ... caught you, sir."

He smiled, setting the brake again. "And I'm sorry to have caused you to overexert yourself on my behalf, madam."

She held up a hand. "It's all right ..." The burning in her lungs gradually lessened. "I'm simply ... unaccustomed ... to running."

He laughed and climbed from the carriage. "And I'm unaccustomed to having lovely young women pursue me across massive estates. So that makes us even." A twinkle lit his eyes. "While also making this old man's day."

Olivia smiled, finding the ease with which he bantered both surprising and engaging.

He gave a slight bow. "To what do I owe this pleasure, Mrs. Aberdeen?"

There it was again, the way he said her name and that feeling they'd met before. "By chance, Mr. Pagette, have our paths had opportunity to cross before today?"

A fleeting look clouded his expression. "No, ma'am, we've never been properly introduced, but ..." His voice softened. "I knew your father. We served on a number of committees together through the years. I had the utmost respect for him, God rest him. And your mother, as well. Whom I had the pleasure of meeting on several occasions."

Maybe it was being here at Belle Meade all these months, cut off from the outside world, or maybe it was the fact that he'd known her parents, but she felt a connection to the man.

"I've also seen you in town on occasion, Mrs. Aberdeen. Though it's been some time. At social events ..." He glanced away briefly, before looking back. "When you accompanied your late husband."

Olivia read awareness in his eyes. So he knew who she was. Or more rightly, whose widow she was. "Did you know him, sir? My late husband?"

"Not personally, no. But I am familiar with … the circumstances, of course."

The circumstances. The words prompted a sense of melancholy as her smile came and went. "Of course."

"Please allow me to extend my condolences, ma'am, for the pain you must be enduring upon your husband's passing."

"Thank you, Mr. Pagette. You're most kind." But his sincerity cut her to the quick. She wanted to tell him he needn't feel badly for her, that she hadn't loved her husband. But such honesty with a stranger hardly seemed proper. And yet, this man hardly seemed like a proper stranger.

"Pardon me for rushing our conversation, Mrs. Aberdeen. But I have another appointment to make yet this afternoon. Dare I presume your pursuit of me pertains in some way to my discussion with General Harding?"

"Yes, sir. It does."

He waited.

Contemplating what she was about to propose, Olivia felt her pulse kick up a notch. "It's about … starting a freedmen's school."

He sighed. "I sensed you felt badly for me in that regard. But I knew the odds of the general granting my petition weren't in my favor when I came here. So his disposition on the topic—as cool as an iceberg, you might say—wasn't surprising. Still … I had to try."

"Mr. Pagette?" She took a deep breath. "If you had a building in which to meet, would you be able to start the school?"

He studied her for a moment, and she could see his thoughts churning.

"A place to meet is necessary, of course, ma'am. But the bureau also needs to find a teacher. Then there's the business of books, which are quite expensive and—"

"If you had a teacher"—Olivia felt a quickening inside her—"and if that teacher somehow found a way to provide books …"

Gradual understanding deepened his gaze. But to her surprise, he shook his head.

"No, ma'am. *No* … The bureau would never agree to that. Nor would I."

"But why? I'm capable of—"

"Do you have any idea how dangerous that would be for you, Mrs. Aberdeen? A white woman? Teaching freedmen? Just last week, a male teacher in Memphis was beaten almost to death. Pardon my candor—and I don't mean to offend you—but you think the city of Nashville shunned you over what your husband did?" He looked down at the ground, then back up. His eyes were fierce. "Taking into account current public opinion, they'd likely do to you what they did to him, if they ever found out."

Olivia fought back a shudder, the images of Charles's body burned into her mind. "Then, we'll make sure they don't."

"You don't know what you're saying, ma'am. I'm not unaware that your personal ..." He clenched his jaw tight as if trapping the words before they leaped free. But Olivia could guess at what he'd been about to say, and considering what she was proposing, she felt it important for him to know the truth.

Surprisingly, her voice came smooth and strong. "Mr. Pagette, since we're speaking with candor ..." Seconds passed. He nodded. "You offered your condolences a moment ago on my late husband's passing, and I appreciate them. But it always feels so false to respond with 'thank you,' as etiquette demands, when my feelings are ... quite the opposite. The truth is, I haven't suffered as greatly in my late husband's death as I did while he was living."

The lack of surprise in Mr. Pagette's expression revealed she'd guessed correctly.

"I appreciate your honesty, Mrs. Aberdeen, and will certainly keep your confidence. When I stated that I didn't know your husband personally, that was true. But I did know personally of his dealings, more so than the newspapers reported. And ..." A sheepish, almost regretful expression swept his face. "It's not difficult for me to imagine what a woman such as yourself might have suffered at the hand of such a man. And since we're being so honest ..." He smiled. "It was *that* pain for which I was truly offering my condolences moments ago."

Olivia slowly returned his smile. "So we've come full circle then, Mr. Pagette."

Neither spoke for a moment. A cool breeze rustled the trees lining the road, and Olivia caught the first sure hint of fall on its wings.

"I realize you suffered at the hand of your husband, Mrs. Aberdeen. And for that, I'm deeply sorry. But you've lived a sheltered life in comparison to what these recently freed—"

"I know that, sir. Though I didn't know it ... until coming here. And until ..." Her throat tightened. She motioned past him. "Until going to church there."

He glanced behind him, then turned back. "*That's* where *you* go to church, ma'am?"

She nodded. "They welcomed me ... when no one else would. I'm already teaching two of the children. They're very bright. They're learning to read and write. We've started arithmetic now too." She told him about how Jimmy stood up in church the previous week and read a series of verses they'd practiced. But she could tell he wasn't impressed. "What I'm saying to you, Mr. Pagette, is that I'd appreciate the opportunity to at least be considered as a teacher for a freedmen's school."

A moment passed, and she felt her hope passing with it.

He glanced back in the direction from which she'd come. "How will General Harding feel about your teaching, ma'am?"

"I ... hadn't planned on telling him. But remember," she hastened to add, "he said himself he wouldn't stand in the way of it. Only that he couldn't be party to it. And one thing I would insist on, out of respect for him—and I *do* respect him, Mr. Pagette, even though I don't agree with him on this issue—is that the school could not be on Belle Meade property."

Mr. Pagette looked off in the distance. "A freedmen's school burned over in Alabama last month. Killed fourteen people. Most of them children. If anything like that were to happen to you, the daughter of a trusted friend ..." He turned back. Emotion lent a sheen to his eyes, and Olivia felt the same in hers.

"And yet," she whispered, "these people deserve the right to learn. To have the chance to improve their lives."

"I agree," he said softly.

"So please, sir ... Let me help them learn. Allow me to have a ... meaningful purpose for my life again."

She searched his expression and saw compassion and gratitude, along with his struggle. But no clear answer.

He climbed into the carriage and gripped the reins. "You're a brave woman, Mrs. Aberdeen."

"No, sir. I'm nothing of the sort. I simply know what it's like to live under someone else's rule. Then to have a taste of freedom. However briefly."

Mr. Pagette looked beyond her, toward the mansion. "Even a brief taste of freedom is a powerful thing, isn't it, ma'am?" He released the brake but held the reins taut. "I'll contact you again, Mrs. Aberdeen.

Though, it may be a month or so. And it will definitely be through someone else. A trusted third party. It's best for you if we aren't seen together. Do you understand?"

Olivia nodded, already wondering who that third party would be. Susanna, perhaps. Or Jedediah. Even Uncle Bob.

"The fewer people who know about this, ma'am, the better. But from what I've learned about you, Mrs. Aberdeen, I'd wager you know how to keep a secret."

"Yes, Mr. Pagette. Keeping secrets is something I do very well."

Chapter
THIRTY-SEVEN

No sooner had Ridley started hitching Old Gray to the miniature cart, than he spotted Olivia coming from the mansion. She paused on the front porch to speak with Mrs. Harding and Mary, who were seated in rockers.

He still had no idea what had changed Olivia's mind about taking the extra work for the quarries, but he intended to pry it out of her. Whatever her reasons, he applauded her willingness to give the horse cart a try.

While he was glad to see her facing her fear, he was hesitant because it meant they'd be spending more time together. Something he'd once thought he would never get enough of. But after what she'd said to him that afternoon a couple of weeks ago—*What I'm trying to say is you're an honest man ... You always tell the truth ... Those are qualities I greatly admire*—he'd gotten a glimpse of the man she thought he was. Her words, spoken with such sweetness, haunted him, burning a hole in his conscience and making the time they *did* spend together increasingly uncomfortable for him.

Thankfully, they'd both been busy in recent days. Her with something Mrs. Harding was working on for a women's committee, she said, plus teaching Jimmy and Jolene. And his own days began well before dawn and often went late into the night. What with the fall harvest, training the yearlings, the recent races at Burns Island track, and working with the stallions, he had more on his plate than he could manage.

And even though he knew it was probably best they see less of each other ...

He missed her.

It was so easy for him to lose himself with her. To enjoy the moment, her laughter, her smile, and the way she sometimes looked at him. And of course, he always enjoyed looking at her. He'd made it no secret that he was leaving for the Colorado Territory after the yearling sale, and she'd made it no secret that the Colorado Territory was the last place on earth she'd ever like to be. So, that pretty much left them at odds with each other. Only, *at odds* did not describe his feelings for Olivia Aberdeen. Or what he felt right now as she leaned down to give Mrs. Harding a hug, the comely shape of her bustle drawing his eye. And what about the churning he felt each time he imagined leaving her when he headed west in a few short months?

"Lots goin' on up at the big house this mornin', Ridley?"

Hearing Uncle Bob behind him — and not missing the man's playful sarcasm — Ridley went back to work hitching up Old Gray. "Not that I know of. Why?"

Uncle Bob wiped his hands on his apron. "Oh ... I don't know. Just seemed like you was enjoyin' the view."

Ridley shook his head. "Not at all. I was just ... checking those clouds." He motioned. "Think we might be in for some rain later today."

"Mmm-hmm. Checkin' them clouds. That's what I thought you was doin'."

Ridley smiled and pulled a strap through the harness, then secured it. "But what if I *was* ... enjoying the view, as you said? Would that be so wrong?"

He looked over, expecting to see Uncle Bob's customary grin. But the man wasn't even close to smiling.

Ridley straightened. "Something wrong?"

Uncle Bob glanced toward the house, then back. "This ain't none of my business, sir. That's why I ain't said nothin' up to now."

His curiosity roused, Ridley eyed him. "What are you talking about? Up to now ...?"

Uncle Bob scratched his whiskered chin. "White folks," he said, his voice barely above a whisper. "Sometimes they talk 'round us. Almost like they forget we's even in the room."

Ridley got a funny feeling, like he was about to hear something he wasn't going to like. And the solemnity of Uncle Bob's gaze confirmed it.

"Word is, Ridley ... The general's plannin' on marryin' her off to one of his war buddies. Whichever one makes the best match. I hear tell he's already got an officer in mind."

Ridley had trouble hiding his surprise on two levels. First Uncle Bob had picked up on his feelings for Olivia ... He thought he'd done a fairly good job of masking all that. But Ridley didn't know which surprised him more—Uncle Bob's perceptiveness or that General Harding had taken the fatherly role upon himself to find Olivia another husband long before her mourning period would end.

"I'm guessin' she ain't said nothin' 'bout all this to you yet, sir."

"No." Ridley glanced back toward the house and saw Olivia walking toward them, still some distance away. She waved, and he waved back. "She hasn't."

"I don't know if I's right or not in tellin' you that. But I figured if it was me in your shoes, I'd wanna know."

Ridley nodded, not liking the sour feeling creeping up on him inside. It wasn't as if he'd never thought of Olivia marrying again someday. She was young, beautiful, intelligent. What man wouldn't want her for his wife? It was just that he didn't *like* thinking about it, so he chose not to. Most of the time. Except for now. When he couldn't think of anything else, thanks to Uncle Bob. And General Harding.

"There's somethin' else, sir. Somethin' I need to ask you."

Ridley looked over, not liking the caution in Uncle Bob's voice.

"You ain't said nothin' to her, have you? 'Bout the war or which side you—"

"No." Ridley shook his head. "I wouldn't do that to you. I wouldn't endanger your position here at Belle Meade. Or with the general. You can trust me on that, Uncle Bob."

Uncle Bob nodded. "Only reason I'm askin' is 'cause ... if you *was* to start ... *enjoyin' that view*, sir, then it'd only be right to tell her. It's true, she ain't thought of too highly right now by folks in town, but she also ain't just *some woman* either. She's a proper lady, livin' here under the charge of General William Giles Harding, and she—"

"I know who she is, Uncle Bob." The words came out harder than he'd intended. He sighed. "What I mean is ..." He offered a placating nod, the truth twisting his gut like a knife. "I understand what you're saying."

Uncle Bob walked over and put a hand on his shoulder. "That was me talkin' to you like the head hostler at Belle Meade Plantation and a worker for the general. But this is me talkin' to you like a man." He squeezed Ridley's shoulder. "If that woman was to chose you, sir, she couldn't chose no better."

Ridley heard the creak of the gate, then the rustle of a skirt, and Uncle Bob glanced beyond him.

"Mornin' there, Missus Aberdeen."

As Uncle Bob greeted Olivia, Ridley finished hitching up Old Gray, working out a knot in the reins, as well as in his gut.

Fifteen minutes later, Ridley still hadn't managed to coax Olivia into the cart, and he was all but ready to give up. "Olivia ... do you want to do this or not?"

"Yes, I want to do it. I'm just ..." She put a hand to her stomach. "The cart is so close to the horse. I just need another minute to ..."

He started unhitching Old Gray.

"Wait!" She tugged at his sleeve. "Why are you so impatient today?"

"*Impatient?*" Ridley exhaled a laugh. "I've been standing here waiting, watching you walk back and forth, picking at your skirt and then your hair, talking about this and that. Just get in the cart, Olivia. Before Old Gray dies of old age. And me along with him."

Her mouth fell open. "I can't believe you just said that to me. You know how I feel about horses. I'm just a little more nervous about this than I thought I'd be, but—"

"I understand. But that's why it's best to just do it. Just take a deep breath and get in."

She eyed Old Gray. "What if he strikes off across the pasture like Copper did that day?"

"If this decrepit gelding strikes off anywhere, I'll douse Uncle Bob's hat with Susanna's gravy and eat it for lunch." Tempted to smile at the look on her face, he didn't. He remembered how her late husband had pressured her to ride a stallion and knew he was taking a similar tactic. Only, the chances of Olivia getting hurt doing this were next to nothing. And riding in this cart—so close to the horse—was a definite step in the right direction. "Now, please ... get in the cart."

"Ridley," she whispered. "I really want to do this, but—"

"I'm going to count to three, then I'm putting Old Gray out to pasture. Literally. One—"

"Ridley, please, I just—"

"Two—"

"This isn't very gentlemanlike behav—"

"Three!"

Giving him a scathing look, Olivia stepped into the cart, sat down, and gripped the edge of the seat, then stared at the back of the horse as if the animal might turn on her at any moment.

Ridley climbed in beside her. "See? That wasn't so bad, now was it?" Feeling a little guilty about pressuring her, yet knowing she could do this—and would be glad about it later—he gathered the reins and released the brake.

He was taking out his frustration on her when really he was frustrated with himself. Why he'd ever allowed his feelings for this woman to grow into what they were, he didn't know. Caring about her the way he did, wanting her like he did—even now, with her wedged up beside him. *Very* close beside him. Turns out the miniature cart was probably better suited for one person than two. Not that he was complaining.

Old Gray sidestepped—or tried to—and the cart rocked.

"Ridley, I think I'm going to be sick."

He curbed a grin. "That's fine. Just lean over your side."

She nudged him hard with her shoulder. "You're mean today."

That made him smile. This woman could go from sweet to sassy in nothing flat. And he loved that quality about her. Just like he loved all the rest. "I'm sorry, Olivia. I don't mean to be *mean*. I just have a lot to do and—"

"Well, if you don't have time today, then …" She started to get out, but he quickly reached across the short bench.

"Oh, no you don't. You're not getting out of here until we've taken a turn around the meadow."

Looking more rebellious now than scared, she exhaled.

"You ready?"

She gave the faintest nod. He seized the moment and slapped the reins. And Old Gray set off. At a snail's pace. Yet with the way Olivia held on, watching Old Gray's every move, one would've thought they were rounding the final turn at Burns Island track.

As the ancient gelding took them around the meadow, Ridley was certain he could've counted every blade of grass if he'd wanted to. But he didn't mind too much. He enjoyed being with the woman beside him.

A late-October breeze bowed the knee-high grasses feathering the pasture and stirred the sweet scent of sunshine through wild-flowers dotting the meadow. The soft *whoosh* of wind through the field grass reminded him of the faint echo of waves from home, and in his memory, he caught a whiff of ocean and sand. A pang of homesickness hit him hard. That happened from time to time, and he guessed it would always be that way.

Instinctively, he reached for the seashell in his pants pocket, but sitting so close to Olivia, he quickly gave up the idea. She shifted beside him and her thigh rubbed the length of his, sending heat like the dog days of summer spiking right through him. He tried to move over, but there was nowhere to move. Why on earth had he made this bench so doggone narrow? Every time Olivia moved, her thigh brushed his. If she didn't stop shifting around, he was going to have to get out and walk. Either that or burn alive.

Needing to think about something else, he peered over at her. "May I ask you a question?"

She nodded, her grip on the seat easing.

"What made you change your mind? About taking this extra job at the quarries? And what about being even closer to a horse?"

She looked out across the pasture. "Several things. Aunt Elizabeth, for one. A while back"—the cart hit a gopher hole, but Olivia only gave a fleeting frown—"she and I were talking. And she told me about their son ... Nathaniel. Who died," she added softly, "just before his tenth birthday."

Ridley listened as she spoke, but he also watched as her body relaxed against him. He'd noticed that about her before. If he could get her talking, or maybe sparring with him, she would all but forget her nervousness about horses.

"So," she continued, "I figured if Aunt Elizabeth—after losing a son that way—could be around horses again, then surely I should be able to as well." Ridley nodded. He hadn't known that about the Hardings. "It's odd, isn't it?" She brushed a strand of hair from her face. "How learning about someone else's past and what they've been through makes you look at your own life so differently? I've felt the same way sometimes on Sunday morning when ..." She looked around. "We left the pasture?"

Ridley smiled. "I wondered when you were going to notice."

He guided the cart down the long driveway they'd first walked up together months ago, their conversation coming easily, like it always did. Enjoying the time together, he guided it back to where they'd started, set the brake, and helped her out.

"That wasn't so scary after all, was it?"

"At first, yes. In the end ..." She pretended to have to think hard. "No." Her eyes lit from within. "Much as it pains me to say this to you, I rather enjoyed it. Thank you, Ridley."

"You're welcome, Olivia."

His gaze lowered to her smile, then to the rest of her. She wore a skirt and jacket he'd seen many times, and the outfit suited her. But it was the color that caught his attention today. Gray, for mourning. Over a man who had been shot and hung for being a traitor to the South. Which is what Ridley knew he was. Not in his own heart. But in the hearts of most everyone else here at Belle Meade. And in Dixie. And in her heart. If she only knew the truth.

Reminded of what had brought him here and of how quickly he'd be gone, Ridley bowed at the waist and bid her good day, playing the part of the Southern gentleman he would never truly be. Not in Olivia Aberdeen's eyes.

Not after what he'd been. And done.

"An invitation? From Mrs. Adelicia Acklen?" Not certain she'd heard the general correctly, Olivia glanced at Elizabeth beside her at the dinner table, glimpsing the same note of surprise in the girls' expressions. She knew of Mrs. Acklen, of course. Everyone who lived in Nashville knew the richest woman—and widow—in the Confederacy, if not the entire country. Olivia simply hadn't realized Mrs. Acklen and the Hardings were close acquaintances.

"Yes, dear. That's right." Aunt Elizabeth exchanged a look with her husband at the far end, her smile faltering. "Apparently Mrs. Acklen has returned from her grand tour of Europe and is hosting a reception. On the eighteenth of December. For Madame Octavia LeVert."

"*The* Madame LeVert?" Selene's voice rose almost a full octave. "And our family has been invited?"

The general nodded.

Selene, Mary, and Cousin Lizzie all exchanged smiles, and Olivia didn't blame them. But she sensed a reticence on the part of her aunt *and* the general, which made her suspect. Growing up in Nashville, she'd heard about the Belmont Mansion—Mrs. Acklen's home—and had longed to visit. Her family had never received an invitation, of course, and she was certain this invitation didn't include her name either. Not that she could attend anyway, still officially in mourning. But it was a nice thought. To be invited to a reception at Belmont in honor of the famed Southern socialite, Madame LeVert.

Elizabeth rang the bell for dessert.

"From what I hear," the general continued, "it's going to be the social event of the season. Reportedly, Mrs. Acklen is inviting over a thousand guests."

Cousin Lizzie's eyes widened. "Her home must be enormous!"

Selene sighed. "I hope General Jackson can attend with us."

"With *you*, you mean," Mary said beneath her breath. Then she sat forward in her chair. "Mother! May I please be excused? I want to see if I have anything suitable to wear."

Looking slightly irritated but not enough to argue, Elizabeth nodded. "Yes, dear, that's fine. You may all go, if you like."

Mary was the first to exit the room, but Selene and Cousin Lizzie were hot on her heels. Olivia remained where she was.

Susanna arrived with the dessert tray and stopped short. "We done lost the girls already, Missus Harding?"

"I'm afraid so, Susanna. And ..." Elizabeth pushed her chair back from the table. "If it's agreeable to the general, I suggest we retire to the front porch for dessert this evening. It's so nice out."

"That's fine, ma'am. I go back and get the coffee and bring it all outside."

Olivia intentionally loitered behind, waiting for the general and Aunt Elizabeth to take the lead. She wanted the opportunity to speak with Susanna. Or rather, give Susanna the opportunity to speak with *her*, if she wanted to.

It was the third of November—four weeks since she'd met Mr. Pagette and discussed starting a freedmen's school with him. She was still waiting to hear from the trusted third party. She'd been so hopeful this would work out. She'd taken on the additional responsibilities at the limestone quarries, saving every penny she'd earned in anticipation of teaching and enjoying every minute of extra time with Ridley—even if it meant being in the horse cart.

He'd been far quieter lately, but no wonder with the long hours he was keeping. It frightened her, seeing him working so closely with the stallions like he was. Rachel had joined her and Elizabeth for a walk the other day, and the stories the women told her about past incidents in which stable hands had been injured—or worse—made Olivia wish Ridley wasn't so bent on learning from Uncle Bob like he was. Yet, watching him, it was impossible not to see his love for those animals.

Susanna returned with the tray set with dessert and coffee for three.

"Susanna, is there something I can help you with?"

"No, ma'am, Missus Aberdeen. I got it."

Olivia followed alongside her in the dining room. "You've been doing well then?"

Susanna glanced over. "Yes, ma'am. You been doin' well?"

"Yes, I have. Thank you for asking."

Susanna paused for Olivia to precede her into the front hall.

Olivia stopped just short of the front door, the general and Aunt Elizabeth already outside. "Susanna," she whispered, "is there, by chance, something you'd like to tell me?"

Susanna paused, holding the tray. "I don't reckon so, ma'am," she whispered. Then her eyes got a twinkle. Her head lowered a little. "Unless ..."

Olivia perked up.

"Unless there's somethin' you *want* me to be tellin' you?"

Olivia glanced up the spiral staircase to make sure they were alone. "I only want you to tell me ... if you're ready to tell me."

Susanna's forehead wrinkled. "Is we talkin' 'bout the same thing, ma'am?"

Olivia nodded, then paused, remembering what Mr. Pagette had said about not telling anyone. But surely it was all right to talk to Susanna. Still ... "Why don't you go first," she whispered, feeling that was safest.

Susanna glanced through the open front door, then back. "She give 'em to her, ma'am. Just like you said you was gonna talk to her 'bout doin'." Susanna smiled. "I was there too. And Miss Mary? Mmmm ... That child, she was so happy."

Olivia stared for a second. "The boots," she said softly, realizing they weren't talking about the same thing.

Susanna nodded, then stopped. "That *was* what you was talkin' 'bout, right, ma'am?"

Thinking fast, Olivia touched her arm. "I'm so glad Mary liked them."

Susanna smiled. "That was a good thing you done, Missus Aberdeen. Mary's a good girl. She just needs to come into herself a little more. She will."

Nodding, Olivia continued to the front porch and, for the next hour, listened to the general talk at length about the upcoming yearling sale. But all the while, in the back of her head, a nagging certainty told her Mr. Pagette wouldn't be contacting her after all. And that she would never teach in a freedmen's school.

Chapter
THIRTY-EIGHT

*L*awd, sir! You all right?"

Ridley staggered back a step from Jack Malone—his world reeling, his body numb. Dazed, he saw Uncle Bob running toward him across the corral and could barely make out the hazy outline of the prized stallion who had just tried to take his head off. Jack Malone stared down at him as if the animal knew exactly what he'd done. And was proud of it.

"I ain't *never* seen him rear up so mean-like, sir! Bent on doin' harm. What'd you do to him?"

Ridley squeezed his eyes tight, trying to focus, a dull ache starting on the right side of his head. "I just looked at him like you told me to."

"Did he clip you?"

Uncle Bob reached up to touch his head, but Ridley brushed his hand away.

"I'm fine." Ridley took a deep breath, slowly regaining his balance. "But I'm pretty sure that horse tried to kill me." He forced a laugh. "And still might."

The stallion snorted and pawed the ground, every move defiant, powerful. The horse was twenty times a man's strength and stamina, and Ridley would've sworn the thoroughbred was flaunting the fact.

He winced. Everything had happened so fast.

Every day for the past couple of weeks, he and Uncle Bob had worked with the stallion. Jack Malone's temperament made Seabird look like Old Gray by comparison. And Ridley had thought he was starting to get the hang of things.

Uncle Bob tried again to touch Ridley's head.

"I said I'm *fine*."

But Uncle Bob's persistence won out, and his fingers came away bloody. The man muttered something beneath his breath that Ridley couldn't hear and didn't need to.

"How many times I done told you, sir? Don't *ever* take your eyes off a stallion! 'Specially not one like this. One kick to the head, and you's gone. Time you know what hit you" — Uncle Bob snapped his fingers — "you already be checkin' in upstairs, lookin' up your name in the Book o' Life!"

Ridley laughed.

"It ain't funny!" Huffing, Uncle Bob gave him a dark look.

Only then did Ridley realize how truly shaken the man was. "He grazed me, Uncle Bob. That's all. My head's a little fuzzy, but I'm all right."

Eyes fierce, Uncle Bob stared up at him, then slowly shook his head. "Ain't even three o'clock yet, and I be needin' a drink of cider. And I ain't talkin' that sweet stuff Susanna and them other women serve at church neither." Releasing a breath, he removed his black derby and scrubbed a hand over his head. He gave Ridley a sideways look, the barest hint of a smile beginning to show. "Scared me so bad I 'bout lost it in my britches."

Ridley laughed again, but paid for it when the right side of his head throbbed even harder.

"This gonna be hard, Ridley, but you gotta get back in there right now and stand up to Jack. Else next time, all he gonna 'member is how he won today. You feelin' up to it, sir?"

Ridley started to nod, then caught himself. "Just tell me what I should do."

Ridley listened, aware of stable hands who had apparently seen what happened and were staying to watch. Cresting the hill was General Harding astride his stallion. But it was seeing Olivia, standing by the stable, stone still and staring at him, that narrowed his focus. Maybe it was the kick to his head, but he felt a surge inside him. Every time they were together now, all he could think about was how she should be with somebody else. Yet the only man he could ever see her with ... was him. He wanted her more than ever. But even more than that, he wanted what was best for her. What would make her happy in the long run. He wanted her to have the home and security she deserved and was far from convinced that he was the man who could give it to her. But that still hadn't stopped him from accepting her invitation to go walking with her later tonight. Which told him he hadn't given up entirely.

"Ridley, you listenin' to me? You get what I'm sayin' to you?"

Pulled back, Ridley nodded. "Yes, Uncle Bob. I do."

"It ain't 'bout physical strength, sir. You just gotta get him to heed you. Get him on your side by showin' him what to do. And 'member what I said ... What's the one thing a stallion wants more than anythin' else?"

Ridley smiled, glancing back at Olivia. "A mare."

"And if you start fightin' with a stallion, what's he thinkin' y'all is fightin' over?"

"A mare."

"And what's the three times you stop payin' attention to a stallion?"

"Never, never ... and never."

Uncle Bob patted him on the back. "All right then. Go get him."

Olivia moved to the fence for a better view, then almost wished she hadn't. Ridley was approaching the stallion *again*, even after what she'd just witnessed. Had the man lost every shred of good sense God gave him?

"Hey there, Missus Aberdeen."

Olivia looked up at the mountain of a man sauntering up beside her and nodded. "Ike." She knew what everyone else called him, but—when speaking to him—she felt more comfortable using his given name. She looked back at Ridley. "Please tell me Mr. Cooper knows what he's doing."

Big Ike's slowness to respond didn't instill comfort, neither did the blood she saw smeared on Ridley's forehead.

"Jack Malone's 'bout as spirited as they come, ma'am. And he's mighty particular 'bout who handles him. But Uncle Bob ... There ain't nobody better at teachin' than him. And Mr. Cooper, he done good so far."

"But he's bleeding ..."

"Yes, ma'am. But he still standin', holdin' his own. That's mighty good after gettin' kicked in the head by somethin' like Jack. Most men go down like a stone. Don't get up either."

She glanced beside her to see if Big Ike was smiling. He wasn't.

Three times, Ridley approached the stallion. Three times, the stallion reared. And three times, her heart nearly stopped. Ridley reacted quickly, but she sensed his reflexes were impaired. What was it about these animals that made him want to work with them like this? That instilled such determination—at cost of physical injury or death—to learn what Bob Green was teaching him? But one thing was certain, though she loathed the certainty with which the realization came: Ridley Cooper was made for the wilds of a place like the Colorado Territory, and it for him.

Uncle Bob called something out to Ridley, but Olivia couldn't make out what he'd said. But apparently Ridley had. Because he nodded. Then he stopped.

"What's he doing?" she whispered, glancing at Big Ike.

Big Ike leaned forward on the fence. "I ain't altogether sure, ma'am."

Then Olivia heard it. Ridley was whistling. And not the way you would to call a dog. He was whistling a tune. A song. Gradually, hearing it, she smiled. It was one they sang in the Negro church. One she especially liked.

With measured steps, Ridley moved off to the side and approached the stallion from that direction. Jack Malone followed Ridley's progress as he drew closer.

Twenty feet, fifteen ...

Without warning, the stallion charged him.

It all happened so fast, the scream was still working its way up Olivia's chest when the stallion skidded to a halt just feet from Ridley, who looked tense and ready to react. Yet he was still whistling the tune, low and sweet.

This happened again and again. Like some sort of terrifying dance. Each time, the stallion came closer than before, as though testing Ridley's courage. And each time, Ridley looked poised to act. Until finally, the thoroughbred seemed to weary of the sport. Then Olivia watched—nerves raw and throat aching—as Ridley took patient, purposeful steps toward the horse. *No, Ridley, don't* ...

Not the least hesitant, Ridley closed the distance, continuing the low, sweet whistle.

And the stallion let him come.

He grasped the thoroughbred's harness, and for a moment, man and beast simply stared. Olivia had never seen anything like it.

Glancing around at the stable hands' expressions, she judged they felt the same. A swell of pride and admiration rose within her, and she couldn't help but wonder if what Ridley felt in that moment was anything like what she felt when she saw Jimmy and Jolene learning how to read and write and work their sums.

Thinking of Jimmy and Jolene made her think of Mr. Pagette. Mid-November now, and still no word from him or that trusted third party. She told herself to accept it and move on. But part of her still wouldn't let go. A faint flicker of hope kept burning.

"He done good," Big Ike said beside her. "Didn't he, ma'am?"

"Yes, he did."

"And … if you don't mind me sayin' it, Missus Aberdeen," he said softly. "You doin' good too, ma'am. With lil' Jimmy and Jolene."

Olivia turned and looked at the hulk of a man beside her and felt the flicker of hope burn brighter. Perhaps *he* was in contact with Mr. Pagette.

"My wife speaks real high about you, ma'am."

"That's very kind of her. I think very highly of Susanna too."

He smiled, and Olivia waited, wondering if he would say something about the freedmen's school outright. Or maybe speak of it in a secret way.

"Well, I best be gettin' back to the stable. Good to talk to you, ma'am."

Olivia's hope deflated.

"Fascinating creatures, these stallions. Aren't they, Mrs. Aberdeen?"

Not recognizing the voice behind her, she turned. And blinked. *"Colonel Burcham?"*

The Colonel's eyes narrowed ever so slightly, and she knew her tone hadn't communicated a pleasant surprise on her part.

"What are you doing here? I-I mean … in town? You said in your last letter that—"

"I know. I said December. But I've long held that—just as in battle—the element of surprise can be a valuable one." His gaze moved beyond her. "That stable hand there … What's his name again?"

She followed his line of sight. And bristled. "That's Ridley Cooper. And he's one of General Harding's *foremen* here at Belle Meade. Not a stable hand."

The colonel smiled. "A foreman who works with horses. In a stable." He looked at her as though his point were made.

Olivia's dislike of the man doubled a hundredfold.

"Everythin' all right, Missus Aberdeen?"

She turned to see Big Ike still there. He was eying the colonel, whose stony expression said he didn't welcome the interruption.

"Yes, everything's fine," she whispered, remembering the distasteful opinions the colonel had expressed at dinner earlier that summer and how the man had treated Susanna. She wondered—seeing Big Ike stare at the man—whether Susanna had shared the colonel's comments from that evening with her mountain of a husband.

"Go on now." The colonel stepped closer, gesturing to Big Ike. "Get back to work. I'll take care of the lady."

Wincing at the condescension in the man's tone—and ashamed for the colonel, even if he wasn't—Olivia looked at Big Ike and tried to communicate an apology with a glance. Then she spotted General Harding astride his stallion, watching from the hill, and knew without a shred of doubt that the colonel's visit hadn't been a surprise to *him*.

The colonel held out his arm and Olivia—stomach curdling, but not wanting to cause a scene—accepted.

It was no use. Olivia pushed back the covers. She couldn't sleep. Not with the general and colonel sitting on the porch just below her bedroom window, outside the general's office, smoking cigars and swapping war stories. But mostly sleep wouldn't come because of wondering about Ridley and how he was doing. Earlier that evening, she'd learned Uncle Bob had called for Rachel to suture Ridley's head. The wound had been far worse than Ridley had let on that afternoon.

Silly, foolish man.

At dinner, General Harding had taken great pleasure in recounting the event with flourish, much like he had the story about Davy Crockett. But Olivia hadn't enjoyed this tale in the least.

"Mark my words," he said, lifting his glass. "People will come for miles around to see 'the man who got kicked in the head by Jack Malone ... and lived to tell about it.' I've asked Mr. Cooper to head up the yearling sale come June. And what's more ... we'll make certain he's the one to lead Belle Meade's prized stud out to center ring, so they can *both* take a bow."

The comments—not rudely meant, Olivia knew—had drawn laughter. But what the general said next had inspired her to hope Ridley might consider staying at Belle Meade after all, if given the proper motivation.

"Ridley Cooper is turning out to be a fine foreman. The other men respect him and respond to him well. Who knows but what he might have a future here at Belle Meade."

Colonel Burcham, seated beside her at the table, had leaned close to her. "Hmmm ... That may be, but helping with a yearling sale, leading a horse around ... still sounds like a stable hand to me."

Anger rippled through her again just thinking about it. Colonel Bryant Burcham was so much like Charles. To anyone looking on, he was dashing and charming, obviously a man of means. A man worth pursuing. But every time he touched her ... The small of her back as she preceded him through an entryway; his elbow brushing hers at dinner; the way he always, *always* offered his arm, then drew her close—so close her breast brushed his arm. She shivered and felt Charles touching her all over again.

She kicked the covers back and rose from bed, her nightgown sticking to her body. November had brought cooler temperatures. But today, as often happened this time of year, summer seemed to be rearing its head again, and the air in her room felt stagnant and constricting. Standing at the side window, the one that allowed the view of the old Harding cabin, she breathed in the night air, *flouncing* her gown, as her mother used to call it. Billowing the fabric to force air up inside, she enjoyed the few fleeting seconds of blissful, heavenly cool.

It had to be well after midnight by now, and the cabin was mostly dark, except for a window at the front where a warm glow dispelled the night. She wondered if Ridley was still awake. Most likely not. Rachel would have given him something to help him sleep. Still, she wished she could check on him herself. She was growing far too accustomed to their time together and missed him when she didn't see him.

Like now.

She glanced behind her at the window on the adjacent wall, hearing Colonel Burcham's voice and wishing he and the general had stayed in the library for their little military *tête-à-tête*. If not for them,

Olivia was certain she could have sneaked down the stairs and back up without being discovered. Especially since Elizabeth, fatigued from the day's events, had retired early. But the staircase emptied directly onto the porch outside the general's office where the men were reliving their glory days.

Sighing, she turned back. Her gaze dropped to the wisteria whose blooms had long since vanished, then to the lattice. And slowly, stealthily, an idea began to form. An idea that almost felt as if it had been lingering nearby, merely waiting for the right opportunity to present itself. Hearing the thought plainly now, Olivia pushed back from the window.

No ... She couldn't. Ridley wouldn't be here to catch her if she fell.

But—an internal voice countered—*you didn't fall last time. You made it fine.*

But last time, she'd had Ridley there to help her, which had bolstered her confidence. This time she had no one. And if she *were* to fall, she could lie there on the ground all night. *No.*

She looked back at the door again. That wasn't true. The general and colonel would surely hear the ruckus and come running. At which time—if she weren't dead—she would be in a world of trouble.

Which simply meant one thing ...

She couldn't fall.

She never would have entertained the thought of sneaking out like this before coming to Belle Meade. *Before meeting Ridley Cooper.* Just the thought of him cinched it for her.

She couldn't get dressed fast enough.

Chapter THIRTY-NINE

*O*livia tucked the back hem of her skirt in the front of her waist-band, just as Ridley had taught her, then gripped the window-sill, her hands sticky from nerves. Snatches from the general and colonel's conversation drifted toward her from around the corner on the porch below, and she caught an occasional whiff of their cigars. Pipe smoke, she'd never minded. But the smell of cigars turned her stomach.

She leaned her face out the window and took deep breaths, try-ing to work up the courage she lacked. She sent up a quick prayer, fashioning it after prayers she'd heard Bob Green offer in church. She didn't know Uncle Bob well, but she knew him well enough to know he knew the Almighty better than most. And he spoke to God more honestly than anyone she'd ever heard.

She eased her leg out the window—the rhythm of her heart kick-ing up several notches—and could hear Ridley's voice in the back of her head. *Don't look down. Just concentrate on where you're going to put your other foot.*

Holding on for life and limb, she finally managed to locate a foot-hold. Then, hearing Ridley's silent counsel, she put her weight on it to make certain it was the lattice and not the vine. She got a firm grip on the lattice with her left hand and took a steadying breath. It was much cooler outside than in her room, and she welcomed the breeze—on the half of her that could feel it. She licked her lips and tasted fear. Then squeezed her eyes tight.

She could do this. She'd done it before.

Going against instincts she trusted, she maneuvered her other leg out the window, wishing for the first time in her life that women could wear trousers. At least while scaling the walls of—

Her right hand lost grip on the window, and she slipped.

Her body arched wide, giving her a sickening weightlessness that sent her stomach to her throat. It only lasted a second or two, but it felt like an eternity. And it gave her a glimpse of the ground far below she never wished to see again. Momentum propelled her back toward the house, and she knew she'd only have one chance.

She hit the lattice hard and clawed for a grip.

Branches tore at her right palm. She grappled for hold and something sharp pierced the soft inside of her hand. But she held on, struggling to find purchase with her right boot. Finally she did, and—body shaking—she pressed her forehead into the vine, clinging to it. "Oh, sweet Jesus," she breathed out, hearing it the way Uncle Bob said it and doubting her heart would ever regain a normal rhythm.

She clung there, willing her body to calm, to stop trembling—while watching for General Harding and Colonel Burcham to round the corner of the house and find her. She couldn't hear them talking anymore, but she couldn't hear anything over the roar in her ears. So she waited. But with every slowing beat of her heart, her hands lost strength. She either had to climb back in the window or climb down. She couldn't stay here.

Finally, she heard laughter. From which decorated Confederate officer, she didn't know. But she decided she wasn't about to climb back in the window after coming this far and risking this much. The rest of the way down was more her body knowing what to do rather than her telling her body what to do. When she reached the bottom—legs shaking, fingers aching—she untucked her skirt and looked up, not exactly eager to retrace her path but knowing she could do it. Her right palm burned and was sticky with sap from the vine. But she'd have to see to that later.

At least she could say she'd conquered the lattice!

Even with moonlight, the mansion grounds were darker than she remembered on the walk with Ridley, and she looked around for the man on night patrol. She didn't see anyone. Still, it was comforting to know she wasn't out here alone. When she reached the stretch of meadow leading to the cabin, however, she grew nervous again and decided she'd rather not risk surprising any animal that might not want to be surprised. So she stomped through the field grass, making as much noise as she could.

The light in the cabin window still shone in the distance, and as she drew closer, she caught the scent of pipe tobacco mingled with cherry and something else familiar. On the other end of the pipe was Bob Green.

He rose from his chair on the porch. "Missus Aberdeen?" he whispered. He took a couple of steps. "That you, ma'am?"

"Yes, Uncle Bob. It's me." Olivia kept her voice soft, like his, in case Ridley was asleep. She climbed the steps to the porch.

Uncle Bob glanced beyond her. "Everythin' all right at the big house?"

"Oh yes. Everything's fine. I just came to check on Mr. Cooper. To see how he's doing."

Uncle Bob didn't answer immediately, and the trickling melody of the creek behind the cabin filled the pause. "You come all this way?" he whispered. "In the dark? By your lonesome?"

She grinned, proud of herself. "Yes, sir. I did. All by my lonesome."

He smiled big, and so did she. She'd left out the part about climbing out the window but had a feeling he'd be impressed with that too, if he knew.

"Well, come on then. He's inside. Still awake, last time I checked."

She'd walked by the old Harding cabin countless times but had never been this close. The porch opened to a dogtrot that split the dwelling right down the middle, and she followed Uncle Bob into the left side of the cabin. A single oil lamp gave light to the room, and Ridley lay on a bunk by the stone hearth, his eyes closed. She might have thought him asleep, if not for the seashell he fingered in his right hand.

The lyrics of the creek were even more pronounced in here than on the front porch, and when she saw a back window open, she realized why. Her gaze returned to Ridley and to the thin straw-stuffed mattress and rolled-up blanket beneath his head. She thought of her own bedding in the Hardings' home — same as that of her childhood and the home she'd shared with Charles — filled with goose down and fluffed daily by servants. She'd never given it a second thought.

Until now.

"Ridley, you got company, sir."

Ridley smiled, eyes still closed. "Sure I do. Is it Jack Malone ... here to finish the job?"

"Not exactly," Olivia said. "But I'm guessing that with a head as hard as yours, you'd be fine even if it was."

Ridley's eyes came open. *"Olivia?"* He tried to sit up. Then paused, holding his head.

"Please don't get up, Ridley." She came alongside the bed. "I won't stay but for a minute or two." She directed the comment to Uncle Bob as well. "I just came to see how you're doing after that ... *display* of yours this afternoon. Which nearly scared me to death."

Ridley smiled. "You were frightened?"

She nodded. "For the horse."

Uncle Bob snickered behind her.

Ridley lay back down, his dark look unconvincing. "You're one heartless woman. Coming down here to try to rile me up. And with my head already about to explode."

She warmed at the comment, knowing it was his way of thanking her. Hearing the shuffle of steps, she turned to see Uncle Bob standing just outside the door. He nodded once, then left, the door still slightly open.

She took in her surroundings. *Rustic* described the cabin well and might have even been a little generous. The walls were paneled wood, as was the floor, and a small table with three mismatched chairs sat off to the left by the window. A clock adorned the wall above it, and a wash basin hung unceremoniously on a nearby hook. Maybe it was the stark contrast of having lived in the mansion for months now, but the cabin felt so small. And she couldn't stop thinking ...

This was where General William Giles Harding had been born?

"Welcome to our humble abode."

"It's very nice," she said a little too quickly, and could tell by his expression he'd already read her thoughts. Yet he didn't seem the least put off.

He gradually turned onto his side. "The general and Mrs. Harding must be sleeping soundly tonight if you were able to sneak down the stairs."

"Who said I used the stairs?"

Slowly, his easy smile faded to doubt, then disbelief. He rose on one elbow. "Olivia Aberdeen, *please* tell me you did *not* climb out that window by yourself."

"All right. I won't tell you." She grinned, scrunching her shoulders. "But I did!"

He exhaled. "Do you have any idea how dangerous that was? You could have—"

"Ridley Cooper!" She huffed. "I expected you to be proud of me!"

"Proud of you for risking your neck just to—"

"What happened to 'Climbing's just like walking, except you're going up or down'?"

"That's different, Olivia. That was when I was with you to make sure—"

"And what about 'I want you to know you *can* do this'? Or did that mean something different then too?"

He stared at her, pressing his left temple. "You're the most headstrong woman I've ever met in my life."

He didn't intend it as a compliment, yet she couldn't help but smile. "And that's about the nicest thing anyone's ever said to me."

A hint of humor shone in his expression before he groaned and lay back down. "You're going to be the death of me, woman."

She laughed, not knowing exactly what he meant but liking that he cared enough to think his life hinged on her actions. She spotted a thatched-seat rocker by the hearth. The chair sagged with the weight of time and use but looked sturdy enough. She pulled it a little closer to the bed and sat carefully, wincing at a pain in her right hand. She glanced down at her palm, then almost wished she hadn't. An ugly gash, not quite an inch long, was caked with dried blood. *The vine* ... Apparently, the stickiness she'd felt earlier hadn't been sap. So much for conquering the lattice. She buried her hand in her lap, not wanting him to see.

"I hope you had dinner," she said, wishing now she could have brought something. Or had at least thought about it before coming.

"I did. Betsy brought something over for Uncle Bob and me." He gestured. "She made those biscuits you like. We have some left. Help yourself, if you want."

Olivia spotted a cloth-covered plate on the table. "Are you sure?"

He looked over at her, smiling. "Very. But only after you help me sit up."

"You're making me *work* for my biscuit?"

"You bet I am. Those are good biscuits."

Careful of her injury and of him seeing it, she helped him to a sitting position, then rolled up a thin blanket and stuffed it behind him for support.

"Thank you." He leaned back. "Feels good to sit up."

"Where are the sutures?"

He pointed toward the right side of his head. "It only took nine or ten."

"*Only* nine or ten?" She helped herself to a biscuit, using her left hand, and eased back into the rocker.

The quiet settled around them.

"Thank you for coming to see me, Olivia. Despite how you did it."

She gave him a smart look.

"It's actually quite scandalous on your part, you know. Visiting the private quarters of an unmarried man."

The way he said it made her smile. But she realized, with no small surprise, that he was right. She looked around. She'd never been in the private quarters of an unmarried man before. It felt a little rebellious and definitely beyond the bounds of propriety. But what she found most telling was how she hadn't even given it a thought. Until now. She was a different woman when she was with Ridley Cooper. And she rather liked who she was becoming because of him. But she didn't like seeing him hurt like this.

"You could have been killed today," she said softly.

He looked at her. "But I wasn't."

"But you could have been."

"But ... I *wasn't.*"

Though his tone was serious, the look in his eyes said he understood her concern. And appreciated it. And that was enough. For now.

She finished her biscuit and brushed the crumbs from her lap, her right hand aching. "I understand from General Harding that you're in charge of the yearling sale. The way he spoke about you at dinner tonight, I'd say he thinks very highly of you."

"Really?"

She nodded.

"That's nice to hear. And while I'm grateful for the opportunity ..." He sighed, half smiling. "I'm under no illusion that I'll be in charge. We both know who's always in charge around here."

She nodded, conceding the fact.

"What he's put me 'in charge of' is coming up with a way to sell the yearlings that will result in the highest sales."

"What are you planning to do?"

"I'm not sure yet. I've got some ideas, but I'm glad I've got some time to think about it."

"Who knows? Your ideas might be so good he'll make you an

offer you can't refuse." She tried for a casual tone, as though this next thought had just occurred to her. "Either that or … you may end up liking it so well here that, come June, you won't want to leave."

He held her gaze, his own deepening with an intensity born only from truth.

"Come June, Olivia …" He swallowed, the sound pronounced in the quiet. "Regardless of what happens with the yearling sale, I *will* be leaving. I hope I've never given you cause to think otherwise."

The quiet of his voice and the honesty in his face made it impossible to maintain his gaze, so she lowered hers. Then saw, again, what was in his hand.

She gestured, grateful for the distraction. "I've wondered if you still had that."

He held up the seashell. " 'Course I do. I'll never part with it. At least not willingly."

He looked at the shell then back at her. She nodded, and he held it out.

It was just as pretty as she remembered. The inside smooth against her thumb and pinkish like the dawn. With her thumbnail, she counted the outside ridges. *One, two, three …*

"Twenty-eight," he said. "There are twenty-eight ridges."

He leaned forward to adjust the padding behind his back. She paused from counting to help, but he held up a hand.

She went back to counting. "Twenty-six, twenty-seven … twenty-eight! You're right!"

"Which obviously is a fact you doubted, Olivia." He wasn't smiling, but she heard the teasing in his voice.

"*No* … I just wanted to be sure."

"My point exactly."

Ignoring his comment, she studied the shell. "You said you found it along the beach near your home."

"That's right." He carefully leaned his head against the headboard, closing his eyes. The clock on the wall behind her ticked off the seconds. "The day before I left to join the army … I went for one last walk along my favorite stretch of beach. It was late afternoon, high tide was coming in. The sun lay so pretty on the water. And I looked down, and there it was. Been carrying it with me ever since."

Fatigue edged his voice, sadness too. And she realized she'd overstayed her welcome.

She rose. "I'm sorry. I've stayed too long. I'll let you rest."

She held out the shell and he took it, but he reached for her right hand as he did and wove his fingers through.

"Olivia, I—"

She sucked in a breath and pulled her hand back.

He looked up at her. "What's wrong?"

She shook her head, trying not to grimace. "Nothing."

"Did I hurt you?"

"I'm fine, Ridley, I just ..." He reached for her hand again, but she slipped it behind her back.

He sat straighter in the bed. His gaze lowered. "Let me see your hand."

"It's nothing. I just scraped it when I—"

"Olivia," he whispered. "Please."

Dreading the look of I-told-you-so in his eyes—a look she'd seen so many times from Charles—she reluctantly did as he asked.

He turned her palm up. "Oh, Olivia ..."

She tried to make a fist, but he prevented it.

"Did you do this climbing down?"

"Yes, I did." She sighed. "Go ahead. Tell me I shouldn't have done it. Tell me how foolish I am and that—"

He eased his legs over the side of the bed.

She stilled. "What are you doing?"

"Sit down." He gestured to the rocker, then moved slowly to a side table, poured water from a pitcher into a basin, then brought the basin and some cloths back with him.

Reading his intention, she shook her head. "No, Ridley. Get back in bed."

"Sit down." He eyed the rocker, then her, and smiled. "Before I fall down."

She sank back down in the chair.

He knelt beside her, took her hand, and began washing it, his movements tender, caring. But still, it hurt. Tears rose to her eyes, more due to his gentleness than the pain.

"I wish the water was warm," he said softly.

"It doesn't matter," she whispered.

"I don't think it needs suturing, but if Rachel thinks it does ..." He looked up. "Just take a swig or two of her cider." He winked. "You won't feel a thing."

Olivia laughed, tasting her tears.

The wound, once clean, started bleeding afresh, and he gently applied pressure until it stopped, then rubbed a salve on her palm. She recognized a smell similar to the concoction Rachel had given her for her feet. He wrapped her hand in a fresh cloth and gently tied it off. "There. That'll keep it until morning."

He set aside the soiled rags and the basin of rust-colored water, then stood slowly, closing his eyes for a minute before helping Olivia stand. He pressed a kiss to her forehead, and she slipped her arms around him. It seemed so natural a response, and when his arms came around her, she'd never felt so safe. So … *loved.*

He walked her outside. The front porch was empty, Uncle Bob apparently having retired.

"I'll see you home."

Olivia put a hand to his arm. "No, you won't. You'll get halfway there and collapse. And then what will we do?"

"I can't let you walk all that way by yourself. Or climb back up that lattice with your hand hurt. I've got to know you're safe."

"You will. I'll take the stairs back up, then I'll wave my lamp in the window so you'll know I'm all right."

She started down the porch steps.

"Olivia?"

She paused.

"I'm proud of you for climbing down. I could wring your pretty little neck for doing it. But I'm proud of you."

It was dark, but she could hear his smile. "Climbing out was the hardest part."

"Taking that first step always is."

Olivia fairly floated back over the meadow to the mansion where everything was quiet and dark. She slipped up the back staircase, walking as lightly as she could and cringing when the creaking planks snitched on her a time or two.

Once in her room, she lit the lamp, as promised, and waved it — *once, twice*—in front of her window. Then watched Ridley do the same from the front porch of the old Harding cabin.

Careful of her hand, she changed into her nightgown and snuggled into bed, thinking again of the thin straw-filled mattress Ridley slept on. She prayed he'd rest well and heal quickly. Closing her eyes, she relived what it felt like to be in his arms. To feel so safe and so—

Her eyes came open.

The darkness around her seemed less so than when she'd turned down the lamp a moment or so earlier, and a thought she wished had never come refused to leave. She had two men pursuing her hand in marriage and didn't have the least bit of interest in either of them. While another who held more of her heart than she'd ever entrusted to anyone hadn't indicated a formal pursuit of any kind. Though he'd had plenty of time and opportunity—and encouragement—Ridley hadn't asked for her hand in marriage. He hadn't asked to court her. He hadn't asked for anything at all. Quite the contrary.

His words replayed again in her mind: *Come June, regardless of what happens with the yearling sale, I will be leaving.*

The silent, obvious question hovered at her bedside. Why, if he cared for her like she knew he did, had he not formally acted on his feelings for her?

She turned onto her back, the goose down molding to her form, cool where her body hadn't been yet. Was it because of what Charles had done and her lack of standing in the community? As quickly as the thought came, she dismissed it. No one cared less about others' opinions than Ridley. He was his own man. He acted on personal conviction, no matter what others thought.

Was it because of his … *misgivings* about the South? She knew the war had taken a toll on him, as it had every man, woman, and child. But his disappointment, his unrest, ran so deep. She'd seen it in him again tonight as he'd fingered that seashell. But the South was changing. Maybe not as quickly as he'd like. But change was happening. Didn't the freedmen schools show that? And Jimmy and Jolene learning to read and write like they were? Ridley was part of that change too. What about the increase in pay he'd gotten for the Negro men? Susanna had told Olivia all about that.

The flurry of thoughts kept sleep at bay until she ruled out every possible answer to her question save one… Ridley didn't want to stay in the South, yet he knew she would never follow him to the Colorado Territory. And he was right. *This* was where she was meant to be, for so many reasons. But she knew something he didn't. This was where *he* was meant to be too. The South was his home. Or would be again. She simply needed to prove it to him.

And would. Before the yearling sale.

Chapter
FORTY

*R*idley stood just inside the stable watching the handsome couple stroll the estate in the distance. He didn't like Colonel Burcham to begin with or the uniform the man insisted on wearing. But he especially didn't like his spending time with Olivia. For the past few days, much to Ridley's irritation, he'd had to endure the colonel's attentiveness to her, as well as the man's all-too-frequent visits to the stables and his arrogance with the workers. Especially young Jimmy.

The only bright note about the colonel being here—something which gave him great pleasure—was seeing Olivia's almost-comical attempts to keep her distance from the man. Even now as she walked beside him, she kept at least a foot of space—if not two—between them, something the colonel persistently tried to lessen and Olivia—equally persistent—resisted.

Like now. Ridley bristled as Burcham reached for her arm and tucked it through his. Tasting metal, Ridley counted the seconds, anticipating Olivia's response. She hadn't disappointed him so far.

One ... two ... three ... four ... fi—

Right on cue, Olivia knelt and picked up a leaf, effectively disengaging herself from the colonel. She studied the leaf as though it were a work of art and not at all similar to the one she'd stooped to pick up moments earlier—right after the colonel had attempted the same fruitless maneuver. No doubt Burcham saw through Olivia's polite rejection, but from all appearances, her rebuttals weren't discouraging his efforts.

Growing more rankled the longer he watched, Ridley turned and went back inside, hoping the colonel would take Olivia's hints and leave. *Soon.*

He picked up a bridle that had slipped from the hook, grateful when his world remained steady. He fingered the side of his head. The wound was still tender to the touch and would be for a while, but at least the constant ache had abated.

He joined Jedediah and a few of the stable hands out back and worked with the foals, turning ideas for the spring sale over and over in his mind. During the course of the afternoon, it became obvious that some of the men had developed favorites among the colts and fillies. And watching the hands who were more experienced, Ridley could already see a difference in the quality of those foals and the trainable demeanor of the animals. The observation took his thoughts about the yearling sale down an entirely different trail.

A while later, brushing down Seabird in her stall, his thoughts churning as the idea took shape, he heard the crack of a whip somewhere outside, followed by what he could only describe as a primal scream.

"I said keep her still, you lazy—"

Ridley bolted, grabbing gloves from a shelf as he ran. He reached the stable's side door in time to see Colonel Burcham raise a whip—for the second time, judging by the bloody welt on the mare's haunch.

Jimmy, sprawled in the dirt, scrambled to his feet with Uncle Bob's help. "Colonel, please," the boy cried. "Don't whip her, sir. I get her for ya!"

Uncle Bob tried to grab hold of the colonel's arm, but Burcham flung him aside and let loose a string of obscenities that boiled Ridley's blood. Burcham brought the whip back a third time, his face mottled in fury. The thin strip of leather cut the air with a sharp whistle—

But Ridley was ready. He caught the tail end of the whip in his gloved hand and jerked hard. Colonel Burcham lost his grip and stumbled a step but didn't go down. When he turned and saw Ridley, his expression hardened with rage.

Uncle Bob picked himself up just as Jimmy started toward the mare, but Burcham grabbed the boy by the scruff of the neck.

"If you'd have just held her still, you ignorant little nig—"

Ridley brought the whip down with a crack. The colonel stumbled back from Jimmy, holding the sleeve of his uniform.

"You touch either of them again, Colonel, and next time, I'll go for skin."

Burcham looked ready to explode. "How *dare* you!" The colonel started toward him. "Do you have any idea who I am or what I could do to someone like you?"

Ridley brought the whip down a second time, skimming the tip of Burcham's boot. The colonel stopped cold.

"I don't care who you are, *sir*. No one takes a whip to General William Giles Harding's horses — or *workers* — here at Belle Meade. Is that clear?"

Ridley heard the shuffle of steps behind him and grew aware of stable hands gathering.

"The only thing clear to me, *Cooper*, is that you're about to lose your ... position here."

Ridley smiled at the smugness in the man's tone. "That may be, Colonel. But something tells me I'll be around long enough to see *you* gone. Which ..." He nodded beyond Burcham to where General Harding strode toward them. "Should be anytime now."

Ridley leaned against the porch railing outside the general's office, feeling a little like he had when he and Alfred and Petey used to get into trouble at school. Thinking of his brothers, he closed his eyes for a second, feeling a sigh work its way up from down deep. *Lord, I hope they knew how much I still loved them. And that I never stopped being proud to call them brothers.*

He stared out across the meadow, not surprised by the thought, but deeply surprised in the form it had taken. Not so much a thought as a prayer. Whether the general fired him or not — Ridley smiled a little — he was going to have to find a new place to live. Because living with Uncle Bob was apparently rubbing off on him more than he'd realized.

The door to the general's office opened, and Ridley straightened. Colonel Burcham walked out, his features set, his manner still seething. Ridley wondered what it would have been like to have faced him on the battlefield. Then just as quickly wondered if he already had. But guessed he'd never know.

Burcham shouldered past him, then turned. "You're a disgrace to the Confederacy, Cooper."

Wanting to say something he knew he couldn't, Ridley merely glanced down at the clean slice in the colonel's sleeve. "Might want to get that sewn up, sir."

"Mr. Cooper!" General Harding stood in the doorway. "Come in, please. Now."

Ridley did as the general requested, feeling daggers in his back.

Harding closed the door. "Have a seat."

Ridley did, his head beginning to throb.

General Harding reached for his chair as though to sit, then gripped the back of it instead. "Mr. Cooper, I'm certain you have no idea what a precarious position you've placed me in."

Ridley nodded, having already thought this through. "He wasn't one of your superior officers?"

"Of course not. But he *was* a potential partner in a business venture who has now"—Harding's laughter came out bitter—"needless to say, suddenly decided to withdraw his support."

"I'm sorry, sir."

"Are you, Mr. Cooper? Because what I just witnessed out there on the porch did not sound like someone who regrets what they did."

Ridley sat a little taller. "I don't regret what I did, sir. The colonel's actions were wrong."

"I know they were wrong, Mr. Cooper. But there was a way to handle that situation that would have allowed the colonel to save face."

"Save face, sir? He was whipping one of your mares. And would have likely done the same to Uncle Bob and Jimmy if given the chance." Ridley stood. "I apologize for any repercussions my actions have brought upon you personally, General. But allowing a man like that to save face is the least of my concerns. He was wrong. I don't regret doing what I did. And with all due respect, sir ... I'd do the same again."

Harding stared across the desk. "You're a stubborn-minded man, Mr. Cooper. With a streak of pride that runs deep. I knew that the first time I laid eyes on you. I simply didn't realize how costly those character traits would prove to be for me. Both personally and professionally."

Sensing what was coming, Ridley felt his Colorado Territory dream slipping away, along with everything he'd worked so hard for. Yet he'd done the right thing, no question in his mind. But choosing to do the right thing didn't always get a person what they deserved or even what was *fair*. The war had taught him that well enough.

He turned to leave.

"Fortunately for you, Mr. Cooper ..."

Ridley stopped.

"Those are character traits which I have long admired. And if you listen to my critics, ones I also share."

Ridley turned back.

General Harding took his place in the chair behind the desk and gestured for Ridley to return to his. "Now let's get down to business, Mr. Cooper. By my estimation, your actions today cost me approximately ... seven thousand dollars. So I'm very interested to know ... What are your ideas for the yearling sale? And I hope, for your sake, they prove to be lucrative."

Chapter
FORTY-ONE

*O*livia had never laughed so much in her life or seen people more eager to find joy in the everyday. Even in the painful parts. After what had happened earlier that afternoon, Ridley was the talk of Belle Meade—at least among the servants—and Julius and Betsy's tiny cabin was overflowing with folks who'd come to thank him.

Standing by the window with Rachel, sipping cider, Olivia enjoyed watching several of the men who'd witnessed Colonel Burcham's comeuppance take turns reenacting the event. Much to Ridley's chagrin, it seemed. But it was Big Ike who made everyone laugh until they could scarcely draw breath.

"You got any idea who I is," Big Ike thundered, mimicking what Colonel Burcham had supposedly said. "Or what I could do to the likes o' you?"

Jimmy jumped up, brandishing a towel high over his head like a whip. Then he tucked his chin tight against his chest, obviously trying for his lowest voice. "I don't care who you is, sir. No one takes a whip to the general's horses or workers here at Belle Meade!"

Jimmy brought the towel down with a *snap* against Big Ike's boot, and the comical look of surprise mixed with terror on Big Ike's face drew a fresh wave of cheers and applause. Uncle Bob laughed and patted Ridley on the back. Ridley just smiled and shook his head again, then sneaked a look in Olivia's direction. She was so proud of him her heart ached with the force of it.

Some time later, Ridley rejoined her side. "It's getting a little late. Are you ready to go?"

She nodded. "If you are."

It took another ten minutes to say good-bye and thank Betsy and

Julius for their hospitality. As they walked out the door, Olivia drew her shawl closer about her, and Ridley offered his arm. Mindful of the bandage on her palm, Olivia slipped her hand through. The gash hadn't needed stitches and still hurt a little, but it was healing nicely.

She glimpsed Rachel walking ahead, and as if reading her mind, Ridley called out.

"Mrs. Norris!"

Rachel paused and waited for them. Ridley offered his other arm when they came close. With a grin, Rachel accepted.

"Been a long time, Mr. Cooper, since I been escorted all proper-like. But you quit callin' me Mrs. Norris right this minute! Makes me feel old as the hills."

They laughed and talked all the way back to Rachel's cabin. Rachel let herself in and lit a lamp by the door.

"I thank you both for walkin' me home. Bein' with everybody like this tonight sure makes me look forward to the shindig next month."

"Shindig?" Olivia looked between them.

Rachel smiled. "You ain't heard 'bout that yet, ma'am?"

Ridley laughed softly, but Olivia shook her head.

"Oh, Missus Aberdeen … You got to come. It's only the biggest party of the year." Rachel winked. "This year we havin' it on the same night the Hardings are goin' to some rich lady's fancy house across town. It's *our* time to get all fancied up and act like we's the kings and queens of the world." Rachel lifted her nose in the air, then laughed. She glanced at Olivia's gray dress, her expression softening. "You got somethin' else to wear other than them mournin' clothes, ma'am?"

Olivia shook her head a second time. Then thought better of it. "I have a dress that belonged to my mother. It's beautiful, but … She was a good deal shorter than I am." She gave a tiny shrug. "And it doesn't matter anyway. Because … I'm still *officially* in mourning." She felt a little odd saying it, especially with her arm still linked with Ridley's. But it was the truth.

Rachel gently touched her hand. "This is the *one* night we take all year long to forget about all the bad and live like there's only good. And, no offense, ma'am …" Rachel arched a delightfully caustic brow. "But none of us want to see you comin' in this drab ol' raggedy thing."

Olivia giggled, Rachel's smile warming her heart.

"So you bring me that dress from your mama, Missus Aberdeen. And you and me, we'll work to get it right."

Olivia was grateful for the few moments alone with Ridley as he walked her back to the mansion. The house was dark save the warm glow coming from Cousin Lizzie's bedroom window. When they reached the staircase leading to the second-story porch, Ridley brought Olivia's hand to his lips and kissed it.

"Thank you for coming with me tonight," he whispered. "The whole ... *debacle* ... was embarrassing." He laughed. "But it was also nice to have you there."

"I'm grateful you invited me. And I'm so proud of you." She looked down at their hands clasped between them. "I only wish I could have seen what happened for myself. Although ... thanks to Big Ike and Jimmy, I think I have a fairly good idea."

That made him laugh again.

She wanted to tell him how much his actions today meant to her personally. But she hadn't yet confided to him about General Harding's determination to find her a second husband. Specifically, Colonel Burcham. The topic wasn't one she was eager to discuss with Ridley.

The abrupt manner in which Colonel Burcham had departed, leaving without a word to her, instilled hope that whatever interest the colonel had in her had quickly abated. Burcham's pride had been sorely bruised, and she knew only too well that a man like that, who fed on the constant affirmations and fawnings of others, was like a wounded animal looking for a place to lash out. And she never wanted to be on the receiving end of that kind of wounded pride again.

Ridley touched the side of her face, and she turned toward his hand and kissed it. His lips parted, his gaze dropping to her mouth, and she knew he was going to kiss her. And oh, she wanted him to. He leaned down and she closed her eyes, remembering what he tasted like and wanting to feel his arms around her again like when they—

He kissed her forehead—*once, twice*. Olivia opened her eyes in time to see him step back.

"Good night, Olivia," he said softly.

Staring up, swallowing back disappointment, yet determined not to show it, she managed a smile. "Good night, Ridley."

She walked up to her room, the stairs feeling steeper than before.

She paused by the railing and followed his silhouette as he crossed the meadow. More than once, the darkness swallowed him. When he reached the porch of the cabin, he turned and raised his arm, like she'd hoped he would.

She waved back, telling herself that his choosing not to kiss her was nothing to be upset about. But somehow, it didn't feel like nothing.

"Olivia?"

Clutching her shawl, Olivia glanced up to see the general on the front porch.

"Mrs. Harding and I would appreciate it if you would join us for tea, please."

Olivia paused. She and Aunt Elizabeth had shared tea in the afternoon countless times. But with General Harding? She'd just returned from her first official trip to the quarries with Ridley, and her preference would be to freshen up first. But the general wore an insistent look. "Of course," she said, reaching for a smile. "I'd love to have tea."

Negotiating the porch steps, she tried to imagine what news the general had for her. Whatever it was, it surely couldn't be good. And this, after she'd enjoyed such a lovely day with Ridley. All the way to the quarries and back, they'd asked each other questions and taken turns whistling bird calls, then trying to guess which was which. Games, Ridley had said. Ones he was especially good at. But she'd found herself either chirping or talking almost the entire time. So much so, she'd all but forgotten to be nervous about being in such close proximity to a horse. Ridley's intentioned design, perhaps. She didn't regret taking the additional work for the quarries. Besides spending time with Ridley, it would allow her to be more generous to Jimmy and Jolene—and perhaps others.

Inside the front parlor, she claimed a seat beside Elizabeth on the settee. Her aunt smiled, looking remarkably rested after playing hostess to a houseful of family and friends during the Thanksgiving holiday the previous week. Elizabeth's string of good days was gradually lengthening.

Betsy wheeled in a cart, and when Olivia saw the silver tea service and Susanna's pecan cheese wafers, her heart fell. The news must be worse than she'd thought.

"Olivia." The general settled into a chair opposite them. "A letter arrived today. From Colonel Burcham."

Olivia stiffened at the name, but the general held up a hand as though to say, *Let me finish, please.* Her throat suddenly parched, Olivia craved a cup of tea. But the steaming silver pot must have been heavy because Betsy poured each cup slowly, methodically.

"The colonel has written to inform me that despite the ... *unfortunate* circumstances under which he departed Belle Meade two weeks ago, he's still very much taken with you. And he wishes to see you again at his earliest—"

"No." Olivia shook her head. "No, General Harding, I cannot." Disapproval darkened the general's eyes, and she hurried to temper her too-hasty response. "What I meant to say, General"—she included Elizabeth with a glance— "is that I have no interest whatsoever in Colonel Burcham, or in him pursuing a—"

"Olivia." General Harding's somber tone held warning. "Would it be asking too much to allow me the courtesy of expressing my thoughts on the subject *in entirety*, before you seek to assert your own?"

Her face burning, Olivia shook her head, knowing better than to offer further argument. "I beg your pardon, General. And no, sir. Not at all."

Betsy handed her a cup of tea, and Olivia avoided the woman's eyes.

"Will there be anythin' else, Missus Harding?"

"Not right now, Betsy. This is all very nice. Thank you."

Betsy nodded once and left the room.

Waiting for the general to speak, Olivia sipped her tea and sneaked a look beside her. Elizabeth's hands were clasped tightly around her tea cup, her aunt's gaze confined there as well, and Olivia felt a twinge of regret.

The general cleared his throat. "As your guardian, Olivia, I assure you I have carefully considered Colonel Burcham's professional *and* personal attributes. I've also weighed the sentiments expressed in his letter, which, I believe, ring true. I also think that ..."

Olivia felt sick. She struggled to listen while also scrambling to find the words that would convince the general to change his mind. That would convey to him the heartache of living with a man like Charles Aberdeen. And like Colonel Bryant Burcham.

She wouldn't do it. Not again. She willed Aunt Elizabeth to say something, to speak in her defense. But Elizabeth—silent, submissive—said nothing. And Olivia couldn't blame her. She knew only too well the cost of crossing a husband's opinions.

"The Colonel and I have long been friends, as you know, Olivia." The general's voice registered again, and Olivia blinked back angry tears. If she wanted a choice in this, she'd have to fight for it. However much in vain her efforts might prove to be. "And this decision," he continued, "was not an easy one for me. But my opinion on the matter is fully formed. And I am of the mind ..."

Olivia took a deep breath, the words of her rebuttal forming swiftly now.

"... that Colonel Burcham is not the best match for you."

"General Harding, I greatly respect you and appreciate your generosity, but I simply *cannot* agree to ..." Olivia blinked, suddenly hearing what he'd said. Yet, seeing his scowl, she was slow to embrace the relief lest she'd misunderstood. She swallowed. "My apologies again, General, but ... did you say that you *don't* think Colonel Burcham is the best match?"

"That's precisely what I said, Olivia. And it's what I believe is best. For all involved." Shifting in his chair, the general shot a quick—but telling—glance at Elizabeth, and the simple gesture revealed a counsel his words had not.

Relief pouring through her, Olivia couldn't help but wonder if Aunt Elizabeth had spoken to him on her behalf after all.

The general set aside his empty cup. "Let me be clear, Olivia ... My decision does not diminish my obligation, nor my determination to find a suitable match for you. Which, of course, I immediately began pursuing again once I believed the colonel had withdrawn his interest."

As swiftly as relief had come, Olivia felt a portion of it flee. There was only one other person he could be referencing. "General Meeks," she said softly, remembering the gentleman well. *Feeble, paunchy, and dull ...*

"Yes, precisely! General Meeks was under the impression, from the colonel, no doubt, that your affections were engaged elsewhere. However, I've written to him and he's already responded. Very enthusiastically, I might add." The general smiled. "You can expect a visit from him no later than Christmas."

Later that evening, Olivia crawled into bed earlier than usual and pulled up the covers. The trip to the quarry and back had been enjoyable, though tiring, but tea with General Harding and Elizabeth had drained what little stamina she'd had left. Feeling the tears coming, she turned her head into the pillow and wept. Yet even as she did, she felt a trace of guilt. She had so much compared to many who had so little. Still, she hurt.

She gave herself one full minute to empty herself of tears — then another, because one hadn't been enough — then she took a deep breath and turned onto her back, determined to view her situation in a brighter perspective. Marrying General Percival Meeks wasn't the worst thing that could happen to her. She knew that from having lived with Charles. And judging by what she knew personally about General Meeks — and based on stories the general had shared about the man over dinner tonight — he actually seemed like a very kind and decent person. The Hardings had both known the late Mrs. General Meeks, Sarah, which Olivia hadn't realized.

Twenty-nine years ...

That's how long Percival and Sarah had been married. Olivia found the number unfathomable. She was only twenty-four and sometimes it felt like she'd been alive forever.

Wishing the pounding in her head would stop, she applied pressure to her temples and prayed for God to remove her desire for the handsome face, laughter, and smile of the one man who filled her thoughts every day and her dreams every night. Because while she could marry a man she didn't love, she couldn't live the rest of her life loving a man she wasn't married to.

She didn't know when she'd started loving Ridley Cooper. She only knew that she did. But since that day in General Harding's office when he'd found her hiding behind the chair, he hadn't even attempted to kiss her. Not once. Well, not on her lips anyway. Remembering what he'd said about her bustle that day warmed her heart — and made her cry all over again. She *knew* he felt more for her than friendship. Or had, at one time. But apparently something had happened to change —

A knock sounded on her door.

She sat up in the bed, her breath coming hard. She sniffed and swallowed and hoped she sounded halfway normal. "Yes? Who is it?"

"It's me, dear. Aunt Elizabeth. May I speak to you for a moment?"

"Of course." Wiping her cheeks, Olivia quickly lit the lamp on her bedside table, then checked her reflection in the mirror. *Oh ... a mess.* She smoothed her hair, took some deep breaths to clear her head, pasted on a weak smile, and opened the door.

Chapter
FORTY-TWO

Aunt Elizabeth took one look and drew her into a hug. "Oh, Livvy, dear ..."

"I-I'm fine," Olivia whispered, knowing she didn't sound it.

Elizabeth closed the door, and they sat together on the bed like Olivia and her own mother used to do.

"I'm sorry to be so late, Livvy. I wanted to come to you after dinner, to see how you were faring after the news this afternoon. But the general felt it was better to let you have some time alone. *Men ...*" Elizabeth gave a short laugh. "So I waited until he was asleep!"

Olivia smiled. "Such a rebellious spirit, Aunt. It's almost scandalous. But truly ... Thank you for checking on me ... I'm fine."

Elizabeth shook her head. "My dear, you are *not* fine. Not yet. But I trust that in time, you will be."

Olivia bowed her head.

"General Meeks is a good man, Livvy. Oh, I know ... He's not quite dashing or engaging or handsome in the way a youthful girl—or young woman—dreams about. Except, perhaps, for being enormously wealthy and having a mansion on a hillside." Elizabeth squeezed Olivia's hand. "But he's caring in every way Charles Aberdeen was not, my dearest." Fierce love deepened Elizabeth's eyes. "And he will never hurt you in that way, Livvy," she whispered. *"Never."*

Tears Olivia thought were drained dry began again. "I know," she whispered. "But ..." She glanced downward. She wanted to share with Elizabeth about Ridley. But what good would it do? None. And with the way things stood between her and Ridley now, what did she really have to tell? From all indications—both public and private—they were friends. Perhaps good friends. But still ... *friends.*

"I realize," Elizabeth continued, "that getting married again isn't something you would choose to do. Many a woman in your position, Livvy, would marry for the money alone. But you ..." She brushed a strand of hair from Olivia's forehead. "You're different. And those qualities are so commendable. You want more from life than a marriage such as this. Which, believe it or not, is something I can understand. But the fact remains ..." Elizabeth glanced downward. When she looked up, her eyes glistened. "The general and I won't always be here. And you're so young, Livvy. You have so much of life ahead of you. And you need to live your *own* life. Not live in the shadow of a cloistered life here."

Olivia didn't respond, afraid if she did, she'd start crying again.

"When I look at my girls and the world in which they're growing up" — Elizabeth's laughter came softly — "or have grown up in ... It's very different from the world I knew when I was their age. And yours."

The wind whipped around the corner of the house, whistling as it went. Finally, December was delivering on the promise of winter.

"Would you make me a promise, Livvy?"

Surprised by the question, Olivia squeezed her hand. "Anything."

Elizabeth searched her gaze. "Mary is so much like you. Even as a young girl, she wanted to go her own way, to brave the untrod path, as it were. So unlike Selene."

"But so like her father," Olivia whispered.

Elizabeth offered a nod, then seemed to focus on a point somewhere beyond the confines of the room. "I don't worry so much about Selene. Selene will never leave Belle Meade. Not that the general would allow it, even if she wanted to." She laughed softly. "But Mary ... Mary has always been different. She's got a courage, a strength inside her, much like you." Elizabeth gripped her hand. "Promise me that when the time comes, you'll help Mary find her way. You'll help ... give her wings. I see her watching you. In a way she's never watched me."

Hearing an earnestness in her aunt's tone, Olivia was quick to nod. But something in Elizabeth's eyes, in her manner, also gave her pause. "I'll do anything I can to help Mary. Though I'm not certain she'll welcome it, coming from me. I don't think she likes me much."

"It's not you she doesn't like, Livvy." Elizabeth's brow furrowed. "It's me. And perhaps, the closeness you and I share." She exhaled. "Looking back over the years, I see how I could have done better with her. *And* Selene. But I was either sick or grieving, it seems. Thank the Lord for Susanna. She was there for them when I wasn't. But ... I'm determined to change that ... for however much longer I'm here."

"Which is going to be a very, very long time, Aunt. You're going to see your daughters marry and have children. You and the general will grow old together and sit out there on the front porch, rocking and watching your grandchildren play. You have many happy years ahead. Don't doubt that. All right?"

Elizabeth's gaze grew wistful. "Of course, my dear. I'm sure you're right."

"And don't for a moment think Mary doesn't watch you, Aunt Elizabeth. She does. Every day. She loves and admires you more than you know."

Elizabeth drew in a breath. "Thank you, Livvy," she whispered. "I'm so grateful God brought you here when he did." They rose and hugged again, and Elizabeth walked to the door. She paused, hand on the latch. "However much things may still seem the same, Livvy, they are changing. The war alone has seen to that. And I, for one, welcome many of those changes."

"As do I," Olivia said softly, thinking of the freedmen's school but not daring to mention it. "I simply wish I could be more a part of them."

Elizabeth held her gaze. Olivia tried to read the emotion in her expression. Sadness? Fear? She wasn't sure.

"Your mother, God rest her," Elizabeth whispered, "was the dearest friend I've ever had. Every time I look at you, Livvy, I see her, from years ago when we were younger. And not a day goes by that I don't wish she were still here. If anything were to happen to you ..." She shook her head, firming her lips. "I'd never forgive myself."

Olivia's heart warmed, both at her concern and at how Elizabeth saw her mother in her—something Olivia had never been able to see. "Nothing's going to happen to me, Aunt Elizabeth. As you said yourself, General Meeks is a kind man. He'll never hurt me."

A single tear slipped down Elizabeth's cheek. She didn't wipe it away.

"Mr. Pagette contacted me two days ago, Livvy. The board reached their decision. You start teaching the freedmen's school on the first of the year. And ... while we'll talk further about all this soon, I couldn't be more proud."

Chapter
FORTY-THREE

Olivia awoke early the next morning and was up and dressed before sunrise. *Teaching ... in a freedmen's school.* She could still hardly believe it. And Aunt Elizabeth ...

She'd underestimated the woman, in so many ways. She still wondered though—considering the firm stance General Harding had taken with Mr. Pagette on the subject—how her aunt was managing to help. Whatever her reasons, Olivia was indebted to her. And had so much to do before January.

She slipped her shawl around her shoulders and peered out the window, the chilled pane cool against her scarred-but-healing palm. Across the meadow, smoke curled from the chimney of the old Harding cabin, a pale gray against a swath of purplish dawn.

Ridley.

Only hours earlier, she'd grieved the loss of him, in a way. Yet with morning came renewed hope. Because if God could open a door for *her* to teach at a freedmen's school, what else might he do? But as soon as the whisper came, she warned her sensibilities to pay it no mind. She wasn't naive to the honor-bound traditions, duties, and expectations surrounding a woman in her situation. In securing a match between her and Percival Meeks, General Harding would profit in some form. Financially, most assuredly. That was how things were done. A daughter enhanced her family's status through her appearance and accomplishments and later by marrying well. It was a Southern rite of passage. A daughter's—or a ward's—hand in exchange for stocks, bonds, or a promised alliance. Like a game of chess, only with flesh-and-blood pieces. And feelings. It was one tradition that wouldn't be changing anytime soon. Not soon enough for her, anyway.

As unsettled as her stomach had been at dinner the prior evening, she was hungry this morning, and the aromas wafting up from the kitchen caused her mouth to water. Susanna's beaten biscuits and country ham and Betsy's diced potatoes with rosemary and onions. Her taste buds knew the savory scents by heart. She crossed the open second-story porch and hurried down the stairs. Almost overnight, it seemed, winter had arrived. But fall had given them a memorable showing.

Even with the chill in the air, the kitchen door was open.

"Morning, ladies!" As she always did when she visited the kitchen, she hugged Susanna from the side, gave Betsy's apron a firm tug, and flashed Chloe a smile.

"Well, look at you, Missus Aberdeen." Betsy grinned. "Up with creation this mornin'! What you doin' up so early, ma'am?"

Olivia leaned close to the pan of fried potatoes and inhaled. "I smelled all this and couldn't sleep anymore."

Susanna laughed. "You sure didn't eat much last night, ma'am. You hungry now?"

"Starved!"

Susanna filled a plate, then a cup of coffee, and Olivia ate at the kitchen table, talking with them as they cooked.

Betsy glanced back from the stove. "You ready for the shindig comin' up? It always means a good time and lots o' fun!"

"Mmm-hmm!" Susanna and Chloe remarked in unison.

Olivia smiled, chewing her last bite of biscuit. "I am. And I'm looking forward to it." She sipped her coffee, the brew warm to her throat. She'd thought Ridley might ask her to go with him. Or at least to walk together. But so far he'd said nothing.

She'd seen Rachel several times since dropping off her mother's dress by the cabin, but Rachel hadn't said anything about it. And she hated to be the first one to bring it up. Rachel was doing her a favor, after all, by altering the dress. And if it turned out not to be fixable, she'd already decided to simply wear what she had on today.

"Lawd …" Chloe looked at the clock on the wall. "Where are them two men? They ain't gonna have time to eat 'less they get themselves up here."

Susanna gestured to Betsy. "You best pack it up and take it on down there to 'em. Mr. Cooper told me him and Uncle Bob got to be on the road by seven-thirty."

Olivia looked up. "On the road? Where are they going?" Ridley hadn't said anything to her about leaving.

"Just up to Gallatin. 'Bout two hours from here. Business with the general."

Betsy grabbed a tray and started piling plates high. "I still got to get the tea on for Missus Harding. Then get up there and help Miss Selene with her hair. Her General Jackson is s'posed to come callin' today." She wiped her forehead with her sleeve. "Lawd, it never ends."

"I could take it for you." Olivia rose from the table. "If that would help."

The kitchen fell silent. Betsy glanced at Susanna, who looked right back at her, then over at Olivia.

"You sure you want to, ma'am?" Susanna's tone was hesitant. "This tray be mighty heavy. And it's a long way down to the cabin."

Olivia acted as though she were offended. "You don't think I can carry a tray?" But she could tell the women didn't believe her. Especially Betsy.

"Oh, yes, ma'am." Betsy nodded. "I think you can carry a tray. With them skinny little arms of yours, I'm guessin' you get almost to the door 'fore they give way."

Olivia laughed but narrowed her eyes. "Give me that tray right now. And put an extra biscuit on it for me."

Halfway to the cabin, Olivia was certain her arms were going to give out. How did the women do this? She saw them carrying trays even heavier than this every day, full of china plates and dishes and platters and silver tea services. Her arm muscles started to cramp, then her shoulders. But as sure as the sun was high above the hills, she could *feel* Betsy, Susanna, and Chloe watching her from the kitchen window, and there was no way she was about to stop and rest.

When she reached the cabin, it was all she could do to negotiate the two steps up to the porch and then set the tray down on a bench beside the window without dropping it. Oh, her arms ached, but it felt so good to be free of the weight.

She smoothed her dress and the sides of her hair, wondering why Ridley hadn't mentioned anything to her about traveling today. Then she saw movement through the window, inside the cabin, of a bare back and broad shoulders and muscular arms that had held her close. Ridley turned toward the window, reaching for his shirt, which hung on a chair. She didn't dare move for fear he'd see her from the corner of his eye. He slipped his arms into the sleeves, then began sliding the buttons through the buttonholes. The shirt stretched taut over his chest.

To say that Ridley Cooper was handsome was like saying the thoroughbreds at Belle Meade were fairly nice horses. She told herself to look away but couldn't.

Or didn't.

She'd seen a man put on a shirt before. But never, in all the times she'd seen Charles dress, had she wanted to reach out to him like she wanted to with Ridley. To see if her slightest touch could stir him like his touch did her.

Ridley turned away from the window, and Olivia did the same. She waited a few seconds, then knocked on the door at the same moment Ridley opened it. "Olivia!" His expression was surprised but happy.

"Good morning, Mr. Cooper. I'm here with breakfast, compliments of the kitchen."

His eyes brightened further. "We woke a little late, so I figured we'd have to go without." He glanced past her. "Uncle Bob! Breakfast!"

Uncle Bob appeared in the door of the adjoining cabin. "And we got about two shakes of a rabbit's tail to eat it!"

Minutes later, still amazed at how quickly two hungry men could make a tray *full* of food disappear, she walked back to the main house with them to the carriage waiting in the drive. General Harding wasn't there yet.

"You'll be back tonight?"

Ridley nodded. "A quick trip. Part of getting ready for the yearling sale." He winked. "Why? You want to go with us? Help us check out the horses?"

If they'd been alone, she would have playfully shoved him. As it was, she narrowed her eyes and leveled a stare, which only made him laugh.

Uncle Bob leaned over. "I hear you's joinin' us for the shindig, ma'am." He smiled big. "Best bring your dancin' shoes. 'Cause we know how to kick up a fair amount o' dust."

The door to the mansion opened, and General Harding strode toward them. Ridley and Uncle Bob waited for him to climb into the carriage first, then Ridley gestured for Uncle Bob to go next before he turned back.

"Thanks for bringing us breakfast, Olivia," he whispered. "That was real sweet."

You're welcome, she mouthed back, hearing only friendship—and nothing more—in his words.

The carriage pulled away, and she walked back in the direction of her bedroom. Then, on second thought, she retraced her steps to the old Harding cabin and gathered the breakfast dishes, stacking everything again on the tray. Recognizing one of Ridley's shirts hanging on a hook on the wall, she momentarily forgot about the dirty dishes, taking a moment to run her fingers down the sleeve. In height, stature, and strength, he was so much like Charles. And yet ...

He was nothing like Charles at all.

Charles would forever be remembered as a traitor of the Confederacy and a cheat. A man who had disgraced himself, his family, and his countrymen. Ridley Cooper, like so many others, was a wounded but loyal *true* son of the South, struggling to find his place again.

And he would, she believed, in time.

The tray wasn't nearly so heavy on the way back. She deposited it in the kitchen with Chloe, then slipped back upstairs to work for a while on Jimmy and Jolene's lessons before she met with them later. She was eager to start planning her lessons for the freedmen's school too.

When she reached the second-story porch, her bedroom door stood ajar. She entered, expecting to find one of the servants, but saw Rachel by the wardrobe instead.

Rachel glanced up, her blue eyes especially bright. "Missus Aberdeen! I'm glad you come by, ma'am. I'm needin' you to try on somethin' for me." With an expectant look, Rachel withdrew a gown from the wardrobe with a flourish.

Olivia's breath caught. She recognized the deep russet-red fabric and knew it was the dress that had belonged to her mother. But she could scarcely believe it was the same gown. Because it wasn't. The dress was ... "Oh, Rachel." Olivia sighed, shaking her head. "It's gorgeous!"

"Thank you, ma'am." Rachel's voice went soft. "But it ain't nearly as pretty now as it's gonna be with you in it. Look here, I added this special." She pointed to the delicate trim of black tasseled lace she'd sewn along the neckline and that appeared to continue on around to the back. "I thought it'd go real pretty with your hair."

Olivia fingered one of the tassels. "It's lovely."

She'd always shied away from wearing sleeveless gowns, what with the scar on her forearm. But she *did*, on occasion, when the event demanded. Charles had insisted she wear evening gloves to cover what he deemed a less-than-comely feature, but she'd have done so anyway. If Aunt Elizabeth didn't have a pair she could borrow, she'd ask someone to purchase a pair for her in town.

She stepped back to better admire the altered hemline of the dress and couldn't begin to fathom how much time and work had gone into adding the length of fabric Rachel had sewn along the hem. Olivia would never have chosen the faintly striped fabric to go with the floral brocade of the dress, but the combination was stunning. And not only that, Rachel had added rosettes with bows, creating a scalloped tier where the two coordinating fabrics met.

Olivia knelt to admire the skilled needlework. "Rachel, I-I don't know what to say. This dress has always been special to me, but now ..."

"So you're pleased then?"

Olivia laughed. "*Pleased* doesn't begin to describe it."

"Oh!" Rachel grinned. "I ain't even showed you the back yet." She turned the dress around to reveal a bow that tied at the fitted waist and trailed the length of the gown. "Now, if you don't mind, ma'am ... Let's get you into it so I can see what final touches I need to make 'fore the big night."

With Rachel's help, Olivia changed into the gown, trying to keep her arm turned so Rachel wouldn't see the scar, while also attempting to sneak peeks at the dress in the mirror.

"No, ma'am!" Rachel giggled, holding her still. "Not yet you don't. First, we need to get you all buttoned and tied up in the back."

Olivia looked down. With her crinolines beneath, the dress extended out from her waist in a bell shape. "You must let me pay you for the fabric *and* for your work, Rachel."

Rachel patted her shoulder. "I 'preciate that, Missus Aberdeen. But somebody already done paid me, ma'am. They swore me to a secret, so I ain't tellin'. And you best not be askin'."

Olivia didn't have to ask. She knew. *Aunt Elizabeth.* She'd never be able to thank the woman for all she'd done.

Rachel nudged her shoulder. "All right now. Get on over there so we can see it!"

Even before Olivia reached the mirror, she heard Rachel's soft intake of breath behind her—and experienced the same reaction when she first saw her reflection. The dress was even prettier on than off. But it was *who* Olivia saw when she first looked in the mirror that stole a breath and caused her eyes to burn.

"Missus Aberdeen?" Rachel came alongside her. "Is somethin' wrong, ma'am? You don't like it?"

"I love it, Rachel. The dress is perfect. It's not that. It's ..." Her smile felt bittersweet. "Aunt Elizabeth has told me many times that when she looks at me, she can see my mother. But ... I've never been able to see it myself. Until now."

Rachel's blue eyes glistened in the morning light. "I understand what you sayin', ma'am," she said softly. "Gives you a funny feelin' to walk by a mirror and catch a glimpse of someone else in your face." She met Olivia's gaze in the reflection. "Or maybe walk by a picture on a wall and see your own eyes lookin' back out at you."

Reading more than simple understanding in Rachel's expression, Olivia remembered the day she'd found Rachel staring at the portrait of John Harding in the entrance hall.

Rachel adjusted one of the black tassels that had gone askew. "Makes you feel a little closer to 'em, in a way, I guess."

"While also making you miss them even more," Olivia whispered.

"Yes, ma'am." Rachel's jaw firmed. "Yes, ma'am ... it sure do."

"I don't think I'll ever tire of this view, Livvy. The hills are so breathtaking."

Olivia paused beside her aunt and shielded her eyes from the sun as she peered out across the meadow. Exactly two weeks before Christmas and it felt more like a day in May than December. But that was one of the things she loved about Tennessee. *Indian summers.* She lifted her gaze to the hills beyond and, in her mind's eye, she pictured the jagged peaks of the Colorado Rocky Mountains tipped with snow as Ridley had described. She wondered whether the Colorado Territory ever had days like this.

Aunt Elizabeth resumed their stroll, and Olivia fell into step beside her.

"Aunt Elizabeth, thank you again for what you did with the dress. Rachel worked wonders!"

Elizabeth's expression turned playfully scolding. "You're most welcome. And yes, she always does. But you've already thanked me once."

"I know. But this dress is dear to me. And I never dreamed I'd be able to wear it."

Elizabeth's steps slowed. A peculiar look came over her face. "But Livvy, you wear the dress all the time. That's why I asked Rachel to work on it. I'd noticed the hem was becoming a little frayed in the back, so I spoke with her about it."

Olivia paused. "We *are* speaking about my mother's dress?"

"I'm speaking about your gray ensemble, dear. The one with the jacket and white piping. Did Rachel work on one of your mother's dresses too?"

Olivia nodded, her thoughts already churning about who else could have paid for those alterations, and it quickly landed on the only other possibility. *That dear man* ... "And she did such beautiful work too. I'll show it to you later."

Elizabeth slipped her arm through Olivia's, and they continued on.

"The other night, Livvy" — Elizabeth looked over — "I told you I was proud of you for teaching at the freedmen's school. And I am. But I also want to urge you again to be careful. Mr. Pagette, an old childhood friend, has assured me he's given this situation his personal attention. The first meeting will be the fifteenth of January. They've located a building." She gestured. "About a mile or so through the woods. Not too far. An old hunting cabin no one uses anymore, he said. Just across the boundary of Belle Meade on a neighbor's land."

"And this neighbor ... they know about it?"

"Oh yes, and were eager to help. But there are people, as we both know, who do not approve of servants being educated in this manner. People who would prefer that schools such as this not exist."

"People like ... the general?" Olivia broached softly, and felt Elizabeth stiffen beside her.

"My husband is a *good* man, Livvy." Elizabeth paused, her voice soft but earnest. "I know you may not agree with some of his ways. But he always has your best at heart, I promise you that. And mine and the girls' and also Belle Meade's."

"I have no doubt of that, Aunt Elizabeth. And while I'm grateful to you for arranging this opportunity for me, I also don't want to place you in a precarious situation. I'm concerned about what the general's reaction would be if he knew. He made it quite clear to Mr. Pagette that he could not support the idea of starting a school on Belle Meade property. So I have to assume he doesn't know."

Elizabeth shook her head. "Though he does know about your teaching Jimmy and Jolene. Because I told him. But, Livvy dear, who do you think started giving Jimmy those old copies of the magazine to begin with?" Elizabeth offered a careful smile. "When the general was in prison during the war, he and Susanna traded letters quite often. He told me that hers were some of the most meaningful he received. And he's often lent her books from his library. Does that sound like a man bent on not allowing servants to learn?"

"No, but—"

"The general has a great many responsibilities resting on his shoulders, Livvy. He also has a great number of men—powerful men on both sides of this issue—watching him as he balances those obligations. The war is over. But in many ways it's still being fought ... in the hearts of men and in their ... vision for this new world." Elizabeth looked across the meadow. "I see the weight of it in my husband's face when he returns from a meeting in town, or when I awaken at night and find him standing at the window, staring into the darkness, unable to sleep for the cares of this world pressing down upon him.

"And don't forget, Livvy ... He has all the servants and employees depending on him. Not to mention his family. And though he would never tell you this, and I only know because I overheard him speaking to a gentleman from the bank, Belle Meade is not as solvent as it appears. My husband has debts, and this is a crucial time for him. For *us.* He's depending on the yearling sale to do well. And ... he's also counting on—"

"General Meeks," Olivia whispered, seeing it in her aunt's eyes.

Elizabeth briefly glanced away. "Yes. General Meeks has shown great interest in investing in Belle Meade, so a union between our families—*if* that comes to fruition—would enhance its future. But it would also enhance your own. Chattanooga is a fine city. It wasn't devastated like Atlanta. The bulk of General Meeks's estate was spared. You'd be able to start afresh there, my dear. You'd have a brand-new life. Something, I fear, you will never have here."

Olivia bowed her head and let a nod be her answer.

"Also, my dear . . ." Elizabeth took hold of her hand. "And you must have considered this by now, but . . . your teaching in the school can only be temporary."

Olivia looked up.

"Should this union come to pass . . ." Elizabeth offered a smile that hinted at *or when it does come to pass.* " — it would hardly be fitting for a married woman, much less the wife of General Percival Meeks, to be teaching in a freedmen's school."

"I understand. And I'm grateful for what you've done. I'll teach for as long as I can."

Elizabeth linked arms again and turned to walk back toward the house, but Olivia hesitated.

"I think I'll continue on for a while, Aunt Elizabeth."

Elizabeth's nod held understanding.

Olivia walked on toward the mares' stable, watching for Ridley, something that had become second nature to her. Her attention was drawn to the pasture where mares were grazing, some lying in the sun. But there was one in particular . . . She looked closer. *Seabird.* The mare was running full out, her mane whipping the air behind her, her hooves hardly touching the earth. Even at this distance, Olivia could see the fullness around the mare's middle, and she counted . . . Five months until Seabird would give birth to the foal of Jack Malone. Oh, how angry Ridley had been that day the mare jumped the corral.

Olivia went as far as the fence and leaned against it, admiring the horse, her speed and agility, and finding it hard to believe the mare had ever sustained a serious injury to her leg.

Such beauty, such power and *freedom* — Olivia couldn't help but feel a touch of envy.

Chapter
FORTY-FOUR

Olivia waited in the front entrance hall with Aunt Elizabeth and Cousin Lizzie. She'd already arranged her hair, but hadn't yet dressed for the shindig. She'd do that right after the Hardings left for the LeVert reception. Ridley had never said anything about escorting her, but she still wanted to look nice for him. Especially tonight. And especially since he'd paid for her dress. Because whether it was sensible or not—and she knew it wasn't—she couldn't seem to convince her heart to stop hoping where Ridley was concerned.

She gave Elizabeth a hug, then Cousin Lizzie. "I hope you all have a marvelous time this evening. I'm certain Belmont will be exquisite."

"Oh, no doubt it will be, Livvy." Elizabeth's eyes brightened. "Adelicia Acklen never does anything on a small scale, and she gives the most wonderful party favors!"

The door to the study opened behind them, and the general emerged. "Olivia." His dark eyebrows drew together. "Bad news, I fear. I've received word from General Meeks that he won't be joining us for the holidays as planned."

Feeling as though she'd been given a Christmas gift a week early, Olivia tried her best not to show it. "General Meeks isn't ill, I hope."

"No, no." The general gave her a reassuring nod. "A bit of rheumatism, I believe, that flares up in the cold. He says he looks forward to seeing us all again soon."

Olivia nodded, glad to hear it wasn't anything serious. She didn't want to marry the gentleman, but she also didn't wish him ill.

"Ah ..." General Harding glanced toward the staircase. "My eldest daughter, in all her glory." Selene descended the stairs looking radiant, as always, shiny curls arranged atop her head. "Daughter." The general placed a kiss on her forehead. "General William Hicks Jackson had better mind his interests this evening, or someone else is liable to steal you away."

Selene smiled and ducked her head.

From outside, the clomp of horses' hooves announced the arrival of the carriage, and the general peered through the window.

"Livvy?" Elizabeth whispered where only Olivia could hear. "I left the gloves for you on my dressing table. I hope you have a wonderful time tonight, dear. That was very kind of Rachel to invite you."

"Thank you, Aunt." Olivia gave her another quick hug. She hadn't mentioned Ridley being invited as well. In light of everything, it just seemed easier that way.

"Oh!" A cry drifted down from upstairs, followed by what sounded like something being thrown against a wall.

Selene sighed. "It's Mary! Chloe fixed her hair but she doesn't like it. I told her it looks fine for her age, but I think she wants it to look more like mine. If her dawdling causes us to miss the opening waltz ..."

Aunt Elizabeth started toward the spiral staircase.

"Elizabeth!" The general shook his head, then looked up the stairs. "Mary Elizabeth! Get down here at once. The carriage is waiting."

"I'm not going anymore," came a weak voice.

Elizabeth turned. "Please ... let me go to her, General. I remember what it's like to be that age, and—"

"Selene and Lizzie managed to be ready on time. There's no reason why Mary shouldn't be as well." General Harding glanced at his pocket watch then toward the stairs again. "You have exactly eight minutes, Mary Elizabeth. At which time I will expect you to be in that carriage."

The general ushered the women out the door before him, then followed. From the porch, Elizabeth looked back and cast a parting glance at Olivia, her look of excitement replaced by one of distress. The second the latch clicked on the door, Olivia hiked her skirts, sprinted up the staircase, and down the hall to Mary's room.

Slumped at the dressing table, Mary lifted her head as Olivia entered. Tears streaked the girl's cheeks.

"If Mother sent you up here, then—"

"She didn't." Olivia put her hand to her chest, out of breath. "I came of my own volition. To fix your hair ... if you want me to." She filled her lungs again, the words spilling out. "But we only have eight minutes! Actually ... more like seven now." Olivia smiled at her in the mirror. "But I'd love to help ... if you'd let me."

Mary stared, her gaze suspicious, her struggle evident. But if what Aunt Elizabeth had said about their similarities was true, Olivia knew she and Mary stood a good chance of being friends. *If* they could start again.

"Six minutes, thirty seconds," Olivia whispered, praying Mary could feel her sincerity.

Mary sat straighter in the chair, but teared up again. "Yes, please," she whispered. "But we have to hurry! Papa will be angry if I'm not down there on time."

Beyond thrilled, Olivia had no time to show it. "Would you like your hair to look like Selene's?"

Mary shook her head. "I want it to look like yours."

Olivia felt a flood of love for the girl. "Well, you're in luck then. Because this is a style I could do blindfolded." She took inventory of the hair accessories atop the dressing table. "Where are your hair combs? Some long ones ..."

Mary's shoulders slumped again. "Selene used them. All I have are these."

Seeing the tiny clips in Mary's hand, Olivia took one look at herself in the mirror ... and pulled the combs from her own hair.

Mary gasped. "What are you —"

"Just do exactly as I say, all right?" Olivia winked. "And keep track of the time."

Hinting at a grin, Mary nodded. "Five minutes!"

Olivia grabbed the brush.

With seconds to spare, she and Mary all but flew down the stairs. At the door, Mary turned. "Thank you, Mrs. Aberdeen. I feel so ... pretty!"

"It's *Olivia*, remember?" Olivia touched her face. "And you *are* pretty, Mary. Now please, remember every detail about tonight. I've always wanted to visit Belmont."

Grinning, Mary nodded and raced out the door. Olivia followed as far as the porch, tensing when she saw the general waiting by the carriage. *Please ... let him be gentle with her.* But to her surprise, it was Mary who took the lead.

"I'm sorry for having kept you all waiting, Father. It was foolish and selfish of me, and ... I hope it won't spoil our evening."

From where she stood, Olivia could see the general's surprise.

"Yes, Mary Elizabeth," he said sternly. "You have kept us waiting." Mary bowed her head. "But obviously"—the general urged her chin up a fraction—"with good reason. Because you look lovely tonight, my dear."

Mary beamed, and so did Olivia.

"Thank you, Father." Mary gave a little curtsey.

The general held his daughter's hand as she ascended into the carriage. Then he turned back toward the house. "Good evening, Olivia. We won't be home until daybreak, I'm sure."

Olivia curtsied much as Mary had done. "Good evening, General Harding. And have a wonderful time."

"There you go, Missus Aberdeen. All fastened, ma'am."

"Thank you, Rachel." Mindful of the scar usually hidden by her sleeve, Olivia kept her arm close to her side as she craned her neck to see the back of the dress in the mirror and to admire Rachel's handiwork again. An idea suddenly came, and she decided to test her theory about Ridley being the benevolent fashion financier. "Are you certain, Rachel, that you were compensated adequately for your work on this gown? Because if not, I'd be happy to give you something as well. Who was it again who paid for the alterations? I've forgotten."

Slowly, Rachel smiled and wagged her finger. "That is *the* most *pitiful* try at gettin' to the truth I ever done heard, ma'am. You should be ashamed."

"I am." Olivia grinned. "Mostly ... But I do wish you'd tell me so I could thank them properly."

"Some gifts are meant to be given in secret, Missus Aberdeen. And I think this is one of 'em. And don't you worry, I was *compensated adequately*, like you said."

Olivia nodded, determined to let that be the last word on the matter. At least until Ridley arrived.

Rachel frowned. "You plannin' on wearin' those this evenin', ma'am?"

Olivia saw her looking at Aunt Elizabeth's gloves laying on the bed, and could guess what she was thinking. The gloves—more gray than a true black like Aunt Elizabeth had remembered—didn't match the dress very well. In fact, they almost detracted from it. But Olivia wasn't about to parade around with her arm bare for all the world to see. It was her own fault. She should have asked to see the gloves before tonight.

"Yes, I thought I would." She tried for nonchalance. "They might come in handy if it gets too chilly."

Rachel didn't smile or nod. She just looked at her. And Olivia would've sworn the woman could read her thoughts. "With you lookin' like you's lookin' in that dress, Missus Aberdeen ... Ain't nobody gonna be lookin' at your arm, ma'am." Rachel's gaze lowered. " 'Sides, it ain't that bad. No need to be ashamed. How did it happen, ma'am?"

Olivia ran a finger over the furrow of white puckered flesh. "I was thrown ... from a horse."

A moment passed. "How old was you?"

"I was ten." Olivia finally looked up. "And I've been scared to death of horses ever since."

Awareness dawned in Rachel's smooth brown features. "And here you is ... livin' on a thoroughbred farm. Funny how God works things sometimes, ain't it?"

"*Funny* wasn't quite my first thought when coming to Belle Meade." Olivia smiled. "But yes, I can see the irony in it now, I guess."

"You need help puttin' 'em on, ma'am?"

"No, I can do it. But thank you."

"All right then. I best run and get myself ready. I see you there shortly." Rachel closed the bedroom door behind her.

Olivia finished getting ready, tucking wayward strands of hair back into place. Without her long combs, she wasn't sure how well her hair would hold on the sides, but she didn't regret sharing the combs with Mary. She only hoped the girl's dance card was already filled.

A quick dab of perfume behind each ear, and she wondered again what the party would be like tonight. She assumed food and dancing. What else did you do at a party? Surely she'd be teaching some of Belle Meade's servants in the freedmen's school. Did they know yet that she would be their teacher? She felt both honored and nervous at the prospect.

She slipped the gloves on. They reached past her elbows, three-quarters of the way up her arms. Plenty long enough. And warmer than she'd thought. She reached for her shawl when a coo, like that of a mourning dove, sounded outside her front window. She smiled.

It was dark, but she could just make out Ridley standing below. So he'd come for her after all ... She pushed up the window.

"You ready for the biggest party of the year?" he called in a hushed voice.

"Almost! I can be down in three minutes!"

"But I'm only giving you two."

Closing the window on his smart remark, she wrapped her shawl around her shoulders and took a final glance in the mirror before turning down the lamp.

Moonlight illuminated the second-story porch as she headed for the staircase.

"Not that way, Mrs. Aberdeen. Not tonight."

She stopped and peered over the railing but didn't see him.

"Over here."

She followed his voice to find him standing on the front porch, the gas lamps on the walkway scattering the night. "What are you doing over there?"

"I'm calling for you at the front door, like any proper gentleman would do."

Grinning, she quickly decided to play the part. She hurried through the door leading into the hallway outside the Hardings' bedroom and then down the grand spiral staircase.

A single oil lamp burned low in the entrance hall, its undulating shadows giving the tall-ceilinged room an almost otherworldly feel. She stopped for one last check in the hall mirror and her eyes were drawn to the Harding family portraits. She thought again of Rachel Norris—of "eyes lookin' back out at you"—and recalled a scripture Ridley had read in church last week. Something about being encompassed by a *great cloud of witnesses* while running life's race.

If her father and mother were somehow able to see her now, she hoped they would be proud of her. Although, if they knew about her teaching—and her pupils—she doubted that would be the case. Still, who was to say ... Perhaps heaven lent a perspective on this life that the earthly one had lacked. Maybe her parents were cheering her on even now.

Reaching to open the door, she chose to think so.

Chapter
FORTY-FIVE

*R*idley knew he was staring, but he couldn't stop. He realized in that moment that he'd never known what beautiful was ... until Olivia Aberdeen. The woman was stunning. Especially in that dress. And if what Betsy had told him was right—and if General Harding had his way—come summer Olivia would likely be marrying Confederate General Percival Meeks.

Ridley recalled the general's aging military colleague. Meeks was plenty wealthy and seemed like a kind enough man, but it was still a match Ridley couldn't envision and a possibility he couldn't bring himself to accept. Not that it mattered if he did or not. At least Colonel Burcham was out of the picture, and it felt good to know he'd had a hand in that outcome.

Olivia cleared her throat. "Mr. Cooper, I believe this is where you're supposed to say 'Good evening, Mrs. Aberdeen' to me, at which time I'll say something similar in return. Except with your name inserted, of course."

Tempted to silence that quick-witted, pretty little mouth of hers with a sound kiss, he settled for a bow instead. "Good evening, Mrs. Aberdeen. A pleasure to see you again, ma'am."

"Pleasure's all mine, Mr. Cooper."

She curtsied and extended her hand. He kissed it, preferring the softness of her skin to gloves, but appreciating the way the dress framed her neck and shoulders. And everything else.

"Shall we go?" he asked, offering his arm.

But she merely did a twirl in front of him, holding out her dress on the sides. "Thank you, Ridley. I know it was you."

He frowned, fairly certain it would be convincing. "You know it was me who ... what?"

"Who paid Rachel."

"Why would I pay Rachel?"

"For the alterations."

She grinned, swaying from side to side like the belle she was, and looking so adorable, yet so womanly, he couldn't decide whether he wanted to hug her or take her in his arms and kiss her until she was breathless. Or both. But he knew he'd better 'fess up soon before that last option got the best of him.

He bowed slightly. "You're most welcome, m'lady. And I must say ..." He allowed himself to look at her, aware she was watching him. "I've never seen a more intoxicating sight."

He offered his arm a second time, and she slipped her hand through.

Conversation came easily as they made their way across the property. Uncle Bob had told him this event was usually enjoyed only by the servants, so it was an honor that he and Olivia had been invited. Soon, they met with others walking in the same direction. The couples greeted them, and Ridley nodded in return, thanking them for the invitation. Olivia did the same, which made him proud. Without fail, all of the servants called her by name, which wasn't surprising.

As they drew closer to the building where they met for church, fiddle and mandolin music greeted them, joined by the lively tune of a harmonica. The succulent aroma of a roasted pig, compliments of General Harding, drifted toward them from a deep pit dug nearby.

Ridley had a fairly good idea of the frivolity that would go on here tonight but doubted Olivia did. Watching her eyes widen in church when someone said a loud *amen* or *thank you, Jesus!* had become a favorite Sunday pastime for him, so he could hardly wait to see her reaction.

The building had been emptied of pews and chairs, and a crowd of couples stood on what was now the dance floor, paired off and waiting. Magnolia leaves, still waxy green in winter, had been strung together into wreaths and hung from the ceiling. Hay bales lined the walls, and the only furniture was a makeshift table of lumber and two sawhorses, laden with the most delicious-looking food he'd ever seen.

He led Olivia to the dance floor and leaned close. "In case I forget to tell you, you look radiant this evening, Olivia."

She smiled up at him. "Thank you, but ..." She glanced down at her dress. "I feel a little out of place."

Only then did he notice what the others were wearing. The men either had on suits of varying styles, similar to his, or trousers with freshly pressed shirts. But the women ... they looked the most different. Many of the ladies wore dresses similar to Olivia's, though not as fancy—likely hand-me-downs from the Harding family. A handful of others wore vibrant-colored clothing that draped around their bodies like togas. Still, he couldn't quite place what it was that—

Then it occurred to him ... Every one of the women was without a head wrap, something usually required for servants. But not tonight. Tonight, the women wore their hair like their crowning glories. He reached for Olivia's hand, eager to ease the worry in her eyes. "You don't look out of place to me. In fact ..." He wove his fingers through hers. "I think you're right where you need to be."

The look she gave him not only made him wish they were alone, but was one he was pretty sure General Percival Meeks had never seen. Or likely would. Not that the elderly man would survive it if he did.

Hollering started from up front where the fiddle and harmonica players were. Ridley spotted Jedediah on the banjo, another man with a washtub bass, and Julius climbing atop a hay bale, holding onto Betsy's hand.

"It's time to grab your partners, men!" Julius yelled.

Some of the women squealed as though their partners had taken Julius's suggestion literally, and laughter filled the room. Ridley grinned, especially when Olivia's eyes went wide. She tried to hide her smile behind her hand.

"All right, now," Julius continued, raising an arm, attempting to quiet the crowd. "Everybody knows how this works. Our first dance tonight"—he raised his chin a little—"be the waltz."

People clapped, including Olivia.

"Oh, good," she whispered. "I know this one."

Ridley just nodded, reading humor in the faces around him and already guessing where this "waltz" would lead.

"All right, fellas." Julius briefly turned to the musicians. "Do it all proper-like now ... And all y'all out there, get your places!"

Ridley clasped Olivia's hand with his and brought it up, then placed his other hand on the back of her shoulder, while she rested hers on his arm.

"No matter what happens," he whispered, giving her a wink. "I won't leave you. Just follow my lead, all right?"

She nodded as the music started.

The fiddles' sweet strains filled the building and the harmonica joined in, providing the downbeat. Couples whirled and twirled in proper form, elbows held high, shoulders stiff, women's heads angled beautifully, if not slightly too much. Ridley had all but decided he'd assumed incorrectly when the twang of a banjo broke in—

And the tempo of the music changed on a dime.

Olivia felt her jaw drop as couples around them started breaking hold. Men and women began to clap and swing their arms and hips from side to side. Some of them even kicked up their heels. This wasn't any waltz *she* knew.

Men jumped and moved like they were standing on hot coals. Others started in with high-stepping antics that looked a little like a quadrille, but that was done with greater enthusiasm. Meanwhile, their partners danced around and around, clapping and laughing. Olivia had never seen anything like it in her life. The closest thing was church here on Sunday mornings. But church was tame compared to this.

She heard Ridley laughing and looked over at him. She yelled to be heard over the commotion. "What are they doing?"

But Ridley didn't answer. He just smiled and began moving. She looked down. His feet were shuffling so fast she didn't know how he kept his balance. He'd apparently done this before. And he was good! She giggled, but when he reached for her hand, she shook her head and backed away—and bumped into someone. She turned to apologize when Betsy's grin greeted her.

"Come on now, Missus Aberdeen," Betsy shouted. "I know you can do more than them stuffy ol' fancy dances!"

Olivia shook her head again, but felt Ridley grab her hand tight.

Big Ike jumped up on a bale of hay and yelled something, and couples began forming lines. Ridley steered her through the crowd to join Chloe and her husband at the end. Olivia didn't know what on earth they were doing, but Ridley had said to stay close, so she figured that was best.

"Give your partner a quick little hug," Big Ike called out in time with the music. Ridley did just that, as did the other men with their women. "Then turn her around and give her a tug."

Olivia raised a hand to object, but Ridley already had her spinning before giving her a bustle a quick yank. She felt her mouth slip open, then saw Uncle Bob and Rachel watching her from the side. Rachel was laughing so hard tears rolled down her face. And Olivia laughed too, trying to fix her hair where it had fallen down on the sides.

"Let it go," Ridley whispered. "You look beautiful."

"Pick up your ladies and give 'em a twirl," Big Ike called out, and Ridley obliged without a second's hesitation. "Then give her a kiss and make her your girl."

Seeing husbands and wives exchange quick but full-on-the-mouth kisses, Olivia started to panic … until Ridley placed a chaste little peck on her cheek. That earned him playful jeers from the men on either side of him, but he just grinned.

"Right foot up and a left foot down …"

Olivia did her best to follow along, taking cues from Ridley and Chloe, who had obviously done this before.

"And make that big foot jar the ground."

She pounded her right foot on the floor, out of breath but determined to keep up.

"Chew your tobacco and pinch your snuff …"

Feeling more than a little conspicuous, she mimicked those around her, chewing like an old woman.

"Now gals, meet your honey and show him your stuff."

She joined hands with Ridley but had no idea what "show him your stuff" meant. She tried to walk sassy like Chloe was doing, but her imitation only drew more laughter from those around her. From Ridley especially. But she didn't mind. Like that night at Julius and Betsy's cabin, she was having more fun than she could remember.

The song went on and on, and she was certain after a while that Big Ike was just making up phrases as he went. That dance led to another and another. And the later the night got, the funnier and more nonsensical the phrases became. But Ridley always acted the gentleman and, true to his word, stayed close to her, even when other couples parted to dance separately. Olivia had never danced or moved like this in her life, and she loved every minute of it.

"Would you like something to drink?" Ridley finally asked over the music, leading her to the side.

She nodded and claimed a seat on a hay bale, holding her hair up and fanning the back of her neck. "Yes, please!"

Ridley returned moments later with some cold cider that tasted like heaven—with a kick! With the back of her glove, Olivia dabbed her forehead, burning up. It might be mid-December outside but it felt like July inside.

"Why don't you take those off?" Ridley moved to help her take off the gloves.

"No!" she said, pulling away. "I mean … I'm fine. They … go with my dress."

"Olivia," he whispered. "You've already told me you have a scar." He glanced down. "May I see it?"

"No." She shook her head and tugged the left glove higher. "I'd prefer you not. It's … not attractive."

He leaned close. "Olivia, no scar of any kind could ever make you unattractive to me," he whispered, then brushed a feather-soft kiss on her cheek.

Whether it was the warmth of the room or her last defenses melting in a puddle at her feet, Olivia couldn't be certain. But she felt herself sway.

"If I show you my scar," he said softly, his tone playful while his expression was anything but, "will you show me yours?"

She stared, searching his eyes, and the curiosity was too much for her. She nodded. Having already shed his jacket, he unbuttoned the first four buttons of his shirt, then pulled it to the right. Her breath left her.

"You were shot … in the war?" she asked, already knowing the answer.

He nodded.

Instinctively, she reached out to touch the scar about the size of a coin on the upper right side of his chest, in his shoulder. Then pulled back, thinking better of it.

"It's all right." He took her hand. "It doesn't hurt anymore."

Gently, she touched the healed wound. She'd seen him shirtless before, but only at a distance. The puckered skin looked so familiar. Only her scar was much bigger. And jagged. And ugly. Yet, she felt him waiting. And she *had* agreed …

She edged the left glove downward, one inch at a time, feeling as if the marred flesh might go on forever. She watched his face and, to his credit, his features didn't change.

He held her arm, his thumb moving slowly, gently over the furrowed flesh. "It wasn't a clean break."

"No. Not at all."

"Was it painful?"

She nodded. "Though no more than yours, I'm sure."

He lifted her hand as though he were going to kiss it. Or even worse, her scar. She quickly pulled the glove back on. The look Ridley gave her said he thought her actions uncalled for, but he didn't argue.

They danced the next two dances, slower tunes this time, and she felt a difference in the way he held her. Closer, more possessive, and she liked the change.

The twang of a banjo announced the next tune would be another lively one, and Olivia politely waved off Ridley's invitation, wanting to rest. He led her to the side.

"Would you mind if I asked Rachel to dance?" he asked.

She looked over and saw Rachel standing against the wall, smiling but alone. "Not at all. My feet will thank you."

He grinned and squeezed her hand. "I'm so proud of you. Thank you for coming tonight. And for being with me."

"I'm always proud to be with you, Ridley."

He stilled and touched her face. "I'll be back," he whispered.

She enjoyed the chance to sit and watch but was glad when Uncle Bob made his way over. He pointed to the empty space on the hay bale beside her, and she motioned for him to sit. She hadn't seen him dancing at all. Maybe he had an aversion to it. Some men did.

"You enjoyin' yourself, ma'am?"

Olivia grinned. "Doesn't it look like it?"

He laughed. "Yes, ma'am. It sure do. It's good to see you havin' fun, Missus Aberdeen."

She might have been imagining it, but she could almost hear a silent *after all you've been through* tacked onto the end of his sentence. "Thank you, Uncle Bob. It feels good to laugh."

"Hmmm." He nodded. "Laughter sure helps you through the hard times. And makes the good ones even better."

She studied his profile, imagining what hard times he must've seen in his life, here, at Belle Meade. "Ridley says you've taught him so much. He admires you a great deal."

"He's a good man, ma'am. And I feel the same 'bout him. Wish he wasn't leavin' come June."

Wishing the same thing, Olivia sought Ridley out in the crowd. He was still dancing with Rachel. If anyone knew Ridley, it was Uncle

Bob. Maybe the man could shed light on why Ridley seemed so bound and determined to leave here. And to leave her.

"Who knows, Uncle Bob. Maybe something will happen and he'll choose to stay. Maybe he'll decide he likes the South, after all."

Seconds passed. Uncle Bob finally turned to her. He studied her with old-soul eyes and a careful regard that told her he knew she was fishing.

She bowed her head.

"You ever said that to him, ma'am? What you just said to me?"

She looked up and nodded. "He said that come June, no matter what, he *will* be leaving."

Uncle Bob turned back to the crowd. She waited and had all but given up on his responding when she heard his voice.

"Life is full of choices, ma'am. Most we live once, then move on and forget. But others" — he narrowed his eyes — "we live a thousand times over and remember for the rest of our days. What's important is knowin' how to tell 'em apart. And then decidin' if you's willin' to pay the price. 'Cause choices ... they always come at a price."

Olivia stared, knowing they were still talking about Ridley but not understanding what Uncle Bob meant. She could easily see her own life in light of his words. Charles Aberdeen had been a choice made *for* her. General Meeks was a choice being made *for* her. When would it be her turn to choose? Or would that time ever come without *her* making a choice first?

She'd chosen to teach at the freedmen's school, and God had opened that door. She glanced back at Uncle Bob, wondering if he knew about the school and that she'd be the teacher, and if maybe that was part of his reason for talking about choices just now. Something told her yes. She looked around, wondering if others here knew as well.

"Ho!" Uncle Bob grinned. "Finally! It's a slow one comin' up, Missus Aberdeen. You best get yourself back on out there, ma'am. Ridley's gonna be lookin' for ya."

Hearing the music, Olivia had a thought. "Do you like to dance, Uncle Bob?"

"Sure I do. Just some nights I can't get this ol' leg of mine" — he gripped his right thigh — "to stay up with me."

"Well." Olivia rose and fluffed her skirts. "They're playing a slow one now."

He looked up at her like she'd suddenly grown a third eye.

"Life is full of choices, Mr. Green. Is it not?"

He stared at her for the longest time, then stood. "Yes, ma'am. It is. But they come at a price, like I said. Some of 'em awful high." Her heart fell a little, and she moved to sit back down. "But once you make a choice, ma'am, you got to stand on it. Firm and strong. Can't let nothin' move you from it."

Understanding even more now why Ridley admired this man so much, Olivia took her place on the dance floor and slipped her hand into Uncle Bob's.

Chapter
FORTY-SIX

*H*er stomach in knots, Olivia was so excited she could hardly stand it. Her first real class tonight. Well, their first *meeting*, anyway. She checked the clock on the dining room mantle. Twenty-five minutes past seven. She still had thirty-five minutes before the appointed time, and it was only a twenty minute walk through the woods to the cabin. She'd timed it a week ago. Though she'd never walked it in the dark before.

She glanced around the table and caught Mary's eye. The girl smiled, and Olivia returned it. Ever since the night of the reception, things had been different between them. In a good way. Over brunch that next day, Mary had given Olivia a lengthy and delightful summary of the evening, complete with details of Adelicia Acklen's home. But it was what Mary had done—or was doing—with the party favor the Harding family had received that truly touched her.

The clock on the mantle chimed. Olivia looked over. Half past the hour. She glanced around the table. They'd started dinner later than usual, and she couldn't very well ask to be excused while others were still eating.

But she still had time …

The meeting tonight was an opportunity for her to introduce herself and meet the students. She only hoped people showed up. What if, after all this, it was only Jimmy and Jolene?

Guilt chided her. She knew she was making a difference in their two lives, but was it so wrong to want to do more? Obliging Mr. Pagette's and Elizabeth's counsel, she hadn't told anyone about her teaching. Not even Ridley. Though she'd wanted to tell him many times during the past month, imagining how proud he'd be.

Since the night of the party, she'd thought often about what Uncle Bob had said to her about choices. She glanced down the table at the general.

She could choose to object to this arranged marriage with General Meeks. But in doing so, she'd not only be spitting, as it were, in the face of tradition, but in the face of this family's honor and generosity. She'd had nowhere to go and they had taken her in. They'd given her a home and welcomed her into their family. A union with Percival Meeks would provide for Belle Meade's financial future. How could she *not* agree to this?

Especially when Ridley had said nothing about desiring a future with her. Nor had he indicated any intention of changing his mind about leaving. So what choice did that leave her?

"Thank you for dinner, Mother."

Across the table from her, Selene tucked her napkin by her plate. Olivia checked the mantle clock again. Seven-thirty-five.

Mary and Cousin Lizzie asked to be excused, and Olivia quickly followed suit.

"Thank you for dinner, Aunt Elizabeth." Olivia smiled. "You as well, General."

"Olivia, do you have a moment?"

Hearing the general's voice, Olivia hesitated in the doorway.

"It won't take long, I assure you."

Biting the inside of her cheek, she nodded and followed him into the library. General Harding stood before the mantle, above which hung a recently commissioned, near life-sized portrait of himself that stared down in austere fashion. It was as if there were two of him. And for a moment, Olivia couldn't decide which one was more intimidating.

"General Meeks tells me you've been exchanging letters, Olivia. He also shared that you've been rather ... forthcoming in yours."

Able to guess now why he'd requested to speak with her, Olivia resisted the urge to look away. What she'd done, she'd done with pure motives. "Yes, sir. I have. I believe General Meeks has a right to know who I am and ... what my past has been. Just as I have inquired about his."

"Yes, I know." The general picked up an envelope from the table behind him. "He's written me in detail, quite eloquently in fact, about what you wrote to him. Were you under the impression, Olivia, that I was attempting to hide from him the details of your ... *situation,* as it was, before you came to live with us?"

"No, sir. Not ... hide, exactly." Seeing the arch of his eyebrow, she hurried to explain. "But I know how easy, even tempting, it can be to ... frame details in a certain light when a person desires a specific outcome. I was merely attempting to be honest with him, General."

The general's gaze grew appraising. "Very well stated, Olivia. But I'm not naive to the fact that you don't want to marry General Meeks. Are you certain the tiniest part of you didn't reveal this to him with the hope that he'd change his mind about you?"

Feeling a tad exposed, and with good reason, she had to smile. "At first, yes, that was my motive. But I tore up that letter, General, and started again."

Surprise sharpened his features.

"I did my best to be honest and forthright, without attempting to color General Meeks's opinion of me. If I had the letter I sent him, I would happily let you read it."

General Harding pulled a folded piece of paper from the envelope. She recognized the stationery. "I have read it, Olivia. General Meeks returned it to me. With the purpose, he stated, of crediting your character. After reading your letter—and hearing you just now—I, too, wish to convey my appreciation for your candor with him and for how you're approaching this entire situation. It's"—he briefly looked away—"of significant importance to me. And to you too, of course," he added quickly.

She nodded. "Of course." Seeing the time, she turned to go.

"One last caution, Olivia ... And I share this only because I'm aware of how others can sometimes form false impressions."

That drew her attention back.

"Take care in who you spend your time with. Friendships, even those most innocent, can often be misconstrued by others and seen in a very different light."

It took a moment for what he said to sink in, but when it did, she realized who he must be talking about. *Ridley.* Knowing the general was aware of their friendship gave her pause. But not overly so. Because as she watched him—his head lowered, his brow furrowed as he fingered the letter—she glimpsed a side of General William Giles Harding she'd not seen before. One Elizabeth had told her about. And she realized she wasn't the only one agonizing over the decisions facing her. The only difference was ...

After all was said and done, *she* would be the one living with the choice a thousand times over. Not General Harding.

Olivia tugged the collar of her coat closer about her neck and headed in the direction of the stallions' stable, then kept walking. She only had ten minutes to get there, and it was so dark. She hadn't stepped ten feet into the woods when she heard something rustle in the trees beside her.

She turned, hand raised in defense.

"Missus Aberdeen, it's me, Big Ike."

She breathed again.

"I come to see you there safe, ma'am."

"Bless you, Ike." She laughed, but it came out high pitched and stilted. "I guess I'm a little nervous."

"I guess you got reason to be, ma'am."

She didn't find his admission comforting.

With an ease surely born of experience, Big Ike led her through the woods, holding branches back and helping her over a fallen log until, finally, the hunting cabin came into view. The windows were dark, and Olivia wondered again if anyone had come.

Then she caught a whiff of woodsmoke.

Big Ike opened the door and the palest sliver of light jumped out, illuminating the darkness. She realized then that they probably had curtains on the windows. Readying her expression so her disappointment wouldn't show, no matter how few pupils, she stepped inside and felt her fragile hope split wide open.

The room was packed. People stood shoulder to shoulder. Sixty, at least. Maybe more. And of all ages. Most of the faces were familiar, but some were not. Men, women, boys, and girls. Even ...

"Rachel," Olivia whispered, grasping Rachel's outstretched hands.

"Welcome to your class, Missus Aberdeen." Rachel gestured to everyone gathered. "I think I can say for all of us, ma'am, that we's grateful you came."

But Olivia shook her head, knowing the far greater truth. "I'm the one who's grateful ... for all of you."

Chapter
FORTY-SEVEN

Mindful of Seabird being with foal, but knowing the exercise was good for her, Ridley kept the mare to an amble and urged her back up the meadow toward the main house. A thin dusting of snow that would be gone by mid-morning lay across the land like lace on a freshly made bed, and he cut across the south pasture, his and Seabird's breath puffing white in the cold.

When he topped the hill, the sun peeked through the clouds causing the iced tree limbs to sparkle like diamonds. Belle Meade rose in the distance like a crowning jewel. How he'd happened into all this, he didn't know. Then again — his gaze moved to the old Harding cabin — he did. And he knew it wasn't by accident.

Near the end of January, almost two weeks ago, he'd ridden up to the high pasture, just him and Miss Birdie, and after scouting the hills, he'd finally found the ridge where he and Uncle Bob had first met. He'd camped there for the night, needing some time to think. It had been good for him. It wasn't until he'd unpacked his bedroll that he found the Bible Uncle Bob had sneaked in before he left. The Bible he'd been reading from at night, at Uncle Bob's request.

He felt a stirring inside him. So much for that book being just words dried on a page, like he'd thought that first Sunday when he'd read aloud in church.

As he neared the main house, he thought he heard someone yelling. He cocked his head, listening.

But ... nothing.

His gaze trailed up the lattice to the bedroom window on the second floor. It'd been five days since he'd seen her, and it felt like a lifetime. He couldn't imagine how it would feel come June, just four short months from now. Winter months at Belle Meade were busier than he'd thought they would be. Olivia seemed busier too. But also happier than he'd ever seen her. Which bothered him a little, seeing as he missed their time alone together. But the evenings she visited him and Uncle Bob at the cabin were good ones. And it wasn't as though he could just go calling on her at the mansion.

He reined in by the kitchen, having foregone breakfast before riding out earlier, and heard laughter—or more like a commotion— coming from inside. He recognized Betsy's cackle above it all.

"Oh, come on, Missus Aberdeen. You can do better than that!"

"Hit it harder, ma'am!"

"Smack it good this time!"

"Show it what for, ma'am!"

He dismounted, looped Seabird's reins around a limb, and peered through the partially opened kitchen door. He couldn't believe his eyes.

Olivia wielded a rolling pin high above her head and—with a grimace—brought it down with a *thwack* on a mess of dough spread out over the table. All while Susanna, Betsy, Chloe, and Rachel cheered her on.

He pushed open the door. "What in the world are all you women doing in here?"

Olivia looked up, saw him, and beamed. "I'm making biscuits, Ridley! This is the part where we beat them!"

Betsy laughed even louder, holding her side. "Oh Lawd, I ain't laughed this much in ages. You here just in time, Mr. Cooper. She been namin' everybody who ever done her wrong!"

Ridley laughed. He reached over to wipe the flour from Olivia's cheeks before realizing it would be a losing battle.

She held out the rolling pin. "Do you want to have a try?"

He backed away, hands raised in a truce. "Unfortunately, I have a meeting with the general."

Her shoulders sagged.

"But!" He smiled. "I'll stop by later for one of your biscuits."

"Is that a promise, Mr. Cooper?" she said, one pert little eyebrow raised.

He didn't miss the looks the other four women exchanged. But he knew they were good at keeping secrets. The secrets that mattered, anyway.

"It's a promise, Mrs. Aberdeen. I *will* be back for that biscuit."

He closed the kitchen door on their laughter, wondering if Olivia had any idea how little she resembled the oh-so-prim-and-proper young woman he'd pulled from the carriage on the road to Belle Meade. And yet how much more of a lady—strong, confident, and caring ... not to mention, desirable—she was in his eyes.

A woman fit for the Colorado Territory if he'd ever seen one.

"Before you share *another* new idea with me, Mr. Cooper ..." General Harding eased back in his chair, the creak of fine leather competing with the crackle of fire in the hearth. "I'd like a report on the progress of the yearling sale."

"It's progressing very well, sir. Uncle Bob tells me he's never seen a finer group of yearlings here at Belle Meade. The stable hands are taking the training and care of the yearlings more seriously too—or most of them are—since they have a vested interest in the outcome."

"Most of them?"

"Some of the men, a handful of the white men—"

"Grady Matthews and his like," the general said, a scowl forming.

Ridley nodded. "They don't like the Negroes being paid the same amount they are."

"I pay all my workers fairly, Mr. Cooper. And I'm proud of my contract system. So if any worker doesn't like it, he can speak to me."

"That's precisely what I told Grady and the other men. But ... I wanted to make you aware of it."

The general nodded, eying him. "Now ... about that *vested interest* for the stable hands ..."

Ridley's defenses rose. How many times had they discussed this before the general had finally signed off on it? If the man changed his mind now ...

"I'm wondering, Mr. Cooper ... You designed an incentive for the stable hands by assigning a specific foal to each of them whereby the more money the yearling brings, the higher percentage they earn. And yet ... you ignored the most important part of the overall equation."

Not following, Ridley shook his head. "Sir?"

"You failed to incorporate a similar incentive for yourself." Hinting at a smile, General Harding wrote something on a sheet of paper. "So I'd like to propose that if the overall earnings on the yearling sale exceed a set amount, then you will personally receive 5 percent of that total."

Ridley knew better than to get excited. "And just what would that set amount be, General Harding?"

The general turned the paper and slid it across the desk, and it was Ridley's turn to smile.

"That's a very ambitious goal, General Harding. Has anything near that amount been earned by any yearling sale you know of?"

"Belle Meade is known for doing what no other thoroughbred farm in the country can do, Mr. Cooper. After all, those silver cups and trophies lining the entrance hall didn't just walk in here by themselves."

Ridley tried not to think of the money 5 percent would amount to if they reached the general's goal. But the figure popped into his head and wouldn't leave. That would go a long way toward building a ranch in the Colorado Territory. But they'd never reach that goal through a typical sale, which provided the opening he needed.

"I told you, sir, that I had another idea I wanted to discuss with you."

"Another incentive, Mr. Cooper?"

"No, sir. It's actually a different way to approach the sale itself. Remember the thoroughbred sale we traveled to in Gallatin? Although it wasn't a yearling sale, you said it represented every sale you'd ever been to."

The general's hurried nod hinted at impatience.

"I propose, sir" — Ridley leaned forward — "that we have an auction instead of a sale. We could invite buyers to come early in the day, view the stock, ask whatever questions they may have about the foals' lineage. Maybe we offer to give them a tour of the plantation, in case they don't know what else Belle Meade offers. Then that afternoon, we'll present the stock for the bidding."

Harding nodded slowly. "Go on."

"We could advertise not only in the Nashville papers, but Lexington, Mobile, and Charleston, as well as the Southern markets, which everyone knows have been hit hard. But also in the New York papers. And Chicago, Philadelphia, and Washington, DC. Up north where more of the money is. And instead of making it an event where only men come to buy yearlings, let's invite the wives too. We'll roast a few pigs. Maybe ask Susanna and the other women to make some of those beaten biscuits everybody loves."

The image of Olivia wielding that rolling pin like a weapon earlier came to mind, tempting him to smile. But seeing the thoughts churning behind Harding's eyes, he continued.

"I'd also suggest having a meeting, or maybe a dinner, say—a couple of nights or so before the event, for your primary Southern buyers. A chance to show them the stock and explain the auction process, should you decide to go that route. While you're inviting breeders from the North, I still think it would be wise, in the interest of local relations, to make sure Belle Meade's neighbors feel a special invitation. Even if they're outbid in the end, the hospitality will go far in relaying your gratitude for their support."

For a long moment, the general studied him over tented hands. Then he rose. "Mr. Cooper." General Harding reached across the desk to offer his hand. "With men like you, I don't see how we lost the war."

The comment hit Ridley like a blow square in the chest. Slowly, heavily he came to his feet, staring at the general's hand. The room grew warmer, and he found himself confronted with all the opportunities he'd been given since coming to Belle Meade. He thought about how different his life—his future—would be without them and about how every one of those opportunities could be traced back, in some way, to this man.

Not wanting to, but feeling as though he had no choice, Ridley shook the general's hand.

Harding rounded the corner of the desk. "Frankly, your understanding of this business surprises me, Mr. Cooper. It's quite impressive."

Ridley cleared his throat, working to find his voice again. "Thank you, sir. But most of what I've learned, I've learned from Uncle Bob. The ideas I presented are all ones he and I have discussed at length together. He's a good man. Belle Meade's fortunate to have him."

The general nodded, reaching for the door. "Yes, I know. Now, about that percentage for you, Mr. Cooper. I believe the goal I set forth is realistic, especially with the idea of the auction."

Ridley followed General Harding outside to the covered porch, listening as the man expounded on the details. He welcomed the chill in the air, his conscience still stinging. It wasn't as if he'd directly lied to the man. He'd simply never allowed their conversations to drift too deeply into areas he knew could cost him his job.

As the general continued to discuss possibilities, Ridley followed along, nodding on occasion, commenting when necessary. All while trying to come to terms with why his omission of a very few—yet quite consequential—facts about his past hadn't bothered him before nearly as much as they did now. And when he finally realized why, the reason struck him as humorous.

"Is something about that idea amusing to you, Mr. Cooper?"

Ridley looked beside him. "Not at all, sir. I think it's a very good idea. The men will certainly appreciate it."

"Very well, then. Have Mrs. Aberdeen order whatever's necessary."

"Yes, sir. I'll do that." Ridley turned to go.

"By chance, Mr. Cooper ... Have you given my job offer further consideration?"

Ridley looked back.

"It still stands, by the way." The general fingered his beard. "Most firmly."

"I appreciate that, General Harding. More than you realize, sir. But—"

"But you believe something better awaits you out west. Is that it?" Doubt thickened the general's voice.

"Yes, sir." Ridley nodded. "I'd like to think so."

"What if, come June"—General Harding peered across the meadow—"assuming all goes as I believe it will, I were to offer you the position of *head* foreman? Would that be of interest?"

"Belle Meade doesn't have a position of head foreman."

"It can. And will. If I deem it so."

Not in a thousand years could Ridley have imagined this set of circumstances. The situation was full of irony. Here he was, a former Union soldier being offered the top position at the grandest plantation in Dixie, by a man who—at one time—was one of the largest slave-holders in the South. A position which he'd never have been offered, much less have been qualified for, without the help of Bob Green, a man enslaved by General Harding for almost the whole of his life.

Ridley felt that sharp sting of guilt again and, with all traces of humor gone, acknowledged what it was. Even with all the differences between him and this man—and there were plenty—he'd come to genuinely respect General William Giles Harding.

"I greatly appreciate your trust, General. But even if you were to offer me the position of head foreman, I would still politely decline, sir."

To his surprise, Harding grinned, something he didn't see often.

"You never disappoint, Mr. Cooper. But not to worry, I always get what I want ... in the end."

Chapter
FORTY-EIGHT

These biscuits are even better now than they were two days ago."

Olivia glanced up from her notes. "You're just being nice, Ridley. But thank you."

"No, I'm serious." He shook his head, looking more like a little boy than the ruggedly handsome man he was. "I like them better when they get a little crunch to them."

Olivia smiled her thanks and looked back at the page, searching for the next entry. Though she was warm enough in her coat and gloves, the supply room in the mares' stable did little to keep out February's chill. She felt the urge to yawn. The late nights at the old hunting cabin were catching up to her.

She'd been teaching for a month now, and she'd never done anything that gave her more satisfaction and a greater sense of accomplishment than teaching. The children—who she taught five mornings a week—were like little sponges, soaking up the knowledge. There were a handful of adults, Rachel and Jedediah among them, who were progressing well too. But the majority of the adults were taking longer to grasp reading and writing than she had anticipated. But who could expect otherwise when they worked all day, then attended classes for three hours at night, three nights a week, only to get back up a few hours later and start all over again? The schedule was demanding. Yet their dedication and enthusiasm was infectious. And Olivia was loving every minute of it.

She found the entry she was looking for and made a check mark. "I've ordered the shirts General Harding wants for all the stable hands, so you can mark that off your list."

He did. "And when will they be ready?"

"In a couple of weeks. No later than the first week of March."

"Very good." He jotted something in the margin. "I came by last night but you didn't answer."

Feeling his attention, Olivia kept her gaze on her notes, knowing her eyes would betray her. She didn't like hiding the fact from him that she was teaching in the freedmen's school. It didn't feel right. But she'd given her word.

"You came by? Do you mean … you knocked on my bedroom door?"

"No, on your window," he said softly. "But not to worry, I didn't peek."

She lifted her head and, seeing his grin, she had to smile. "I'm sorry I missed you coming by. What time was it?"

"Mmmm …" He shrugged. "Around eleven or so."

She returned her attention to the page. "Aunt Elizabeth and I visited late into the night, I'm afraid." Which was true. But they'd visited *after* she'd returned from teaching her evening class, which hadn't been until close to midnight.

She stifled another yawn.

"You sure seem tired recently. I'm sorry that a lot of the extra work for the auction is falling on you."

"Don't be. I'm enjoying it." She pointed to his notebook. "What else is on your list?"

She watched him as he read silently, looking at his hands, then his muscular forearms. She was chilly, yet he seemed comfortable in a chambray shirt with his sleeves rolled up to his elbows. Working on the auction was adding to the weight of teaching, managing the plantation's inventory, and still being a part-time companion to Aunt Elizabeth. But it also added to the time she could spend with him, so she wasn't about to complain.

But she *did* feel the clock ticking.

Her motivation for wanting to make the auction the best it could be wasn't selfless either. If the event was as successful as she anticipated, General Harding would surely make Ridley an offer he couldn't refuse. One that would make Ridley realize the South was still his home.

At least that was her hope.

Her other hope was that General Meeks—whose rheumatism, per his last letter, had seen some improvement, perhaps due to his recently employed live-in nursemaid—was a proponent of faithful yet *very* platonic marriages. Because try as she might, and she was trying, she simply couldn't imagine living with the man as husband and wife.

Not after having been kissed — and quite thoroughly — by the man in front of her, who was the last man on earth who needed a nursemaid.

"Olivia?"

She blinked.

"You look a little dazed. Are you sure you wouldn't prefer to do this later?"

Glad her thoughts were hidden from him, she gave him a tiny smirk. "Not at all. I'm just waiting on you." She eyed him. "Why? Are you trying to get out of work, Mr. Cooper?"

He smiled. "You finally figured me out, Mrs. Aberdeen."

She looked at him, wishing that were the case.

Over the next few weeks, as February slipped into March and March into April, the daylight hours lengthened, yet the days themselves seemed to grow shorter. No matter how long Olivia worked, there was always more to do. But she welcomed the busyness. It made it easier not to think about what was coming.

In so many ways.

After teaching an early morning session, she dismissed class and walked with the children as far as the edge of the woods. She returned to the mansion as she always did in the daylight, by way of Rachel's cabin. Sometimes she stopped to visit. But not today.

Back in her room, she deposited her books and teaching materials in a drawer, and as she turned to leave, she spotted the unique hand-painted candy box on her desk.

That sweet Mary ...

The candy box was a party favor from the reception the Hardings had attended at the Belmont Mansion. And following that night, Mary had taken to sneaking the little box into Olivia's room and leaving her something inside. A note, one of Rachel's caramels, a flower petal. Olivia would wait two or three days and then sneak it right back over to Mary's room, with something inside for her. It had become a game of sorts. A way — at first — to mend the once-tenuous relationship. And now, to show acceptance and appreciation without words.

Eager to discover what Mary had left this time, Olivia carefully lifted the lid to find a fragile blue robin's egg inside. At first glance, she thought it was an unbroken egg. But looking more closely, she saw tiny cracks.

Gently, not wanting to crush it, she lifted the eggshell from the box. It was no heavier than a fluff of down. She held it up to the light and turned the eggshell this way and that, appreciating its vivid color. She marveled at the minuscule fissures that revealed the struggle of the chick who had bravely fought its way through the barrier of one tiny, confining world into a much larger, freer one. How Mary had put the eggshell back together, she didn't know.

Olivia returned it to the hand-painted box, and as she left her bedroom to go meet Ridley for their monthly excursion to the quarries, she thought about what she could put into the box next, while doing her best not to think about how she and Ridley had only one month or so left together. A thought that never strayed far.

A short while later, as Ridley guided the tiny horse cart up into the hills—their conversation spare, their bodies touching—Olivia worked to memorize everything about him. A cool breeze carrying the promise of spring lifted the hair at his collar, and she resisted the urge to reach over and touch him.

Thinking again of the brave fledgling who had pecked its way from the eggshell, she searched every low-hanging limb and bushy shrub they passed, wondering if the plucky little chick was still here at Belle Meade or if it had flown away to find a new life.

Chapter
FORTY-NINE

$\mathscr{C}$hin up and chest out, Jimmy!"

Jimmy did exactly as Ridley said, only to an extreme.

Holding back a smile, Ridley snapped the boy a smart salute before continuing down the center aisle of the stable. Each of the men who'd been assigned a foal in recent months stood outside their respective yearling's stall. And with humor, Ridley noticed how all of them, without exception, now had their chins up and chests puffed out.

He could scarcely believe it, but in just two weeks, all the months of work—the training and planning, the endless hours of exercising the foals, watching their health and diet better than they watched their own—would come down to one day. Saturday, June the first. The day of Belle Meade's first yearling auction.

This dress rehearsal, as they were calling it, was actually Uncle Bob's idea, and it was a good one. The stable hands, decked out in their matching tan trousers and crimson-colored shirts, all stood proudly at attention. Seeing their expectant expressions and knowing how hard they'd all worked, Ridley felt a swell of pride—both in them and in what they'd accomplished together.

"Well done, men. *Well* done!"

Smiles broke across their faces, and a few hollers went up. As Ridley walked back down the aisle, he shook each man's hand and looked him squarely in the eye, appreciating how each man did the same with him.

Yet as difficult as it was for him to imagine the auction being almost here, it was even harder to wrap his mind around the fact that it had been a year—almost to the day—since he'd first walked up the long road to Belle Meade. And only two weeks remained until he'd retrace his steps and leave it behind him forever.

"Cooper!"

Ridley turned to see Grady Matthews walking toward him, along with three other men. He was surprised he and Matthews hadn't come to blows again, as they had on his first day here. But he figured his position as foreman had corralled Grady's temper. While Uncle Bob's patient nature had, no doubt, harnessed his.

Matthews planted himself firmly in front of him, arms crossed. "Me and my men, we decided we want to be part of this auction, after all. We might work mostly with the stallions, but we figure we got a right to it, more so than these darkies. So you need to give us a job and whatever you're paying them."

"And just how do you figure that, Matthews? These men have been working for months with these yearlings. You had the same opportunity they did to sign up to be considered for training one of the foals. But you chose not to."

"I ain't gonna *compete* with some darkie for a job."

"That's your choice, Matthews. But realize that's what it is." Ridley looked at each of the men. "*Your* choice."

Ridley made to leave, but Grady stepped forward.

"It ain't fair, Cooper. And if you don't do somethin', we're takin' it to the general."

Ridley motioned, aware of Uncle Bob coming up from behind. "There's the door. Be my guest, gentlemen."

Grady went red in the face. "This ain't the last of this, Cooper. And this ... auction?" He laughed beneath his breath. "Just between us ... It may not turn out as good as you think."

Ridley stepped closer. "I'll be sure and pass along that threat to General Harding, Matthews, just in case anything should go wrong with this auction. As will Uncle Bob."

The men turned as a group and strode off, Grady muttering under his breath.

Ridley watched them. "I know the connection between Grady's father and General Harding, but I don't know why Harding keeps him around."

"Don't let Grady Matthews worry you none, sir. He's a hard talker but when it comes to it, he ain't got the stuffin', much less the smarts, to do much harm."

Ridley had to smile.

"But some of them buddies o' his ..." Uncle Bob sighed. "Them fellas is mean."

All Ridley could think about was how hard everyone had worked on the auction. If Grady Matthews and his men—

"But you know what, sir?" Uncle Bob clapped Ridley on the shoulder. "We ain't gonna talk 'bout them no more. 'Cause everythin's lookin' real good, ain't it?"

"It sure is." Ridley held out his hand. "Thanks mostly to you."

Uncle Bob's grip was oak-tree strong. But he shook his head. "Oh no, sir. I ain't even nearly done this by myself. You and me ... We just make a good team."

They walked outside together. The last hour of sunlight lay golden over the fields. The warmth of May had returned a lushness to Belle Meade that winter had thieved, and Ridley breathed deeply, catching traces of lilac and hay. He loved this time of evening. Dusk fell so gently here, making the onset of night feel almost like a gift.

Seabird nickered from the corral and sauntered toward them, heavy with foal. Ridley met her at the fence and rubbed her behind the ears.

"Don't you worry, sir. She gonna do fine this time." Uncle Bob pulled an apple from his pocket.

Ridley nodded. "I think she will too."

Still two weeks—maybe three, the doctor had said—before she was due to foal. The timing of that with the auction and his departure was far from perfect, but Seabird hadn't much taken that into account the day she jumped the fence. He knew Harding would be fine if he asked to stay for a few extra days for the mare and foal to gain strength enough to travel. Ridley just wanted them both to come through it all right.

He looked toward the main house, to Olivia's window, and felt that tightness in his chest again.

What would she do if he told her everything outright, confessed it all, asked her to forgive him for not being honest with her from the start about his past? What if he did all that, then asked her to come with him? To leave all this behind—Aunt Elizabeth and the Harding family, her new home, the relationships with the servants, and her all-but-guaranteed marriage to a very wealthy Confederate general—all to start a new life with him in the shadow of the Rocky Mountains. There were moments when he almost thought about doing it. And rarer moments when he thought she might actually consider it. Then he'd quickly come to his senses.

Why would she leave all this to live in a one-room cabin in a land that was as rugged and brutal as it was beautiful?

But the main thing that kept him from telling her—the thing that felt like a saber between his ribs, even now—was imagining what it would be like to see himself through her eyes as a traitor, a turncoat, a deserter.

"Head foreman of Belle Meade, Ridley?" Uncle Bob's voice pulled him back. "That ain't nothin' to spit at, sir."

"I'm not spitting at it." Ridley looked over at him. "I appreciate the general's offer. But you know I couldn't accept it without telling him the truth. And if I told him the truth ..." His laugh came out flat.

"If you go and tell the general that, sir ..." Uncle Bob sighed. "You might as well have your bags already packed and waitin' at the station. 'Cause you ain't gonna be stayin' round long after that. And for sure not once other folks get word."

Ridley nodded, getting in one last rub before Seabird moved on down the fence.

"But Ridley, one thing you got to know ... There ain't no doubt in my mind, the Lawd led you to the mountain that night. Any other man would o' took the general's thoroughbreds with nary a thought. Might've even shot me in the back. But not you. No, sir. Way I see it, you was meant to be here at Belle Meade, Ridley. Least for the time that you was. And I sure—" Uncle Bob's voice broke. He looked out across the pasture. "And I sure am thankin' him for that 'bout now."

It took a moment for Ridley to speak. "Just like I'm thanking him for you ... for all you've given me."

Uncle Bob nodded, his gaze still averted.

"But if I don't go to the Colorado Territory now," Ridley continued, "I don't think I'll get the chance again. Not like this. I've got one more year to make improvements on my land there before it goes back to the government. Last summer when I checked, the land and title agent told me there were over a thousand names on his list just waiting for prime land like mine to open." Ridley would have felt funny saying what he said next to anyone other than Uncle Bob. And maybe Olivia. "But what makes me more sure is that I think I'm meant to be out there. Looking back, I can almost see how God's been working things. Even ... working in my own heart to—"

"Mr. Cooper!"

Ridley turned, his guard rising again when he saw who was walking toward them. "General Harding, how are you, sir?"

The general nodded to Uncle Bob before swinging his focus back to Ridley. "Plans are coming along well, I take it? We're going to be ready?"

"Yes, sir." Ridley included Uncle Bob in his acknowledgement. "We'll be ready."

"Good." Harding gave a satisfied sigh. "Very good." He turned to go, then paused. "At the dinner we're having … the night before the auction …"

"Yes, sir?"

"I want you there. To explain the process to everyone, to answer questions."

Ridley hesitated. Social events such as that weren't high on his list. But it also bothered him that Uncle Bob wasn't being included and would likely never receive an invitation to such a gathering. "Perhaps, instead, sir, Uncle Bob and I could meet with the—"

"I said I want *you* there, Mr. Cooper. Is there a reason why that isn't possible?"

Ridley stared, feeling the none-too-subtle challenge. "No, sir. No reason. But I *would* appreciate the chance for—"

"Uncle Bob," the general said, shifting his attention, "would you be available the morning of the auction to give tours of the stables to the guests? I think a great many of them would be interested to see the champion thoroughbreds. *And* to meet the head hostler of Belle Meade."

Uncle Bob nodded, smoothing his apron. "Why, yes, General. I be happy to. Real happy."

Harding threw Ridley a brief but pointed look of satisfaction as he walked away, and Ridley had to smile. Yes, there were definitely things he would miss about Belle Meade.

Later that evening, after dark and under the guise of needing to confirm a detail about the auction, Ridley finally gave in to the desire to see Olivia. He left the cabin and headed for the main house. Or namely, the window above the lattice.

He was nearly there when—he couldn't believe his eyes—there she came around the corner of the house, heading straight for the old Harding cabin and him. He paused by the dogwood tree, not wanting to frighten her, but more than a little pleased that she'd had the same idea.

She cradled something against her chest — books, he guessed — and she glanced behind her as though making sure no one was watching. He waited, biding his time, when, not ten feet from him, she veered and headed in the direction of the stallions' stable.

Confused and a little disappointed, he waited a few seconds, then a few more, then followed her. Past the stable and the corrals and — into the woods? Where on earth was the woman going?

The woods were thick and dark, and he couldn't see more than a handful of yards ahead of him. But following her wasn't hard. Not with the carpet of wintered leaves and branches littering the ground, and not with her wide skirt robbing any chance of her moving stealthily through the foliage. He hadn't followed her but a few yards when he realized ...

She wasn't alone. He heard hushed voices.

He followed her for at least a half mile, then another, and was about to make his presence known when, just ahead, the woods opened into a small clearing. He made out the palest outline of a cabin and saw Olivia going inside — by herself — just as a vice-like grip clamped hard around the back of his neck.

Chapter
FIFTY

*T*ired from teaching yet invigorated at the same time, Olivia stood at the door and whispered a word of encouragement to each of her students as they left, so proud of their progress. But she still wondered why Big Ike hadn't joined them like he usually did. He was always a little late. After walking her to the clearing, it took him a few minutes to check in with the men keeping watch in the woods. But she thought she knew the real reason for his tardiness.

Susanna had confided earlier that week that Big Ike sometimes got frustrated, because he wasn't learning as quickly as he wanted to. Olivia had tried to encourage him on their way here tonight, and he'd admitted to recognizing a few words in the newspaper now. Hearing him say that told her a lot. Ike Carter would learn to read and write soon enough. He just needed to be reminded that people believed in him. Something she understood only too well.

After the last person left, Olivia gathered her teaching materials and, one by one, blew out the lanterns set randomly on the floor. No desks yet, but Mr. Pagette had said those should be coming within a month, depending on available funds. She considered them fortunate to have as many books as they did. The additional money she'd made from the quarries had helped purchase those.

Kneeling to blow out another lamp, she heard Big Ike walking in behind her. He always waited to walk her back. She rose. "Ike, I wondered where you—" She blinked. *"Ridley?"*

"Olivia." He stood just inside the doorway. "How was your *class* this evening?"

His voice sounded ... flat. *Different.* She sensed his surprise. "Class went very well, thank you." She couldn't blame him if this had caught him a little off guard. She smiled, eager for him to understand what part he'd played in her decision to do this. "Ridley, I've wanted to tell you about this. *So* many times, but . . ." Aunt Elizabeth's name had been on the tip of her tongue before she caught herself. "But I was asked to keep quiet. Not tell anyone. Now that you know, I want to th—"

"Why do you think you were asked that?"

She blinked, hearing a coolness in his tone. "I beg your pardon?"

"I said . . . why do you think they told you to keep things quiet? To not tell anyone?"

She couldn't see his expression well in the dim light but didn't need to. His hands fisted, his stance firmly planted, told her enough about his state of mind, and summoned memories she wished she could silence forever. She slowly met his gaze, feeling her own narrow.

"Ridley, are you angry with me?"

He moved closer but unlike the times Charles had tried to intimidate her—and succeeded—she didn't back away. Not because Ridley wasn't angry. That much was apparent. But because Ridley was *not* Charles.

"Yes, I'm a little angry, but mostly I'm disturbed about this . . . decision you've made. And frankly . . ." He looked around. "I'm a little surprised you didn't mention it to me first."

Old defenses snapped to attention with surprising fierceness.

"Mention it to you first?" Her smile felt anything but genuine. "Do you mean . . . *discuss it* with you before I did it? Do you discuss all of your decisions with me?"

He leveled a look. "Olivia, what I'm trying to say to you is that this is not a safe situation. Far from it. Do you realize what could happen to you as a teacher in a—"

"Freedmen's school?" she finished for him. "Yes, I do. And I considered those risks before making *my* decision to teach." She saw him bristle. "But you also have to realize, Ridley, we're not in a town. Look around you. We're in the middle of the woods."

"It doesn't matter, Olivia. People talk. And when the wrong people find out—"

"*You're* the one who encouraged me to do it."

His eyes darkened. "I would never have encouraged you to do something like this. Teaching Jimmy and Jolene in the back room of a stable is one thing. But this? This smacks of foolishness, Olivia."

The air in her lungs went flat and she drew in another breath, determined not to show how much his words hurt. *In the back room of a stable* ... He made it sound like what she'd been doing was so insignificant. And only fools were foolish.

She knelt down and blew out the last lamp. Darkness crowded close again, and she stood. "I'm sorry you don't agree with my decision, Ridley. But it's mine to make. And I've made it. And ... I prefer to see it as noble rather than foolish."

She brushed past him, but he caught hold of her arm and drew her back. His grip was tight but not enough to hurt.

"I know you're doing this because you care. And yes, it's noble. But please, Olivia"—his deep whisper bulleted past her defenses—"think about what you're doing. About what this could cost you. Think about the Hardings and how this would reflect on them. I believe we both know how the general would react. And what about your aunt? This is too much, Olivia." His grip tightened briefly, possessively. "It's too much."

Maybe it was the tender thread of appeal underlying his voice. Or maybe it was being this close to him again. Or maybe it was how he was deliberately touching her, something he hadn't done in far too long. But she began to wonder if he wasn't so much angry with her as he was genuinely worried about her.

A creak at the door begged their attention.

Big Ike dwarfed the entry. "Y'all ready to be gettin' home? It's awful late."

The walk back to the plantation was the longest Olivia could remember. Big Ike led the way, and Ridley followed behind her. Twice she looked back to make sure Ridley was still there. He moved through the woods with scarcely a sound.

Regardless of what he'd said or how well intentioned he was, she wasn't going to stop teaching. Yes, there was risk involved. But he, of all people, should understand risk. They were nearly back to the mansion when he caught up with her and touched her arm. She paused.

"Big Ike," Ridley said softly, then offered his hand when Ike turned. "Thank you for not snapping my neck clean in two earlier."

Accepting, Big Ike smiled. "Sorry I gave you a fright, sir. Didn't know it was you."

Ridley shook his head. "Under the circumstances, you were doing what you needed to."

Even in the moonlight, Olivia caught the brief but pointed look Ridley gave her. But that made her even more determined to hold her ground.

"We workin' hard to take good care of Missus Aberdeen, sir. And of all our folks. Best we can."

"I know that." Ridley nodded. "You made that clear tonight."

Smiling again, Big Ike tipped an imaginary hat and walked on.

"Good night, Ike," Olivia whispered. "And thank you."

For a moment, neither she nor Ridley spoke. Then he sighed, fatigued or frustrated—or both—she couldn't tell.

"Olivia, some of what I said earlier might not have come out as I'd intended. Your desire to teach and help others is the furthest thing from foolish."

Seeing his attempt to make amends, Olivia softened. "Thank you, Ridley. I appreciate—"

"But that doesn't change my opinion on the issue." He held up a hand. "Because I'm right about this. It's too dangerous. Not only for you, but for those around you."

She stared at him. "Too dangerous? You, who leave for the Colorado Territory in two weeks, are telling me something is too dangerous? Have you read about this place where you're going, Ridley?" She exhaled. "Every time you've talked about the Colorado Territory in the past, you were encouraging me to do this. Whether you realized it or not." He opened his mouth as if to respond, but she beat him to it. "Along with every time I've seen you work with one of the thoroughbreds. When you first started training Seabird, she was so skittish. She about pummeled you in the face. I saw it myself. Numerous times!"

"That's different. Training a—"

"*And*," she went on, her turn to hold up a hand, "when you were working with Jack Malone ... I'll never forget watching you that day he reared up on you. My heart all but stopped. So please, don't speak to me about not doing something because it's too dangerous." She took a quick breath, grateful for an opportunity to say one more thing to him while she could—even though she was using it against him, in a way. "*You're* the reason I'm teaching, Ridley. You're the reason why I first believed I even could. Or have you forgotten?" She felt the touch of a smile. "That I'm stronger than I look?"

For the longest time, he said nothing, only stared. "Are you finished?" he said finally.

Wishing his voice held even a hint of playfulness, she nodded.

He glanced toward the house. "Then may I walk you the rest of the way?"

She accepted the offer of his arm and they strolled side-by-side. But even with him right beside her, she *missed* him. Missed him maybe even more than she would once he'd left Belle Meade for good. Then again, no ... She didn't believe that for a minute.

He walked with her around to the front of the house and paused by the staircase leading to the second-story porch. "You *are* a strong woman. It's something I admire in you—most of the time." Finally, a hint of the humor she loved. "But just because you *can* do something, Olivia, doesn't mean you always should. After all, a door may open ... but it doesn't mean you were meant to fall through it."

It took her a moment, but she remembered the night of their first walk. And as long as she lived, she would never forget that carriage door. But that *he* remembered ...

He looked away briefly, then back. "What if I were to tell you that I don't want to see you get hurt. And that I wish you would reconsider. Would you at least think about it?"

She looked up at him, half wishing she could simply nod and agree like she would have done a year ago. Just to avoid seeming quarrelsome. But ironically—thanks in large part to him—she couldn't.

"I appreciate what you're saying, Ridley, and I'm grateful for your concern. But when I made this decision, I felt a certainty inside me I haven't felt but a handful of times in my—"

"Mr. Cooper! Hurry, sir! Come quick!"

They both turned to see Big Ike running full out and turned to meet him in the yard.

"It's Seabird, sir." Big Ike huffed. "She's foalin'!"

Chapter FIFTY-ONE

*O*livia peered into the stall, not at all certain she should be watching. But Ridley had asked if she wanted to, and seeing his excitement, her curiosity got the best of her. The closest she'd ever come to seeing a birth was when she was seven years old and found a cat about to have its kittens beneath their front porch. Her mother had quickly whisked her away before anything really happened. *That's not something a young lady should watch, Olivia!*

But Olivia couldn't stop watching this.

Big Ike had run to get Susanna, and the couple returned and joined her, Ridley, and Uncle Bob outside the stall. Susanna, so tiny, stood on tiptoe to see over the slats.

Seabird lay on her side, bedded down in fresh hay, her swollen belly contracting, then relaxing. Every minute or so, the mare whinnied and rose up and would rock back and forth as though she were about to get to her feet. But instead, she'd lie back down, only to repeat the entire process.

Olivia leaned over to Ridley and whispered, as Uncle Bob had instructed. "Shouldn't you do something? Try to help her along?"

Ridley shook his head. "Not unless something goes wrong. And so far she's progressing well."

"Everythin's goin' just right," Uncle Bob said beneath his breath. "Come on, Miss Birdie. You's a mite early, girl, but not by much."

Over the next few minutes, more servants arrived to stand quietly behind them and watch. Apparently, word had spread. Everybody at Belle Meade knew Miss Birdie had lost her first foal two years earlier. No doubt that was at the forefront of everyone's mind. Especially Ridley's.

Olivia sneaked a look beside her, watching him. The man cared for her, she *knew* it. He'd never said it outright, yet he said it every day in the way he treated her. Like earlier tonight. So why hadn't he verbalized those feelings? Especially since he'd soon be leaving? Then again, that was probably why he hadn't. What could come of those feelings? But Olivia knew he could have a life here at Belle Meade—if he wanted it.

Ridley had to be aware of General Harding's desire to see her wed to General Meeks. Everyone was. That aspect of her private life felt a little like the published racing odds in *American Turf Register and Sporting Magazine*. But surely Ridley knew her better than to think she would ever choose a man like Percival Meeks over him. *Didn't he?*

Her year of mourning had officially ended two weeks ago on the anniversary of Charles's death. But after speaking with Aunt Elizabeth, they'd decided the yearling auction would be the best time for her to make the public segue. So she still hadn't put away the widow's garb, and—looking down on the familiar dark gray—in many ways, it seemed like she should continue wearing it. Because with Ridley leaving and General Meeks on the horizon, it felt like a part of her was dying inside all over again.

Susanna's soft gasp yanked her attention back to the floor of the stall. And seeing the progression, Olivia pressed a hand to her midsection. "Oh, my goodness ..."

"It's all right," Ridley whispered, leaning closer. "That's just the foal's forelegs."

"What's wrong with them?"

He laughed softly. "Nothing's wrong. The foal's still in the birthing sack, that's all. As long as the shoulders clear the birthing canal, we're all but home free."

Olivia nodded, trying to act as though speaking of birthing canals was routine conversation. Seabird raised her head again, whinnied and rocked, then went back down on her side. Olivia kept her eyes on the protruding forelegs, about to ask Ridley what to expect next, when something else began to—

She looked closer ... then grabbed Ridley's arm. "It's a head!" she whispered.

He said nothing but briefly covered her hand on his arm, which she much preferred. Having reached a milestone, the foal began to wriggle.

Ridley pointed. "See how one leg is advancing a little before the other?"

She nodded. "Yes, I think so."

"That's what we want to see," he continued. "It allows the shoulders to pass through one at a time."

The foal squirmed, its face covered in the milky white sack. Its writhing movements conveyed an eagerness to have this over with.

"You's almost there, girl," Uncle Bob said low. "Another few good pushes and you be done."

The shoulders came next, and Olivia could hardly contain herself. "Come on, Miss Birdie," she whispered, willing the foal fully into this world.

Seconds passed. Feeling someone's attention, she looked over to find Ridley smiling at her, the emotion in his eyes confirmed her thoughts of minutes earlier. Now if she could only get the man to say the words.

With a loud whinny and two snorts, Seabird finally pushed the foal free, and Ridley's breath left him.

Uncle Bob clapped him on the back. "A colt, Ridley! You got yourself a colt from Jack Malone hisself, sir!"

A chorus of congratulations went up as mother and colt inspected each other nose to nose. Seabird nuzzled the foal, licking it, gently nudging, her affection tangible. Ridley grabbed some towels, and he and Uncle Bob moved into the stall. Seabird gained her feet, and Ridley whispered something to her, then gave her neck a good rub — as did Uncle Bob — then they both set to work drying off the colt.

Suddenly, Ridley stilled. "Uncle Bob," he said, his tone sober.

Uncle Bob looked over at him, then down at the colt. "Well, I'll be ..."

Olivia tried to figure out what they were looking at. "What is it? Is he all right?"

Then the colt directed its attention at her. *Directly* at her, its black eyes huge, almost ... discerning.

Uncle Bob knelt down. "I ain't never seen a newborn able to key onto people so fast in all my life."

The colt looked, one by one, at each of the faces closest to him, focusing finally on Ridley's again.

"Look at the courage in those eyes, Uncle Bob. The determination. He looks ... dauntless."

"If you mean stubborn ..." Uncle Bob grinned. "Then we's seein' the same thing."

Olivia laughed, and Ridley looked up at her. "Come around and meet him."

Before she could say she preferred to meet the colt later, a path cleared for her to the door of the stall. Everyone was watching, smiling, and Olivia couldn't find the courage to refuse. But as she walked to the door, what she realized was that she didn't want the courage to refuse. She wanted the courage to step inside.

She did so and heard the door close with finality behind her. Seabird turned, saw her, and plodded straight for her. For an instant, Olivia was back in that blasted carriage window—stuck fast—with this same horse coming at her, and she was tempted to turn and run. But remembering what she'd witnessed moments earlier, Olivia found herself less concerned with leaving the stall, and far more intent on not being afraid of this magnificent animal anymore. Trying not to wince too much, she held out her hand as Ridley had taught her, and Seabird nuzzled her palm.

Gradually, Olivia relaxed. Seabird lowered her head as though wanting to make it easier for Olivia to reach her, so Olivia obliged and scratched her behind the ears. Seabird blew out a breath that said *satisfaction* if Olivia had ever heard it.

"Good girl," Ridley said, a smile in his voice.

And even though everyone else probably thought he was talking to the horse, Olivia knew better. His words were meant for her.

Chapter
FIFTY-TWO

Olivia knocked gently on the bedroom door, knowing Aunt Elizabeth was expecting her.

"Come in."

Obliging, Olivia pushed open the door and caught Elizabeth's eye in the mirror.

"Oh, Livvy, how lovely." From the dressing table, Aunt Elizabeth motioned her closer.

Olivia came alongside Susanna, who was putting the finishing touches on Elizabeth's hair. Susanna gave an approving wink.

"Oh." Elizabeth ran a hand across the full skirt of Olivia's dress. "It's even more beautiful on, dear. I can remember, so very well, your mother wearing this. You're right, Rachel outdid herself this time."

"Thank you, Aunt Elizabeth. And, yes, she did."

"And those gloves. They're lovely too."

Olivia fingered the delicate black lace gloves that covered the scar, though only just. At her request, Rachel had picked them up in town for her. "You look lovely this evening, Aunt."

"Thank you, Livvy. But between you and the girls, and the general's handsome crop of yearlings ..." Elizabeth laughed. "No one will be looking at me at dinner tonight or at the auction tomorrow. Thank goodness!"

Smiling, Olivia placed a hand on her aunt's shoulder, trying her best to mask the sense of dread building inside her. The Hardings' twenty-six guests for the pre-auction dinner would be arriving at any time—General Percival Meeks among them. She hadn't seen him since the dinner last fall but they'd exchanged several letters in recent months. And she had to admit that, at least on paper, Percival Meeks actually seemed to be a thoughtful, compassionate, well-read, and intelligent man. In truth, she might have liked him … if she didn't have to marry him.

But what had a vice-grip on her hope was the fact that Ridley was only a few days away from leaving. She'd overheard him tell Jimmy in the stable two days ago that he'd stay a few days following the auction, no more than a week, and then he'd be gone. The boy had been shadowing his steps ever since.

The image of the handsome chestnut colt came to mind, the spitting image of Jack Malone. Dauntless, Ridley had named it. And the name fit. Both the colt and its owner.

Susanna stepped back. "There you go, Missus Harding. All done up right, ma'am."

Elizabeth reached for Susanna's hand. "Thank you, Susanna. I know you had plenty else to do downstairs without seeing to this mess."

Susanna eyed her. "I been fixin' your hair for parties since I's twelve, ma'am. I ain't 'bout to stop now. But I do need to get myself on downstairs." She looked at Elizabeth in the mirror. "You need any more help, ma'am? 'Fore I go?" she asked, her voice taking on an unaccustomed tenderness.

"Not at all." Elizabeth made a playful shooing gesture. "Now go see to your kitchen and that wonderful dinner you're preparing."

Susanna left, and Elizabeth dabbed a spot of perfume behind each ear. "You're nervous, Livvy."

Olivia held her aunt's gaze, wishing she could talk to her more openly about what was going on inside of her. About Ridley. But Aunt Elizabeth was firmly entrenched in General Meeks's camp. Understandably so. So Olivia simply nodded, then turned her attention out the window to where the wrecked carriage once sat, the fragments of chopped wood and bent metal long gone. But *nervous* didn't adequately describe the falling-forward feeling inside that caused her stomach to ache even now.

"If it helps, Livvy, I don't think General Meeks will propose tonight, dear. Tonight and tomorrow are about the auction. My husband confided in me that Percival will be in town for several days. He's indicated he desires to spend more time with you before moving forward."

Again, Olivia nodded, not comforted by the news. Because whether it be tonight or days from now, the question was coming. And though she knew the answer she wanted to give, the answer she should—no, *must*—give pressed hard.

Seeing Elizabeth struggling with her necklace, Olivia helped her with it, fitting the tiny clasp inside the hook. Then she noticed ...

"Aunt." She gently took Elizabeth's hands in hers. "You're trembling."

"It's nothing, dear. I've been having these little *tremors*, the doctor calls them, for years. They come and go. But recently, they come. It's not painful." She smiled. "Only frustrating."

Footsteps sounded in the hallway and General Harding entered the bedroom. Then stopped almost as quickly. "My goodness," he whispered. "Don't you two ladies look lovely. May I escort you both downstairs? The guests should be arriving any time."

Olivia accepted the general's left arm. Typically, she'd have been surprised by his compliment. But the closer the auction came, the more chipper he'd become. And it wasn't hard to understand why. The auction—but far more, her marriage—would help Belle Meade recover from the war years and become solvent again.

She walked beside him and Aunt Elizabeth until the spiral staircase turned and narrowed. Then she slipped her arm free and nodded for them to continue on. She had paused for a moment, waiting for the train of Elizabeth's dress to clear the stairs below when she looked down into the entrance hall and saw Ridley coming through the front door.

Dashing in his suit and tie, he glanced up, saw her, and the look on his face—one of undeniable pleasure and approval—made her heart race. She gripped the banister to her right but had scarcely negotiated the next stair when he was by her side.

He wove her arm through his. "I was hoping you would wear that." His gaze moved over her with deliberate, and welcomed, leisure. "Intoxicating yet again, Mrs. Aberdeen."

"Precisely what I was thinking," she whispered, catching a whiff of bayberry and spice as they descended and loving how his eyes narrowed the slightest bit.

He was clean shaven. His hair, reaching just past his collar, had grown longer than he usually wore it. But it looked good on him and was reminiscent of when she'd first seen him—all wild and untamed—that day on the road. He would fit in well in the Colorado Territory. And yet ... viewing herself through his eyes, she was the furthest thing from a woman fit for such a place.

This was her world. Empty and foreign though it felt at the moment.

When they reached the landing, he turned. "Olivia, after the auction tomorrow night, do you think we could—"

"Yes."

Playful warning lit his gaze. "Careful. You don't know what I was going to ask."

His comment elicited a smile. "You were going to ask me to take a walk, were you not?"

He studied her for a moment. "More or less."

"Then, more or less, my answer is still yes."

The clomp of horses' hooves and the squeak of wheels announced the arrival of their guests, and she caught the general's glance aimed in her direction. So, apparently, did Ridley.

"Duty calls?" he asked softly.

"I'm to stand with the Harding family and greet the guests. It's part of the official end of my mourning."

He merely nodded, his features revealing nothing. He started to go, then paused. "Thank you again, Olivia, for everything you've done to make this auction come together. Same thing for inventorying the stables. I couldn't have accomplished what I have here without you."

His gratitude felt painfully like the beginning of good-bye. And using a skill rusty from disuse but which polished up surprisingly quick, Olivia stuffed her emotions down deep.

"You're so welcome, Ridley. It was my pleasure." She forced a laugh, daring to voice an ever-thinning hope. "And as I've said before, if the auction goes well—as we all know it will—the general might offer you a job you simply won't be able to refuse."

He reached for her hand and brought it to his lips, not a trace of a smile touching his. "Until tomorrow night."

Over the next half hour, standing at the end of the receiving line with Mary, Olivia greeted the Hardings' guests and swiftly realized the road to reentering society in Nashville would be a bumpy one. If it could be navigated at all.

"Welcome to Belle Meade," she said softly as a couple passed her in the receiving line.

The gentleman barely glanced her way before turning. The woman angled her head slightly as though about to nod, then delivered a discreet but scathing glance that caused Olivia's face to burn.

Olivia tried again with the next couple in line, and the next, but with similar results. After a while, she simply smiled, then quickly averted her gaze so as to avoid their contempt.

Then she saw him. General Percival Meeks. Coming up the walkway. At least ... she thought it was him.

"General Meeks." General Harding greeted him with a handshake. "What an honor to have you in our home again, sir."

"The pleasure is all mine, General Harding. I assure you."

Though no one would describe him as svelte, the man was a shadow of his former self. Since she'd last seen him, he'd reduced his girth by close to half. And he didn't appear sickly either. Quite the contrary. The hairy laurel he'd sported was gone too. And she had to say, bald was a vast improvement.

As he visited with General Harding and Aunt Elizabeth, the man's focus drifted down the line and connected with Olivia's. He smiled and nodded kindly, then returned his attention to the conversation.

"Is that the man you're going to marry?" Mary whispered beside her.

Olivia looked at her, wishing she could answer with a resounding no, but deciding it best to respond vaguely. "We'll see," she whispered, then looked back to see General Meeks working his way down the line.

When he reached her, he clasped her hands in a fatherly like fashion. "My charming correspondent. How wonderful to see you again, Mrs. Aberdeen."

Olivia offered a curtsey. "General Meeks, nice to see you again, sir." Only then did she notice a woman following behind him. Short, a little roundish about the middle, with kind eyes.

"May I introduce Mrs. Fairbanks," he said. "My nurse. Mrs. Fairbanks ... Mrs. Olivia Aberdeen."

Olivia nodded, not quite believing he'd brought his nurse with him. Unless he wasn't as well as he appeared. "Nice to meet you, Mrs. Fairbanks. Welcome to Belle Meade."

Mrs. Fairbanks smiled and dipped her head. "Mrs. Aberdeen, a pleasure. General Meeks speaks so very highly of you, ma'am." Then she lowered her eyes.

General Meeks stepped closer. "I'll explain more privately, Mrs. Aberdeen. But suffice it to say the doctor gave me an ultimatum last fall, and I chose to make some changes in my daily regimen. He assigned Mrs. Fairbanks here to assist me with those."

Olivia nodded. "Well, sir, if I might say, the regimen seems to agree with you."

He beamed. "Thank you. And whatever you've been doing most definitely agrees with you."

Once the last of the guests arrived and were greeted, a bell sounded from the main dining room. Everyone began moving in that direction, and as Olivia did likewise, making her way beside General Meeks, she saw women glancing behind her. Again and again. Finally, curious to see what drew their attention, she turned. And couldn't blame them one bit for their ongoing stares. Ridley Cooper was well worth a second look. And a third.

"He's so handsome," Mary whispered.

At that moment, Ridley glanced their way. His gaze connected with Olivia's, and he smiled. Mary gave her a discreet nudge, and Olivia saw the glint of mischief in the girl's eyes.

Mindful that whatever opinions Mary formed would no doubt be passed along posthaste to Aunt Elizabeth, Olivia affected a serious tone. "Mr. Cooper and I are friends," she whispered, hoping no one else was thinking what Mary was.

Mary quirked a doubtful brow.

Olivia quickly nodded. Then, thinking better of it—and thinking, too, about all that Ridley truly did mean to her—she added, "We're very good friends. And Mr. Cooper leaves for the Colorado Territory in one week."

Mary's teasing smile dimmed a little, and she nodded. But still looked far from convinced.

Following plates of fresh fruit, the main course was served and dinner conversation flourished. With General Meeks on her right and Mary on her left, Olivia did more listening than talking, which suited her fine. Ridley was seated opposite the table from her, one seat over, and she caught him sneaking looks at her, almost as often as she sneaked looks at him.

With the exception of Ridley, each of the men at the table had served with the general in the war, and each had stories of valor and bravery they shared. Some stories drew tears, others applause, while more lighthearted stories drew laughter. Occasionally Olivia caught snippets of other exchanges that proved more than a little interesting.

The woman who had earlier delivered the most scathing stare at Olivia was seated directly across the table from her—just to Ridley's right—and was in deep conversation with one of the many Confederate generals in attendance. But apparently the woman had never perfected her whisper.

"Well, you *do* know that General Harding contributed five hundred thousand dollars to the Confederate cause. And, of course, my husband and I did nearly that much as well." The woman huffed. "Those dirty, filthy Yankees. Look at what they did to us, General. To our lives! And they dare call *us* traitors to the Union." The woman slid a brief but well-aimed glare across the table at Olivia. "My husband says that if any of them have the *gall* to show up here tomorrow, he will outbid them all!"

Olivia confined her gaze to her plate. Two years since the war had ended and still such bitterness. In the thrum of conversation around her, a quiet realization came, and she searched her heart to make sure it was true. And to her amazement, it was. When had she put away the sharp bitterness and loathing she'd had for Charles? She still thought of him, on occasion, but although the memories were far from pleasant, neither were they drenched in animosity. She felt a stirring within, and her gaze was drawn across the table.

Maybe that's why God had brought Ridley into her life. To help her forgive, to heal, and to let go. In one sense, it felt a little cruel. To dangle something so beautiful in front of her. A relationship she could never have. And yet she wouldn't want to go back to being the woman in that carriage. The woman she'd been before she met him.

"Susanna!"

Olivia blinked at the name, then dabbed her eyes with her napkin.

Susanna refilled a gentleman's water glass down the table. "Yes, sir, General Walker. You need somethin', sir?"

The older man winked at the woman beside him. "I need you to confirm to my wife here that you did indeed hide the Harding family silver during the war. At the general's request. And that General Harding wasn't the least concerned that he didn't know where you'd hidden it."

Susanna stood a bit straighter. "Yes, ma'am, that's what happened, all right. Them Yankees were camped out in the deer park, been takin' everythin'. So the general, he asked me and Uncle Bob to hide it for him. So we did."

The wife nodded as though still not quite believing. "And he didn't ask you to tell him where it was?"

Susanna shook her head. "No, ma'am, Missus Walker. General Harding, he trusts me and Uncle Bob." Susanna glanced down the table, and General Harding gave her a kind smile.

"Would you tell *me* where you hid it, Susanna?" Another man asked, humor in his tone.

"Why, no, sir. I will not." Susanna winked. "There might come another war, and we need to be keepin' that silver safe."

Laughter filled the room, followed by the telling *tink* of silver on china, and one of the general's friends stood and raised his glass. "To our gracious host, General William Giles Harding, owner of the finest plantation and thoroughbred farm in the country, and one of the best men the South has ever known."

His remarks were met by affirming nods.

"A true son of the Confederacy, he set an example and made us proud by choosing prison rather than signing the Oath of Allegiance to a Union he didn't support and a cause he did not believe in. To General William Giles Harding ..." He lifted his glass. "A man among men."

"To General William Giles Harding," everyone repeated. "A man among men!"

"Hear, hear!" rose up throughout the room, and everyone drank a toast.

"Now if we could only get him to cut that scraggly old beard!" another man said, but the comment drew only the shallowest of laughter.

And the room grew quiet.

General Harding merely smiled. "The war may officially be over, gentlemen ... and ladies," he added with a nod. "But my allegiance to my true country, to my South, will never end or be diminished in my heart." His smile faded, his attention focusing on the man who'd made the comment. "And I swear to you, my good friend, that I will wear this beard proudly until the day the South has won, or—if the Almighty wills it—until the day I die."

Seconds passed in awkward silence.

Olivia looked down the table at Aunt Elizabeth, whose carefully arranged smile couldn't mask the concern—and love—she felt for her husband. She also glimpsed the weight of worry and stress that her aunt's letters during the war had so painfully reflected.

General Harding rose from his seat, and all eyes turned. "Before we continue with dinner and with what I'm certain will be one of Susanna's delicious desserts, I want to offer my gratitude to all of you for coming here tonight. And for helping us to celebrate Belle Meade's *first* annual yearling auction."

Applause followed, sprinkled with congratulatory remarks.

"I've asked one of my foremen, Mr. Ridley Cooper, to join us this evening with the purpose of giving you an overview of the auction tomorrow. As you're able to visit with him tonight following dinner, or tomorrow during the auction, know that he has my full confidence and therefore full authority to deal with you on any account. I've also instructed him to teach you how to bid high and bid often, which is something I highly encourage."

The guests laughed, and any momentary awkwardness from earlier faded.

"And now, without further ado, ladies and gentleman … Mr. Ridley Cooper."

Olivia's eyes burned with quiet pride as Ridley rose to his feet.

"Thank you, General Harding, for that introduction. I'm honored not only to be here with you tonight, but to be here at Belle Meade. As the general said, if you have any questions, seek me out. But something you must do while you're here tomorrow is visit the stables of Belle Meade. When you do, you're going to meet a gentleman by the name of Bob Green. But within five minutes, you'll be calling him Uncle Bob, as we all do. Uncle Bob is the head hostler here at Belle Meade and is the finest horse trainer in the country. Maybe the world, but I haven't traveled that far yet."

More laughter drifted up from the table, and as Ridley continued speaking, Olivia watched the people in the room respond to him. He was a natural-born leader. People followed him, because Ridley Cooper knew where he was going.

After he sat down, Susanna, Betsy, and Chloe cleared the dinner dishes and served warm carrot cake, a Belle Meade specialty, as Susanna called it. Conversation ensued but most of it, Olivia noted while listening to General Meeks beside her, was directed toward Ridley.

"Where are you from, Mr. Cooper?" One of the generals asked.

"From South Carolina, sir. Near Hilton Head."

The man nodded. "Beautiful area. Nothing like the ocean, is there?"

Ridley shook his head. "No, sir, there's not."

"I bet you miss it," a woman added.

"I do." Ridley shot Olivia a look. "But I keep a seashell with me, as a reminder."

Olivia warmed at the silent, personal exchange and was glad when General Meeks turned to Mrs. Fairbanks on his right.

A gentleman three seats down from Ridley leaned forward. "I served with a few of the regiments from South Carolina, Mr. Cooper. Which regiment were you in?"

Olivia tensed at the question, knowing Ridley didn't like talking about the war.

Lifting his water glass, Ridley took a long drink, then cleared his throat. "I served with the 167th, sir."

The man frowned. "I don't recall that regiment. But you were stationed here in Nashville?"

Ridley nodded. "For the majority of the time, yes, sir."

"What was your rank, Mr. Cooper?"

"I was a first lieutenant, sir."

"My gracious, dear," the gentleman's wife interrupted. "Would you stop badgering poor Mr. Cooper and give him a chance to eat his carrot cake while it's still warm?"

Smiling at the woman, Ridley took a huge bite.

"We're not badgering him, ma'am," another man offered. "We've just heard all of our stories, so we want to hear his."

People laughed, even the woman who had done the gentle scolding. But Olivia didn't.

"A first lieutenant, you say, Mr. Cooper?"

"Yes, sir. That's right."

"I bet you saw a lot more hand-to-hand fighting than the rest of the old men sitting around this table, myself included."

Ridley looked down at his plate. "Yes, sir. I ... guess I probably did."

Olivia sensed the desire from the men in the room for Ridley to share his stories. But while she had long wanted to know more about his experiences in the war and to understand why he wanted to leave here so badly, she wished they would stop peppering him with questions. If only they knew how hard it was for him.

"So were you with us at the Battle of Franklin, Mr. Cooper? Horrible night that it was," the man said softly.

Ridley laid his fork aside. "No, sir, I wasn't at that battle."

"The Battle of Nashville then?" an older general asked from down the table, his voice somber. "I lost 237 men from my company that day. But we made a valiant last stand."

"No, sir." Ridley bowed his head. "I wasn't there either."

Conversation at the table fell silent, and Olivia felt much like Aunt Elizabeth must have moments earlier as she'd watched her husband hurt so silently, yet so publicly.

One of the men at the far end of the table, at least twice Ridley's age, leaned forward. "So tell us, son. Where did you fight?"

Ridley lifted his head, and to Olivia's surprise, he looked at her, then looked with resolve at the man who had asked the question. "I was stationed in Nashville at the start of the war, sir. But I spent the majority of my time toward the end ... at Andersonville."

Chapter FIFTY-THREE

*T*he room went still.

Ridley felt like he'd been kicked in the gut by Jack Malone. His heart hammered, his breath would hardly come. The faces around the table were a blur. All but one: Olivia's. He sought her gaze and held it, finding strength in the compassion and understanding in her eyes.

Although, he knew she didn't fully understand. Not yet. But she would. Before he left.

An older gentleman a few seats down looked Ridley's way. "I was stationed at Andersonville for a while too, Mr. Cooper. Three of the hardest months of my life," he said, his voice barely above a whisper. "I know we needed prisons. And both sides had them, but ..." He looked down. And when he looked up again, his gaze was watery. "That place was brutal. And ... I'm sorry to say, Lieutenant Cooper, but I don't remember seeing you there."

"That's all right, General." Ridley acknowledged his kindness with a nod. "With all respect, I don't recall seeing you either."

The distant clank of pots and pans drifted in from the kitchen and, slowly, Ridley's heartbeat returned to a normal rhythm. He hadn't planned on admitting he'd been at Andersonville. But when the questions kept coming, the only way he knew to silence them was with the truth. Or part of it. Now he weighed the cost—not only to himself, but to General Harding—of revealing the whole.

The woman beside him scoffed. "All this talk of Andersonville being brutal ..." She shook her head. "Of course it was brutal! It was a prison, for heaven's sake. And for thieving, lying Yankees. The men who ..." Her voice caught, her features twisted. "Who killed *my son*! We can never allow ourselves to forget what they did. How they—"

"Mrs. Stewart!"

All eyes turned to Elizabeth Harding. Ridley had never heard the woman raise her voice in such a manner. He'd thought earlier that she looked weary. But now she appeared almost too fragile to sit upright.

"Mrs. Stewart," Elizabeth began again, softer this time. "My heart grieves with yours over the loss of your precious son. I did not lose a son to this war, but I've lain seven children to rest, so I am familiar with grief. But let us not forget that *all* the men who fought and lived, and who fought and *died*—on both sides—were someone's sons. Now ..." Lifting her chin slightly, she directed her gaze to the opposite end of the table. "To my husband and all the gentlemen in this room, I extend my heartfelt gratitude for your devoted service to our beloved South. But please ..." Her voice strained to the point of breaking. "At least for the remainder of this one evening I beg of you..." She smiled or tried to, "Let's have no more talk of war."

A while later, retired to the central parlor, Ridley fielded questions from the gentlemen about the auction and the yearlings, always aware of where Olivia was. Which, so far, had been across the room from him and consistently by General Meeks's side.

Ridley hardly recognized the man. But he didn't have to think long to understand the motivation behind the changes Meeks had made in his life—*and* his person! General Meeks was smitten. It was written all over his face. And with good reason. What man in his right mind wouldn't move heaven and earth to have Olivia Aberdeen beside him? Even if it meant not going to the Colorado Territory.

And yet, Ridley *knew* that was where he was supposed to be.

"Making foreman in so short a time, Mr. Cooper. That's impressive."

Ridley turned back to the group of gentlemen. Specifically General Maddox, the man who'd been stationed at Andersonville. It was sobering to stand face to face with one of his captors, even though he didn't recognize the man. "Thank you, sir. I'm grateful for General Harding's trust and appreciate working here."

"If that's the case, Mr. Cooper," another man said, his tone hinting at tongue-and-cheek, "then explain the rumor I heard a few moments ago about you wanting to give all this up for some plan to go to the Colorado Territory."

Ridley managed to smile. "I see you've been speaking with our host." He glanced at General Harding across the room, who merely lifted his coffee cup in mock salute. "The answer is simple, gentlemen. I've always wanted to see the Rocky Mountains and have been making plans to do that for some time."

"Still," the man countered, "why not wait two or three years until the railroad is built and go then? I'm fairly certain the mountains will still be there."

The men laughed.

Sensing an ambush, good-natured though it may be, Ridley shook his head, eager to put the topic to rest. Especially with Olivia just across the room. Thinking of leaving was hard enough for him without seeing that look she always got whenever they discussed it.

"I purchased land in the Colorado Territory four years ago, gentlemen. And if I don't go now, I'll lose it. So while I appreciate the opportunities General Harding has given me, I'll be leaving within a week."

"I believe I heard my name mentioned." General Harding joined them. "I hope it was being used in the best sense."

General Maddox smiled. "Not to fear, Harding. We'd never talk unkindly about you. Not in your own home, anyway," he added.

The comment drew laughter, as intended.

"Mr. Cooper here," General Maddox continued, "was telling us about his plans to go west. I think a few of us — myself not included — were questioning his decision. If I were his age and without attachments, I'd be tempted to hop on a wagon and join him."

"You always *have* been a bad influence, Maddox." General Harding smiled, stroking his beard. "I would appreciate you men working on Mr. Cooper here. I've done everything I know to encourage him to stay. I even created a new position."

Ridley tensed. He purposefully hadn't shared Harding's offer with Olivia, afraid it would hurt her further if she knew he'd turned it down. If she had her preference, he'd stay here at Belle Meade. But she didn't know the whole truth. Yet. He looked across the room to where she'd been sitting, but she was gone. He looked around. She stood only feet away now with Mary and Selene and a handful of other women.

"And what position was that, Harding?" Maddox asked. "If Mr. Cooper's declination is final, I might be willing to come work for you. For the right price."

Harding laughed. "My friend, there is no price right enough for me to hire you."

The men laughed all the more, which drew the women's attention.

"The position I offered Mr. Cooper was that of head foreman of Belle Meade. I offered it to him awhile back. But he turned me down flat."

Even without looking back, Ridley knew Olivia had heard. He sensed it from the silence behind him. But he knew it for certain when he turned and saw the hurt in her eyes.

Olivia closed her bedroom door behind her and leaned against it in the dark, grateful the evening was finally over. She'd wanted answers to questions, and she'd gotten them tonight. But they weren't the answers she wanted.

The general had already made an offer to Ridley. Supposedly a very good one. Yet Ridley had refused. That told her plenty right there. Learning he'd been stationed at Andersonville told her even more.

Every Northerner and Southerner alike knew about Andersonville. Reports describing the deplorable conditions of the Georgia prison and the inhumane treatment of Union soldiers there had circulated in newspapers for months following the war. She remembered the public outcry from the North for one officer of the Confederate prison to be hung for his offenses. And he had been.

The things Ridley must have seen and orders he'd had to carry out. She couldn't imagine.

She had wanted to see him privately tonight, but with all the guests—and General Meeks—that had proven impossible. As soon as General Meeks had left, she'd looked for Ridley, but he'd already gone. Other guests were still here, visiting in the central parlor or on the front porch in the rockers. But she'd excused herself.

She wanted to see him. Needed to see him. And by the time she looked toward the side window, her decision was already made. She changed out of her dress and into a simple skirt and shirtwaist.

Halfway down the lattice, she heard voices coming from around the corner. And froze. It wasn't a full moon but she was hanging from the side of the mansion, something that would be a little hard to miss. Much less explain. She scrambled down, watching the side of the house, and as soon as her foot touched the ground, someone clamped a hand over her mouth.

Chapter
FIFTY-FOUR

Olivia started to struggle, then caught a whiff of bayberry and spice at the same time she heard his voice.

"It's me," Ridley whispered. He loosened his hand and pulled her with him into the shadows against the house. Just then, General Harding and two of his colleagues rounded the corner. "I didn't want you to scream," he said, mouth against her ear, his breath warm on her neck. "I was on my way up when you climbed out."

Pressed against the house—and him—Olivia scarcely breathed as the men approached. General Harding looked in their direction and her heart all but stopped. Ridley tensed beside her. The general said something and laughed, which drew similar responses from his friends, then they continued on, deep in conversation. Pulse still racing, Olivia waited for Ridley to move first.

"Come on," he finally whispered, then grabbed her hand and set off across the darkened meadow.

All but running just to keep up, she welcomed the strength of his grip, wondering if the sense of adventure buzzing through her veins was anything like what the children she used to watch from her bedroom window felt as they ran and played in the meadow below. *Young ladies do* not *tromp around in fields like livestock, Olivia. You'll dirty your dress.* Remembering her mother fondly, Olivia still couldn't resist running a little faster. And harder.

Only when they reached the edge of the woods did Ridley slow. He took a path leading down a slight incline, and when Olivia heard the soothing tumble of the creek, she guessed where he was going and felt a sense of déjà vu.

They sat by the edge of the water on a slab of limestone. The same spot where he had washed the blisters on her feet. How long ago that seemed.

He sat quietly beside her, and her feelings were so mixed at the moment she had trouble sorting out what she wanted to say to him first. She was angry he hadn't told her about the position the general had offered. Head foreman of Belle Meade. Then hurt that he'd turned it down. And in the midst of it all, she wanted him to know that since learning about Andersonville, she understood better now why he didn't think he could stay here.

But he was mistaken. And she was going to prove it to him.

"Ridley, I—"

"Olivia, I—"

They both paused, then smiled.

"Usually, I would say ladies first. But ... in this instance, I think it would be better if I took the lead."

Detecting an unsettled quality in his tone, she reluctantly nodded. Seconds passed before he spoke again.

"To say that you have ... *captivated* me, Olivia, would be an understatement." Surprised by how he'd started out, she was glad now he'd spoken first. "The first time I saw you ..." He exhaled. "You took my breath away. Then, trapped inside that carriage like you were, then stuck in the window. But still all prim and proper to the hilt, telling me your driver would be back *posthaste*." He looked over at her, his voice harboring a smile.

Remembering, Olivia grinned.

"Then we got here. I somehow managed to get a job, thanks to Uncle Bob ..." He turned toward the darkened woods. "And to God for knowing what he was doing even when I didn't. Then I started seeing you around the plantation, and I thought to myself, 'It sure would be fun to give that woman a hard time for a while. See if I could loosen her up a little.' "

"You did *not* think that..."

"I did too."

She swatted him. "That wasn't nice. I was in mourning!" Even as she said it, she knew he would take it the way she'd intended.

"I *know* you were. And sometimes I felt bad about doing it—"

"But you did it anyway."

"I couldn't help myself. I'd see you with all that propriety bustled up so good and tight ... quite literally ... and you just brought the worst out in me."

"So it was my fault then, our becoming ..." She grinned and faltered over the word. "Friends."

He turned to her, and though the darkness hid the precise definition of his features, she was certain whatever humor his expression held, faded.

"First," he said softly, "whatever we've been, at least for me, we've been more than friends. *Much* more. And second, nothing has been your fault. There *is* fault to be assigned, but it's mine and mine alone."

Hearing him use past tense — *we've been* — she sensed the goodbye she'd been dreading inching closer. For a moment, neither spoke and the timeless trickle of the creek filled the empty space.

"When I first got here," he continued, leaning forward. "I was only planning to stay for a few weeks, and sparring back and forth with you became almost a game. You were so easy to rile, which I found irresistible." Tenderness softened his voice. "But there came a time when I realized it wasn't *playful* for me anymore. It wasn't a game. I knew if I wasn't careful, *very* careful ... you were going to turn my world upside down. And me with it. And that was something I couldn't afford to have happen."

Anticipating what he was going to say, Olivia felt cut to the quick. A pain twisted her chest. "But I ..." She shook her head, forcing out the words. "I didn't turn your world upside down ... did I?" She took a tattered breath. "Not like you did mine."

He moved closer and took her hand in his. "But that's just it, Olivia. You *did* ... You turned my world — and *me* — inside out."

Hot tears filled her eyes, and she was grateful for the shadows. She wanted to ask him why, then. *Why* didn't he care about her enough to stay? *Love* her enough? But she couldn't push the words past the tangle of emotion in her throat.

His grip tightened. "The problem is ... you don't know me. It's not your fault. I haven't allowed you to see who I am. Or ... at least who I was during the — "

"That's not true." She swallowed, wiping her eyes. "I do know you, Ridley Cooper. Better than you think." She squeezed his hand. "I don't know what you saw at Andersonville, or what you were forced to do there, or what horrible things you experienced during the war. But that's all over now. You fought for your country, for the South you loved. You did all you could. No matter where you were stationed."

"But that's what you don't understand, I wasn't — "

She put a finger to his lips. "I do understand. More than you realize. I saw the pain in the faces of the men around that table tonight. I saw it in yours too. How you wish the outcome had been different. I do too, in so many ways. Yet the changes that are happening now … They wouldn't be, without the war."

She let her hand drop and took a breath. "But it was wrong what the North did. The Federal army was brutal and cruel, coming in the way they did, stealing and taking everything. Destroying families and homes, tearing lives apart. You saw Aunt Elizabeth tonight. The war took such a toll on her. Especially when the Yankees locked the general in prison."

Ridley leaned forward and rested his forearms on his knees, his head bowed. And her heart ached for him.

"Ridley," she whispered. "The North took from you too. But you can have your life back, if you want it. You're a good man. You don't have to go to the Colorado Territory to start over. You can do that here. At Belle Meade. With Uncle Bob and the servants and the Hardings and …" She reached for courage to speak past the rubble of the wall now crumbled inside her. "With me."

Hands knotted in her lap, vulnerable and exposed even in the dark, she watched him, waiting. And slowly, he sat up and looked back at her.

"If there were a way to do that, I would. But … I can't."

He rose and stepped toward the creek. She followed.

With disappointment knifing deeper, she sensed the struggle in him and believed she knew how to help. She reached for his hand. He resisted at first, then finally relented. She brought his hand to her face and smiled when he cradled her cheek.

"When you touch me," she whispered, the tears returning. "You help me forget."

"Forget," he said softly. "Forget *what*?"

"What my life used to be like … with my late husband."

He stilled, then tried to pull away, but she held his hand where it was.

"Every time you touch me, Ridley …" With unaccustomed boldness, she guided his hand from her cheek down to her neck.

"Olivia," he whispered. "Don't."

"Every time, you erase a little more of the hurt Charles left behind, the pain that comes from being the wife of a traitor. And from the disgrace and shame he left me to bear alone."

Again, Ridley attempted to pull his hand away, but again she held it fast.

"I think I can do that for you too, Ridley. Help you forget. Forget the war, and all you went through. We could help each other. If only you'd —"

He took her face in his hands, but not gently like before. *"Olivia."* His voice came out rough, anguished. "I wasn't stationed at Andersonville ... I was a prisoner there."

Certain she felt the bedrock shift beneath her feet, Olivia took hold of his arm. She searched his face, wishing now for light instead of darkness. She needed to see his eyes. *A prisoner?* "That's not possible," she heard herself say.

"It is. I fought for the North. With the 167th regiment ... out of Pennsylvania."

"But ..." She struggled to form a thought. "You told me yourself ... about that night, on the beach, when you found the seashell. You said you found it before you left to join the Confederate Army."

He shook his head. "I said *army.* I never said which one."

Stark realization squeezed the air from her lungs. Even as her mind raced, another part of her was numb. She couldn't believe it. He'd taken up arms *against* the South? He'd lied to her? To everyone? No matter how she rearranged the pieces, she couldn't make them fit.

In a matter of seconds, the last year of her life — *their* lives — came painfully into focus. The way he treated Uncle Bob and Susanna and the other servants with such ... sameness. Why he didn't care what others thought. Why he couldn't wait to leave the South. His impatience for change. She even recalled conversations she'd overheard between him and General Harding and filtered them in a new light. But mostly she understood without question why he was so bent on leaving. Why he couldn't stay. And what that meant for her — for *them* — and it felt as if someone had reached inside her chest and wrenched her heart out.

Just as quickly, her thoughts jumped to what could happen to him if certain people learned this truth. Horrific images returned on a wave of dread. She tried to step back but he wouldn't let her go.

He lifted her face to his. "I'm sorry, Olivia. For not telling you sooner. For not being honest from the start. I have my reasons for doing what I did. You're probably not interested in hearing them right now, but —"

"Let go of me," she whispered.

He did, and she backed away, needing space between them. She couldn't think with him so close. She rubbed her arms, not cold but feeling a chill all the same.

"You fought for the Federal Army." Saying it aloud somehow made it more real.

"Yes. I did."

He took a step toward her, but she put out a hand. He stopped. She'd pictured him before in Confederate gray, but never Union blue. Yet somehow, looking at him, she could see it.

"How long were you at Andersonville?"

He didn't answer immediately. "I was captured by Confederates on August 18 of '63 and was moved to Andersonville in February of the following year."

"And you were there …"

"Until the end of the war."

She shook her head, scarcely able to keep up with her thoughts as they turned over and over upon themselves. "Who else knows about this?"

He hesitated. "Uncle Bob."

"*Uncle Bob?* Do you have any idea the trouble he could get into if anyone were to find out?"

"They won't."

Another thought came. She went weak in the knees. "General Harding doesn't know …"

He shook his head.

"And you can't ever tell him, Ridley." She shuddered to think of how the general would react. How angry he'd be. "Everything you've worked for here would be gone. And his colleagues. If they knew, the general would become a laughingstock. And Aunt Elizabeth …" She winced, imagining the ripple of repercussions of those who would be hurt. "And you wouldn't be safe either. People will brand you a traitor. You'll be just like Charles …"

She caught herself. Only, too late. And not even the darkness could hide the hurt her words had inflicted.

Ridley studied her in the dark. He'd known she would be hurt and angry, and she had every right to be. But the bullet he'd taken to his shoulder that night on the mountain four years ago had hurt less than what she'd just said to him. *You'll be just like Charles* ...

That's how she thought of him now. And he knew only too well how she felt about her late husband. However much he'd imagined it would hurt to have her looking at him like this, the reality was a hundred times worse.

"Ridley, I didn't mean for it to come out like that. What I was trying to say was that people will look at you, and they'll see—"

"A turncoat. A deserter. You can say it, Olivia. It's nothing I haven't heard before."

She bowed her head, hands knotted at her waist.

"Believe me, I weighed that cost before I put on the uniform. And I'd pay it again, if God called me to. Although ... I sure hope he doesn't. I just couldn't fight for a cause that would allow a man like Bob Green or Big Ike, or women like Susanna or Betsy, to be auctioned off like we're auctioning off the yearlings tomorrow." He wished she'd look up at him. "I don't blame you for being angry. And hurt. But everything that happened between us was true. Don't ever doubt that, Olivia."

All around them, the night sounds rose to a steady hum. He willed her to look at him. But she didn't.

"I'll walk you back."

Wordlessly she fell into step beside him. He knew her well enough to know she was battling tears and losing. But he also knew better than to try to comfort her.

When they got as far as the old Harding cabin, she raised a hand. "I'll walk the rest of the way by myself."

"I don't mind going with—"

"I *prefer* to walk by myself."

He nodded.

Sniffing, she wiped her cheeks and continued on.

"Olivia?"

She paused but didn't turn back.

"I know this doesn't change anything, but ... I never meant to hurt you."

She finally looked at him. "I know you didn't mean to, Ridley. But you did."

Chapter
FIFTY-FIVE

Well, Mr. Cooper. We're almost there! Do you think we'll reach our goal?"

"I don't know, sir. It's going to be close." Ridley had never seen General Harding look more pleased. And while he was pleased, too, and wanted the auction to do well, the outcome wasn't nearly as important as it once had been. "But if that gentleman from New York City buys any more of your yearlings, he's going to need his own railroad to get them back."

Harding laughed. "And since *that gentleman* owns the Hudson River Railroad, I believe we can assume he'll manage quite well."

Ridley motioned for Jedediah to take the next yearling out to the corral—and spotted Grady Matthews standing at the edge of the fence. He hadn't heard another word out of Matthews about the auction and hoped that boded well.

"Two yearlings left?" the general asked.

Ridley nodded, and Harding walked back toward the crowd.

Scanning the crowd of over seven hundred people, Ridley sought Olivia out again. She was where she'd been the last time he'd looked, seated with Elizabeth, Mary, Selene, and several other ladies at tables and chairs spread out across the front lawn beneath the trees. And wearing the dress he loved. Complete with gloves again. In June.

But knowing why she wore them only endeared her to him more. Even if she wouldn't let him see her scar.

He'd glimpsed her walking with General Meeks following the barbecue lunch. He'd also had opportunity to speak with the gentleman alone earlier. From all appearances, Percival Meeks was a good and decent man. He would provide well for Olivia and give her security, a well-respected name, and the Southern way of life she longed for.

But the man would never make her happy. Not like Ridley knew *he* could, if she could only find a way to forgive him. To accept him *and* the choices he'd made.

He'd only seen her from afar. They hadn't spoken. But after she'd left him last night, he'd been given reason to keep hoping on her account.

Unable to sleep, he'd sat on the front porch until the wee hours going over and over their exchange by the creek, until he'd finally figured out what was puzzling him. Thanks mainly to Uncle Bob.

"So she didn't yell any?" Uncle Bob had asked after joining him well after midnight. "She just got real quiet like?"

"*Real* quiet. Wouldn't let me come near her. Said she understood that I didn't mean to hurt her, but that I did anyway."

"Was she loud when she said it?"

Ridley exhaled. "No. Quiet as the night."

"Oh, Lawd ... that ain't good. But we done knew she wasn't gonna like hearin' it, sir."

The creak of their rocking chairs marked off the seconds, the aroma of Uncle Bob's pipe rising like an offered incense.

"Then you say Missus Aberdeen done asked who else knew about it?"

Ridley nodded. "She told me I couldn't ever tell General Harding or anybody else. Told me I wouldn't be safe."

"Safe?" Uncle Bob stopped rocking and took the pipe from between his teeth. "She started in talkin' 'bout you bein' safe, sir?"

Ridley nodded again, and that's when Uncle Bob grinned.

"Well, *shoot* ... You ain't lost her yet, sir. Not altogether, anyhow. Any female goes to talkin' 'bout you bein' safe ... hmmmph. There still be somethin' left in her heart for ya."

Gesturing to the auctioneer to begin the bidding, Ridley prayed Uncle Bob was right. The man hadn't steered him wrong yet.

Still, the way Olivia had looked at him ...

In the center of the bidding corral, Jedediah stood tall and proud beside the yearling he'd trained. At the signal, he led the yearling around the corral, showing him off for the crowd, who applauded enthusiastically. Jedediah's talent was evident both in his manner and in the young thoroughbred's, and the bidding was swift and fierce.

By the time the auctioneer brought the gavel down, Jedediah's yearling had brought a price that put them well over the amount General Harding had set as their goal. Which meant not only did Jedediah's incentive add up nicely, but Ridley had made his too. His 5 percent alone would be enough to pay for the wagon and supplies to see him west, with a little left over.

His only question was ... if Uncle Bob was right, and Olivia really did still feel something for him, was what she felt enough for her to say yes when he asked her to leave with him? Because he knew beyond a doubt now: Olivia Aberdeen was the one woman he did not want to live without.

Hurt and frustrated, her heart still tender, Olivia watched Ridley give the signal for the last yearling to be led into the corral. She'd cried herself to sleep last night and when she'd awakened this morning, her pillow was still damp.

As angry and hurt as she was, one thing she realized ... Regardless of whether or not Ridley had told her from the start about his fighting against the South, the end result was the same. He'd still be going to the Colorado Territory. But, no, that wasn't quite true. Yes, he'd still be going. But if she'd known about him from the beginning, she'd never have allowed herself to love him like she had. Like she still did.

The crowd applauded and she joined in, peering over their heads to see the yearling. But when she saw Jimmy leading the young thoroughbred, she came to her feet. *Jimmy* had trained a horse? He led the horse around the corral, looking handsome in his shirt, which matched those of the other stable hands.

She heard his name being called and spotted little Jolene standing off to the side by the fence, cheering on her older brother. Beside Jolene, their mother did the same. But when Olivia looked back and saw Jimmy looking so small and innocent in the middle of the corral beside the thoroughbred, she thought again about what Ridley had said last night. About how he couldn't fight for a cause that would allow people to be auctioned off like thoroughbreds. And a wave of pride swept through her for him, washing up against her frustration and hurt and causing the dull ache inside her to hurt afresh.

"Livvy, dear. Are you all right? Have the week's festivities been too much for you?"

Olivia turned, pasting on a smile. "Too much for me, Aunt? What about you? You've hardly stayed still for more than two seconds in recent days."

Elizabeth smiled, and the brightness in her eyes all but masked the shadows beneath. "I wouldn't change anything about today. My husband is realizing the fruition of a long-held dream." Elizabeth breathed deep, her gaze on the general some distance away. "I learned long ago, Livvy, that a wife must love her husband's dreams as much as she loves him. Because the two are inseparable. If a wife can't embrace the desires of her husband's heart, he will never become the man he could have been, if only she had."

Hearing the devotion in Elizabeth's voice, Olivia felt her gaze drawn back to Ridley. She certainly knew what his dream was and still envied his passion for it. Yet she could hardly embrace it. That very morning, she'd read a newspaper article about another Indian uprising out west. But as dangerous as the Colorado Territory seemed to be, wasn't it equally dangerous for him to stay here?

The bidding for the last yearling commenced and scarcely ten minutes later, the final winning bid of the auction drew a hearty round of applause. Jimmy tipped his cap to the crowd as he left, giving them his trademark grin and enjoying the attention.

"The general tells me," Aunt Elizabeth said softly, leaning close, "that General Meeks has formally requested permission to speak with you this week, Livvy." Elizabeth took hold of her hand. "It's going to be a good match, my dear. For so many reasons."

Nodding, Olivia turned back and spotted General Meeks making his way toward them through the crowd. She fought the ridiculous urge she had to run—which didn't bode well for the future she and General Meeks were slated to share. But forcing herself to look at her circumstances in a more practical light—including what she'd learned last night—she knew this marriage was a sound choice. She'd be well cared for. It would benefit Belle Meade and the Hardings, who had given her her life back. How could she reject it? She couldn't. And Chattanooga wasn't two hours from Nashville by rail. Certainly General Meeks wouldn't begrudge her visiting Aunt Elizabeth on occasion. He could certainly afford the train fare. She took a steadying breath. Aunt Elizabeth was right. This would be a good match.

Yet no matter how many times she told herself that, she still couldn't imagine marrying the man. Not while Ridley Cooper was still in the world.

"Mrs. Aberdeen, wasn't that exciting?" General Meeks pulled a handkerchief from his pocket and swabbed his moist forehead, then continued on up and over his shiny scalp. "Mrs. Harding, may I offer my congratulations, ma'am, as I did to your husband just now? A splendid day for Belle Meade! Just splendid."

"Thank you, General Meeks. We're deeply honored to have you in attendance, sir."

"Ah! Mr. Cooper!" General Meeks looked past Olivia and held out his hand. "Join us."

Ridley came toward them and reached to shake the general's hand. Ridley looked as tired as she felt, and Olivia wondered if he'd gotten any sleep at all last night.

"Well done today, Mr. Cooper."

"Thank you, General Meeks. I appreciate your contribution to the winning bids. You got yourself two fine horses."

"Yes, I did. And I'll be by for them." General Meeks paused, eyes wide. "Mrs. Harding, are you all right, ma'am?"

Olivia recognized the pallor of Elizabeth's complexion only too well. But before she could even react, Ridley had Elizabeth in his arms.

Waiting in the entrance hall, Ridley heard footsteps on the staircase and looked up. Olivia descended, looking beautiful but weary, as though the weight of the world rested on her slender shoulders. She seemed determined to look everywhere but at him.

He met her at the landing. "How is she?"

"She's resting now. The doctor and the general are with her." She glanced down at her hands. "The doctor said it was another spell. A little worse than those she's had before ... But he's given her some laudanum to help her rest." She lifted her gaze, still not looking at him. "She told me to thank you again, for coming to her rescue."

She smiled that polite, distant little smile he hadn't seen in a long time, and he was surprised by how much it hurt to see it again.

"Olivia, look at me."

She shook her head. "No, Ridley. I can't. It's over."

"It's not over. I'm still here."

"But not for long." Her face crumpled. Her breath came hard. "You're leaving, and I—"

Footsteps sounded from above, and Ridley drew her with him into the parlor and shut the door. When he saw her tears, he took her in his arms, and to his surprise, she came willingly. Her shoulders shook with silent sobs, and any trace of doubt that she was meant to be with him fled.

"Come with me," he whispered. "I love you, Olivia. I've loved you ever since you told me where to put that advertisement. The one for the teaching position, remember?" He kissed the crown of her head. "If memory serves, I *think* you told me I could put it with the horse droppings."

Her shoulders shook harder, whether from laughter or tears he wasn't sure.

"That's what *you* said," she whispered against his chest, then held him tighter.

"I'll take care of you," he promised softly. "We'll build a life together, just the two of us. We won't start out in a mansion on a hill, but ... you'll never be cold in the winter, you'll never go hungry, and ..." His throat tightened with emotion, his promises sounding flimsy compared to what Meeks could lavish on her from the start. "You'll never wonder whether your husband loves you more than his own life. Or whether you're the first thing he wants to see in the morning and the very last thing he wants to hold as he turns down the lamp at night."

"Oh, Ridley ..." She took a shuddering breath and drew back, her head bowed.

Ridley smoothed her hair and tilted her face to meet his, and the look in her eyes punctured a hole in his chest and told him everything he didn't want to hear.

"I love you too," she whispered. "And I ..." Tears traced her cheeks. "I *want* to be with you, but I can't leave Aunt Elizabeth. She needs me too much. And with my teaching ..." She shook her head. "With all my heart I wish you didn't have to leave. I wish you could stay. Here. With me. But" — she hiccupped a sob — "just as you've tried to tell me, all along, that you couldn't stay, I've tried to make it clear to you ... that I can't go."

How long they stood that way, he couldn't say. He only knew that when she slipped her hand around his neck and drew his mouth down to meet hers, he realized for the first time what bittersweet tasted like.

Chapter FIFTY-SIX

Monday morning, Ridley steeled himself and knocked on General Harding's office door. Hearing the man's reply, he entered.

The general glanced up from his desk. "Mr. Cooper. Right on time, as always. Have a seat. Have you had a chance to review the figures from the auction?"

"Yes, sir." Ridley laid the report on his desk. "It's all in here. The expenses, the yearlings, their trainers, what the winning bids were, what percentage each man is due."

"Well done, Mr. Cooper. So tell me ..." Harding leaned back in his chair. "Have you changed your mind yet?"

Ridley shook his head. "No, sir. I'm leaving this week. Wednesday, at the latest. I've got a few more ... loose ends to tie up. Then I'll be on my way."

Harding studied him for a moment. "You're somewhat of an enigma to me, Mr. Cooper."

"How's that, sir?"

"Because I've done everything I know to do to get you to stay. And, within reason, I'd do more. Yet at the same time, I'd be almost disappointed if you changed your mind. There's something about a man deciding to do something, and then doing it no matter the odds or obstacles. It demonstrates character, which is sorely lacking in so many these days."

Ridley couldn't even come close to smiling. "No worries about me changing my mind, sir. How is Mrs. Harding today?"

"She's doing better. Still weak, but that's been an ongoing struggle for some time, as you know. But thank you for your concern. She thinks mighty highly of you, Mr. Cooper. As do I."

Ridley met General Harding's gaze straight on. "Thank you, sir. I return the sentiment."

"You told me where you're leaving from before. To head west ..."

"St. Joseph, sir. At the end of the month."

"And yet you're leaving Belle Meade so soon."

"I've got plenty to do to get ready for the trip."

"I'm sure you do. Well ..." The general sighed and turned back a page in his ledger and withdrew an envelope. "This is, I believe, all the money that is owed you from the auction, plus a few days of work this month, minus boarding expenses for Seabird *and* Dauntless, of course."

That made Ridley smile. "You never miss a penny, General."

"Not when one is stood to be made." The man grinned.

Harding held out the envelope. But just as Uncle Bob had predicted that morning—after they'd talked and laid things out, settling on what was best to do—Ridley couldn't bring himself to take it.

Harding eyed him. "Is there a problem, Mr. Cooper?"

Ridley knew he could take that envelope and leave, never having said a thing to the general about the war or what side he'd fought for. But he also knew in coming days and months—even years—he would think back to this moment and wish he'd been honest with the man. And yet ... he also remembered how doing the right thing had turned out for him in the war and how that decision was still costing him. His thoughts turned to Olivia, and he tried to steer them elsewhere. He needed to be clear minded for the next few moments and thinking about her made him anything but. Yet thoughts about Olivia Aberdeen were nearly as persistent as the woman herself.

He was certain about his feelings for her and thought he'd been certain about hers for him. He saw the affection in her eyes and felt it in the urgency of her kiss. He *knew* she loved him. But she'd made her choice, and he'd made his—painful though they were.

"General Harding, I appreciate the opportunity to work at Belle Meade. But before I accept that check"—his gut knotted up—"*if* you still choose to give it to me, I need to tell you something ..."

As he spoke, painstakingly revealing more of who he was and of his part in the war, Ridley watched Harding's expression. The only indication of General William Giles Harding's anger was the beard reaching halfway down his chest. It began to tremble.

"It was never my intention, General, when I first came here, to stay as long as I did. I was going to be here a month, maybe two, then be on my way. But one thing led to another, and two months led to a year. And the only reason I'm telling you all this now is because ... during that time, I've grown to respect you, sir. Far more, I'm hesitant to admit, than when I first came."

A full moment passed.

Then Harding slowly, deliberately, came to his feet. "*Why* did you come to Belle Meade, Mr. Cooper?" He circled the corner of the desk. "To exact some sort of vengeance? To rob me of my honor? On my own land? In my own home?"

"No, sir. I give you my word, I ..." Seeing Harding's eyes darken, Ridley continued. "I came here because I wanted to learn from Uncle Bob."

Harding scoffed. "And just how did you know about the talents of my head hostler?"

"Because, sir ..." Ridley drew in a breath. "I found him hiding your thoroughbreds up in the high pasture ... back during the war."

Harding's eyes narrowed, and Ridley could almost see the shards of truth jarring into place for him. General Harding walked to the window and stared out, his spine rigid as a post. After a moment, he turned back.

"Andersonville," Harding whispered.

Ridley held his gaze. "They shot me coming down the mountain. After I left Uncle Bob."

"And after *not* confiscating my thoroughbreds."

Ridley gave a nod.

"So ... in an odd twist of fate, Mr. Cooper, it would seem that I have you to thank for the champion thoroughbreds on my plantation."

"No, sir. I'm not the one to thank. There's only one reason I didn't take those horses that night ... Robert Green. He's the reason you have what you have, sir. Not me."

Harding stared at him long and hard. Then finally walked back to his desk. Ridley glanced at the check again, then back at Harding. And received his answer.

He headed for the door.

"Mr. Cooper."

Ridley turned.

Harding reached for the envelope and held it out. "A handshake is as binding a contract as any words dried on paper."

Remembering the general having said that, Ridley reached for the check. Then Harding pulled it back.

"But I want you off my land by noon today. Is that clear?"

"Yes, sir."

Ridley took the check and walked to the door.

"One more agenda item before you go, Mr. Cooper."

Ridley waited, detecting a glint in the general's eyes.

"Remember our agreement with Seabird. If she ever races again, I want fifty percent. No cap on earnings. For her lifetime."

"You may want fifty percent, General. But we shook on twenty-five." Halfway out the door, Ridley looked back and caught the tail end of a smile on General William Giles Harding's face. "I like a man with a sense of humor and a touch of stallion in him too, sir."

Ridley closed the door behind him.

Chapter
FIFTY-SEVEN

You feel a little warm this evening, Aunt Elizabeth." Olivia pressed a hand to Elizabeth's cheek, then dipped the cloth in the basin of water, wrung it out, and laid it across her aunt's forehead.

"Mmmm . . ." Elizabeth sighed. "That feels good. You're so kind to me, Livvy. I'm so grateful you're here with us."

Olivia scraped together a smile. "I'm . . . grateful to be here too, Aunt."

Elizabeth's brow furrowed. "Dear, it's Monday," she said in a softer voice. "Don't you teach class tonight?"

"Yes, ma'am, I do. But I wanted to make sure you were feeling better before I left."

Elizabeth waved off Olivia's concern, her delicate wrist even thinner than Olivia had realized. Olivia adjusted the cloth on Elizabeth's forehead, and her aunt's eyes slipped closed.

Elizabeth had been embarrassed about fainting at the auction. But Olivia assured her Ridley had carried her inside quickly and only a handful of people witnessed it.

Ridley . . . Olivia sighed. Even thinking his name hurt.

She looked out the window toward the hills where approaching dusk settled in folds of purple and gray over the trees, the sun making its slow descent. Although she'd seen him at a distance, she hadn't spoken with him again since they'd shared those few moments in the central parlor on Saturday. She'd wanted to go to church yesterday and had hoped to see him then, at least briefly, but Elizabeth had asked her to sit with her.

But really, what more was there to say between them? He would leave on Friday to start his way west, and she would stay here at Belle Meade with Elizabeth and the Hardings before marrying General

Meeks. A sickening weight pressed down inside her at the prospect. And for as long as she lived, she knew she would never, ever forget the promises Ridley had whispered to her.

Even now they played tug-of-war with her heart and made her want to run and find him. To see him while she still could, before he left.

"I've had a dream, Livvy ..." Elizabeth's voice was soft and breathy. "Twice now. And each time I awaken thinking of you."

Olivia leaned closer, noticing the crepe-like lines wreathing Elizabeth's eyes. "Why me?"

"Because it reminds me of something you told me." Elizabeth smiled faintly. "When you first came here. About that door ... in the carriage. The one that flew open. Do you remember?"

Olivia nodded, thinking of the night she and Ridley had taken their first walk and of his opinion on why she hadn't fallen out the door that day. Swiftly on the heels of that thought, clambered another, reminding her of how much the Hardings had done for her—Elizabeth, specifically—and of how much she owed them.

"In my dream ..." Elizabeth's eyes closed again. "There's a door. And somehow, I know what lies beyond is lovelier than anything I've ever seen. And I want to see it. So badly." Elizabeth frowned, her eyes opening. "But I can't, Livvy, because the door is always locked."

Olivia smoothed the lines of worry from her aunt's forehead, eager to reassure her, knowing it was the laudanum talking more than Elizabeth. "You don't think that has anything to do with the walk we took last week, do you? When Mr. Hunsaker warned us to keep the door closed on his prized roses?"

Elizabeth blinked. "You know ... It actually might, at that." The furrows in her brow gradually lessened. She glanced toward the door. "You need to go, Livvy. But, before you do ... I want to thank you again for being a friend to my Mary. She is ... quite changed in recent months, thanks to you."

Olivia reached for her hand. "Mary is a delightful person. Intelligent and spirited, much like her mother."

Warmth softened Elizabeth's eyes. "You're giving her wings to fly."

Olivia shook her head. "*We* are."

Hearing the anticipated footsteps in the hallway, Olivia rose and pressed a kiss to Elizabeth's cheek. "I'll stop by again in the morning."

The door opened and Mary entered. "I'm here to spend some time with my favorite mother." Mary tossed Olivia a look, pointedly touching the brooch at her neckline before giving her mother a hug.

Olivia had splurged on the little treasure she'd put inside the painted box for Mary recently. But Mary's reaction then—and since—had been worth it.

Mary held up a newspaper. "I thought I'd read today's news to you, Mother. There's an article about Mrs. Acklen." She tapped the front page and arched her eyebrows. "And also …" Her gaze swung to Olivia. "About the auction."

Aunt Elizabeth feigned sadness. "Susanna beat you to it, I'm afraid, dear. But I'd love for you to read more from this."

She held up a novel, and Mary laid the newspaper aside.

Her own curiosity piqued, Olivia gestured to it. "May I? For later?"

Mary nodded, opening the book.

On her way to class, Olivia looked over at the old Harding cabin as she passed. No sign of Ridley, or Uncle Bob. Most likely, they were still working in the stables. If Ridley didn't seek her out by tomorrow, she would seek him. Maybe even later tonight, if she saw a light in the window on her way home.

With a flat stretch of meadow in front of her and the sun's last rays reaching over the hills, she scanned the front page of the newspaper. She found the article about the auction and grew excited when she read the words "generous array of sumptuous food" and "yearlings second in excellence to none." The servants would enjoy reading that after all their hard work.

An adjacent title drew her attention …

FETTERMAN MASSACRE
81 SLAUGHTERED IN INDIAN UPRISING

The words *Nebraska* and *Colorado Territory* jumped out at her. She slowed her steps as she read. Then finally stopped, her lips moving silently. *Captain W. J. Fetterman gave orders to attack … small group of Sioux warriors … Soldiers from Fort Kearny pursued over the ridge* … She swallowed. *Two thousand Indians laid in wait … stripped and mutilated bodies … found by patrol.* The newspaper crinkled in her grip. *In retaliation for soldier attack … Sand Creek Massacre … Colorado Territory … Killing 163 Cheyenne, mostly women and children …*

She read the remaining paragraphs, then lifted her gaze. And *this* was where Ridley was going? Where he wanted to start a new life? Such savagery and barbarism. It made no sense. And fear clutched at her throat. *Please, God, keep him safe.*

Not wanting to be late for class, she hurried on, tucking the newspaper in her book and pushing the all-too-vivid images from her mind.

Big Ike was waiting for her as usual. He didn't seem much in a mood to talk, which suited her fine tonight. By the time they reached the clearing, the sun had set and the brisk walk had helped to clear her mind. Hearing the laughter and conversation coming from inside the cabin did her heart good.

She paused at the door. "Will you be joining us tonight, Ike?"

"I don't know, ma'am." He glanced down at his feet, then toward the cabin. "I ain't sure I was meant for this."

"Ike." She waited for him to look at her again, remembering a similar moment when she'd doubted herself. "It's fine if you don't want to learn to read or write. I won't blame you one little bit if that's what you decide. But!" She smiled. "I want you to know that you *can* do this. You're *able* to do this ... even if you choose not to."

He stared, his expression all but lost to the dark. "You in cahoots with my Susanna?"

Olivia grinned. "If you come to class tonight, I'll tell you."

His laughter was deep and hearty. "I be in directly, ma'am."

"... and the Belle Meade ... auc —" In front of the class, Betsy squinted at the newspaper, sounding out the second syllable of the word.

Holding the oil lamp higher so Betsy could see, Olivia liked how some of the other students, both young and old, leaned forward, waiting expectantly. A few of the older ones doing so from new desks. Well, new to them anyway.

Off to the side, little Jolene sat on the floor, having come by herself tonight. Her mother felt poorly and Jimmy had chosen to stay home with her. Olivia gave Jolene a little wink and that earned her a grin. They'd already decided to walk home together.

Olivia leaned closer to Betsy, but Betsy glanced up.

"Now don't go tellin' me, Missus Aberdeen. I can get it."

"I know you can," Olivia said. "Because you've seen part of that word before." She glanced back at the door, wondering where Big Ike was. He'd had plenty of time to make his rounds. She hoped he hadn't changed his mind.

"I got it!" Betsy suddenly turned. "Auc-*tion!*" she said, and did that little dance she always did when she got a word right.

People clapped. A few whooped and hollered.

Betsy held up a hand. "I got a few more words, y'all." She looked at the newspaper again. "And the Belle Meade *auction,*" she said with some sass, "was a great ..." She squinted again, then made a face as if to say this was easy. *"Success!"*

Everyone laughed and clapped as Betsy curtsied, holding out one side of her apron—until a rifle shot sounded outside. Followed by another.

The room went silent.

Olivia started for the door when a window exploded somewhere behind her and fire rained in. People screamed and grabbed their children as the door to the cabin burst open.

Big Ike strode through. "Run for the woods! Don't stop!"

Olivia took a few steps and felt a hot wind behind her, breathing up her legs, like she'd stood too close and too long by the hearth. Then she smelled something.

"Missus Aberdeen!" Betsy jerked her arm. "You *burnin'*, ma'am!"

Olivia looked behind her to see the bottom of her skirt on fire, and while the world around her moved at a fever pitch, her own motions felt slow and lethargic.

"Turn 'round, ma'am!" Betsy screamed, untying her apron. She whipped at the flames, then knelt and covered the back of Olivia's skirt. She briefly grabbed Olivia's hand. "Come on!"

Smoke burning her eyes and throat, Olivia reached the door and heard a deep, throaty rumble behind her. She turned to see the flames devouring the old cabin. Then caught sight of something moving behind one of the desks. Not something—some*one*!

Jolene ...

Seeing Betsy already halfway to the woods, Olivia turned and ran back inside. Jolene cowered behind a desk, coughing and covering her head. "Come here, honey! I've got you!" Olivia scooped her up, and Jolene's thin little arms clamped tight about her neck.

Almost to the door, Olivia heard glass breaking and another

explosion behind her, but she didn't turn back. She ran for the woods like Big Ike had said. Betsy was there, waiting, with the others. Betsy put her arms around little Jolene and kissed her head.

Jolene cried and pointed. "Them men with guns ... They ain't got no faces, Missus Aberdeen!"

Olivia looked up. At the top of the ridge to the west stood four men. The blaze illuminated their silhouettes and though their clothes appeared normal, Jolene was right. They had no faces. They were all wearing hoods, with only black sockets for eyes.

Chapter
FIFTY–EIGHT

*T*his is how you repay my family's kindness, Olivia?" General Harding stood over her in his office, the control in his voice contrasting the fury in his eyes. "You sneak behind my back to teach in this school and knowingly endanger the lives of my servants. And their children!"

His voice rose, and Olivia jumped.

"Not to mention yourself!"

Still shaken from the incident, her hair and clothes reeking of smoke, the hem of her skirt in burned tatters, Olivia steadied her voice and her emotions. "I didn't decide to teach in a freedmen's school to spite you in any way, General Harding. Or to endanger anyone. I simply wanted to help."

"To help?" He gave a harsh laugh and began pacing. "How is this helping? Do you realize that last week one of these schools north of here was set on fire just as this one was tonight?" He stilled. "But they *shot* the men, women, and children as they fled *that* building. Including the white teacher."

Olivia closed her eyes, not having heard of that incident but able to imagine it only too clearly after this evening. "I didn't do this naively, sir. I knew there was danger involved. But … every choice comes with risk. And a cost." How well she was learning that lesson.

He leveled a stare. "Rest assured, Olivia … Today, of all days, I am most fully aware of that fact." Sighing, he sat heavily in his desk chair. "Big Ike says there were four men, but their faces were covered."

"Yes, sir. Once we all got out, we met in the woods and accounted for everyone. Then hurried back here."

"There was nothing recognizable about any of the men?"

Olivia shook her head. "It was dark, and they were a ways off."

"Injuries?" he asked, voice solemn.

"A few have minor burns, but … it could have been much, much worse as you know. Rachel is treating those with burns."

No one at Belle Meade had seen the flames or, with it being dark, had detected the smoke, since the old hunting cabin was over a mile away. Still, word spread quickly and a small crowd had gathered near Rachel's. Olivia had expected—hoped—to see Ridley there. But neither he nor Uncle Bob had shown.

"You're not to speak a word of this to my wife, Olivia. I will not have her already-weakened health further compromised. Do I make myself clear?"

"Yes, sir," she answered, not quite sure how she'd manage that but determined to follow his wish. She didn't want to upset Elizabeth either. And it was her aunt's prerogative whether or not to tell the general about her own part in the school. Not Olivia's.

"This is certain to be in the newspapers later this week." He rubbed his temple. "I pray they don't include your name. Or mine. But they likely will."

That reminded her of something. "Sir, I want you to know that when looking for a site for the school, we specifically chose somewhere not on Harding land. To help protect you."

"How considerate." His smile was cool. "If only you would have chosen not to involve my servants and my wife's personal companion, who is also a guest in my home."

She realized nothing she could say would change his opinion. And looking at it from his perspective, she understood.

"You say 'we' about the freedmen's school, Olivia. I'm no simpleton. I assume Mr. Pagette was involved, since you met him in my office that day. Who else assisted in this?"

"I'm sorry, sir, but I can't tell you that."

"Can't? Or won't?"

"Won't, sir."

"It was one of the servants, wasn't it? Betsy, perhaps? Big Ike? Jedediah?"

"General." Olivia moved to the edge of her seat. "These people did nothing wrong. And none of them deserve to be punished. They simply want to learn, to better themselves. To have an opportunity at a richer, more meaningful life."

Seeing the surprise on his face, Olivia was a little surprised herself at the tone she'd used. Not harsh. But certainly not … submissive.

And what she'd said about the servants' lives wasn't lost in relation to her own either.

"None of the servants will be punished, Olivia. But neither will I tolerate any further involvement in a freedmen's school. From them. *Or* from you."

"But, General, teaching is something I've come to love. And ... I'm good at it. I'll never be allowed to teach in one of the—"

"Perhaps the way I phrased it left the issue open for debate. So let me state it again ... As long as you are in my home, Olivia Aberdeen, you will *not* teach in a freedmen's school or be associated with one in any way. Not and remain under my household and my guardianship."

She knew only too well what he meant by guardianship: His financial support. "I understand, General." He opened the door for her. "Good night, General Harding."

"Olivia ..."

She paused.

"Big Ike told me what you did. Going back inside to save Jolene ... That was a very brave thing to do."

"Thank you, sir. But I didn't feel very brave at the time."

"One rarely does when one is doing something brave."

She was still thinking about that when she walked into her room and got ready for bed. Wishing she could have washed the smoke from her hair, she looked out the window and could barely see the outline of the old Harding cabin. No light in the window. But it was late, and she was exhausted anyway.

She climbed into bed and an inexplicable loneliness settled over her. And she realized what it was ... She wanted to talk to Ridley, to tell him all that had happened, to see his reactions, his eyes when he smiled, his scowl when he got cross with her. Which he surely would after learning about tonight. He hadn't been in favor of her teaching at the school, at first. But he would know exactly what to say right now to lift her spirits. Only, there was nothing he could say to cure what she was feeling.

Because *he* was the cure. And he was leaving.

The loneliness inside her fanned out. *Oh, Lord, what am I doing?* She could scarcely breathe. She sat up in bed and took several deep breaths, the events of the night crowding close, like the smoke clinging to her hair, and the forthcoming proposal from General Meeks.

She laid back down but sleep evaded her. She kept thinking about how there would be no more freedmen's school for the servants here, and her heart ached for them. And for herself. Then she realized …

A number of them had already learned to read and write. Quite well. So even if she never got the opportunity to teach any of them again—or anyone else for that matter—the people she'd taught could teach each other.

The realization brought a momentary slice of peace, until she thought about how she still wanted to share all this with Ridley.

The next morning, not feeling hungry, Olivia skipped breakfast and— with Betsy's help—washed her hair instead. She towel-dried it as best she could, put it up in combs, then visited Aunt Elizabeth as promised.

With her encouragement, Elizabeth decided she felt well enough to sit up in a chair in the bedroom and take an egg and half of a biscuit. When Elizabeth inquired about class the previous evening, Olivia went into great detail about Betsy reading the article and tried to mimic what Betsy had said and done, much to Elizabeth's delight. But as the general had requested, she shared nothing more.

And surprisingly, that sufficed.

But the simple act of sitting up proved to be too much, too soon, for Elizabeth, and Olivia helped her back into bed just before Mary arrived.

Olivia made a beeline for the stallions' stable, knowing Ridley would be there by this time of morning. But he wasn't. She asked one of the stable hands about him but the man hadn't seen him. Surely Ridley would have heard about the fire by now from either the general or one of the servants. That would prompt him to come and find her, to see how she was.

She worked in the supply room on the inventory until noon, at which time she'd almost begun to think Ridley was avoiding her. Not a difficult thing to do at Belle Meade, she knew from experience. Yet also not easy in the long run.

But when she walked into the mares' stable and saw Seabird's empty stall, she relaxed.

He was out riding. A little late in the day to still be gone, but heaven knew the man did the work of two men. He deserved a little time to himself. After lunch, she made her way back to the mares' stable when she spotted Uncle Bob in one of the corrals with a pretty little bay mare. "Uncle Bob!" she called.

He looked up and waved. Then promptly went back to work. She hesitated for a moment, then continued on inside. But when she saw Seabird's still-empty stall, she retraced her steps and let herself inside the corral.

Uncle Bob looked up as she approached, absent his usual smile. "How are you, Missus Aberdeen? I done heard 'bout what went on last night, ma'am." He shook his head. "I sure am sorry. You all right?"

"I'm fine." She nodded. "Thanks to Betsy and Big Ike."

"Them's good people. Both of 'em."

"Yes, they are."

He reached into the pocket of his apron, pulled out a small apple, and offered it to the mare. The horse grabbed it.

Olivia stepped closer to rub the mare on the forehead. "Uncle Bob, do you know where Ridley is? I've … been looking for him."

"Yes, ma'am," he said, his gaze elsewhere. "I do. But first …" He reached into his shirt pocket this time. "I'm to give you this."

Instinctively, Olivia held out a hand, but when she saw the seashell he placed in her palm, her world began to narrow until, finally, all she could see was the shell. And suddenly she was back in the cabin, on the night Ridley had been injured.

I've wondered if you still had that, she'd asked him.

'Course I do, he'd said. *I'll never part with it. At least not willingly.*

His response echoed in her ears—*I'll never part with it,* reverberating inside her. And without being told, she knew. Her fingers closed tightly around the shell as an unseen fist closed tightly around her heart.

"When did …" But she couldn't finish the question. She looked at Uncle Bob through tears, an unseen chasm threatening to swallow her whole.

"Yesterday, ma'am. The general, he …" Uncle Bob blew out a breath, his bottom lip quivering. "He give Ridley 'til noon to clear out … after Ridley told him."

"*Told* him?" Olivia felt a flush of hot, then cold. "You mean … about—"

"Yes, ma'am. Told him everythin'. Said he couldn't leave here, much less take the auction money, without settin' things straight 'tween 'em as men."

Oh, Ridley…

"But it's all right, ma'am. I already knew he couldn't, 'cause I know Ridley Cooper. I done gave him permission to tell my part too."

She frowned. "Your part?"

He nodded. " 'Bout that night Ridley and me first met on the mountain …" He glanced south. "Back durin' the war."

"You and Ridley met during the war?"

His eyes widened. "Oh, Lawd, ma'am … He ain't said nothin' 'bout that when he told you the rest?"

She shook her head, seeing by the look on Uncle Bob's face that he was wishing he hadn't either. But he was sure going to.

Gone. Ridley was gone.

Olivia paused in the meadow and looked behind her to where Uncle Bob still stood on the front porch of the old Harding cabin. He lifted a hand, and she did the same, then continued toward the mansion, her thoughts in a tumult. Ridley had met Uncle Bob during the war, with orders to confiscate the thoroughbreds. And yet…he hadn't. No matter how she tried, she couldn't stop crying. She was so proud of him. But a part of her was angry too.

Angry Ridley hadn't told her he was leaving. That he had just up and—

No sooner had the thought formed than its flaws showed themselves. If there was one thing Ridley Cooper had made clear to her from the start, it was that he was leaving. He'd never left any doubt of that.

"He done left me half his auction money too," Uncle Bob had told her. "I ain't got no idea what to do with all that money. Got everythin' I need right here."

She fingered the treasured seashell, running her thumb nail over the twenty-eight ridges, fitting her thumb into the smooth underside. This had been with Ridley through so much living—and near dying. Through the war, through Andersonville, and the year following, and through the time he'd been here, with her. Ridley couldn't have given her anything more precious than this. Or left her with anything that would make her want him more.

But surely, he'd known that. Which, for some reason, made her hurt all the worse.

Chapter
FIFTY-NINE

Walking back from the lower pasture days later, Olivia looked toward the house to see Mary smiling and waving at her from the front porch. Olivia lifted a hand in response, but couldn't mimic Mary's enthusiasm.

Fingering the seashell as she'd done almost constantly in recent days, she slipped the shell back into her skirt pocket and dried her eyes. No matter where she went on the plantation, she saw him. As clearly as if he were standing in Seabird's empty stall or leaning down to give Dauntless a rub or working in one of the corrals with a horse. He was everywhere. And yet, she had no idea where he was. Had he left St. Joseph yet? He'd told Uncle Bob he wasn't going west until the end of the month. But had that changed? Had he decided to leave earlier, the way he'd done here? And where was he going once he got to the Colorado Territory? He'd mentioned Denver, but nothing more.

The same sick, lost feeling welled up in her again, and her legs felt heavy as she walked up the meadow toward the mansion. In her mind's eye, she saw Ridley standing by the front door, depositing her trunk there as he had that first day. *Oh, Lord ... I was trying so hard to do the right thing*. For Elizabeth, the Hardings, for duty and honor. But whatever this was, it didn't feel right. She couldn't eat. She could hardly sleep. Yet sleep was what she craved because it erased the pain for a while. Made her forget. Until she awakened, and it started all over again.

Mary gestured for her to walk faster. "Hurry!" she said in a stage whisper. "He's here!"

Olivia's hope renewed in a rush. "Mr. Cooper?" she whispered.

Mary frowned and looked at her funny. "No, General Meeks. He's in the parlor. He's been waiting for you."

Olivia had known this moment was coming, though she wished she could run and hide from it forever. She was ready to give him her answer, but she wasn't looking forward to it.

General Meeks stood when she entered the room. "Mrs. Aberdeen, how nice to ..." His eyes narrowed with concern. "I hope you're not unwell, ma'am."

"Welcome, General Meeks. And no, I'm not unwell. At least, not in the way you mean. But thank you." Olivia perched on the edge of the sofa and gestured for him to return to his chair, catching a telling creak of a floorboard out in the entrance hall.

A moment passed.

"Mrs. Aberdeen ..." He offered a gracious smile. "You have honored me with your attention both in the engaging exchange of letters and in the delightful enjoyment of your company. You are a fine, lovely young woman who has so much to offer a man such as ..."

Unable to listen to the kindnesses, Olivia reached for strength beyond her own and held up a hand. "General Meeks." She attempted to soften the interruption with a look. "Forgive me, but I need to say something to you that is ... most difficult. And that does not reflect in any way upon your character, your conduct, or your good name."

The warmth in his eyes clouded, but she pushed on, her stomach giving her fair warning.

"I've searched, General, and there is no easy way to say this, but ... I've firmly come to believe—even more so in recent months—that marriage should be a union between a man and woman who not only have mutual respect and admiration for each other, as we obviously do, but ... who share a special affection for each other as well." The knots in her stomach tangled further, and it was all she could do to maintain his gaze. "And while I admire you very much, my feelings do not extend beyond—"

"Mrs. Aberdeen, before you say another word ..."

He came to sit beside her on the sofa, but Olivia detected the emotion in his eyes and felt guilt creeping forward.

"Please, General. I fear if I stop now, I'll never see this through."

"And I fear if you don't stop now, we'll likely end up needing to call a servant to clean the Hardings' lovely carpet."

Her mouth slipped open even as his smile turned sheepish.

"Mrs. Aberdeen ..." He glanced toward the open door leading to the entrance hall, then back at her, then winked. "Would you do me the honor, ma'am, of accompanying me on a walk? It's very fine out, and I believe you and I have much more in common than you might suppose."

"You're not too upset with me, Aunt?" Olivia leaned close, seeing the worry in Elizabeth's eyes.

"No, dear, of course not. But ... he's in love with his nurse? That sweet little roundish woman?"

Olivia laughed, relief flooding her all over again. "The very one. He told me they were friends at first and that their love gradually grew over time. That it almost sneaked up on him, in a sense." Which she understood only too well. Even if too late.

The bedroom door opened and Susanna entered with a tray. "Am I interruptin', ma'ams?"

Olivia shook her head. "Not at all. But I think it's going to take both of us to get this woman to eat." She motioned to the breakfast tray sitting untouched on the desk. No matter what she did, she couldn't seem to get Elizabeth to eat more than a bite or two at a time.

After General Meeks had left yesterday afternoon, Olivia had slipped in to see Elizabeth, but she'd been sleeping and had slept through the night. Even now, her color was pale, and Olivia didn't like the gauntness in her face. Perhaps if she asked Rachel, they could try another tea ...

But even as she thought it, she knew better. And she felt so helpless. Just as she had when she'd watched her own mother die. Life was full of choices. But sometimes, as she was learning, there were no choices given. God, in his kind-yet-unfathomable nature, narrowed the choices down to one. And most times, it wasn't the one she would have chosen. But mostly, Olivia had learned—the hard way—that some choices, once missed, were gone forever.

Susanna set the tray on the bed. "Well, I got me some warm chicken soup and biscuits slathered with butter. Brought my peach preserves too. That'll give her a good temptin'."

Elizabeth looked between them as if silently challenging their conviction. Then the concerned expression returned. "But, Livvy,

General Meeks had an obligation to you. He and the general shook hands ... That's as binding to my husband as any contract."

"But I released General Meeks of his obligation, Aunt. As I told you at the very first, I have no desire to ..." She stumbled over the words, knowing they weren't true. Not anymore. Not since Ridley. "To be married again."

"Hmmmph."

Olivia and Elizabeth both looked over at Susanna, who glanced up, obviously feigning surprise and doing a very poor job of it.

"What, ma'ams? There be somethin' wrong?"

Giving her a warning glance, Olivia continued, forcing a cheeriness to her voice she didn't feel, aware of Susanna's discerning gaze. "Belle Meade is my home now, Aunt. I'm going to stay right here with you. And I'm going to help you get better!" But even as she said it, tears revealed the truth. Olivia rose and pretended to smooth the bed covers.

"My dearest Livvy ..."

The soft whisper was Olivia's undoing. At Elizabeth's urging, she returned to her side.

Elizabeth touched a curl at Olivia's temple. "So much like your mother. Having you here has been like having her with me again. But, Livvy ... It seems we've both been trying to take care of each other. Perhaps a little too well. After all, not everything is up to us."

Olivia saw the look Elizabeth exchanged with Susanna.

"Livvy, dear ..." Elizabeth's lips trembled. "I'm dying. Oh ..." She waved a hand. "The doctor hasn't said anything to me, and I haven't told the general, but ... I can feel it. And I've known it for some time. That's why it's been such a wonderful adventure to watch you teaching at the freedmen's school. It was like living a dream through you."

Olivia looked over at Susanna, who gave her an almost imperceptible shake of her head, yet whose expression bore not a trace of surprise.

Elizabeth took her hand and squeezed it tightly. "Livvy, I have a little money put aside. I'm going to give it to you, and I want you to go somewhere—Charleston or Savannah, maybe even Richmond—and start over again. Start a new life, dear. Let me have the gift of knowing you're doing that before I go. Just as you've given my Mary wings, let me help give you yours."

Olivia shook her head. "I can't leave you."

A peacefulness slipped into Elizabeth's expression. "Remember the dream, Livvy? The one I told you about?"

Olivia nodded.

"I had it again. Last night."

Olivia's throat tightened. "Was the door ... unlocked this time?"

"No," Elizabeth whispered. "It was open."

Chapter
SIXTY

June 10, 1867

*O*livia turned and took a last, lingering look behind her at Belle Meade, the sun barely touching the horizon, the grounds still quiet but for the birds awakening the dawn.

"You ready, Missus Aberdeen?"

"Yes, Uncle Bob ... I am." And she was.

Over the past two days—and after Elizabeth's repeated prodding—she'd made ready for the trip and said her good-byes. Rachel, Susanna, Betsy, and Chloe had made pan after pan of beaten biscuits yesterday. For Ridley, they said. And for their trip west. Olivia held fast to that hope.

General Harding's reaction to her decision to leave had been less cordial. He'd been upset about General Meeks's pending nuptials—mainly that they weren't with her—but his frustration lessened once he learned that General Meeks still wanted to invest in their business venture. But mostly, he seemed relieved that Elizabeth finally knew her days were numbered... Olivia witnessed a resignation—an acceptance—in the man that she hadn't seen before. She'd underestimated how much he'd dreaded telling his wife the truth.

When she'd said her final goodbye to him last night, he'd seemed almost relieved to see her go, which she understood. After all, it hadn't been his idea for her to come to Belle Meade. She'd always known that. And yet, he had *still* allowed her to come.

She turned to the buggy, about to climb in, when she noticed a cloth bag in the seat and looked over at Uncle Bob.

"Just some things people wanted you to have."

She picked up the bag, which had some weight to it, and accepted Uncle Bob's help up to the seat. She couldn't help but notice the horses. What beautiful animals they were. All chestnut sleekness, muscle, and grace. Magnificent creatures. If she found Ridley—no, *when* she found him—she had a request for him. It was time to face a very old fear, one she knew he could help her conquer.

As Uncle Bob snapped the reins, she held on with her free hand, then purposely let go.

Uncle Bob was quiet beside her, and she knew he missed Ridley, probably as much as she did, in his own way. "That cabin's way too quiet now," he'd told her a couple of days ago. "Never knew how much that man talked 'til he left. Lawd, it's a wonder I ever got anythin' done with him jabberin' on the whole time."

But she saw the fondness in his eyes and the way he kept looking back over at the cabin steps—just like she did—where Ridley used to sit.

She didn't know if what she was doing was brave or the most foolish thing she'd ever done. The only thing she knew was that she had one last chance. And she was taking it. *Lord, let him still be there. Help me find him. And please, Lord . . . Let his heart toward me remain unchanged.*

Curious as to the weight in the bag, she peeked inside, and when she saw the rolling pin, she giggled and pulled it out.

Uncle Bob smiled. "Betsy's always sayin' . . . Rollin' pin got two uses . . . beatin' biscuits and beatin' husbands!"

They both laughed.

Next, Olivia pulled out a leather pouch. *Rachel . . .* She opened it and breathed in the herbal scent before closing it again. She peered down into the bag and saw pieces of paper in the bottom. She took one out. Then another. Letters and notes from the servants. Her students. And even one from Mary. What treasures . . . She tucked them safely back inside. There'd be time enough to read them later.

She sneaked a look beside her, wondering why Uncle Bob had never attended one of her classes or asked for help in learning to read. But she figured he had his reasons and kept the question to herself.

The buggy rounded a bend in the road, and Olivia looked up. She instantly recognized the rock wall up ahead where the carriage had crashed. As they approached the exact spot, a tiny part of her almost thought that if she hoped hard enough, Ridley might be standing there waiting for her, at the place where they'd first met. But she knew better. Those kinds of endings were the stuff of stagecoach novels, not real life.

The train station was surprisingly crowded this early and by the time she purchased her ticket and stood on the platform to board, her fears wrestled against hope. She'd ridden on a train before, years earlier, but never this far and never with no one waiting for her on the other end.

"I'm frightened, Uncle Bob."

He peered at her beneath the rim of his worn black derby. "Then you's prob'ly right where the Lawd wants you to be, Missus Aberdeen. He always doin' things to make me shake my head and wonder." He smiled, his brown eyes warm and certain.

The train whistle blew in quick succession and steam billowed from the engine down the track. Olivia gripped her ticket, looking back at him.

"Thank you, Uncle Bob ... For everything you've done for me."

"Oh, I ain't done nothin', ma'am. Just carried you to the train station is all."

She eyed him until he smiled.

"You welcome, ma'am. And I thank you too, for all you done for us. Now ..." He nodded toward the porter waiting to help her board. "Go search out your new life, Missus Aberdeen. And when you find him" — he winked — "you be sure and tell him how proud Uncle Bob is of him and what he done."

"I will," she whispered.

Then on impulse, knowing some people wouldn't consider it proper, she offered Bob Green her hand and was delighted when he kissed it.

Six days, four trains — two with "unforeseen" mechanical problems — and three hotels later, Olivia wandered the streets of St. Joseph, Missouri, weary, hot, and sooty. Satchel in hand and with the bustle of her new dress sagging, she never dreamed so many people would be living — seemingly thriving — this far west. Everywhere she looked men, women, and children crowded the streets along with wagons, horses, oxen, mules, and endless barrels and crates of supplies. It felt as if everyone had suddenly decided to go west.

She searched every face she passed, praying to see those blue eyes staring back at her and that wry grin she loved tipping one side of his mouth. She reached into her skirt pocket, making sure the seashell was still there. Drawing strength from it, she willed it to act as a compass, of sorts, and lead her to him.

Uncle Bob had told her to check the liveries first. "Everybody headin' west gotta have a wagon," he'd said. So that's what she'd done. Two liveries so far, with two to go, according to the train porter. But so far, no one at either place had heard the name Ridley Cooper. Still, she refused to give in, no matter how much it looked like fear and defeat might win.

She spotted the next livery at the far end of the street on the opposite side and dodged wagons, stagecoaches, and numerous animal "deposits" to reach the boardwalk, all while praying beneath her breath. *If not this one, Lord, then the next.*

Her back and shoulder muscles ached from endless hours spent on the train either being deluged with cinders and soot or waiting for the engine to be repaired. But she had to admit, even with the mishaps and inconveniences, the trip had been exhilarating. And to think she'd made the journey on her own! All by herself ...

A tender yet timeless chord resonated against the thought, and Olivia slowed her steps on the boardwalk. Standing there in the midst of the hustle and the noise, she silently acknowledged the gentle yet firm reminder: Never *once* had she walked alone. Never once had God left her. He was so faithful, even when she was not. Even when she couldn't sense his presence, he was there. The past year had shown her that.

She lifted her eyes. The name on the aging shingle above the open double doors was faded but still legible: Ashford's Livery. The first thing she noticed upon entering was how neat and tidy the tools were hung on the wall. Everything had its place. She liked that.

A girl of perhaps twelve or thirteen stood oiling a saddle, intent on her task.

Olivia looked around for the owner but didn't see anyone else. "Pardon me ..."

The girl turned. Her smile came easily. "I'm sorry, ma'am. I didn't hear you come in. What can I help you with? You need a horse?" She motioned toward the back. "We have some real gentle mares and a couple of fine geldings."

Olivia couldn't help but admire the girl's assertiveness and spunk. Especially in one so young. "Actually, I just arrived in town, and I'm looking for someone. A Southern gentlemen." She warmed thinking of how true that was. "A man by the name of Ridley Cooper. He might have purchased a wagon from your establishment. He's heading west in a few days."

The girl shook her head. "Can't say I know that name, ma'am." Her expression hinted at apology. "But what you said just now pretty well accounts for almost everybody who walks through those doors."

Realizing how true that was and feeling foolish for not having thought of it herself, Olivia felt her spirits sag. "You're right, of course." She looked around again. She didn't want to slight the girl but also didn't want to leave any stone unturned. "Is the owner of the livery here, by chance? Where I might speak with him?"

The girl nodded, not seeming the least offended. "That'd be my father. He's in the back. But he'll be out directly." She went back to her polishing.

Olivia laid her satchel aside, admiring the girl's tenacity. "You're doing a very good job."

"Thank you, ma'am. I can make you one too, if you want."

Olivia looked at the saddle, then back at her. "*You* made that?"

As soon as she said it, she wished she could take it back, but the girl just grinned, nodding.

"My father taught me, ma'am. He's real good at it." She stepped to one side as though inviting Olivia to take a closer look.

Olivia ran a hand over the fine leather and fringe along the bottom. The detail work was superb. If General Harding saw this, he would order one for every thoroughbred at Belle Meade. "It's beautiful."

The girl's smile deepened, and she stood a little taller. "Thank you, ma'am. I'm making this one for a real pretty horse in the back."

Olivia noticed something carved into the leather flap and felt a quickening inside her. "What is this?" she whispered, pointing.

"Oh." The girl picked up a leather tool. "I'm almost done with it. It's a bird. Like one you'd see near the water. The man who ordered the saddle last week wanted something special. I told him I can do most anything. I drew this out for him and he liked it."

Olivia leaned closer, looking at the bird, its wings outstretched as if soaring over the water, and the same resonance she'd felt moments earlier returned with greater urgency. *Oh, please ... let it be him.*

Her pulse ticking up a notch, she looked toward the back of the livery. "Would you mind showing me this 'real pretty' horse? The one you're making this for?"

"Sure."

They started toward the back of the livery when a door opened and a man stepped through.

"McKenna, would you help me with ..." He saw Olivia and stopped. "I'm sorry, I didn't know we had a patron."

"Papa, I'm taking this lady back to see—"

"Don't let her talk your ears off, ma'am." The man looked at Olivia. "She'll do it if you let her."

He didn't crack a smile when he said it, but his young daughter did, which told Olivia much about their relationship.

Following the girl down the line of stalls, Olivia's hope mounted with each step, even while the taint of past disappointment cautioned against it. She breathed in the familiar smells and a pang of homesickness for Belle Meade washed over her.

McKenna stopped and gestured. And Olivia held her breath as she looked around the corner. Then broke into a grin.

Stretching for miles on the prairie west of town, hundreds of pristine white wagon canopies billowed in the afternoon breeze. And for a moment, all Olivia could do was stare, trying to take it all in. The excitement was almost tangible, the dreams waiting to be pursued hovering in the warm air over the camp, tugging at unseen reins.

Mouthwatering aromas drifted from cook fires as she walked past wagon after wagon. William Ashford had told her to search the north side of the camp, but she'd never dreamed of anything like this.

After an hour of searching and asking, overly warm and exhausted, lost in the maze of wagons and people, she slipped off her jacket and draped it over her left arm, arranging it just so. She slipped the shell from her pocket. Two weeks since she'd seen him. Yet it felt like a lifetime. Seeing the horses told her Ridley was still here. But it didn't answer the question still lingering in her heart, the fear pressing at her chest.

Would he welcome her after the choice she'd made at Belle Meade?

She walked on and soon came to the end of the wagons. All that was left was boundless prairie and sky. Knowing it was silly, she shielded her eyes against the sun and looked as far west as she could see. But ... no Rocky Mountains.

"Olivia?"

Hearing the hoarse whisper behind her, and the love and hope wrapped up in the sound of her name, in that voice, she turned. She scarcely had a chance to take in the sight of him before Ridley took her in his arms. She clung to him as though he might disappear in a dream if she let go. He whispered something against her hair—a prayer, she thought—but she couldn't be sure.

Still holding her, he drew back slightly, touching her face, her hair as though trying to make sure she was real. "You don't know how many nights I've sat right here, staring out into the emptiness and praying you were with me."

Seeing the emotion in his eyes only encouraged hers. "I wanted to go with you so badly, but—"

"I know," he whispered, understanding in his tone. His expression sobered. "Is Elizabeth …"

"I don't know." She teared up again. "If not yet … soon."

He searched her gaze. "And yet you came."

She ran a finger over his stubbled jaw, drinking in the sight of him. "You're my life, Ridley Cooper. I don't ever want you to leave me again."

"That's not a difficult promise to make, Olivia Aberdeen."

He kissed her, long and deep, and Olivia lost herself in him. Even more. Then remembering, she smiled.

"Ridley," she whispered against his mouth.

He drew back.

"I have something for you."

She reached into her pocket, withdrew the shell, and handed it to him. He looked at it, stilled for a second, then pressed it back into her palm. With gentle resolve, he brought her left hand to his lips. Too late, Olivia realized her jacket had slid to the ground. Ridley kissed her hand, the top of her wrist, and slowly, determinedly, moving up her bare arm, his breath warm, he kissed the length of her scar.

"You are the most beautiful thing I've ever seen," he whispered. "Except for one thing."

She looked up at him.

But he leaned around her, inspecting what, she wasn't sure.

When he looked at her again, that spark she loved so dearly was in his eyes. "You're the only woman for miles with a bustle that size."

She grinned.

"But not to worry." He winked. "I'm good with bustles."

Dear Reader,

Upon visiting Belle Meade Plantation some years ago, I knew I wanted to write a story that included the plantation's history, as well as that of the Harding family and the former slaves. One of those slaves, Robert Green, immediately captured my attention, and the more I learned about him, the more I wanted to know. According to history, he was a horse whisperer and is largely responsible for Belle Meade's success. When you visit Belle Meade, you'll discover that the staff considers him a "rock star" of sorts. And with good reason, considering that what's recorded in the prologue of *To Whisper Her Name* is rooted in truth. He really *did* hide those thoroughbreds.

Writing historical fiction against the backdrop of real history is challenging, to say the least. And attempting to sketch the character of someone you've never met is too. I went to great lengths to remain accurate to history but did take occasional liberties for the sake of story. For instance, the first yearling auction was actually held in August 1867 (not June), and Elizabeth Harding died only two days after that auction, shocking the citizens of Nashville. Also, General William Giles Harding (not Ridley) is the man credited with inaugurating the auction system of selling thoroughbreds in Tennessee. Harding's ingenuity contributed to creating the most successful breeding and distribution of thoroughbred stock in the state's history. Incidentally, the letter in the story from Mary Selena McNairy Harding (General Harding's first wife) is a real letter penned by her the winter of 1836–37. Thank you to Belle Meade for the permission to share that in my story.

To learn more about Belle Meade, visit the Belle Meade Plantation novels page on my website (www.tameraalexander.com). While there, view video vignettes filmed on location at the plantation, discover how current-day Kentucky Derby winners trace their lineage to the 1870s stud farm, and learn about upcoming books in the series.

Sharing these stories with you makes writing historical fiction extra special, and the connections we make are precious to me. Thank you for reading.

Until next time,

Tamera

Galatians 3:28

With gratitude to . . .

My family, Joe, Kelsey, and Kurt—for understanding when I'm "in the zone," for helping me get there, and for making it all worth it.

Alton Kelley, Jenny Lamb, John Lamb, and the staff at Belle Meade Plantation—for opening the personal letters from the Harding family to me and for answering my endless emails and questions.

Ridley Wills II, a descendant of the Harding family—for his book *The History of Belle Meade: Mansion, Plantation, and Stud*, which proved to be an invaluable resource as I wrote this book.

Sue Brower and Leslie Peterson, my editors—for your insight, encouragement, and patience as this story took shape.

Deborah Raney, my writing critique partner—for doing what you do so very well. And for always being just a click away.

Natasha Kern, my agent—for representing me with such integrity and loyalty.

Stan Williams, award-winning video producer, filmmaker, and show creator ... and "Master of Story Structure"—for your book *The Moral Premise* and for sharing your extraordinary gift with me. Thank you, friend.

Jason Ingram, Matt Redman, and Tim Winstall for your song "Never Once," which I listened to countless times as I wrote this book. Thanks for sharing your giftedness. (www.fellowshipsongs.com)

My readers—for loving these historical characters and settings with a passion that rivals my own. You encourage me in ways I can't begin to describe. I'm so grateful for you.

And to Jesus Christ—for whispering my name so faithfully. Mold my heart, Lord, to hear and love you more.

Susanna's Tennessee
BLACKBERRY COBBLER

INGREDIENTS

2–3 cups fresh-picked blackberries
   (or thawed from your "icebox" will do nicely)
1½ cups sugar, divided
1 cup sweet milk (whole milk)
1 cup flour (all purpose)
1½ teaspoons baking powder
½ teaspoon salt
½ cup fresh butter
Fresh heavy cream (for serving)

DIRECTIONS

Place butter in 8x8 baking dish, and place dish in oven while oven heats to 350°. Once butter is melted, remove dish from oven. Place blackberries on top of melted butter and sprinkle with ½ cup of the sugar. Stir.

In a medium-size mixing bowl, stir together remaining sugar, flour, baking powder, and salt until just blended. Add milk and stir until smooth. Pour batter over blackberries but do not stir. Some blackberries and butter may float to the top. Bake at 350° for 45–50 minutes or until golden-brown.

To serve, spoon generous servings into bowls and pour fresh cream over each serving, just like Susanna Carter did!

Compliments of Christy Jordan and SouthernPlate.com

TAMERA ALEXANDER is a bestselling, award-winning novelist whose deeply drawn characters, thought-provoking plots, and poignant prose resonate with readers worldwide. She and her husband live in Nashville, Tennessee, where they enjoy life with their two adult children, who live nearby, and also a twelve-pound silky terrier named Jack.

Tamera invites you to visit her at:

Her Web site	*www.tameraalexander.com*
Her blog	*www.tameraalexander.blogspot.com*
Twitter	*www.twitter.com/tameraalexander*
Facebook	*www.facebook.com/tamera.alexander*

Or if you prefer snail mail, please write her at the following postal address:

Tamera Alexander
P.O. Box 871
Brentwood, TN 37024

Discussion questions for *To Whisper Her Name* are available at www.tameraalexander.com, as are details about Tamera joining you for a virtual book club visit.

Daily Guided Tours

TOUR / SHOP / WINE / DINE

615-356-0501

5025 HARDING PIKE / NASHVILLE, TENNESSEE

WWW.BELLEMEADEPLANTATION.COM

Share Your Thoughts

With the Author: Your comments will be forwarded to the author when you send them to *zauthor@zondervan.com*.

With Zondervan: Submit your review of this book by writing to *zreview@zondervan.com*.

Free Online Resources at

www.zondervan.com

Daily Bible Verses and Devotions: Enrich your life with daily Bible verses or devotions that help you start every morning focused on God. Visit www.zondervan.com/newsletters.

Free Email Publications: Sign up for newsletters on Christian living, academic resources, church ministry, fiction, children's resources, and more. Visit www.zondervan.com/newsletters.

Zondervan Bible Search: Find and compare Bible passages in a variety of translations at www.zondervanbiblesearch.com.

Other Benefits: Register to receive online benefits like coupons and special offers, or to participate in research.